THE RIVER
December 10, 2013

James McCurry

FROM
THE RIVER
TO THE ENDS
OF THE EARTH

PSALM 72:8

Lyons, Colorado, 2013

PO Box 131, Lyons Colorado 80540

Copyright © 2013 James McCurry
All rights reserved.

ISBN: 1493585207
ISBN 13: 9781493585205
Library of Congress Control Number: 2013920495
LCCN Imprint Name: CreateSpace Independent Publishing Platform, North Charleston, SC

Dedicated to
The River
Christian Community Church
Lyons, Colorado

Dear reader,

Flood of 2013: Our church family remains whole, but our church building and many homes have been badly damaged or destroyed along with the water, sewage, roadway and electrical systems of Lyons. Many of us are working very hard on the restoration of our church building and town. Give us a year and then come to visit the new Lyons. While in town, come to The River and worship with us.

Know that God loves you even in the storm,
J.J. McCurry

Church office 303-823-6469
Temporary office location: 630, 15th Avenue, Suite 100, Longmont, CO
Temporary mailing address: PO Box 6043, Longmont, Colorado, 80501

Email: *mccurry2570@centurylink.net* (or) *info@therivercolorado.org*
website: *www.therivercolorado.org*
facebook: *www.facebook.com/theRiverColorado*

TABLE OF CONTENTS

ACKNOWLEDGMENTS	xiii
INTRODUCTION	xv

PART 1—THE WORD — 1
WHEN WE WERE DRUIDS	5
THE TARNISHED BRONZE AGE	18

PART 2—THE WRITTEN WORD — 23
IN THE BEGINNING	27
PROTECTED	34
THE SILVER AGE OF MIDIAN	62
THE BETRAYAL	69
THE HOMECOMING	78
WARRIOR PRINCESS	86

PART 3—LIVING THE WORD — 119
HERETIC PRINCESS	121
MADE IN HEAVEN	140
THE ENEMY WITHIN	149
TRUTH IN ALL THINGS	154
THE VOYAGE TO ROME	164
ROMANS	178

PART 4—THE LIVING WORD — 187
A BRIDGE IN TIME	189
ONE HANNAH—TWO MASTERS	211

PART 5—SPREADING THE WORD — 231
THE FIRST MISSIONARIES	233
RUMORS OF WAR—CALIGULA	272
THE HUNGRY BEAR—CLAUDIUS	285
AGRICOLA	299
CONCLUSION	307
GLOSSARY	309
BIBLIOGRAPHY	325

CHARACTER LIST

PART 1—THE WORD

Nova's paternal family
- Nova, the central character of the story
- Madad (MA daugh), a Gaelic man's name meaning *father*
- Star, identical twin sister

Nova's maternal family
- Elcurr, mother
- Jacurr the Elder, great-grandfather, lovingly known as Poppy
- Jucurr, grandmother
- Curr, grandfather and Curr clan chief
- Elymas, granduncle and the clan's Druid priest, also known as Uncle Eli
- Makcurr, aunt, also known as Stag Slayer and Master Warrior
- Hancurr, aunt, Curr clan diplomat
- Conan, uncle and second Curr clan king
- Sandy, Nova's dog

PART 2—THE WRITTEN WORD

- Hannah, the central character of the story renamed
- Atina, Nova's stepsister
- Monyah, Nova's stepmother
- Teacher Abraham
- Sarah, wife of Abraham
- David, Jonathan, Israel, and Esau, sons of Abraham and Sarah
- Haggai and Leah, friends of Abraham, Sarah, and Nova/Hannah

- Caoimhe (KUEE vu), a Gaelic woman's name for *kind* or *tender*
- Marsha, Nova's best friend
- Captain of the Asbury Guards
- Nate, Nova's friend and the captain's son
- MacDuff, Asbury Guard
- Peatcurr, Tomcurr, Barthcurr, Joncurr, Judcurr, and Mattcurr are Hannah's cousins
- Leocurr, Hannah's uncle
- Goblin, Nova's horse friend
- Nee and Miah, Nova's dog friends
- Faolan (Fool an), a Gaelic man's name for *wolf*. He is the gang leader.
- Latharn (LA urn), a Gaelic man's name for *fox*. He is second in command of the gang.
- Rook, a gang member
- Queen of Asbury
- Lars, King of Asgardshire

PART 3— LIVING THE WORD

- Ruth, Hannah's adopted daughter
- Joseph, Hannah's friend
- Gaius, Roman commerce chairman

PART 4—THE LIVING WORD

- Captain Noah of the *Hannah*
- Chief Priest Caiaphas
- Gamaliel, law student and Samuel's friend
- Hillel, Gamaliel's grandfather and founder of the Hillel School
- Rachel, Hannah's friend
- Jesus and his apostles: Peter, Andrew, John, and Matthew
- Followers of Christ: Mary Magdalene and Martha
- Simon the tanner
- Julia, wife of Joseph
- Aquila, friend of Joseph
- Priscilla, wife of Aquila
- Marcus, Roman centurion
- Orpha, Hannah's friend

PART 5—SPREADING THE WORD

- Maon (Moon), a Gaelic man's name that means *hero*.
- Cornelius, Roman centurion
- Moses, Marsha's grown son
- Epona, Moses's horse
- Phoenix, Hannah's horse
- King Cunobelinus of Britons
- Prince/King Adminius, son of King Cunobelinus
- Guards of the Sarah House
- Caligula, Roman emperor
- Claudius, puppet Roman emperor
- Senator Cleverous, actual Roman leader
- Aulus Plautius, Roman military commander
- Agricola, Roman governor of Caledonia
- Gideon, the warrior prince

ACKNOWLEDGMENTS

FIRST EDITOR JUDITH McCURRY

Editors Judith McCurry and Heidi Chanlynn Parrott gave endless hours to the readability of the story. Sandra K. Stedman and Harriet Spector Edelstein went beyond reasonable expectations to provide edification, insight, focus, and encouragement. Adrienne Holmquist and Gary Erickson provided technical assistance.

INTRODUCTION

This book is a two-thousand-year journey back to a time when the Romans expanded the known world with their roads, culture, and technology. In doing so, they trampled over every family, tribe, nation, and culture that stood in their path. This imperialistic drive was determined to subjugate an otherwise barbarian world into civilization no matter how many people had to be murdered. Rome exploited conquered territories and their people for the glory of Rome. While the mighty Roman roadway system made global expansion possible, it also made a way for the rapid spread of knowledge and the eventual contraction of the empire. These imperialists could only see the extraction of great wealth flowing down those ancient channels back to Rome. Consequently, all those roads led the barbarian hordes directly to the heart of the empire. Today the Appian Way is gone, and the victorious Romans are gone, yet the Word of God continues to be the truth, the way, and the life against the evil that was once the glory of Rome.

The momentum of expansion continued beyond where the ancient western roads stopped on the shores of Gaul. (A large part of ancient Gaul is now France.) From there, the Roman legions launched their invasions to the edge of the world into the land they called Britannia, which the ancient Celts knew as Albion.

Roman Emperor Gaius Caesar Germanicus (Caligula) threatened Britannia with Roman wealth, the best-trained, battle-hardened warriors, and the cutting edge of military technology in AD 40. On the other side of the channel, the ill-prepared barbarian forces of Albion braced themselves to face the Romans in all their military grandeur. The Roman forces were ready to invade the land that they could see across the water from western Gaul. It would be a much-needed victory for them after their recent failure of conquest along the Rhine River in the north. Thousands of Roman soldiers hesitated at the western front and did not cross the water now known as the English Channel. The historical record remains unclear about why Caligula failed to follow through with his conquest of Britannia. Historians can only offer possible reasons, such as he could not be certain of victory. Exactly why he did not cross the channel in AD 40 remains a historical mystery.

Another Roman invasion mystery took place four decades later in the Grampian Mountains. The Romans reported that Agricola, the Roman Governor of Caledonia, conquered the Celts known as the Picts of Aberdeenshire in a final battle high in the mountains. Thereafter, the remaining Roman troops retreated southward to the area known today as Stirling and built massive defensive walls for protection against the conquered Picts. This book offers plausible answers to these invasion mysteries.

Large extensive sections of the defensive Hadrian Wall still stand in southern Scotland as a monument to the Celtic tenacity that would not surrender to tyranny. The following picture shows the trace evidence that remains of the Antonine Wall.

Falkirk is located in central Scotland, where only the
following historical marker stands today.

ANTONINE WALL—WATLING LODGE

*The Antonine Wall was built by the Emporor Antoninus Pius AD 142-143.
It ran for thirty-seven miles from Bridgeness on the Forth to Old Kilpatrick
on the Clyde and consisted of a ditch with a turf rampaert behind it. The
material from the ditch was thrown onto its north side to form a mound.
Forts, fortlets, and beacon platforms were placed along the wall. The fort at
Rough Castle lies one and a half miles along the road. The section of ditch
running through the wood is the best surviving stretch of the wall.*

PART 1—THE WORD

PART 2—THE WRITTEN WORD

PART 3—LIVING THE WORD

PART 4—THE LIVING WORD

PART 5—SPREADING THE WORD

The River attempts to imagine the exceptional life of a Celtic woman as she engaged the people and events of her time. Her story begins in a time before Christianity. For Celts, Druidism was their only connection with the spiritual realm. Celts are an ethnic group of Indo-Europeans who spoke the Gaelic language. These ancient Celts and their Druid priests did the best they could to provide social, spiritual, and moral leadership to their people. It is unlikely that the Celts of Eastern Europe were exactly like the clans of northern Scotland. The Celts were similar to all people, in that they tried to live their lives lovingly, taking care of their families and friends while maintaining hope for a better future.

Of course, there have always been those who want something for nothing and think only of themselves. The greatest among those were the Romans. Today, we have their written bias of what the Celtic people were like two thousand years ago. Please do not believe everything they have reported. After all, you would not want your worst enemy to define you for posterity.

WHEN WE WERE DRUIDS

Nova's Age: Birth to Age Seven

The central character in this book is a Celtic girl named Nova. This child grew to become a mighty warrior able to lead her nation to stand and face the Roman invasion of AD 40. Even before the invasions began, life was difficult for Nova's Stone Age Albion Highland Celts known as Picts. The technology of Nova's Curr clan was far behind the Roman advantages that existed in their time. They may have been backward, but the mountain people of Currcroft village had one timeless quality: They had an abundance of love for nature, for one another, and for their homeland. That love carried them through unspeakable hardships, generation after generation, but one question remained. Would their strength of character be enough to see them through the coming centuries of consecutive foreign invasions? Yes, it would be strong enough. The Romans have faded into history, whereas the Celtic people have remained in Scotland, England, Wales, and Ireland as a remnant of a mighty warrior nation.

Elcurr and Madad named their twins Star and Nova because there was a very bright star in the eastern sky on the night that they were born. It was an especially desperate time. Several nights earlier, a renegade clan had slipped into the Currcroft village during a storm and stole all the Curr clan cattle. In response, every available hunter willingly went out into the barren, wintry landscape to search for anything to eat. The story opens with a Druid priest named Elymas talking to his father, Jacurr the Elder, on the same cold, winter night that the twins were born.

PART 1—THE WORD

THE STORY

"My son, thank you for your prayers. I have never told you how important you are to me. I am very proud of you and the man that you have become."

"Father, you make it sound so serious. Go now. If there is anyone who can save us, it is you, Jacurr. I know that you will have a successful hunt."

"Yes Elymas, it will be successful, but I will not be the one to save the clan. It will be Makcurr. As you know, I often dream, but I remember only a few of my dreams. Those that I remember actually take place in the future, and I had such a dream last night. Makcurr will become known as Stag Slayer. As for myself, I'm no longer much of a hunter if I cannot even find my own cattle. I would have given all the cattle to the thieves if they had only left my bull. He is more than a bull. He is my friend."

"Yes, the beasts have always known you as a friend. Go now, I will rest my body at this gate where I will pray and await the moment of your return to the other side."

Soon the hunt was on, and Jacurr the Elder was holding the lead with a new generation of hunters close behind as they approached the mountaintop. With him, were his two granddaughters, Hancurr and Makcurr. As usual, his grandson Conan was at his side. Earlier, Jacurr the Elder had only wounded a stag, and now they must make the kill. This was a pivotal moment for the survival of the clan because they had not eaten in two days. Even the stag could sense their desperation as the hunters and death came ever closer. The runners were very high on the mountain now in a place so cold that they did not dare stop.

Jacurr the Elder directed the attack. "Hancurr, you go left. Makcurr, you go right. Conan, stay with me. Everyone, take the shot when you can, but not too soon. Take that extra moment, and then kill."

Man and hound were closing in from three sides. Makcurr had gone right, which took her directly to the prey. She focused her thoughts on survival. *Forget the pain and fatigue...forget the hunger and thirst...ignore the cold...oh, the cold—I am so numb that the cold is forgotten. Easy now, take a deep breath. See it; kill it.* Makcurr's spear only seemed to hang in the frigid air in search of its mark. It was over in a moment. Her deadly aim secured the clan's survival and that of every generation to follow. Months of practice had paid off. Makcurr made her first kill.

A proud and breathless Jacurr needed to rest before he could put an arm around the champion and in a whispering voice manage to say, "Well done, girl of mine."

Then to the entire hunting party, Jacurr said, "Quickly, everyone together—we must hack off these legs. You lassies pull while Conan and I hack. All right, that is enough. Everyone eat some of this hot liver, and let's get off this mountain before we freeze."

Conan turned away from the grisly feast and hoisted his share of the meat over his shoulder. "Come, let us just go. I cannot stand this cold any longer."

"Conan, eat that liver while it is hot. You need it to stay strong."

"No, Grandfather, it is disgusting. I would rather starve. You should see yourselves."

PART 1—THE WORD

Jacurr paused to look at the other hunters and himself and then laughed. "Conan is right. Look at us. Everything that we eat looks good on us.

Come now, my children. We must go **now**—no, not that way! Come this way. We are leaving a blood-scented trail behind that wolves could be following. We will return home another way, but we must hurry. Watch every step you take. There will be no time to help anyone who falls. Keep moving. The clan must have this meat tonight."

Even while running, Hancurr could not ignore the bite of winter. "Jacurr, it is so cold here!"

"It is only cold if you are not wearing enough clothes."

"That old joke of yours never was funny, especially now."

"True, but it made you stop thinking about being cold for the moment."

The winter sun began to fade as they drew closer to home, and each of them still carried twenty pounds of meat over their shoulders. "Let your Poppy Jacurr take the lead. I can run this trail with my eyes closed." At that very moment, the clouds parted, and the star in the east was so bright that night became as day.

Conan's voice lifted everyone's spirit. "Way to lead, Poppy, but you can open your eyes now!" The four hunters laughed with renewed strength as the entrance to Currcroft came into view.

"Home—we are home. I cannot wait to tell everyone how I killed that stag."

As he had promised, Druid Elymas was waiting at the gate for his father, Jacurr the Elder. He was sitting on the ground covered only with his robe in the bitter cold. He was there in body while his eternal being was waiting for the arrival of his father in the Otherworld. Jacurr stopped beside him, and then he turned to face his grandchildren and said, "I am so proud of you, and I love each of you very much. Go on home without me, but please send one of the men to help your Uncle Elymas and me. Go now and get warm!"

The three young hunters gladly ran toward the warmth of the hearth, but Makcurr stopped and turned for one more look at her grandfather. Although it was snowing very hard, she could still see him through the blizzard when he called out to her and said, "I will love Makcurr the Stag Slayer forever!" Jacurr faded from her sight a little with each word until disappearing in a cloud of snow with, "This is your day to remember!"

"Poppy?" Makcurr called out, feeling confused and a little frightened, and then she turned and ran to catch up with the others.

A belief of their Druid religion was that a soul star was reborn when a person died, and Jacurr's star really lit up the sky that evening. They also believed that a soul star fell to the earth when an eternal being was reborn on earth. Two stars fell to earth when the twins Nova and Star were born into the Curr clan that same night. They were born into a clan that had hearts filled with love but now two more stomachs to feed.

"Mother, I did it! I made my first kill!"

"Makcurr, I knew it would be you! Now, the three of you get out of your wet clothes and into dry ones before you get sick. And where is your grandfather?"

"He said that he had something to do with Uncle Elymas at the gate and that we should go home without him."

As though suddenly awakened, Mother Jucurr stopped and turned toward a haunting sound. "Quiet, children; what is that sound?"

Hancurr answered, "It is the sound of the hounds. They are making a frightful sound."

"Drat!"

Everyone knew that an evil spirit sat on the left shoulder and a good spirit sat on the right. Tears began to fall from their mother Jucurr's eyes. From the right eye flowed tears of joy for the successful birthing and hunting that night. Both of these events ensured that the clan would not die out anytime soon. From the left eye flowed tears of sorrow, for she knew that Jacurr's soul had lit up the night sky.

PART 1—THE WORD

Clan survival always was first priority. With that in mind, mother Jucurr was quick-witted to organize the clan into action, beginning with her husband. "Curr, take some of the other men to bring your father and the meat home from the entrance gate. Conan, go and find the sin-eater. Makcurr, go tell the women to begin preparing the feast, for a star has been lit and two souls have come home to Currcroft."

Hancurr immediately caught her mother's meaning and went outside followed by Conan and Makcurr. The three hunters ran to where Jacurr finished his life race and found him there in the arms of his son Elymas. The Druid was no longer transfixed, chanting, or praying. He was simply holding his father's body for the last time. Grandfather Jacurr the Elder died happy that night, knowing that a new generation would live to hunt another day.

Jacurr's last words had been, "I love my granddaughter Makcurr the Stag Slayer! This is your day to remember!"

Instead of feeling comforted by her grandfather's words, Makcurr fell asleep sad and angry that night. She was saddened over the loss of her Poppy and angry because the birth of the twins caused her special moment as clan hunting champion to go unnoticed. What should have been her best day ever seemed to be her worst day to remember.

Makcurr's father, Curr, became clan chieftain with the death of his father Jacurr the Elder. His first act as chief was to awaken his daughter Makcurr before the following dawn.

"Do you think that you can show me where you made the kill?" he asked her quietly.

"Yes, Father. Do you think we might be able to find some of the carcass?"

"That would be wonderful. However, we are going after something else that is important. Bring your spears."

"What could be so important this early in the day?"

"Your rightful trophy and place of honor as clan champion."

Makcurr easily found the kill site, and from there, hunters and all the clan hounds tracked the deer carcass to a wolf den. Outnumbered, the wolf pack abandoned the prize allowing Curr to collect the antlers. Then he commanded the hounds to eat, and the remains vanished in moments.

Later that day, a ceremony recognized Makcurr as clan champion, where she received the title of Makcurr the Stag Slayer. She reenacted that midwinter hunt for the next forty-five years. During that time, she had twelve warrior sons, and they all lived to have twelve warrior sons. Their fierce mad-dog style of fighting put fear into the hearts of many Roman soldiers who gave them the collective name of the Makcurries.

The life of Nova, Makcurr's niece, was off to a good start when she survived her first four years in the harsh and brutal climate of the highlands. It is difficult to imagine how a four-year-old cave-girl could have survived without the love and support of her clan. Then came a day when Nova's mother, Elcurr, died and another star was reborn. The Currcroft hounds began their mournful harmony, and weeping followed with the words, "Go fetch the sin-eater, and prepare the celebration meal."

"Grandmother, where is Mother?"

"She has become a new shining star in the night sky, Nova."

"Why?" It was a question that Nova's grandmother could not answer honestly.

"Druid Elymas, do you think that Nova will be all right?"

"Oh, Jucurr, she will be fine. Children are resilient."

For the next three years, the clan of Currcroft met all Nova's needs except for the best of what life has to offer: a mother's love. It had vanished to light the night sky. Was heaven's need of Elcurr greater than the needs of her twin daughters? A great light went out in Nova's world when her mother died, but not before passing her faith, hope, and love to the next generation.

This was an especially difficult time for Nova. In general, people take the most essential things in life for granted until they are lost. Love, friends, and family are the essence of life. The inconvenience of death and the rituals of religion that accompany it mark its poignant effect on our lives. In these moments, even a small child will listen more carefully with the hope of understanding the purpose of death. Four years of age is too early to awaken to this dark side of life.

Nova listened as the elders attempted to explain the reason for her mother's death, but nothing made sense to her. Their groundless superstitions had nothing to do with a mother's life or death. Stars, reincarnation, shape-shifting, fairies, goblins, spirits, ghosts, spells, omens, good, evil, reward, punishment: what do these things have to do with the loss of a mother? What evil had Elcurr ever done? What sin had she committed? What does punishment have

PART 1—THE WORD

to do with such a self-sacrificing person as a mother? No one had answers to these deep-rooted questions, and yet the sin-eater was called.

The sin-eater's whole purpose in life was to take away the life-long accumulation of a person's transgressions and place them on his own eternal being. Could there possibly have been an easier task for this man than to bear the sins of Nova's mother? He was desecrating her memory with his grim presence, without ever having known her. What sin of any consequence could there have been in such a dear person? Surely, Elcurr was a friend of the good spirits and was not in need of an intercessor.

"Nova."

"Yes, Grandmother?"

"She is gone, and she is not coming back to us. Right now, capture all your memories of her in your heart. Remember all the things about her that you can, and know that she loved you very much. Remember that in your heart, and try to be the girl and the woman that would make her proud. Can you do that?"

"I will try, Grandmother. But I just want her back."

"Me too, Princess, me too."

In a sense, Nova lost both parents when her mother died. Her father needed to get away from the place that had once made him so happy. Madad had made some coastal friends during his travels, and in time, they invited the entire clan for a summer seaside visit. It quickly became the favorite family thing to do each summer. One time, most of the clan walked down out of the mountains while Nova rode on the shoulders of an oxen friend. Once down, the clan stopped along the riverside to rest and camp for the night.

Chieftain Curr called everyone together with his resonant voice projecting to the outer reaches of the group. "We are going to rest here tonight. Please stay in the area."

Nova saw the respite as an opportunity to explore the area and search for flower nymphs (butterflies). They kept urging her ever southward away from the river encampment. Her grandfather Chief Curr grew worried at Nova's absence, so he found her father and asked, "I do not see Nova. Do you know where she is? Have you seen her?"

"Now that you ask, no, I have not seen her," Madad replied. "Oh, wait, there she is under that tree playing with the other children."

WHEN WE WERE DRUIDS

"What is wrong with you, Madad? They are twins, but anyone can see that is your daughter Star, not Nova."

Frustrated that Madad could lose sight of his own daughter so easily, Chief Curr called out, "Listen, everyone: I cannot find Nova! Has anyone seen Nova?"

Silence was his answer. She was not in the camp. The older men and woman stayed with the children while the others searched along the river and toward the south. No one would say it, but everyone thought she had fallen into the river and was lost forever.

"Curr, my brother, in all our days, I have never seen you weep," said Elymas.

"Elymas, it was hard losing her mother, but I cannot bear the thought of losing my Princess Nova. Let me not see the death of this child. The sun is low over the mountains now. We ought to go back. Maybe she has already been found in the camp."

Intuitively, Elymas knew that was not true. "What if she is not in the camp? I refuse to stop searching! Let us continue looking for her even into the dark of night."

The two men grew more frustrated with each step until Elymas saw something familiar in a field. "Curr, look over there under those trees. Do you see that bull? No, it could not be. That was years ago."

PART 1—THE WORD

"What do you mean?"

"That old bull over there; for a moment it reminded me of Father's bull."

"Yes, I see it now! Brother, look...seated on the grass in the shadow of the great bull. Isn't that...?"

Elymas cupped his hands around his mouth and shouted, "NOVA!"

"She sees us!"

"She thinks that all animals are her friends."

"Nova, stop! Stop running!"

"Curr, the bull is not chasing her. He is following her! What goddess is this that even the beasts call her friend? How strange, bulls such as these are known to be dangerous."

Casting all concern aside for his own safety, Curr ran to his granddaughter with his brother Elymas yelling after him. "What are you doing, you old fool? That bull will kill you!"

"Grandfather!" Nova cried out with joy.

"Nova, my princess!"

The chieftain placed his granddaughter on his shoulders once they were clear of the fence. "Elymas, I think we can reach the river by dark if we hurry."

"Hi, Uncle Eli!" Nova said joyfully, and then to her grandfather, she said, "Grandfather, please don't leave my old friend here!"

Her plea left both Curr and even Druid Elymas mesmerized. "Dear child, what did you say? Did you say that he is your old friend?"

Dusk settled over the camp when Madad saw the two men and his little girl in the distance. He immediately ran to her and scooped her up in his arms, and then he kissed her. He turned and called out, "Everyone, come! My daughter Nova was lost and now is found!"

Curr drew close to Madad and spoke to him in a stern, low voice. "And you better make sure that she stays that way. Do you hear me?"

"Yes, sir, I will."

The entire clan sat around the campfire all that night discussing what they should do about the cattle thieves of Belmar Village. Most of the men wanted to attack the village, kill the inhabitants, and take all the cattle. Finally, Chief Curr stood and announced, "Today we thought that we had suffered a great loss. In the end, we found both our lost princess and our stolen cattle. Our dear goddess Brigit has been merciful. This is what I propose we do. Tomorrow evening, the older men and women will stay here with the children. Our warriors will encircle Belmar Village under the command of Master Warrior Makcurr and capture it at dawn without killing anyone. Druid Elymas and I will speak with their chief and their Druid once the village has been subdued."

Unfortunately, execution of the plan resulted in the deaths of several villagers. As planned, the Belmar chief and Druid priestess knelt prostrate before Chief Curr, who kept his composure and stated firmly, "Our demands are few. Replace the cattle that you stole from us. What cannot be replaced will be compensated. You will make an oath in the name of the goddess Brigit and in blood to never enter our lands again without an invitation unless you need our help."

These demands left the Belmar clan with half the cattle. As generous as the terms were, Chief Mor objected to the taking of the great bull. "That bull does not belong to you!"

Curr simply ignored Chief Mor and called out a command in response to her claim. "Where is Nova? Bring Nova here!"

Nova ran to her grandfather's open arms. "Princess Nova, do you see your friend out there in the field?"

"Yes, Grandfather."

"Would you please go and bring him here?"

PART 1—THE WORD

Makcurr the Stag Slayer stopped Nova and spoke out against her father. "Father, what are you thinking? That kind of bull is a man killer and you are going to send this child to fetch him? Is she to be a human sacrifice?"

Mor joined the rebuke against Curr. "And I already told you that he does not belong to you."

This time, Curr responded to the chieftain in a less than polite voice. "Mor, someone will die here today. You would be wise to be silent as my granddaughter claims what is hers."

Crouching down to be eye level with his granddaughter, he said, "Nova, don't listen to them. I know that you will be safe. Go and bring the bull to me. We will wait here for you and your friend."

"Yes, Grandfather."

Tension filled the air as the small child walked through a pasture where no man dared to enter. Instead of death, she met an old friend that lay down before her. Nova mounted the great beast without hesitation and returned riding the bull to where her grandfather was waiting.

"Thank you, Nova. You are a brave girl. Stay up there, and you can ride your bull all the way back to our camp."

"Thank you, Grandfather."

As he turned away from his granddaughter, Curr's demeanor transformed from glowing warmth to icy cold. "Now, Chief Mor, I think that you will agree that Nova will be taking the bull home to Currcroft where he came from. The gods have restored our herd. That leaves the blood oath and compensation of the irreplaceable. Consequently, you should know that your night raid on Currcroft resulted in the death of my father, Jacurr the Elder. You will compensate his life with a life of equal value. I regret the lives that have been lost here today. However, the next death will be a deliberate execution. A life for a life; is there anyone of your clan willing to pay this debt?"

Druid Sorcha stepped forward to offer herself, but Curr refused her offering. "I will not take the life of a woman and especially not the life of a Druid priest."

Curr fixed his eyes on a regal-looking man standing close to Chief Mor. "Yes, Master Warrior Makcurr, there is to be a human sacrifice today."

A moment later, Makcurr mercifully ended the man's life. Curr stood patiently by until calm returned to the Belmar clan. "Now for the blood oath, do you swear by Brigit and on the blood of your clansman to never enter our lands again without invitation unless you need our help?"

A tearful Chief Mor struggled to maintain her composure as she answered, "I do."

"As of this day forward, the debt of your clan has been paid in full. Let our clans live in peace once more."

From there, the Curr clan warriors and their cattle returned to the river encampment for a change in plans. Chief Curr knew that the herd was a tempting prize for would-be thieves. "We will not be going to the shore this summer, Madad. We must stay together to protect the clan and the herd. I am sorry if this disappoints you."

"I understand. May I have your permission to continue on to the shore with Star and Nova? My friends will worry otherwise. We will stay for a few days before returning home."

"Certainly; spend the whole summer if you wish. Nova has earned a special reward. Nevertheless, do not forget that I have warned you about keeping your eye on your children."

"Yes, sir, I promise that I will protect them."

Thereupon, they agreed that the clan would return home with the cattle while Madad, Nova, and her twin sister, Star, would resume their seaside journey. Once there, the trio stayed the whole summer at the shore digging clams, crabbing, swimming, and fishing. Still, Nova anticipated going home to a nice, fatty lamb chop with mouth-watering delight. There is only so much sand, surf, sunburn, and fish that a highland lass can take. However, Madad did not return with Nova and Star to Currcroft at the end of the summer. Instead, their lives took a traumatic turn to the south. Madad had knowingly lied to his chief, and in doing so, he had broken the first law of Druidism: *the truth in all things.*

THE TARNISHED BRONZE AGE

Nova's Age: Five to Six Years

A person does not have to travel very far before finding people of a different culture. It is unsettling for anyone to enter a foreign society where one's values, beliefs, and the comforts of home are absent. Five-year-old Nova was about to suffer this type of cultural shock as a new Bronze Age town replaced her Stone Age village.

Since the death of her mother, her father always seemed to be looking for something he could not find. He stayed away from Currcroft for months at a time. He gradually separated himself from the clan by following the Currcroft spring to a stream that joined a river that led to the ends of the earth. Fortunately, the mountain cave was the safest place on earth for his children to await his return. It was a harmonious and loving home. That was all about to change. Madad found what he was looking for in a new wife for himself and a mother for his daughters. This marriage included a bonus package containing a stepsister and a large, strange house made of wood and mud with a straw roof.

"Madad, will the clan be there?"

"No, we will have a new and smaller clan called a family."

A saddened child began to think. *First mother, and now my entire clan except for Madad and Star are lost. Will I ever see the clan or the village again? What would Grandmother say to me? She would say, "You are gone, and you are not coming back to us. Right now, capture all your memories of us in your heart. Remember all the things about us that you can, and know that we love you very much. Remember that in your heart, and try to be the girl and the woman the clan would be proud of. Can you do that?"*

Nova burst into tears. "I'll try to, Grandmother, but I just want you all back."

In her mind, she could hear Jucurr's voice saying, *"Us too, Princess; us too."*

Her father's questioning voice startled her back into the moment. "Nova, who are you talking to? What is wrong with you now?"

"I want to go home, Madad! The clan did not say good-bye. They don't know where we are, do they?"

"Nova, be quiet," her father said sternly.

Madad, Star, and Nova travelled southward on foot for several weeks along the coast until they came to a village and stopped. "Where are we, Madad?"

"Asbury."

"Are we going to the big house now?"

"Oh no, you can't go there looking like that. You will need at least one bath. Look at your hair! Really, Nova, your hair is a mess. We will find some new clothes for you and burn what you are wearing."

Later that day, Star said, "Madad, we look funny."

"Oh, Star, you are beautiful in your new clothes. Here we are at the big house. Remember what I told both of you: behave!"

"Are we not good enough?"

Upon entering, Madad exclaimed, "Monyah, honey, we are here!"

The stepmother came bursting into the scene exclaiming, "Oh, they are so sweet!"

PART 1—THE WORD

Nova took her father's hand and stepped sheepishly behind him. "Madad, these people look and act strange. They are ugly. That girl has a fishhook for a nose."

"Shhh, be quiet; you'll get used to it."

Nova never did get used to it. As it turned out, according to the stepmother, they were not good enough. Their clan was not good enough. Celts were not good enough, and there was something said about "blood being thicker than water." Still, the village of Asbury, in the heart of Monmouthshire, did offer some advantages. However, the gains did not outweigh the losses left behind on the mountain. Their loving clan was as solid and genuine as their mountains. These new, unloving people seemed to be as fake as their cold, bronze idols. In Nova's mind, the incompatibility between the old and new was irreconcilable. So, where was the logic behind this new blended family? It took a while before the answer finally became clear. Madad had sold his dashing good looks and daughters into servitude for a more secure life for himself. Time would prove him underpaid, and good looks do not last very long.

The seaside town of Asbury was obviously a place of advantage. It had art, music, a market, and places to work. It also had a place to worship with its giant standing stones surrounded by an oak grove. In the beginning, Asbury also enriched their lives in other ways, such as providing a steady supply of food, clothes that fit, and a warm, dry place to sleep. All very grand, and yet it was not home. There was no clan, hunting, or genuine love, and there were no hounds in Asbury. It was a community filled with new ideas, superstitions, and fears. Illiteracy was the one thing that both Currcroft and Asbury had in common. Everything was learned through apprenticeship, experience, and the oral tradition.

The big house was an inn, where coastal travelers could rest and eat along their journey. Servants were necessary to constantly prepare meals, serve food, and clean up after inn guests. Therein, the treasured daughters of the Curr clan became enslaved servants of the inn. The more Nova fussed about having to do something, the more the task belonged to her. One memorable episode was the fit she threw over having to clean the chamber pots. In the end, her stepmother declared the task as a life sentence. It was in this way that Nova came to understand how her duties were assigned. An inn guest put it into whispering words. "When Nova throws a fit, the job will be a fit."

Her opportunity for freedom came when the stable boy quit. "I'm not cleaning up after animals. I am not doing it, and that is the end of it," Nova defiantly announced. It was a performance so convincing that she almost believed the drama. Her screams echoed through the halls of the inn, and the job of stable girl became Nova's theatric reward and purpose for living.

She withheld her contained joy until she was alone in the stable. Even then, she whispered, "I love horses! Thank you, my dear great-grandfather in heaven for my new chamber among these magnificent creatures. I love their smells, I love to curry their coats, and I adore kissing their soft noses. Thank you for the honor and privilege to be with these wonderful beasts. Even this stable smells like home! Yes, thank you dear, sweet spirit, Jacurr the Elder!"

The worse she smelled, the more she stayed out of her stepfamily's striking range. Finally, the household refuse had found a place of refuge. As a result, the inn stables were the cleanest for miles around. It was a safe and healthy place for both horse and girl. Then one day, life became even better. It was the day that a puppy found Nova on the beach and kept her as his very own human. "Thank you, Good Spirit Great-grandfather Jacurr for this stable sanctuary and for sending Sandy to me."

Nova was struggling to make sense of life in her fragile Stone Age world. There were wonders of life that could be seen and even more unseen wonders. Her visible clan and village were as real as the invisible good spirits of Brigit and her great-grandfather Jacurr. The presence of both divine beings gave her much comfort. Surely, God addressed as Brigit or by any other well-intended name would hear the prayers of a little girl suddenly taken from her loving clan. God must hear even the misdirected yet humble pleas of a heartbroken child. Otherwise, who among us is worthy of God's ear? Little did she know that the means to a relationship with God had just arrived in front of the stables in the unlikely form of a merchant named Abraham. *What a funny looking man*, she thought.

PART 1—THE WORD

PART 2—THE WRITTEN WORD

PART 3—LIVING THE WORD

PART 4—THE LIVING WORD

PART 5—SPREADING THE WORD

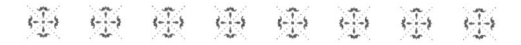

There were many different people groups in Albion in the early first century. Roman roads and the written languages of Latin, Greek, and Hebrew opened trade routes that connected merchants throughout the empire.

IN THE BEGINNING

Nova's Age: Six to Fourteen

Travelers, mostly merchants, from far and wide stayed at the inn. Listening to their stories opened Nova's mind to a much greater understanding of her world. Abraham was among those travelers. Everyone at the inn assumed that he was just another traveling merchant when, in fact, he was an itinerant Jewish teacher—a rabbi, as he called himself. Abraham was different in that he opened hearts and minds to an understanding of the kingdom of God. Here was a man who dedicated his entire life in the service of the one true God. Asbury was only one of three village areas where Abraham ministered to his people. Although scattered along that area of the Albion coast, they needed their beloved teacher for spiritual unity, education, encouragement, and sacred ceremonies.

PART 2—THE WRITTEN WORD

These people were Hebrews who believed in only one deity that created heaven and earth in six days and rested on the seventh day. Man was also to labor for six days, and then rest and worship that one deity on the seventh day known as the Sabbath. The teacher stayed at the inn for a three-day visit closest to the Sabbath of the full moon. He would arrive on the Sabbath eve and leave on the following third dawn. Abraham made this journey faithfully, thirteen times a year.

The cleanest livery stable in the land served as a rehearsal podium for Abraham's latest message. Even so, it was a shame that the best the world could offer to a messenger of God was a stable. As he prepared, the teacher would see Nova sitting up in the hayloft watching and listening for the message in her native Gaelic language. He made the message so simple that even an uneducated Celtic stable girl might understand. One day, teacher and student were already friends when his opening words turned both of their worlds upside down.

"In the beginning, Yah (God) created heaven and earth."

"Teacher, I do not understand."

"Nova, I have only spoken the title of the first scroll; what could there possibly be not to understand?"

"I do not understand the words beginning, god, or created. Everyone knows that there was no beginning. Life as we know it will never end. Everything that there is including you has always been and always will be. You only have one god, but my people have many gods."

Abraham smiled as he thought about her questions and Druidic tenets of faith. "Hmmm…all my life I have heard those first words of scripture, and it is only now that I have really listened to them. Please, little teacher, continue to always ask your questions."

"Sir, the gods of my people are many, and they all have names. Most people speak to our goddess Brigit. I prefer to talk with my personal god, Jacurr the Elder. He was my great-grandfather. What is the name of your god?"

"Nova, these are great questions! Out of the mouth of a babe comes my message for next month. For now, let me say that the name of the Eternal One is so holy that we do not dare speak or write it. A man named Moses was the only person to dare ask, and the One replied, "I AM." Give me time to think about the answers to your questions, and we will talk about them next month."

"You said that you dare not write your god's name. What does 'write it' mean?"

Abraham stooped down and used a twig to write N O V A in the dirt. "I would say Nova to speak your name. To write your name it would look like this."

"This is my name in dirt?"

"No, this is your name in writing."

"Why? Nobody can hear it that way."

Months later, Nova prayed, "Dear Eternal One, I am Nova; please hear my prayer. Thank you for your great messenger Abraham. How great you are. How great are you? Your teacher tells me that you have created the wondrous beauty and harmony of nature throughout Albion. Your magical and mysterious signs are everywhere from the tiny honeybee to the mighty bear. My clan worships our ancestors, the giant oak, and all nature. How humbled they would be to know that they only worship the handprint of our creator. This teacher has words written specifically about you. Thank you for my clan, my friend Abraham, and his teachings."

In return, Nova inspired Abraham over the following months and years. Her questions prompted him to write two rabbinical scrolls. Summer, fall, winter, and spring, Abraham always returned to the coastal village of Asbury with a spiritual message of truth, hope, and love.

Those loving words and Nova's prayers were often contrary to her behavior. She would pray with Abraham in the morning and lie, cheat, steal, punch, and damage property in the night. During that time, she and her friends snuck out at night to cause mischief. Deviant behavior was a Celtic-Druid tradition with the celebration of Samhain to mark the Celtic New Year. It was a day when all rules were set aside and crazy behavior was the norm. Over time, one annual Samhain day of tricks and pranks was not sufficient for her band of hellions. What began as playful pranks escalated until darker acts of mischief became criminal. Once, they rowed away on someone's boat and drained a loch all in the same night. Another night, they painted the outside of a home with calf blood. The loch draining was a turning point toward her reformation when Nova learned that people lost their livelihoods because of her fun. She was wrestling with her guilt when her twin sister, Star, stopped by the stable. "Hey, Star. What are you doing here?"

PART 2—THE WRITTEN WORD

"By all the gods, how do you stand the stench in here?" Star asked, covering her nose in disgust.

"Stay out if you don't like it," Nova answered sharply. "Why are you here, anyway?"

"Nova, I wanted to stop by only to say that I am worried about you."

"Really, I do not mind the smell. It reminds me of home."

"I am not talking about the stink. I am talking about you. I do not like the way you are acting lately. You are headed for trouble, and I think you ought to change your direction."

Nova's demeanor changed from defiant to pensive. "Really, Star?"

"I thought that I should tell you that it is up to you to change. It is your choice. Bye, Nova."

As though on cue, a horse named Goblin made a fresh delivery of manure that caused Star to turn abruptly and walk away as Nova's words followed her.

"It was nice to see you again, Star. Please don't wait another five years to come and see me."

Despite her outward bravado, Nova was stunned at the timing of Star's visit. *That was spooky. I was just thinking the same thing, and Star walks in with her words of wisdom.* She weighed the teachings of Abraham with her own guilt and her sister's concern, and she remembered the promise she had made to her grandmother. *Star is right. Mother and my clan would not be proud of what I have become. It is past time for a change.*

A changed heart comes with true repentance. The word no was waiting on Nova's lips when Faolan, the leader among her gang of reprobate friends, announced his ensuing scheme. The gang of young men and women were to attack and rob the late-night drunks stumbling around the town across the river once darkness had fallen.

"No, Faolan! That is a bad idea!"

"No, it's a great idea, Nova. We will take them by surprise! They will not even see us coming, so none of us will get hurt."

"Well, I will have no part of this cowardly act! I have had enough; this is not fun or funny. This scheme involves hurting and possibly killing someone. You can count me out!"

"Oh, you are out, kid."

With that, Faolan and his second, a boy named Latharn, turned on their friend, and suddenly Nova was the victim of their violent rage until a third boy stepped into the fray. "Stop it, lads! That is enough! Let her go, Latharn."

"Shut up, Nate, or we will give you some of the same!"

"Seriously, Faolan, she said no. Let her go! Anyway, we do not need her. You have forgotten that she is only a wee lassie."

Later that night, when they had left her beaten, defeated, and friendless, Nova regretted her decision to take a righteous direction for her life. The following morning, back at the inn, her stepmother assumed that she had received what she deserved.

"What have you been doing? Look at you. You have been fighting again!"

"No, that is not what happened." Nova had gone home hoping for help and sympathy. In their place, insult added to her injuries and to the loss of her friends.

"Do you think that I am the one who is stupid? Do not lie to me. I'm not wasting my good salt to pay a healer for you. See to your own wounds, and thereafter, you will think twice before fighting."

Hearing her husband moving about in the next room, she called out, "Madad, come in here and look at what your daughter has done!"

"Oh, she will be fine. They probably knocked some sense into her stupid head."

Both friends and family punished Nova for making the correct life choice. She retreated from the inn and returned to the barn with reinforced thoughts of regret as she gathered her creature friends for their morning walk to the beach. Experience had taught Nova of the healing power of the cold seawater. She tied off the horses and walked slowly across the strand and into the surf until fully committing herself to the water just before meeting the full force of a breaker. The numbing shock of the icy water overwhelmed any pain she would have felt from the stinging sea salt. Her body adjusted to the cold as her aches and pains melted away along with layers of dirt.

Later that morning, when Nova and her dog Sandy returned home with the horses, they stopped by Asbury Palace to admire its moat of beautiful white roses. Nova felt the need to pray. "Thank you, Almighty One, for these flowers of purity. They are an image of my beautiful life surrounded by its

PART 2—THE WRITTEN WORD

painful thorns. Thank you for the sweet aroma of life, and protect me from its evil. I have no human friends, and I hurt so…."

She was startled when the captain of the guards interrupted the prayer by calling her name. *Oh dear, what have I done now?* She wondered, nonetheless her only response was to look up and say, "Yes, sir."

"Come here, lass. Let me see those wounds."

The captain helped Nova sit down. "Ah, I see that you have had a bit of a wash-up this morning. That is good. Be brave now. This salt is going to burn." As the captain cleaned, stitched, and dressed her wounds, he said, "My son, Nate, told me everything that happened and what you did last night. I am very proud that Nate has a friend such as you."

After a slight pause, he added, "There you go. You will be as good as new with a few scars to add to your character. Wait here until you are called to bring my horse Black Thunder into the courtyard."

Nova was baffled about why he would give her such a directive. "Sir?"

The captain gently cupped his hand against Nova's face and said softly, "Just do it, lass."

"Yes, sir."

The first watch sounded as a battered and frightened Nova led Black Thunder toward the gate as the handsomely mounted guards assembled into formation. When the warhorse stopped at the gate, Nova urged him forward.

"Bring that horse to me!" the captain commanded.

While dwarfed by the giant warhorse, she walked toward the captain. Nova was annoyed. *What is this about? What is going on? I do not belong in the presence of such mighty men. Am I to play their fool?*

"Sir, your horse."

The captain refused to take the reins. Instead, he took hold of Nova and lifted her onto the horse as he said, "Up you go, lass."

"Me, on Black Thunder? Ouch!"

"Oh, I'm sorry. Try to be a brave little soldier. Otherwise, you are going to muck up the mood."

Once she was up and seated, the captain bellowed to his men. "Guardsmen, I have been informed that this lassie has conducted herself with great honor and valor. Her name is Nova. Henceforth, she is Nova, Daughter of the Light. Guards of Asbury, salute!"

IN THE BEGINNING

She was at once shocked and elated when with one voice they cried out, "Hail, Nova—Daughter of the Light!" Tears of joy, pride, pain, and embarrassment poured from her eyes. This was the kindest, most polite act ever bestowed on her. It was as if God said, "Well done, Nova, daughter of my light."

The captain broke her elation when he spoke to her in a stern yet gentle, low voice. "There's no crying on a warhorse, Nova. Come down off my horse, and off with you!"

"Yes, sir."

"Gently, little soldier; down you go."

As she limped away, the captain said softly, "You are the Daughter of the Light, and don't you forget it, lassie."

Later that evening, Nate and a guard came to the inn stables.

"Nate, what is it?" Nova asked, surprised to see him there.

"Nova, I will be cleaning the stalls and paddock from now on. My father says that you should know what you are doing if you are going to insist on being pugnacious. So, once you feel up to it, Guard MacDuff here is going to give you a few lessons in fighting."

Those few lessons continued through the winter. She excelled in the use of every light weapon including the bow and arrow. At first, her hand trembled so badly when drawing back the bowstring that even her quiver quivered. So, MacDuff taught her how to pluck the bowstring with amazing results. Then, early in the spring before the planting had begun, he took her to a farmer's field to demonstrate how to use fire for both defensive and offensive battle tactics. Little did anyone know that it was the perfect education for a Celt preparing to face the might of the Roman Empire.

She promised herself that no one would ever beat her again as Faolan and Latharn had done. She needed an inconspicuous weapon to carry with her for protection. For this purpose, she asked her blacksmith friend to fashion a leather belt with a weighted clasp. When it was completed and ready for its owner, Nova met the blacksmith at his shop. She tried the belt on and found it to be a perfect fit. "This is exactly what I needed. I will not be defenseless again. How does it look?"

Her friend answered, "Smashing!" He slammed his hammer down for emphasis, and they shared a laugh at his play on words.

PROTECTED

Nova's Age: Fourteen

Children are often unaware of the full anguish of victimization because they do not know any differently as they struggle to understand the world around them. They only know what they have learned. Sorting through their thoughts, they might rationalize that all children have been mistreated. Spoiled children are equally unaware of their privilege as neglected children are unaware of what they never had. Ignorance protects children in this way. Their assumption is that all adults tell the truth when, in reality, adults are often dishonest to children.

That is what made Abraham different. He was so honestly different that even a child could see his light. Because of him, Nova's life felt much brighter and positive. He was the one person who took the time to share God's love with her.

While Abraham provided spiritual encouragement, Nate provided sweat to lessen Nova's physical burden. Working together, the inn stables became an equine showcase where guests knew that their horses received proper care. Inn business increased even further with the purchase of four riding horses for both personal use and business. Nova was simply happy that they were her horses to care for and train. Although new people and animals made her life brighter, Asbury was still not her home.

Then one night she heard the magical words, "Nova! Prepare the horses for a ride to Asgard. We leave at dawn."

Asgard? Nova remembered the name and thought, *Asgard is directly down river from my mountains. I know how to go home from there. Home—yes!* She gave her dog a hug and exclaimed, "Sandy, we are going home! I will travel upriver from Asgard to the highlands. We are going home to Currcroft—to freedom, to hunting, to fishing, and best of all, to my clan! All right, fine, let's calm down; we don't want to give the escape away."

Nova, the stable girl, was responsible for the care of horses on extended rides. Everyone knew that the horses performed best in her company. They willingly followed the human who loved them. Of the four, Goblin was Nova's favorite horse, but the one that gave her the most trouble was her stepsister, Atina's, bad-tempered horse, Cheddar.

Nova, Madad, and the horses were ready at dawn and waiting for Monyah and Atina.

"Come on, ladies, we are really late," Madad murmured in frustration.

"Oh, Madad, what is your hurry?"

"We are expected at the Narrows by midday for the ebb tide. Now we are going to miss it. We will probably have to wait until tomorrow afternoon or later to make the crossing."

The journey began with Nova riding Goblin northward toward Asgard with Sandy faithfully following along. She was excited while memorizing every mile that would someday lead her home to Currcroft. Unfortunately, there were Pict bandits roaming the northern coastal territories, looking for easy pickings. These Celts would rob and murder their own clansmen if the price were right. Four horses guarded by a lass and her dog were the right price.

The four travelers from Asbury made camp on the south bank of the firth that evening. Obviously, the Narrows peninsula reached more than halfway across the firth. As previously agreed by courier, a ferryboat was waiting for them. Fortunately, the ferry-deck made a secure place to sleep until morning. Madad was correct about the tide. It was too late to make the crossing. "It would be nice if we could make it through the night without any rain," he said to no one in particular.

One at a time, Nova washed the horses in the firth then tied them to two large trees upwind of the other travelers. Nova grimaced because her butt hurt a little when she sat down to eat with Sandy. As the sun began to set, the pair played and bathed in the firth. It was a bright and memorable moment that was about to be darkened by the deeds of men.

PART 2—THE WRITTEN WORD

"There is only a lass between us and the horses," murmured a highwayman to the others as he peered through the underbrush.

"Yes, I know that one. Do not worry about her. Latharn and I easily beat her senseless one night. We raid the camp at first light, lads."

Meanwhile, down at the dock, a ferryman was comforting the travelers. "Everyone, get some sleep. We will cast off in the morning at high tide and sail to the north side of the firth. From there you should reach Asgard by nightfall."

Nova finally got out of the cold water and sat on the shore. Sandy followed, and after a big shake of his body that sent the water spraying in a spiral of droplets, he plopped down beside his best friend. "Look, Sandy—see the moon rise out of the sea," Nova said as she slung her arm around his neck and ruffled the fur on his chest. He responded with a happy, wide-mouthed grin and lots of panting. "It will not be long now before we are following that moon and the river to our mountain home. I am never going to be able to sleep tonight just thinking about it." Despite her protestations, Nova was asleep moments later as the full moon slipped behind the clouds. And a great night's sleep it was until Sandy began his low growl.

"What is it, boy?" When she saw that his ears were perked and listening, Nova peered into the darkness where shadows were playing with her fears. She slowly reached for the main hitch knot, released it with one tug, and held the horse-line firmly. The horses spooked when the silhouette of several bandits appeared in the clouded moonlight. "Stay, Sandy," Nova whispered as she dropped the line and set the horses free. "Yeah, Goblin! Home, Goblin, home! Bandits, bandits!" The horses bolted as chaos broke the still of the night with travelers screaming and Sandy charging the three outlaws that were rushing toward Nova. One of the bandits began screaming as Sandy's teeth sank deep into her flesh, but Sandy made his last yelp before Nova could join the fight and save his life. "You killed Sandy!" she shrieked. Moments later, the two men were surprised when overpowered by this small-framed girl. The third bandit turned and ran for her life. Later, she reported that Nova shape-shifted into a fierce, fighting giant.

A cry in the dark came from the dock. "I hear them coming. Cast off!"

"Wait for my daughter Nova!"

PROTECTED

A woman's voice pierced the night. "Leave her. She is nothing without the horses. Leave her or we will be killed!"

Loyalty countered disloyalty where Nova could only think about her best friend until she found his lifeless body. That dear flea-ridden, mangy mutt gave his life to save the life of his best friend. "Drat, Sandy. Look at you, buddy. You went and got yourself murdered...," Nova said, trying to ease her pain with a touch of dark humor before the reality of her loss caught in her throat and turned into a low sob. She wept silently until her tears were spent, and then she sealed the moment with a prayer. "Thank you, my Lord, for sending Sandy to protect me."

For the last time, she held him close and gently brushed the sand from his face and mouth. "Goodbye, my dear friend, until we meet again."

The Picts quickly regrouped, and Faolan took charge of his band. "The horses are gone. Come on—we can still overtake them on the ferry!"

"No, Faolan. They are on to us now. It would be a fair fight. Let's get out of here!"

"Yes, you are right. Until today, we have had a good run. Let's split up for a while until things settle down, and we'll meet back here next Beltane Day. There will be easy prey after lambing season next year."

Nova ran to the water thinking, *I know that voice. Faolan, you have killed my dog.* She dove into the water without hesitation when she saw that the ferry was already gone. With cutthroats behind and an open expanse of turbulent seawater ahead, it seemed as though she had chosen death by drowning. She kept swimming in the frigid water and thought about what the clan would say. *Nova, the water is only cold if you are not wearing enough clothes.* The thought gave her a laugh and restored her courage. *Fight, Nova—you can do this. Ignore the cold. You know that it will pass.*

Fearing for their lives, the ferrymen never stopped rowing. They reached the north bank of the firth by first light of day.

"What will happen to my daughter Nova?" Madad asked Monyah.

"Who cares about Nova? What will happen to my horses?"

"Mother, what are we going to do?" Atina whined. "We cannot stay in this dreadful place."

PART 2—THE WRITTEN WORD

"Madad, look out there!"

"Where, Captain?"

"There is something swimming across the Narrows."

Atina looked worried as she reached for Monyah's hand. "Mother, are the bandits coming after us?"

"No, Atina, my darling, it is not the bandits."

"Yes, I see it!" Madad shouted.

A frantic Atina blurted, "They are coming!"

"It is not the bandits! Look there!"

A tiny figure moved slowly toward the shore. Nova could only pray her thoughts. *Abraham's God, save me! I am so scared, cold, and tired.*

Ever so gently, the changing currents nudged Nova to shore as Madad rushed out to save his now precious daughter.

"Take my hand!" he called out over the noise of the surf.

She gasped for breath and screamed, "No! I can do it! I do not need you anymore!"

Madad stayed close to Nova until she collapsed on the rocky shore. He picked her up and gently brushed sand and seaweed from her face and mouth. He wrapped her in his cloak, knowing that he was holding a champion disguised as a stable girl. "I have lost your love, Nova, and I am sorry. I have lost a treasure for an inn and its nags."

Monyah did not hear her husband's lament as she hurried forward to express her own false concern. "I tell everyone that she is a wonderful lassie. I love the way she takes care of my horses. Nova, honey, where are my horses?"

With that, Madad shocked everyone, including himself. "Oh, shut up, woman!"

Later that day, some of the people in Asbury noticed when Goblin led the other three horses back home to the inn stables.

"They all left for Asgard yesterday. Something must have happened to them!"

"Star, go tell the captain of the Asbury guards that the horses have returned without your family. He will know what to do."

Once the captain heard the news, he told his men that he needed six volunteers to search for Nova and her family. He selected six of his best men after every guard stepped forward to volunteer. The rescue party left within the hour with extra horses, and they were able to signal their presence to the family by evening. One of the ferrymen was the first to notice the blue and black Asbury colors waving slowly back and forth on the south side of the Narrows.

"Madad, how did they arrive here so quickly?" a ferryman asked.

"I have no idea. I would imagine that they just happened to be patrolling this area of the shire. Whatever the reason, I am relieved that they are here. How soon can you take us back to the south side?"

"We can leave here late tomorrow morning."

When morning did come, there was only one traveler willing to continue the journey northward. Hence, there was an almost unanimous decision for the guards to escort the travelers back home to Asbury. For Nova, *home* meant an entirely different place in the opposite direction. *Yes, I also wish to return to my home*, she thought bitterly—*to my mountain home*. Determined, she attempted to persuade her father.

"Please, Madad, let's continue on to Asgard. The danger is behind us."

"Nova, did you lose your mind in the firth? Do you expect the guards to stay with us during the entire journey to and from Asgard?"

"The bandits are gone. We are almost there. Asgard is straight on. I'll protect you, Father!"

"Would you please be quiet? How is a wee lass like you supposed to protect me? We are going back home to Asbury, and that is final!"

"Well, at least I got to be your treasure for a day," Nova said with thinly veiled sarcasm, and inwardly, she thought, *Someday I will return to my Currcroft home, now that I know the way.*

It was an easy crossing after a miserable day spent on the north side of the Narrows listening to her family accusing her of another misadventure that resulted in the loss of the horses and the Asgard visit.

Madad was the first person off the boat to greet the guards. "Captain, I cannot tell you how happy I am to see you and your men. From there, he went on to tell what the family decided had happened the night before. He ended with, "Have you seen our horses?"

The captain kept his eye on a shamed Nova as her father told his side of the story. "The horses are safe and cared for in your stable. That is how we arrived here so quickly. My men and I immediately responded when we learned

PART 2—THE WRITTEN WORD

that the horses returned to Asbury without you and your family. Otherwise, it would have been days before we knew that you were in trouble."

Nova gave a weak greeting to her friends who just happened to be guards, and then she began walking away to search for and bury Sandy.

"Where are you going?" demanded her stepmother.

"I'm going to bury my friend. He died saving you and your precious horses."

"You come back here, young lady. We are not wasting any time on a dead dog and another one of your pranks. Let the crabs eat it."

"I would never do such a heartless thing! I will not be long."

When Monyah saw the captain walking away with his guards falling in line behind him, she demanded to know where they were going. She and Atina were now terrified of being without protection, but their haughty demeanor masked their fear—or so they thought.

"Where are you going, Captain?"

"My men and I are going to help a fellow warrior bury a fallen comrade. We believe Nova. You would also believe her if you knew her. She could not do anything to needlessly endanger you or the horses."

Madad joined Monyah's side with, "The queen will hear about this!"

The captain stopped, turned and walked directly to Madad saying, "Every man here would be proud to call her daughter." At this point, he was standing face-to-face with Madad. "And then there is you. The queen will not hear about this if we return to Asbury with Nova and leave the rest of you here."

"You wouldn't dare!"

Fortunately for Madad, their conversation was interrupted by a guard, "Captain, you should come and see this. We have two more bodies to bury."

"Now as I was saying, excuse me, my men and I are going to help a fellow warrior bury a fallen comrade and two of Nova's imagined bandits.

By the time they were safely at home, Atina was thinking dark thoughts about the future. *Nova this and Nova that. Doesn't anyone remember me? I am the princess in this family, and she is nothing more than our stable girl. I'm going to teach her a lesson that she will never forget.*

Meanwhile, Abraham was preparing for a late return to his home in Midian. "Teacher, I have your horse and cart ready for your trip home," Nova said. "However, it is not too late to reconsider and stay an extra night. Although there is no room in the inn, you are always welcome to stay here in the stable with me. I will make a special place for you to sleep on some fresh hay. Please say that you will stay with me."

"Nova, my dear child, I thank you for worrying about me. Yes, it is too late to return home. On the other hand, you have not seen worrying until you have seen my Sarah worry. I am late because one of our people here in Asbury died. Naturally, I could not leave without conducting a proper shomer for him. Oh, what was I thinking? I could have sent a messenger ahead and stayed the night here, but now it is too late. I must go. Besides, it is a full moon, and Horse knows the way. The Eternal One will protect me. I love you for worrying about this old man, but I will be fine.

Oh, by the way, Nova, I want to congratulate you on your victory! Everyone is talking about how you saved your family and fought off hundreds of bandits all by yourself. You didn't use a donkey's jawbone to defeat the attackers by any chance, did you?"[1]

"No, Teacher. And there were no more than ten bandits." Nova spoke bravely, but her voice cracked with emotion.

"Nova, what is it? Why are you crying?"

"My dog Sandy gave his life so that I would have enough time to escape. My best friend, Sandy, was the real hero. I miss him. And yet, even now, his image is fading from my mind's eye."

"Ah, yes, I think maybe you are my hero."

The old man stopped and took a position of reverence and prayed. "Blessed are you, Eternal One our Lord, Who has such as Nova in the universe. May You who are holy bless her and keep her safe. Amen.

"Nova, I bid you shalom, my dear."

"Shalom, Teacher."

Abraham's cart pulled away as Nova's stepsister Atina walked up and said, "Hi, Nova, would you like to play?"

Nova wondered, *What is she up to? This is the first time that she has ever had a kind word for me, and now she wants to play. Oh, I understand. It is because I saved her life.*

"Yes, sure—what do you want to play?"

---

[1] Judges 15:16—Then Samson said, "With a donkey's jawbone I have made donkeys of them. With a donkey's jawbone I have killed a thousand men."

PART 2—THE WRITTEN WORD

"Let me show you." Atina took Nova's hand and began swinging her around until Nova could hardly keep her feet on the ground. Then Atina let go, allowing the smaller girl to slam into the side of the stable.

"Come, I will show you your place around here, stable girl." She reached down to take Nova's hand for a second round of play when the game changed. Normally a broken nose results in facial disfigurement. Fortunately, in this case it did not hurt or improve Atina's looks. Nor did it improve Nova's welcome. The inn was out.

"Come on San...Drat, Sandy."

Nova stopped to grab her possessions and realized that she was wearing them. She mounted Goblin bareback and headed north out of Asbury toward Currcroft then doubled back south through the pine forest of the sand hills toward Midian. She knew that the mountain village of Currcroft was too far, and it would be the first place they would look for her.

"Come on Goblin, let's catch up to Abraham. He will know what to do."

Although beaten and tired, Nova was determined to reach Abraham or his home village during the now weaning-moon night. Her perseverance was soon rewarded when she saw her friend in the distance. At first, she was even more relieved to see that he had stopped and was getting down from the cart. Something in the road had captured his attention, so he did not see the man coming up behind him. When Nova could see two men beating Abraham, she called out, "Charge, Goblin!"

Goblin charged into battle. Nova released her weighted belt to use it as a mace. Moments later, it crashed into the first coward's forehead, and he was down screaming, with blood flowing into his eyes. The second coward ran into the forest and disappeared from view.

"Whoa, Goblin!" Slipping the mace-belt around her neck, she dismounted, secured the horse and cart, and ran to Abraham. The teacher was badly beaten and helplessly unconscious. It took all Nova's strength to lift his upper body onto the back end of his cart. Nova was about to hoist his lower body into the cart when the second man stepped out of the dark for another attack. In response, Goblin bolted forward and knocked him to the ground. A moment later, both front hooves connected on the second bandit's chest.

PROTECTED

"Goblin, whoa! Easy, girl."

Goblin backed off, allowing the man to roll over and crawl off while gasping for breath as the first man was screaming obscenities. He could not see. Blood had filled his swollen eyes.

"Help me! Please help me. There is so much blood!"

"Why sure, let me wipe the blood from your face," Nova said with a note of sarcasm in her voice.

He captured her left wrist at the exact moment she touched his face. In expectation, her right fist was poised for delivery to his ear. The ensuing punch left him screaming more loudly than before. Then she kept her promise, wiped the blood from the man's face, and smeared it across the white of Goblin's mane. She hoped that her step-family would assume she had suffered a terrible death in some unknown place, and perhaps they would not search for her.

"Dear, Lord, I know that you are with us in the shadow of this valley. Please give me the strength to lift the burden of our heavy friend. All right, fine, heavy friend, up you go into the cart. Please, Abraham, don't be dead."

Returning to the man on the ground, she ordered him to take off his clothes. In response, he screamed, "What? My ear—I can't hear you."

"I said strip, or I will finish you. --- I said everything!"

After the man complied, Nova said, "Thank you. These clothes will make a fine blanket for your victim. Oh, and look—here is a stout purse for our trouble. Thank you, kind sir! You are very generous for a coward!"

PART 2—THE WRITTEN WORD

Turning to her horse, Nova said, "Now for you Goblin. I love you, old horse. Nevertheless, you do not belong to me, and it is time for you to go. You are the second beast to have saved my life. How I have loved you both. You animals make for better company than some people. Once more, go home, Goblin—home! Goodbye, my dear friend."

Wiping a tear, she looked heavenward and said, "Now, Lord, help me lift my hungry, tired, and battered body up into this cart."

Meanwhile, one bandit continued to bleed. "What about me? Please don't leave me here. I'm bleeding to death!"

Nova gave away her identity in a thoughtless moment. "And may both of you bleed to death, you cowards!"

And the bandit named Faolan thought, *Cowards…Goblin…Damn, I will kill that Nova if it is the last thing I do!*

Horse was already on free rein when Nova recalled Abraham's words earlier that day that Horse always knew the way home.

"Horse, you poor old thing—what kind of name is Horse for such a noble beast? I hereby rename you Nightrider. Take us home, Nightrider, and let me sleep."

Meanwhile, Abraham's friends were on that same road, looking for their teacher—fearing the worst and hoping for the best. Nova could hear their approaching voices of concern and was struggling to wake up from having been lulled to sleep by the clopping of the horse's hooves.

"Perhaps he broke that wheel I warned him about," one of them said.

"Well, he has never been late coming home."

"What is that coming this way?"

"That's Abraham's cart, but who is driving?"

"Hey, you—wake up and get down out of that cart."

"Here he is! I found Abraham! Look at what some thief has done. Our teacher has been murdered!"

Nova was now awake, but was still sleepy from exhaustion. "Huh? Oh, thank you, God. Please help us!"

"Damn, it's a girl, and look, she has Abraham's purse. A girl highwayman—these people are animals."

"She is a girl thief and a murderer!"

That accusation fully woke Nova. "No, no, you have it all wrong!"

Seething with anger, one man punched Nova in the face while another held her arms before she could explain what had happened. Nameless voices continued to pierce the dark night.

"Tie her and throw her in the back of the cart."

"Put her in the cart with Abraham?"

"You are right. Tie her across the horse."

The night passed, and Nova woke up hungry and with a swollen jaw. She was tied to a tree, and the entire community was standing around pointing as she lay there in her own excrement, and blood. This unusual crowd drew the attention of a Celtic woman as she and a few of her warriors were passing through Midian. They could not help but notice a ragged, young lass with red hair that stood out from the other well-groomed people with black hair.

"I do not like what I am seeing here. That is one of our own tied to that tree as though she were a dog. Cailean, go and return with our other warriors."

The chief then directed her attention to the remaining three warriors. "This is what you are to do. When Cailean returns, station several warriors near each home in Midian. Tell everyone to stay out of sight until you hear my attack signal. Until then, let me learn about the charges against this girl. It could cost all their heads if they take the life of a Celtic sister without a Druid trial."

One of the young tribe members asked, "Why not just take all their heads now and be done with them?"

"Until now, these merchants have lived peaceably among us and have been very generous. There must be more to this scene than we see here. Everyone go now and wait for the others."

In the meantime, back at the tree, one of the villagers shouted, "Praise the Lord! Abraham lives."

Nova prayed aloud, "Thank you, Lord; now they will know the truth."

The Celtic leader joined the outer perimeter of the crowd and learned that the local leader was alive, but he remained unconscious. It was as though the girl's life was in suspension along with and dependent on Abraham's life. She remained tethered in the sun as an accused thief until someone in the crowd said, "Here comes Sarah. Oh, that girl is really going to get it now!"

PART 2—THE WRITTEN WORD

Sarah untied Nova and covered her with a blanket. Then she sat on the ground and held the girl against her. The crowd gasped in disbelief when Sarah gave her broth to drink.

An onlooker cautioned. "Sarah, she is the most murderous bandit ever. What are you thinking?"

"I'm thinking that she is only a girl. I am also thinking that we are better than this. We are different from the others. We are the chosen people of the One Who Redeems. We are held to a higher standard as His people."

The girl managed to say, "Sarah?"

"Yes, I am Sarah."

"I'm Nova."

With that, Sarah drew her closer, wept bitterly, and finally said, "Nova, my dear child, Nova. How will you ever forgive us?"

Those around her asked, "What is it, Sarah?"

"This is Abraham's young friend Nova. She is the stable girl he has often mentioned in prayer. You women there, come help me clean and prepare her for bed. Bring her into my home. I will need someone to look after her while I care for Abraham."

One woman passed by without stopping, and another woman said, "I'm not touching her."

The Celtic woman had been standing close by and watching to see what these people were going to do to her fellow Celt. She could not understand everything they were saying, nonetheless she did understand mercy when she saw it. She casually wiped away a rare and unexpected tear from her cheek. Sarah's act of kindness had unknowingly diverted a serious Celtic retribution against the people of Midian. The stranger abandoned her violent plans and decided to return mercy to Sarah and to bestow mercy and love on Nova. "If you will allow it, Sarah, I will look after her. You go to your man, this Abraham."

Another woman spoke out from the crowd before Sarah could answer. "Sarah, you cannot allow these people to enter your home."

"As you have said, it is my home."

Turning to the Celt, Sarah said, "Of course I will allow it. Please follow me."

PROTECTED

First, the Celtic woman washed and bandaged Nova. Then she carried her into the house and gave her soft food to eat and strong wine to drink. Nova was already asleep when she rested her head upon a pillow for the first time. Hours later, when she did awaken, she was comforted to see the woman still sitting beside the bed. Nova asked her, "What is your name?"

"My name is Caoimhe. Now rest my little sister. You are safe from harm."

Later that morning there was a gentle knock at Nova's bedroom door. Sarah appeared in the doorway saying, "Nova, there is someone here who wishes to see you. Are you up to having a visitor?"

"Yes, but who is it?"

Abraham stepped into the room with Sarah's support. "I told you that you are my hero."

Nova greeted him with raised arms as he took both of her hands and held them to his chest. The funny-looking old man and the stable girl were an odd pair indeed, and both were home safe and protected in the hands of God. This house was Nova's new home, filled with food, shelter, clothing, education, faith, hope, and best of all, God's love.

Amused at the sight, Sarah smiled and broke up the reunion. "All right, you two—Nova, come to breakfast if you can. Here are some clothes that our boys have outgrown. They will have to do until we can make some new clothes for you. Come to breakfast and let us hear how you appeared so far from home in time to save my Abraham."

Sarah turned slightly and addressed Caoimhe directly in Gaelic. "Please help Nova dress, and stay and have something to eat with us."

Speaking painfully, slowly, and slurred, Nova told her three friends the whole story from the moment Abraham's cart pulled away from the stable until his friends found them on the road. She concluded her story with, "There is one other thing. The noble beast Horse has been renamed Nightrider."

The looks of horror on the listener's faces changed to smiles, and Abraham said, "Nightrider—that's a wonderful name, isn't it Sarah?"

Turning his full attention on Nova, he said, "You are a little Moses, and here you are in Midian even. Of course, Moses killed an Egyptian. You only overcame two highwaymen and broke the little princess's nose all within a few

PART 2—THE WRITTEN WORD

hours. And you were not yet fully recovered from routing the thieves of the Narrows."[2]

"She did what?"

"Sarah, that's a whole other story."

Rubbing her swollen jaw, Nova continued to strain to say each word. "Abraham, you are the wisest man that I know. What should I do?"

"Well, Sarah and I have an idea. Listen, I have witnessed how your family maltreated you for years. You have been a slave to your family in Asbury. Since then, you have made some serious enemies in your so-called stepfamily along with two sets of highwaymen. Am I correct so far?"

"Yes."

"All right, Nova, listen to me. You must hide until we can sort out your enemies. So tell me, how do you like these clothes?"

"They are very nice boy's clothes."

"Yes, these will be your new clothes along with a boy's haircut and a bit of walnut husk stain in your red hair. In addition, for a short time, you will have a new name: Moses."

His words left Nova puzzled and slightly piqued. "Moses is a boy's name. I may not be very pretty, but I am a lassie."

"Exactly, Moses; no one will be looking for a boy. And by the way, Moses, could you try to speak with a deeper voice?"

"Yes, Teacher! You are a genius. I understand and agree except for one thing that you have said. I will not be Moses. I am Nova, the Daughter of the Light.

Where will I sleep? Where will I stay?"

"Sarah and I have already discussed that and we have an offer for you."

"What offer?"

"If and when we do sort everything out, would you consider addressing Sarah as Mother and me as Father?"

Nova could not say a word for fear that she would begin to cry and never stop. Instead, she put her arms around Sarah and gave a silent prayer of thanks

---

[2] Exodus 2:11-12, Moses—*He saw an Egyptian beating a Hebrew, one of his own people. Glancing this way and that and seeing no one, he killed the Egyptian and hid him in the sand. Exodus 2:15— Moses fled from the Pharaoh and went to live in Midian.*

to God for her new family, and for the astonishing way that God had provided for their protection.

Caoimhe remained reticent; she observed and listened. The other three had almost forgotten that she was still there until she stood to leave. Nova took her hand and said, "Caoimhe, thank you for staying throughout the night with me. I will always remember you as being true to your name."

"Yes, I have been true to my name of kindness more than you will ever know. Still, it is only in watching Sarah that I have learned its true meaning. Mostly, you have made me proud to be a Celt. I have heard of you before. You are Nova, Daughter of the Light. I will always remember you.

There is one other thing. I am going to have two of my warriors watch over you until these issues are settled. They will make certain that no harm will come to you. You may not see them, but they will be watching over you."

Caoimhe rejoined her warriors, and the people of Midian returned to their normal routine. They never knew that a host of Celtic warrior angels waited for Caoimhe's attack signal. The signal never came because of one elderly woman's act of kindness, which had overcome an act of war.

After a few days, the physical transformation of Nova was remarkable. The once broken girl emerged as a noble-looking Hebrew boy. The change in appearance from filthy rags to suitable clothing was so dramatic that it lent credibility to the Celtic-Druidic belief in shape-shifting.

"Nova, are you strong enough to go for a walk today?"

"Yes, Father."

While walking, Abraham shared his plan. "I have prepared a message to your father and the Queen of Asbury. First, it lets them know that you are safe, and it pleads for permission to allow you to stay here under our guardianship. It also assures them that you will be free to visit with your father in Asbury every full moon. Furthermore, it informs them of what happened on the roadway. It also requests a hearing and judgment on your behalf to settle the runaway, battery and theft charges made against you. Finally, I have requested that the captain of the queen's guards appear as your character witness. Only your disguise will remain publically unknown until the hearing. Our community will gather tomorrow for worship. I will explain everything at that time. In that way, nothing will be hidden from them that can be hidden."

PART 2—THE WRITTEN WORD

Abraham stopped in front of a yellow shack. "This is it. We have arrived at my friend Haggai's place. He will have the messages delivered to Asbury."

"Father, you have thought of almost everything."

"Almost everything; what did I miss?"

"Could we somehow let my clan know that Star, Madad, and I are alive and well? You should know that my father Madad took me from my clan years ago without their foreknowledge. Madad can tell you how to find my mountain family."

"Let me think about it and I will speak to Haggai about what is possible. I can see two problems. First, Haggai might not find a messenger brave enough to go so far way into an uncertain future. Those northern mountains are forbidding to us lowland people. Secondly, I cannot imagine that Madad would reveal information that would bring destruction back to him.

Now return home while I speak with Haggai. Sarah will be waiting to show you how to bake bread for the welcoming of the Sabbath. Later, the boys and I will join you both after sundown."

The next morning, when the time was right, Abraham revealed his plan to the community. The plan left them speechless until one man stood to speak. "First of all, Nova, please forgive me. I am the one who struck you in the face. I am sorry for hurting you and will do what I can to protect you."

The man turned his attention toward the congregation and gave a warning. "However, there are two greater issues here. Our community has always been protected by not bringing attention to ourselves; that is, protection through anonymity. This situation will draw too much attention to us. It is possible that these highwaymen could come here and harm our families. Finally, even if it is for a short time, Teacher, are you asking everyone to live a lie and pretend this runaway girl is a boy?"

Abraham was ready for that question. "Runaway girl, no—she is an escapee, a refugee even. Yes, that is what I am asking. I am asking it on behalf of the one who risked her life to save my life. Think about this: Did Laban give Noah refuge? Did Reuel give Moses refuge? Yes, of course, we all know that they did.[3] This waif sitting before you has accepted Sarah and me as her

---

[3] Genesis 29:1-14 and Exodus 2:15-21

PROTECTED

guardians. Yes, I am asking you as my friends to pretend for a little while until the danger passes and the queen settles the issue. Before Him Who is Holy and before this congregation, I am asking our Lord to place the total weight of this sin on me for the sake of this child. I am willing to step down as your teacher until my sin can be atoned.

There is also the matter of the security of our community. We have three shields of protection. First, we will be safe if we stand together and remain watchful and respectful of the others. The second shield involves the others. Chief Caoimhe of the Darling clan has warriors watching over Nova and Midian until the hearing is over. Finally, and most importantly, our Lord is also watching over His people."[4]

Then Aaron stood and addressed the congregation. "If it is a sin to protect this child the best that we can, then count me as the greatest sinner of all. Can anyone doubt that Yah placed her on that road in the moment of Abraham's need? Who here has doubt? Let him say so now."

Aaron paused before continuing. "And as for you rabbi, please forget this business about stepping down. There is only one teacher for me, Abraham. Who is with me on this?"

Everyone agreed with the plan and began singing psalms of praise to God. They came forward to embrace the adopted daughter of Abraham and Sarah. They accepted her into their community of faith. It was unlike her moment on the warhorse Black Thunder. On this day, her tears were acceptable before these dear people and the Lord. Afterward, Nova told everyone, "I cannot believe that I have been searching for the Eternal One and found Him living next door to me. The Lord is my neighbor."

The Sabbath passed, and two messages from Asbury arrived at Haggai's office, which he immediately delivered himself. The messages were addressed to Nova and Abraham of Midian. Everyone in the family carefully listened to the messages as Haggai repeated them. "First, I will tell you the good news. Nova, your father Madad has agreed to the plan of you staying here. Furthermore, he has offered himself as a character witness on your behalf, and he is very happy and relieved that you are safe.

---

[4] The Darlings are an ancient Celtic clan.

PART 2—THE WRITTEN WORD

"Secondly, the queen has agreed to the hearing on the day of the full moon after the autumnal equinox. She has ordered you and all parties concerned to her court, where a hearing will be held after a palace midday meal."

Abraham's voice quivered as he offered a thankful prayer. "Blessed are you, Eternal One, our Universal Presence, who is good and bestows goodness. Amen."

When he finished his prayer, he said, "Sarah has prepared some saffron tea and bread. Sarah, come and join us."

The family discussed the messages and prayed about them, as well as for direction from the One Who Is Holy.

Afterward, Abraham had a question for his friend. "So, Haggai, my friend, tell me: Why have **you** delivered these messages? What are you paying your messengers for if you deliver the messages yourself?"

"Abraham, if they are your messages, they are important to everyone in Midian. One of my messengers did not come to work today, and the other two messengers are out making deliveries. Therefore, I have brought them to you without delay."

"Haggai, sir?"

"Yes, Nova, what is it?"

"I noticed that your messengers deliver on horseback. If it is all right with Father, could I work for you? I can ride, and I love being around horses. I could also look after Nightrider and the other horses at your stable."

Haggai turned abruptly toward Abraham. "Nightrider? Abraham, who is Nightrider?"

"That would be my horse. Excuse me Haggai.

Nova, you will not be making any deliveries or taking care of horses. We hire goy-boys of the others to do that sort of thing. You are becoming a young lady—a teacher's daughter even. Your horseback riding days are over. You will be helping Sarah cook and care for our home. Keep in mind that there are people who would love to catch you out and alone."

Nova's face looked as horrified as she felt. "Never be around horses again?"

"Of course you will not be cleaning up after horses or delivering messages. You are no longer a slave. You are a young lady, and you will behave as a young lady."

"Then I rather be a slave."

PROTECTED

"Nova, that will be enough. Go home and help Sarah with the cooking where you belong."

She went away thinking, *I must go home where I belong. Home to Currcroft where people know and understand me. I will be around horses again.*

While the entire community waited for the day of the hearing, a new family with a daughter named Marsha arrived in Midian. Nova and Marsha were immediate friends. Marsha stood out from all the other girls with her quick wit, her openness, and her girth. Her genuine friendship was needed at that time more than she could have ever known. She was large but very girly with jewelry, fancy clothes, and girl thoughts. After an awkward beginning, Marsha was Nova's best friend from the first day they met.

It was the Sabbath when Marsha arrived early and sat down in the outer area of the synagogue. She was immediately annoyed to find a young man sitting in front of her. "Hey, you, go sit with the men."

Nova thought, *Oh, this is going to be fun.* Her accent would immediately give her away if she answered.

"You cannot sit here. Go sit with the men. Leave! Don't be crazy!"

Nova turned completely around and greeted Marsha with a wink, and in an exaggerated feminine voice, she said, "Let me introduce myself. I am Nova."

"You are a girl!" With that, the entire congregation could not contain their laughter. It seemed to last forever before calm returned to the synagogue.

"I will explain everything later. What is your name?"

"Marsha."

"Marsha, may I sit with you?"

Later that day, Nova explained everything to Marsha about how God had led her from a highland cave to learning of Him in a coastal stable while on her way to live next door to His house of prayer in Midian. Finally, Marsha learned of the pending hearing.

"Nova, I am afraid. What if they find you guilty?"

Weeks passed and it was almost time for the hearing when another message for Abraham arrived from Madad. The inn stables were in a bad condition, and the horses were waning, especially Goblin. The inn could not afford the cost of horse feed and a stable-boy for so many horses. They were going to sell the four horses and use the stable only for horses belonging to inn guests.

PART 2—THE WRITTEN WORD

"Haggai, I have an idea for you, my friend. You know how you have been talking about expanding your business?"

"I have? I know that I have been thinking about it. At the same time, horses are expensive."

Abraham explained the situation and offered a proposal to Haggai. "Make an offer for the inn horses and their tack for the value of the tack alone. Then, if the horses are beyond recovery, I will buy Goblin from you and you can sell the other horses for meat. So what do you think, my friend?"

With a sly smile on his face, Haggai quipped, "I think you are a better businessman than you are a teacher."

"Oh, thank you, Haggai, and since you call me your best friend, will you do it?"

"I've a package to deliver near Asbury. I will deliver it myself, look into this matter, and await your arrival at our friend Jairus's home in Asbury."

The hearing day arrived, and the summoned participants gathered in the palace courtyard. Meanwhile, a large crowd of onlookers gathered outside the gates. Some were chanting, "Nova, Nova, may your light shine forever," while others were crying for her condemnation. Her many friends were becoming acquainted with one another and sharing exaggerated Nova life stories. At the same time, the event provided her enemies an equal opportunity to conspire and seek revenge.

Abraham had a plan for Nova's safe arrival to the courtyard. First, he had her wear her old stable-girl rags under a messenger's hooded cape. "You will ride alone to the palace as if to deliver a message. Once you arrive, go sit with the pages and messengers until the queen calls for you. Do you understand?"

"Yes, Father, I understand your concern for my safety. What if someone recognizes me?"

"My concern is that they will no longer recognize you when you are called forward. Let us pray for wisdom, justice, and protection for you on this judgment day. Afterward, we will see you again in the palace courtyard."

The palace was the most beautiful place in Asbury. It served as the home and throne to the most beautiful woman in all the land. Only one word could describe the Queen of Asbury: stunning. She did not wear a crown because it would have diminished her appearance. Her radiant amber hair was her crowning glory.

Her Majesty managed to speak to all persons involved in the hearing except for the seemingly missing Nova. The queen addressed the stepmother by asking congenially, "How are you, my dear? Are these delightful girls your daughters? Where did you ever find such lavish furs and that necklace? Are you trying to outshine me?"

"Oh, no, my queen, we simply wore our best clothes to honor your home."

"Well, come sit with me during the meal and tell me all about your stepdaughter—this Nova person."

The queen did not take a bite of food, but instead, she listened carefully to Monyah's account of all that had happened because of Nova. As the meal concluded, the queen withdrew to her private chambers along with her advisors. "So tell me, what have my councilors learned about this child, and what do you propose we do in the case of her adoption and the charges that have been made against her?" Some of the advisors conjured up images of a child possessed by an evil spirit while others raised her to the legendary status of a great, reincarnated warrior.

In summary, the queen asked, "Has anyone seen or spoken to Nova?" She paused for a response and was angered when silence was her answer.

"No one has seen her? How dare she not come today as summoned! King Lars, stay with me. Please, everyone except King Lars, continue your inquiries, and someone find that runaway girl."

The queen's chief councilor was the chieftain of the Asgardshire territory directly north of her Monmouthshire territory. The councilor poured two glasses of wine and offered one to his southern neighbor as she said, "So Lars, tell me your thoughts."

"Her support is strong and it includes many of your court. First, if she is here, immediately give your seal to the adoption that her father has already given his consent. Then afterward, chastise those who have brought charges against her, and dismiss both the charges and those who have made them. Your subjects will know you as their loving and gracious queen. Then wait some time—say, until the winter solstice celebration—and then have her killed. Otherwise, this young woman and her following will grow out of your control."

Then there is a second possibility that she is not here today. In the event that it is her doing, add contempt to the other charges, and offer a reward for her capture."

PART 2—THE WRITTEN WORD

"Once more, our thoughts are the same, councilor," the queen agreed. Turning to the king, she said, "Dear Lars, would you please call everyone together for the hearing."

The queen made everyone wait a significant amount of time until she made her grand entrance and took her seat with a stilted air of regality in her demeanor. "Thank you all for coming to Asbury Palace today. I am greatly grieved that the center of our attention, Nova, has chosen not to be here. Can anyone give a reason for her absence?"

Abraham stepped forward.

"Yes, Abraham of Midian, do you have something to say?"

"Yes, my queen. Nova is here and awaits your bidding."

"Nova, come forward to your queen!"

Nova prayed within her mind as she walked forward and removed her hood. *Dear Creator of heaven and earth, I am frightened even though I know that you are with me. Please give me strength and courage to face my judgment.*

An indignant Monyah spoke out of turn. "That is not Nova. Nova is a dirty and stupid-looking girl. Anyone can see that person is a handsome, young messenger."

Nova calmly responded by removing the cloak to expose her old rags.

"That is Nova. Arrest her!" screamed stepsister Atina.

"Silence!" commanded the queen. "Family of Nova, come forward and stand beside her. Yes, and you, stand beside your stepsister."

"Ah, yes, Nova, I recognize you now in those rags. Horses and dogs followed you past my balcony each morning. Each day of the year, you were dressed as you are now: barefoot and in rags. The sight of you always caused me pain as I thought, *Her master ought to take better care of this slave.* I was enraged back then. It is only now that I have learned that the stable girl is an innkeeper's daughter and not a slave."

Pointing an accusing finger at Nova, the queen proclaimed, "You are the fugitive Nova: the daughter and sister being called to account for your criminal actions.

To her family members, I have this to say: Look at yourselves dressed in such fine clothes, and only this girl is in rags. All I see standing before me is stepsister next to stepsister. One is obviously superior in stature to the other. And yet, the superior claims that the inferior attacked without cause and broke her nose."

The laughter in the courtyard was a relief to an otherwise tense moment, but soon the queen brought the hearing back to order with the command of "Silence!"

Then, directing her attention to Nova, she said, "Nova, you stay where you are. Your so-called family members are dismissed. Leave my palace immediately!"

This time, the courtyard filled with mocking laughter and jeers as the family left with their heads down in shame. This time there was no call to order. There was only cause for celebration.

"Nova, is there a wish that I may grant for you?"

"Actually, my queen, I have several wishes."

"Oh really? Well, go ahead; let me hear them." Instead of gracious, the queen was cunning as she sought an opportunity to dispose of this trouble maker.

"First, please may I live in Midian with Abraham and Sarah?" The queen pretended to care as she thought, *Yes, you may go and live in Midian where I know where to find you.*

"Of course; it is already done. That leaves two wishes."

"The second wish concerns my northern mountain clan. I was taken from them long ago without their knowledge. If there be any way possible, please make it so that they may learn that Madad, Star, and I are alive and well."

Perfect, thought the queen. "I will have several of my guards accompany you to your clan after the coming Beltane celebration, and you can tell them yourself. And you had one other request."

The thought of going home and under the protection of a royal escort was far beyond Nova's expectations. "Thank you, my queen. Might I have a moment to collect myself?"

"Take a moment. Someone give her something to drink."

Nova's hands were shaking so badly that she could not hold the goblet of wine, so she set it down and continued before losing her courage. "Yes, my queen, I have another request. A certain mare in the inn stable protected Abraham and me on the road to Midian. Her name is Goblin. I miss her, and I am sure she misses me."

"Say no more. The mare named Goblin is henceforth your horse. Hearing adjourned. Everyone go home. Nova, you are free to go."

PART 2—THE WRITTEN WORD

Nova ran over to Abraham and asked excitedly, "Father, can we go and get Goblin now?"

"Yes, we can go to her right now."

Once outside, the people were not ready to let Nova go. Most of them shouted words of encouragement. "Nova, we love you!" Still, there were others, especially people such as Latharn, for example, who wanted her dead.

"Latharn, you get to her from the east end, and I will get her from the west end. The first one to reach her does the deed. We will meet afterward at the bridge over Sunset Loch."

As hard as Latharn tried, he simply could not reach Nova through the crowd surrounding her and Abraham. Father and daughter slowly made their way toward the horses. "Look, Goblin is waiting for you under those trees."

"Where, Father?"

"Over there—Goblin is standing beside Haggai. Goblin is the one on the left."

"I did not know that you could be so funny, Father, but that horse is not...." Nova's face turned from joyful to pensive. "Goblin?"

Haggai released the horse toward her lost friend. "Go find Nova."

The horse bristled as though to pull herself together by gaining strength in seeing her friend. She was a bag of bones making her best effort to move forward while Nova could only stand there watching in horror. Goblin was so weak that she suddenly staggered to the right and stepped on a man's foot. Others in the crowd went to help the injured man while Goblin continued moving until she stopped and bowed her head into Nova's chest. The sad sight of these once magnificent animals was a source of anger for all Nova's remaining days. She and Goblin walked together back to where Haggai stood with the other horses.

"Haggai, what are you doing with these horses?"

"So, no Shalom, Haggai? Or, how have you been, Haggai?"

"Shalom, Haggai. So tell me, what are you doing with these horses?"

"Shalom, Nova. I bought the horses and their tack for the value of the tack alone. The horses were extra. It was a bargain."

"I am sure that it was not a bargain. You can also be sure that I love you, and that I love you all the more for what you have done here."

Haggai wrapped his arms around her, and even he could not hold back his tears.

"Haggai, my dear, dear friend, whatever was the price you paid, it was too much."

Just when she thought that her heart could not break any further, Cheddar stood on wobbly legs, walked to Nova, and nuzzled her neck affectionately. "Hello you old mean thing. Yes, I missed you too."

Nova fought desperately not to have an emotional breakdown in front of her many admirers. Turning to an understanding face she said, "Father, these horses are too weak to travel. In addition to starvation, I suspect that someone drove them hard and put them back in their stalls without proper care. Please go home without me, and I will follow slowly behind, allowing the horses to graze along the way. Later, Haggai can decide what to do with the horses that do make it back to Midian."

Abraham, Sarah, Jonathan, David, Haggai, and his wife Leah discussed Nova's plan, and Abraham answered, "We are not in a hurry to go home, and we will not leave you or forsake you. We will be spending the Sabbath here in Asbury. That will give you a few days to strengthen the horses and visit with your father and sister."

Nova thought about the prospect of a family visit. "After today, that is going to be awkward," she murmured under her breath, but Abraham heard her.

"No one at the inn would dare harm you after today. It is important for you to do as the Holy One commanded. Honor your mother and father."

In remembering how she used to worship her great-grandfather, Nova replied, "Yes, the Druids also encourage the people to honor their parents and ancestors."

Meanwhile, back in the palace, Chief Councilor Lars drew close to the queen after the others were gone. "Well done. I promise you that she will never survive her journey through my northern territory. I have several loyal men who will make certain that her clan will continue to think the worst has happened to their lost members. Later, we will tell your people of Monmouthshire that Nova decided to stay in the highlands and that the clan is enraged against Madad. They are angered to the point of vowing to kill him on sight."

PART 2—THE WRITTEN WORD

"I like it, Lars. Although your plan is necessary, I cannot help admiring the lass. Look at her down there surrounded by her friends watching as she treats those pitiable horses with affection and mercy."

"Exactly; it is that public admiration that makes her so dangerous to the future of our rule in these territories."

Elsewhere, the loch rendezvous was unfolding. Where the royals planned, the bandits had already failed. Latharn was growing impatient for the arrival of Faolan at the bridge when he came limping into sight. "What happened to you, Faolan?

"That damn Goblin horse deliberately stomped on my foot. I will kill both of them if it is the last thing I do. What happened with you? Where were you when I needed you?"

"Calm yourself, Faolan. All is not lost," Latharn said. "I could not get through the wall of people surrounding the lass. The good news is that we know where she is living."

Nearby, two Darling clan warriors were sitting on a bench listening to the failed murder conversation. They stood and walked directly to the conspirators. "Hello lads. We have been following you follow Nova and have overheard your intentions. You both will die if you go near her again. Goodbye. Be on your way now. Far away, be on your way."

Nova left Asbury assured of divine protection. Divine protection or intervention, rather than chance, is one of the things that a new believer realizes is different in his or her life. God's protection over Nova became undeniably clear from the moment of the bandit raid at the firth until her arrival in Midian. Even beforehand, Nate had stopped Faolan and Latharn from beating her. These dramatic rescues proclaimed God's protection in her life. They were a clear sign of divine intervention, which is God's way of saying, "I am with you always when you walk with me."

Still, many people who believe in God go through life unaware of the totality of His mighty armor and the hedge of protection He places around us. This can be in the form of a missed appointment, lost money, a wrong turn, an illness, a betrayal, or any one of those moments in life that we perceive as inconvenient or painful. Such moments often turn out to be spiritual roadblocks against physical or moral disaster. These events made Nova realize that for every known protective act, there were many other moments of protection

PROTECTED

known only to God. Who would have ever thought that an assault in Asbury would lead to a roadway rescue on the way to being adopted by God's chosen people? Those same people of Midian would never know that Sarah defended them with her mighty sword called kindness.

THE SILVER AGE OF MIDIAN

Nova's Age: Fifteen

Nova spent that winter in Midian experiencing life as normal daughter, sister, friend, and girl in love. Genuine friendships were forming and growing. Everyone in Midian believed that Nova's enemies were no longer a threat. On the contrary, the number of her enemies was also growing.

Marsha and Nova continued their unlikely friendship. It is difficult to explain the bond between two teen girls who are so completely different other than to say that opposites really do attract. Marsha never treated her best friend as an uneducated Celt, as a lesser person because she was adopted, or as though she was beneath Marsha because she was poor. She simply loved Nova's genuine, rustic nature, as Nova loved Marsha's sophistication.

Still, she faced new challenges in her new life. At least in Asbury, as long as her work was done, she could come and go as she pleased and do whatever she wanted to do with whomever she wanted to do it with. Nobody had cared about her, and so she had been as wild and free as the birds.

One day she said, "Father, I hate being inside of the house all day. I want to be with the horses. I want to ride."

"Nova, it is not the proper behavior for a young lady to do."

"You do not understand. It is who I am. This life in Midian is a greater enslavement for me than it was in Asbury. It has been days since I kissed Goblin's nose. If you will not let me ride Goblin, then at least let me study and learn about Yah with the boys. You let me listen to you in Asbury. Why can I not listen to you in Midian?"

"Nova, it is simply not done here in Midian. People will think that you are our servant and not our daughter if I let you care of the horses or work as a messenger. On the other hand, you are right. It breaks my heart to see you so sad not being with your animal friends. Haggai does have something that you can do.

Secondly, there is the issue of your attending school. What was acceptable in the stable is not acceptable here in Midian. Again, a young woman's place is to stay at home with her mother. Contrary to that, you are my most brilliant student. Therefore, as my daughter, you may sit quietly in the outer area of the synagogue and listen to the lessons. Later, you can ask me questions at home. For all that, you must continue to help Sarah at home."

"Father, I will agree to anything if it would mean that I can ride Goblin again."

Haggai did hire Nova to look after his horses and to make deliveries twice each week to the coastal villages south of Midian. These were unusual activities for a Jewish woman. Notwithstanding tradition, Abraham and Sarah made an exception for Nova because she was equally passionate about the privileges of learning and horseback riding. Not only was she paid, but she got to keep her earnings, too. Abraham always told her to save for the future. For Nova, this was a labor of love. She would have paid Haggai for the privilege of riding Goblin around the countryside.

Yes, they were able to bring all four horses back to full strength, although they did come very close to losing Goblin. The stable population grew further

PART 2—THE WRITTEN WORD

when two stray dogs decided that it would be fun to follow Nova everywhere. She named them Nee and Miah after Nehemiah, a prophet and a great builder. This was to remind Nova that she was rebuilding her life as Nehemiah had helped rebuild the walls and gates of Jerusalem.

Home, synagogue, school, and riding became routine until she suffered a knee injury from a running dismount. It did not seem to be a serious injury at first until her knee swelled and a new messenger had to take her place. She thought it best to introduce herself to the new messenger.

"Hi, my name is Nova. The horse that you are preparing to ride was misnamed Cheddar. The name Demon is more accurate. Here, take my horse Goblin, who should have been named Angel."

"Okay...but why should he have been named Demon? Is he that bad?"

Shaking her head as though the question was immaterial, Nova asked, "Where is your messenger's cape?"

"The man inside said that he would have one made for me."

"Here, take my cape. And don't worry—Goblin knows the way in the dark. If you become lost, just tell her to find Nova, and she will bring you home."

Nova gently kissed the horse's soft nose. "Now, Goblin, you be good and go."

That night she went to bed crying to God, "Why did I have to hurt my leg? What have I done that you are punishing me? Why did you let this happen?"

Sarah comforted her with hot honey-willow tea. "Here, drink this to ease the pain, and I will have some more for you in the morning. Then go to sleep and stop blaming God for the results of your actions."

The following morning, with Sarah's help, Nova was able to hop next door to the synagogue on one leg with some pain.[5] She found Haggai and Abraham there having a serious low tone conversation. "Good morning. Well don't you two look . . . Abraham turned and took Nova into his arms. "Father, you are frightening me. What has happened?"

"The new messenger and Goblin were accidently killed at Rocky Point Bluff sometime last evening."

Everyone heard Nova cry out, "My Goblin and the boy? Oh Lord, why them and not me? Lord, please tell me why them and not me?" She was equally distressed over the loss of horse and rider. That young man had come to them as though from nowhere and had died in her place without family or friend to come forward. There was no father to say, "That was my son." Nobody in Midian knew the boy's name. Nova inherited his torc, and she wore it for the next nineteen years. She wore it in remembrance of God's protection and of the unknown hero who had died in her place. She wore it openly in the hope that one day she would hear a mother say, *That torc belonged to my son.*

Abraham immediately put a stop to her delivery work. "Nova, it is time for you to take your place as a young lady and help Sarah more at home. Besides, some people have been complaining about your behavior."

She was comforted in her grief by her family, friends, and faith. Her brother by adoption, David, was especially attentive and sensitive to the sorrow of his secret girlfriend. Hebrew and Celtic romances were quite different. The Celts had a complicated system of four different types of marriage. The first being the traditional where two equals were married. Most of the time, it simply took two people of equal social class who were attracted to one another. The type of marriage with the greatest imbalance was the type where a peasant married someone of wealth such as Madad's first marriage in comparison to his second marriage into servitude. Chieftains also arranged some marriages to form unity between their clans.

---

[5] Willow stems contain salicylic acid used in the making of acetylsalicylic acid (aspirin).

PART 2—THE WRITTEN WORD

Hebrew romance was a more sacred matter than it was for the Celts. The man and even the woman had the right to refuse the choice of a matchmaker. A betrothal period began once a proposal was accepted, and a chaperone became the constant companion of the woman until the wedding. This was to ensure the purity of the bride. However, the reality is that love will find a way in any culture. As with all parents, Hebrew parents simply thought that they were holding their children to a higher standard than they practiced themselves. A bridal dowry was common in both Celtic and Hebrew marriages. Once married, Hebrew marriages carried a double standard weighted in favor of the husband. For example, the man could divorce the woman for the slightest reason. The woman could only divorce the man if he granted it. In comparison, Celtic marital rights were equal among men and women of equal social class.

Even from afar, school was wonderful, with so much to learn about languages and the *Torah*. Nova's favorite *Torah* character was David. His best friend was a prince named Jonathan. David and Jonathan were also the names of her adoptive brothers. She always imagined them as their *Torah* namesakes where Jonathan was a good friend and David was the prince of Nova's heart. Some of her other favorite characters were Ruth, Deborah, Esther, and Hannah.

Ruth and Nova were both outsiders known as Gentiles who had attached themselves to the nation of Israel.

Deborah was a prophetess and a warrior queen who obeyed the Lord. She was Nova's scriptural war heroine. She could see herself in Deborah's role against the Canaanites. However, it was Hannah's story that touched Nova the most. Hannah was barren, and she had made a promise to God that if ever He blessed her with a son, she would return that child to God. Later, she gave birth to Samuel and kept her promise by surrendering him to the house of the Lord in Shiloh. Raised toward a sacred destiny, Samuel grew to become a great prophet of God under the tutelage of a priest named Eli.

The story bothered Nova. *Eli,* she thought. *What is there about that Hebrew name that is so familiar and yet I cannot remember meeting a Hebrew named Eli?*

One evening at home, Nova asked Abraham to show her the Gaelic written language, only to find out that it had never been written. The Egyptians,

Hebrews, and many other tribes had written languages for centuries, but there was not one written Gaelic notation. This fact gave her a Stone Age inferiority complex that lingered in her mind for years. Nova wondered about this. *Is there a race more primitive in the world than mine?*

One morning, Abraham called the class to attention and announced, "Today we are going to learn more of our history that was put into writing by Moses fourteen hundred years ago. His writings formed our *Torah*. The first line in the *Torah* is, 'In the beginning God created the heavens and the earth'."

Abraham paused and glanced toward the outer area where Nova was listening to the lesson and smiled before he continued. "From the time of Father Abraham to Moses, we were a people of the oral tradition who could not read or write. Who was this Moses, and where did he come from? Well, my children, the pharaoh of Egypt became fearful of the increasingly large numbers of Hebrews in his land, so he ordered the execution of every newborn Hebrew boy. Moses's mother reacted to the decree by placing her baby boy in a basket and floating it on the Nile River to save him from the pharaoh's wrath. Ironically, the pharaoh's daughter found the child and raised him as an Egyptian prince. He learned to read, write, and behave as a royal.

"As it was then, the gift of the Lord's holy written word continues to be important to our survival as a people. Later in life, Moses led our people, the Hebrews, out of Egypt and into the wilderness in search of the land that God had promised. Some people quickly regretted leaving Egypt and cried out, 'Moses, why did you have to bring us out here in the wilderness to die? We could have stayed in Egypt and died!' God remained faithful and provided for the people day and night, even though they persisted in their unfaithfulness to Him.

They stopped in the desert at Mount Sinai, three months after their exodus from Egypt, and Yah called Moses and the people to the foot of the mountain. It was there that The One Who Reveals spoke to Moses and called him to the mountaintop, where the Lord gave the Ten Commandments to Moses.

The first four commandments established a relationship between man and the One Who Is Holy. The fifth through the tenth commandments defines how people are to live on earth with one another. Summarized, the first

PART 2—THE WRITTEN WORD

four commands us to love the Lord with our mind, all our strength, and all our heart. Simply stated, the second part commands us to love one another.[6]

Moses was in the presence of the Lord and received blessings and the *Torah* directly from our Lord. Thereupon, the Lord turned the tragic wrath of a pharaoh into a Hebrew-Egyptian prince who learned to read and write so that we could have the *Torah*. It is fascinating that the Lord has used Moses, who was raised Egyptian, to speak to us for fourteen hundred years while the stone gods of Egypt silently erode into dust."

Abraham hesitated for a moment to let the depth of that fact sink in. His pupils waited with rapt attention to hear what he was about to say. "My dear students, always remember that God's written word is a powerful and specific connection between The One Who Reveals and us. Without it, we are as cavemen, stumbling around in the dark, worshiping the shadows of our own desires."

Nova thought, *Ouch—he is talking about my people when he describes cavemen stumbling around in the dark and worshiping shadows.* It was then she realized that her destiny was to take the light of God's written word to her people in their Gaelic language.

These were Nova's Utopian days of normalcy. She could be human and live beyond struggling to survive from day to day. As humans, we should have time to learn, teach, worship, build, create, recreate, love, and to serve one another. Midian provided such moments for Nova and gave her a solid foundation to build her life on. It gave her life meaning, direction, and purpose. It also gave her the strength to face an uncertain future.

---

[6] The Tanakh contains 613 commandments. Over 200 of them require the existence of the Jerusalem Temple.

THE BETRAYAL

Nova's Age: Fifteen

It seemed as though spring would never arrive. Snowstorm after snowstorm blanketed the landscape, and then springtime blossomed five days after the last snowflake fell on Albion. As promised, six palace guards and Nova's female chaperone arrived in Midian on Beltane eve. It was good to see MacDuff again along with a new palace guard named Nate. Nova proudly introduced her old friends to her new friends, and a going-away party became part of the Beltane celebration. Then the exciting day came to begin their journey to her Currcroft home.

Nova prayed one prayer repeatedly: "Dear God, please let everyone in Currcroft be alive."

Until then, David and Jonathan had never seen much of Albion or many of *the others*. Both young men begged their father to allow them to make the journey to the northern mountains. The real motive behind the adventure was that David and Nova could not bear to be away from one another for the whole summer. They reasoned that it was not really a lie because they were certain that everyone knew of their feelings for each other. Abraham gave in to their overwhelming enthusiasm and allowed his sons to accompany Nova to and from the Currcroft highland village.

Everyone came to the going-away party, and the celebration continued for another day once they reached Asbury. Nova and her brothers began their journey with much love to share with her mountain clan. Even the queen had some encouraging parting words and a gift. She had her court artist draw a family portrait of Star, Madad, and Nova.

PART 2—THE WRITTEN WORD

She immediately recognized the friendly voice that came from behind her. "Well little soldier, you have come a long way from a stable."

Nova spun around with open arms to greet the captain of the Asbury guards. He took her in his arms, held her uncomfortably tight and placed his lips against her ear. "Captain, you are hurting me."

"You must listen to me. Do not trust anything that the queen has told you. She is not your friend. You must be careful."

Nova pulled away as she wondered if he had lost his mind. "Excuse me Captain, but I must hurry. As you know, the queen has given me a royal escort to my home. Isn't this a wonderful family portrait that the queen had made for me. Good bye captain."

"Nova . . ."

"Oh, I see my father Madad over there. I must speak to him and sister before I leave. "Good bye captain." The captain's behavior was both frightening and puzzling. *How could he betray our dear queen like that?* Nova backed away from a man she once respected without question.

Of the three family members, only Nova had the courage to leave the Asbury incarceration. All the more, she desired freedom with great anticipation after her separation from her clan for nine years.

"Madad, I must speak to you and Star before leaving for Currcroft."

"This is not a good time. The inn is very busy."

"Madad, you know that the clan is going to want Star back, and to free her from this servitude. What are you going to do if they come for her?"

Star joined the conversation after overhearing Nova's question. "I know all about how they live in a cold cave deep in the earth. Why would anyone live that way? I want to stay here with my friends. Unlike you, I do not remember any of those people. Just tell them that we are dead, or you could stay here and do your work as we do. Once again, I do not like the way your life is headed, Nova."

"I hope that I can persuade the clan not to come after both of you," Nova replied, not taking Star's bait.

Madad remained silent with his head down in shame as Nova embraced them. "I will see you both in three full moons," she said decisively.

Star made a petulant sound to accompany the stomp of her foot. "Nova, did you not hear me? Come home to Asbury. We need you here. Father and I have to do your work cleaning the stinking stable. All that you think about is yourself."

"Yes, I heard you, Star. Everyone heard you. Now hear me. I will not lie to Grandfather. Furthermore, I have changed my direction. I am sorry that my actions are interfering with your life as a servant."

Meanwhile, there was another less festive reunion on the Firth of the Narrows south bank. As previously agreed, the ring of bandits gathered for another summer of pillaging along the northern coast of Albion. In Celtic tradition, they sat around the campfire, swapping tales of their winter escapades when Faolan stood to tell his share of lies.

"My dear honorable fellow thieves and cutthroats, I have some stories to tell. Latharn and I attempted to kill the Nova witch. We were very close to her when twenty of her demons sprang up to block our path. She escaped before we could kill all twenty demons. However, that did not deter us from our quest. Today, it gives me great pleasure to inform you that Latharn and I did finally kill the giant Nova and her demon horse Goblin!"

An outspoken thief named Rook egged him on. "Ah, go on with you, Faolan. Do you want us to believe that you and Latharn killed the giant by yourselves? That is not believable. Our whole band could not kill her last summer. Tell us, lad, how did you manage it?"

"Well, we tracked the beast for several months and found that she often traveled alone on horseback along a ridge known as Rocky Point."

In a disbelieving voice, Rook continued his chide. "Yes, go on with your tall tale!"

"So we laid in wait in a place closest to the edge of the ridge and sprang a trip-line that brought giant and horse over and down the bluff to their deaths."

"Brilliant! Let's hear it for Faolan and Latharn, if not for their deeds, then for their imaginative storytelling.

You lads look as though you had a rough go of it this winter. Faolan, that is a bad-looking scar on your forehead, and you've got a limp to match. What happened to you?"

"Ah, Rook, look for yourself. They were very large demons that attacked and wounded us. Besides, my scars give me a bit of character."

"Well, it looks as though something or someone really gave you both a beating. Sorry about the scars, you did not need them to give you a bit of character. You are a character."

"Well, back at you, Rook. A man is bound to get a few scars while killing demons and a giant. Nova is dead, and we sent her straight to the underworld on horseback!"

Rook shook his head in derision and glanced away where something caught his eye. "Hey, look on the northern side of the firth! There is an armed patrol over there. Let's get out of here." The Asbury expedition was also heading toward them from the south.

"Good eye, Rook, I'll give you that." Looking westward, Faolan said to his band of thieves, "We better head west, lads. It is becoming crowded around here."

As Nova and David approached the south crossing of the firth, Nova said, "David, isn't this heaven with all the heather and thistle in bloom?"[7]

It was hard to believe that they were actually heading northward along the coast. Nova could not even glance over at David without her sweaty hands shaking and gumming up the reins. Her heart was racing as she thought of

---

[7] The thistle is the national flower of Scotland. its symbolic meaning is "Don't mess with me."

that first kiss. Could there ever be anything better or more exciting than that first kiss? *What will our children look like?* She mused. *Where would we live? In Midian, I suppose. Where could I live until the wedding? Marsha's family would take me in. Or, Haggai and Leah would have me. Whatever, wherever, I would be the best wife in the world and give Abraham and Sarah many grandchildren.*

Nova loved seeing her two guardians, Nee and Miah, running happily along with them all the way to the Firth of the Narrows where the ferry was waiting. It was then that the three Midianites learned that this was the northern boundary of Monmouthshire, and Nate, MacDuff, and the other Asbury guards were releasing them to the protection of the Asgardshire territorial guards. MacDuff's reassurance did little to reduce the uneasy feeling that Nova had about riding off with strangers. Calm returned somewhat to her mind by the third day. The Asgard guards seemed nice enough, and it was a relief that they did not bring a chaperone to hover over Nova.

Riding between David and Jonathan, with the dogs trailing along, added to her comfort as they lost themselves in conversation. That day they laughed and talked about Albion, family, and how much Abraham and Sarah meant to her.

More and more they noticed how drier everything was in comparison to the southern territorial flora. One of the guards told them that they were experiencing the worst drought that anyone could remember. "All wind and no rain." Otherwise, it was a great day riding together until they came to the small village of Glenn Morrah where that uneasy feeling returned to full strength.[8]

The guards were particularly excited to arrive in a place known for its dining, drinking, gambling, and debauchery. The captain took a moment to say, "We are going to spend the night here, folks. You will really enjoy this place. It has the best heather-ale, wine, and mead in all Albion."

The captain's words were not reassuring. "David, I don't like this place."

"Well Nova, we are here now, and we're hungry, thirsty, and tired. It is only for one night, and you will be home by tomorrow night."

"Well, I am tired and hungry. You and Jonathan go ahead and order something to eat. I will tend the horses and come in later after I freshen up."

---

[8] This scene takes place as the second week of May begins. The lowest recorded rainfall for this region in Scotland during the month of April is .1 inch and the greatest amount is 6.1 inches.

PART 2—THE WRITTEN WORD

"Nova, let the stable boy care for the horses. Come on in out of the wind and have something to eat."

"It will not take me long. Both the horses and I need to be properly groomed."

After grooming the horses and herself, she went into the pub where she met the luscious aroma of freshly baked bread, stew, and wine that overwhelmed her weary soul. "Food, at last…."

Neither David nor Jonathan noticed her standing at their table. They were well on their way to being drunk, and each one had a woman on his lap. "David!"

"Hey, Nova! Come, sit, and stay like a good girl! Have a bowl of stew and some of this great bread, and wash it all down with something called mead. Calm down, relax, and have a drink of this stuff. It will make you feel better."

"Jonathan, you know that you do not live by this kind of bread, and I will not drink from this cup." With that, she picked up a loaf of bread and a large bowl of stew, turned around, and walked out the door as the guards were leaving.[9]

"Captain, where are you and your men going?"

"We are going to patrol the area. We will return later. Go join your family inside."

"Patrol in this wind? Patrol for what?"

"There have been reports of bandits operating in this area."

Just then, David came outside calling after Nova. "Where are you going? Come back inside out of the wind, and have a bit of fun for a change. You just might like it!"

"Yes, David, my body would enjoy it at the cost of my soul. We both know that the 'it' that I just witnessed was not something that would be pleasing to the Lord or your parents—or me, for that matter. I will sleep in the barn with the dogs and horses. They have better manners."

"You will have a long wait while Jonathan and I spend a few nights here! We have met some really nice women, and they like us."

---

[9] Deuteronomy 8:3—He humbled you, causing you to hunger and then feeding you with manna, which neither you nor your fathers had known, to teach you that man does not live by bread alone but on every word that comes from the mouth of the Lord.

"Fine David, I can make it to Currcroft Village from here without you or those foreign looking guards. Thank Jonathan for me. You both may return to Midian after your few nights here."

Later that night, an intoxicated David found Nova sleeping in the barn under the hay. "Nova, my darling, I'm sorry."

"Tell me about it in the morning, David."

"Ah, come on, Nova."

"David, what are you doing? David, stop it. David, no!"

Afterward, all Nova wanted to do was to leave that horrible place. She left David saying, "You fool. Nee and Miah would have killed you had I screamed."

Once more, she made a hasty escape after mounting a horse bareback. The pace westward started slowly and quickened as night gave way to the dawn. She comforted herself by talking during the ride. "All right, fine, Nova, stop crying. He is a stupid, drunken boy who stole what you were willing to give him. David, David, David, how can I ever go back to Midian and face you or your parents? I cannot even ask Abraham what to do this time. Well, at least I have my mountain home and clan."

Days before, King Lars had ordered his captain to solve two problems. The first problem was with his Glenn Morrah subjects. The first fruits were the king's share, and the leftovers belonged to his subjects. Farmers, shepherds, and even the Glenn Morrah innkeeper imagined that they did not have to pay their annual tribute because of the severe drought, subsequent crop failure, and livestock loss. The king would not tolerate this disloyalty. His subjects needed to know what happens to those that disobey his laws.

The second problem was with Nova's growing popularity that could eventually threaten both his and the Queen of Asbury's territory. Best of all, the queen had rewarded the northern king handsomely to have Nova killed. *The time is right*, thought the captain. *One action will answer both of my orders.*

He and his men returned in the night to a sleepy Glenn Morrah and torched its buildings. Soon the fires spread rapidly out of their control and the land was set ablaze with the wind waiting to drive the flames westward.

By then, in addition to being hurt, Nova was hungry, thirsty, and mostly too tired to do anything other than rest. She stopped at the base of her mountain where the rolling hills spread out toward the east. Here, the forest would yield everything she needed including a safe place to sleep high in a giant

PART 2—THE WRITTEN WORD

holy-oak tree. "Hello, great tree. Ah, this is as it was years ago, resting up here in your arms safe from beast or man."

She could smell the sweet mellow fragrance of burning grass as she drifted off to sleep. Later, even in her sleep, she could tell that the smoke had become stronger. In her sleepy brain, Nova rationalized the source of the smoke by thinking, *Oh, this must be the day that the farmers burn their fields before spring planting.* Then the dogs started barking, and she yelled down to them to be quiet. She told the dogs that it was only the wind, and then she slept on. Finally, the rushing sound of a stampede joined the wind, smoke, fire, barking dogs, and terrified horse. Nova could no longer rationalize their meaning, but sat straight up, almost falling out of the tree and blurted, "Wildfire!"

Not only was Glenn Morrah Village burned, but most of the Linndee Valley was charred, and the flames continued to race westward over the lowland hills toward the highlands. Animals and people could be seen in the distance, running and losing ground to the inferno. First, the fire consumed David and Jonathan, and then it was coming to claim everything in its path including Nova. She had nowhere to turn except to God. "Oh, dear God, save me!" she called out in prayer with a loud voice. "Fire has consumed our young men, and now I will soon perish. Please help me think and to use what I know. MacDuff taught me to fight fire with fire! No, that is a bad idea. Even if I had a way of starting a defensive fire, it would save me at the cost of certain endangerment to Currcroft Village. Have you brought me this far only to let me die here in this wilderness? No! You are El Shaddai, the Almighty One. You have always been faithful to me, and I will be faithful to you now. I will trust in you, my Lord; I will not be afraid."

She looked once more toward Glenn Morrah, and her whole body turned as cold as ice, even though the air was already uncomfortably hot. She shivered as salty sweat poured down her face, and again she cried out to God in desperation. "In God I trust; I will not be afraid," she proclaimed, and warmth returned to her body. "Elohim, have mercy on me and my people. It is I, Nova, Daughter of your Light. This is your land, your fire, your wind; please spare our lives. Save our souls."

Nova had to admit being delightfully surprised when the wind reversed direction and returned from the west with a fire-quenching rain. "Hallelujah! Let the praise be given to you, Lord! You are a merciful God. On this day, you have spared my life and the lives of my people. On this day, I vow to place the life of my firstborn son into your hands. As your servant Hannah did in Shiloh, my son Samuel will be dedicated to you and raised in your Midian house of prayer."[10]

By now, all kinds of animals were running in panic while Nova prayed and made her sacred vow. Creatures that normally avoid humans paid little attention to her presence in their desperate flight from something they could not fight. Several dogs stopped running and gathered around her encampment out of their instinctual need for safety in numbers and a human to lead them. The fire had driven the animals westward into the hills and up the mountain. "Look at all that food on the run toward home! Nee, Miah—hunt!"

In moments, she went from a weak and wounded victim to an alpha primal predator. They were dog pack, horse, and woman driving a strange herd of animals farther up the mountainside, heading directly for the narrow entrance of Currcroft. Some animals went through the narrow village entrance known as the Eye, while many others took the wide road to nowhere.

"Lord, I am very tired, hungry, and thirsty. Nevertheless, I will trust in you. Restore my soul that I may not grow weary. Give this dear horse the strength to rise up this mountain as though on the wings of an eagle. Take me home, Lord; take me home. Deliver me safely home to my people. Deliver my people, oh Lord."

It was a seemingly endless trek up the mountain. "I remember that old spiral pine tree. Let me see. What did Mother say about it? Yes, I remember. 'See the tree 'n Eye is nigh.' Nee, Miah—come! It is this way."

---

[10] Psalm 78:63—Fire consumed their young men, and their maidens had no wedding songs.

1 Samuel 1:25-28—As surely as you live, my lord, I am the woman who stood here beside you praying to the Lord. I prayed for this child, and the Lord has granted me what I asked of him. So now I give him to the Lord. For his whole life he will be given over to the Lord.

THE HOMECOMING

Nova's Age: Fifteen

The spiral is the most ancient of Celtic symbols. It is possibly associated with the Druid belief that life is an endless cycle.

Within Currcroft, the great meadow suddenly held a menagerie of stray animals. Elymas called out, "Curr, come out here and tell me what you make of this!"

THE HOMECOMING

When Curr rushed out and saw the astonishing sight before his eyes, he said, "Elymas, you foretold of a great event, and it is happening right now. These animals are the forerunners of their queen. I know what it is! All these animals arriving in this way can mean only one thing. It is Nova. Nova has returned home. My brother, the cycle is complete. This is the great event of your prophecy."

"Wait Curr, it could also be an underworld goddess that has come with her army of beasts to carry our eternal beings to the underworld!"

"No, Elymas. I tell you, it must be Nova."

Druid Elymas pointed toward the village entrance. "Curr, look there; a horsewoman and a pack of great hounds have arrived at the gate."

Elymas cupped his mouth and called out toward the village entrance. "Who are you, and what do you want?"

There was no response. "Curr, what goddess is this that the beasts of the field call her friend? This is the second most remarkable thing that I have ever seen. Deer always run from us, and today they are the forerunners of their queen. You are right! It can only be one person, and I can see her face now. Nova has returned home! The cycle is complete."

"Grandfather!"

"Nova, my princess, has come home!"

When Nova's feet touched the sacred ground of Currcroft, her legs almost gave way as she struggled to walk slowly through a herd of deer toward her grandfather. The whole clan had now gathered outside to witness this wonder.

Elymas called after Curr, "What are you doing, you old fool? At your age you will kill yourself running like that."

The grandfather did not hesitate to run and embrace his lost princess. He called to his wife and clan, "Everyone, come. Nova is home! Our daughter was dead and now she is alive!"

Turning back toward Nova, Curr said, "Dear child of my child, I have missed your sweet face. Where are Madad and Star? Are they close behind?"

The entire clan interrupted Nova's answer when everyone rushed forward to greet her. While all Currcroft rejoiced, there was only sorrow in Linndee Valley. Villages, hamlets, inns, crofts, homes, cattle, and crops were gone along with most of their people. There was little remaining for a roaming band of thieves to raid.

PART 2—THE WRITTEN WORD

Faolan and his land pirates gathered on a ridge later named Hannah's Bluff. Normally, it was a natural belvedere offering a panorama of Albion beauty. On this day, it offered a scene of appalling devastation. The band was looking over the charred ruins of a once lush shire. Always the antagonist, the gang member Rook spoke out. "Faolan, you led us west to these mountains away from those guards at the right time. There is nothing left down there to plunder. What are we going to do now?"

"I have sent scouts out to search for the easiest targets, and I see them returning as we speak. The foothills and the mountains have gone untouched by the flames. I would wager that there is gold for the taking in these mountains. I'm thinking that we should be the ones to find it and take it."

Rook's eyes were wide circles of fear. "We have been told that these backward mountain people fight as animals and eat their enemies! Perhaps you have led us away from the flames and into a witch's cauldron!"

"Easy, Rook, let's not get ahead of ourselves. Let's hear what the scouts have to say."

Faolan called out to the riders as they approached the bluff. "What have you found for us, Latharn?"

Latharn dismounted, tied off his horse, and joined the others waiting on the bluff. "I have found a way for us to make a fortune legally."

"How would that be fun for the lads?" Faolan asked with a sarcastic smirk.

"No, really, Faolan. Cattle have overrun these mountains. I say let's gather them into a herd and drive them to the coastal market. We can hold them in a box canyon that is not far from here."

"I have to admit, it seems to be a good idea. The fire has driven hundreds of sheep, cows, and horses this way. What do you say, men? Are you up for an honest living?"

The bandits were trying to imagine doing honest work. "Faolan, what if the work is successful, and we become tied to it? And what should we do if some of those mountain people get in our way?"

"Rook, you and the others should not worry about such little things. We can sell the cattle and then later steal them back and sell them again. As for those mountain people, no one of importance will ever miss them. We will simply kill them."

THE HOMECOMING

Another outlaw led a cheer with, "All right, plunder and murder. That is the life for us."

Things settled down in Currcroft after several days of a mellow reunion celebration. Sadness tempered the joy of the reunion because the clan did not have Madad and Star to welcome home. They also shared Nova's pain over the probable deaths of her two adoptive brothers David and Jonathan. Tears were flowing from both of Nova's eyes. The right eye was tearing for joy and the left eye for sorrow. At the same time, Madad's betrayal was a shameful disappointment to the Curr clan.

"Nova, come sit between your grandmother and me. A feast has been prepared in your honor. Come sit at our table."

"Thank you, Grandfather."

Once the meal was over, Chief Curr's mood darkened. "How could Madad have done this? It was more reasonable to think that the three of you had died somehow. Death was the only conclusion after searching for you for days. The thought of Madad sneaking away without a word never occurred to us. We knew him as an honorable man, not as a criminal. Then again, did we ever really know your father?"

"Grandfather, Madad regrets what he has done and is ashamed to face you. Star did not return with me because she is happy in Asbury. She does not remember any of her past life. As for me, I will never forget my Curr clan, my family, my village, my shire, my people, and especially my grandparents."

Raising her voice to the clan, she spoke her final words as Nova. "Listen to me, everyone. Please listen to me. Thank you. I want everyone to do something for me. I will always be your Nova. However, for personal reasons, I want to change my name. Would you do that for me?"

Grandmother Jucurr spoke softly, but directly to Nova. "It is very serious and possibly disrespectful to change your given name. Tell us the name first."

"Everyone, please excuse me for a moment." Nova lowered her voice to speak to her grandparents. "I am sorry. I did not mean to be disrespectful. There are no other persons I respect more than my grandparents," She conferred with her grandparents, and they gave their consent to the name change. Then, she stood and continued with her public request. "With my grandparents' permission, I wish to be called Hannah because of a vow that I made."

PART 2—THE WRITTEN WORD

Later that evening, Hannah called her grandparents aside and asked them to sit with her again. "Please help me remember my mother. Tell me everything there is to know about her."

Afterward, the conversation returned to the wildfire tragedy. "Grandfather, is there any way to send messages to people in the lowlands? Madad, Star, Abraham, Sarah, and my friends need to know that I have survived the fire. Sarah and Abraham need to know that their sons may not be coming home. Everyone must know that the fire was deliberately set siege style by those northern guards."

"Yes, we can send messages. Your uncle Elymas can arrange that for us. Nevertheless, how do you know that the Asgardshire guards set the fire? Why would they do such a thing?"

"Mostly it is a strong feeling that I have. In the first part of the journey, we rode with friends who just happen to be guardsmen. The Asgardshire guards became our escort in the second half of the journey. Riding with those foreign guards made me feel uneasy. Perhaps it was because of a strange warning from the man that once lifted me up from slave to warrior. He warned me not to trust the queen that had been so kind to me. He told me to be careful. I did not heed those words until the change of guards at the firth. The queen promised that her guards would escort me home and that was a lie. Finally, there is the time and place of the fire. It is exactly how I would have attacked a sleeping enemy."

"Nova—sorry, I meant to say Hannah—these accusations are no more than wild suspicions without proof. Why would anyone want to kill a wee lassie like you?"

"Alas Grandfather, there could be no reason worth burning an entire valley. I cannot imagine why anyone would do such a thing. Although, now that I have thought about it, I do have a suspicion as to the reason for killing a lass."

"Hannah, what could you possibly have done that anyone would want to kill you?"

"Actually, Grandfather, there are many people who would be happy to see me dead. Connected to the fire, I mostly suspect the queen because of my friend's warning and her close relationship with the king of the northern territory. The fire was set during the watch of his guards. It is possible that the

Queen of Asbury would like to see me dead because she is envious of my popularity with her subjects.

To explain, let me tell you a story of long ago in a land far away. Once there was a young man named David who served as a warrior for his king named Saul. One day, Saul heard the women chanting, 'Saul has killed his thousands. David has killed his ten thousands,' and the king became jealous of their love for David. Saul thought, *What more can he get but the kingdom?* From that time on, Saul kept a jealous eye on David. That jealousy grew until Saul wanted to kill the young man. The love for me in Monmouthshire is great enough to enrage a queen to such anger." (See 1 Samuel 18:5-9.)

Curr shook his head and laughed in disbelief. "You think too highly of yourself, young lady. Hannah, do not repeat that story until you have solid proof against the queen. Indeed, go on with you."

"Yes, I suppose you are correct, Grandfather, and yet, here is something more unbelievable. I was held in bondage for eight years. During that time, I never knew that you were a chieftain. Wouldn't that make me a real princess?"

"You have always been our princess."

"Yes, but during those eight years, who would have believed that the filthy slave girl was a princess?"

Curr's face reddened with rage. "I will kill your father."

"Promise on your love for me that you will not harm him, and I will take you to Star." Curr reluctantly agreed with a nod of his head and Hannah continued. "Grandfather, I have a question. In the meadow, how did you know that it was me and not Star when you saw me in the distance?"

"Oh, the usual signs—surrounded by animals, dirty, freckled face; Jacurr the Elder's smile. Besides, I would know you in any place and in any time." Chief Curr then told her the story of how she rode an oxen down the mountain to Belmar where she found the lost Currcroft cattle.

"Yes, now I remember. His name was Heelin' Coo. I thought that memory was only a dream. Yes, I remember riding a great beast. I remember something else about that day; there was another man with you. Who was he?"

"Yes, that was and is my brother Elymas. You always called him Eli. You have seen him. He was with me in the meadow when you arrived."

Yes, of course, Uncle Eli. That is why that name sounded so familiar. I have missed and forgotten so much, but I always remembered my grandparents. I also remembered what you told me about your father Jacurr the Elder. I prayed to great-grandfather for years."

"You prayed to my father Jacurr? That is funny. He would think that was very funny."

Hannah laughed along with her grandparents without knowing why. As though sharing an inside joke, Curr fed Jucurr's laughter with, "I can hear him laughing right now."

His wife returned with, "Me too dear." And their infectious laughter made the three of them laugh all the more."

"Stop it you two and tell me why we are laughing. Was my great-grandfather Jacurr not the clan hero that you told me all of those stories about him?"

"Yes, the eternal being of my father is very good, and he did help save the clan the night that you were born." Curr prompted more laughter from his wife by saying, "The two of you would have been very close to one another."

Hannah sat there pondering the mental state of these dear old folks. Clearly, she had not heard anything that was funny.

Changing the subject, Curr said, "Come in and rest now; it is getting cold out here."

"I will be there soon, Grandfather, and don't worry. It is only cold if you are not wearing enough clothes."

Hannah became annoyed when the old couple broke into laughter again. Finally, Curr calmed down enough to say, "Why am I not surprised that you said that? And where did you hear such a thing?"

"Here in Currcroft Village, of course. I always remember to say it when I am cold. It always makes me remember home and its warmth until now. What is so funny?"

Curr kissed his granddaughter. "Good night, my dear. I have always loved you."

Her grandparents looked at one another as they walked away laughing, and Curr quietly said to his wife Jucurr, "I told you. Only one other person ever thought that old joke was funny."

Hannah, sat alone thinking, *Poor old dears. All of those years of cave living have caught up with them.* She had forgotten about the filthy, cold, diseased, and infested life of the Curr clan. They lived as dogs and smelled that way, too. How ashamed she would have been for David and Jonathan to find out that their sister really was a dirty little Celtic cave rat. Thinking about the contrast of her two different worlds, she prayed, "Ruling Presence of the Universe, please help me show my people a more healthy way to live. No one ought to live in a dark and unhealthy place such as this cave. Help me raise my people up to be better than they can be on their own. Help me ease their struggle for existence, and allow them time to learn of you, my Lord. Still, I thank you for these dear people, for they are only unclean outside their bodies. Here in Currcroft, I have only known love, while the outside world has taught me about the evil thoughts that come from evil, unclean hearts. My clan has only shown me love and self-sacrifice. These also come from the heart and make them clean in your eyes. Madad took Star and me from here to a better world, and our hearts became unclean. My father and I have since repented, Lord. Please help me to show my people how to hold on to their pure hearts and live healthier lives for you. Amen."

Hannah was finally home where she could fully place her trust in her family and friends. She was joyful because of her faith in God, and she chose to be thankful for the blessings of Midian, Asbury, and being home again in Currcroft. Being thankful and joyful was a clear and easy choice because she had powerfully experienced the presence of the Lord in her life. With certainty, she now knew how to rest high on the Rock of her faith whenever new firestorms threatened to destroy her life.

The last rays of sunlight disappeared, and a cold, highland night wind came that would not be ignored. Hannah entered the dimly lit cave, followed the shadows on the wall, and found where her grandparents were sleeping high on their rock. "Move over, Grandmother, and keep me warm and safe." Soon, the princess was asleep and in dreamland where she found herself in the midst of a victorious battle against a foreign king.

WARRIOR PRINCESS

Nova's Age: Fifteen to Sixteen

A clear picture of Currcroft Village landscape is required to understand how the following Battle of Currcroft unfolded. Try to imagine a mountaintop formed by a volcanic eruption millennia before the time of this story. The village was set in a dormant two-hundred-acre volcanic crater suddenly stocked with every four-legged creature known in ancient Albion. This crater was a circular meadow surrounded by walls fifty to one hundred feet high with only one narrow entrance known as the Eye. This entrance was closed during this time to keep the livestock from escaping. It was sealed so tightly that a mouse could not have escaped. In all, the mountaintop was a natural hill-fort, and its Currcroft Cavern was the safest place on earth.[11]

The southern and eastern sides of the mountain were lush and seasonally mild, but the northern and western sides were barren and had continual forbidding weather. The trail leading to the village came up out of the east across the southern side of the mountain until it reached the western side. From there, the trail forked in two about one hundred feet from the entrance. The wide path led nowhere to the left, and the narrow path led through the Eye into Currcroft on the right. The Road to Nowhere circled around the western outer wall for about a quarter of a mile and ended with a one-thousand-foot drop straight down to the left and a fifty-foot wall towering to the right. This road served no purpose other than a place for the children to explore and play hide-and-seek among its nooks and crannies.

One morning, several of those children went out from the village to gather wild flowers and fresh herbs along the eastern side of the mountain. Two of Faolan's men talked with the children and later reported, "We stopped and asked some children where they were from. They pointed to the mountain and said that they lived 'up there in Currcroft.' Croft means that they have cattle ready and waiting for us to take to market."

Leader Faolan found the idea of a cattle raid more to his liking than working to gather cattle. "Good job, men. Let's rest tonight and strike early tomorrow."

Hannah also rose early that morning and left the village for a walk around the eastern side of the mountain to view the charred rolling hills below and to seek the Lord in prayer. "Dear Merciful God, in your presence, I give thanks for this day. Be merciful to my brothers. They were young and foolish, and I loved them dearly. Please do not hold their one moment of sin against them for eternity. I have forgiven David, and therefore, I know that you will forgive him, too, because your mercy endures forever.

How great you are, my Lord. You once changed a shepherd boy named David into a king, and now you have transformed a simple stable girl into a princess. You are the creator of heaven and earth. I am only a mortal of little value, and yet you have adopted me into your family as an almost divine

---

[11] Great Britain is dotted with the remains of over 1,600 Celtic defensive hill-forts.

princess. Why have you been so gracious to me? Here on this mountain, you have made me masterly over of your beasts of the field. Herds of deer seek the protection of my sanctuary. Bulls have bowed at my feet. Horses and dogs have rescued me and made my life whole. You have commanded the wind and rain to save me. Lord of lords, my Lord, how majestic you are. How gracious you have been to your servant and therein I am ashamed to ask of you again. Please, dear Lord, give me this day. Amen."

God did give Hannah that day. She and the dogs were jogging back home when she spotted the band of thieves—a large group of men and a few women on horseback were coming up the hillside below her. A jog broke into a sprint toward home and a scramble to the top of the large rocks that closed the Eye. "Everyone to the Eye, and bring your weapons. Bandits are coming! Bandits are coming! Spread the word that everyone is to keep out of sight. Let the thieves go down the Road to Nowhere!"

Hannah stepped out of the bandits' view as they rushed by the village entrance. She could not believe what she was seeing. She recognized the two leading horsemen. "Faolan and Latharn, we meet once more," she murmured under her breath. Her improvised plan worked. The bandits raced by the entrance, down the road, and around the bend that led to nowhere.

"Quickly, everyone help me move the barricade from the Eye to block their escape from the road, and we will have them trapped!"

After they closed the road, Hannah's heart raced faster when she heard the bandits returning. "All right, fine, that will have to do. Archers be ready. Everyone hurry to the top of the wall! Do not kill anyone."

Chief Curr was already annoyed. His young granddaughter had been home only days and was already giving orders as though she was in charge. Confusion filled the ranks as everyone paused for confirmation from Chief Curr or Master Warrior Makcurr.

"Grandfather, please trust me. Order our people not to kill, at least for now. I have a better idea."

"Hannah, I give the orders in this clan. We are going to kill them and take their heads as trophies. Other chiefs have often ridiculed me for having so few heads. Now, they will be envious and fearful of me because I have so many."

"Wait! Please, Grandfather, trust me! There is a better way. We can use these thieves to make our clan stronger. If my plan fails, then you can kill them."

The clan was becoming impatient over the anticipation of a battle. Their blood boiled with excitement. Someone yelled, "Come on, Curr, let's kill them and keep their horses."

Another yelled, "Curr, let me die with honor for my clan."

Curr faced his clan and raised his arms in a calming manner. "I rather everyone live for the clan."

Turning to Hannah, Curr lowered his voice and said, "It better be a very good plan. So far, I say nicely done, Princess Hannah. We captured them without anyone being killed—so far."

Curr relieved the tension of the moment with a bit of Celtic humor. "Say, that one over there looks tasty."

"Grandfather, please stop it. This is what I want you to do."

In a cautioning voice, Curr responded. "Hannah...."

"Grandfather, this is what I *hope* you will decide to do."

Against traditional values, Curr gave the order not to kill unless a prisoner tried to escape. From there, a now united clan captured and disarmed the band of thieves. The victors confiscated everything from the thieves including all their clothing. Detained on the Road to Nowhere, each prisoner was expecting the worst and could only hope that it would be a swift death or possibly something better. Thereafter, that is what they received: something much better than they expected with plenty of food and only mead to drink. They consumed generous portions of boneless meat, without utensils or bones that they could later use as tools or weapons.

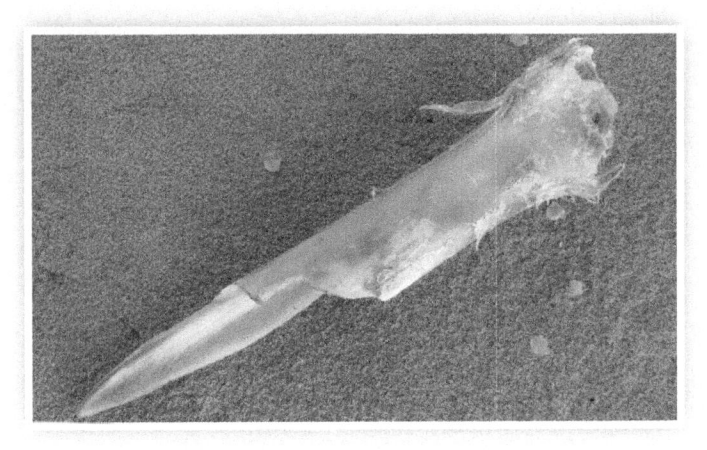

Interrogation began once the prisoners were thoroughly drunk. Curr repeated his command, "Do not kill any of the prisoners. We are going to need them. Question them that you may plunder their camp." Thereafter, the Currcroft villagers found and captured the lightly guarded box canyon corral.

Hannah had begun the day by asking God for mercy for her brothers, and ended the day by pretending to show mercy to her enemies.

A sense of urgency filled the air as Albion greeted a new day. Hannah and Master Warrior Makcurr joined Chief Curr to form a tactical plan. "Father, what is she doing here?" Makcurr demanded to know. "We do not need her and her grand ideas. My warriors are waiting for the order to kill these invaders and be done with them before they can cause us harm!"

"Now, daughter, let us hear what she has to say. Go ahead, Hannah; we are listening."

"No! Father, I object! I am the Master Warrior of this clan! She is little more than an outsider. I am the daughter of a chief, and she is the daughter of a criminal."

"Makcurr, I will tell you what she is doing here. She has earned the right to be here. She has stocked our croft and saved many of our lives in your absence. Her strategy captured an entire band of thieves when you were not here."

"I am sorry sire. I was busy having my twelfth son. I must admit, it is fortunate that she returned home when she did."

"Now, as I was saying; go ahead Warrior Princess, we are listening."

"Thank you, Grandfather. You must immediately send a messenger bearing your plaid colors to the northern king at the Asgard hill-fort. Send three messages. First, send your condolences over the tragic fire that has scorched his people and land. The second message should convey that you have captured the band of murdering thieves that have been raiding his coastal plains. Suggest that they would make excellent slaves to rebuild and farm his lands. Your third message should explain that you are returning thousands of his cattle that were driven into your territory by the fire."

Curr had been feeling quite wealthy and empowered since Hannah returned home. "Why would I do anything that you have said?"

"Grandfather, there are already more livestock here than our land can support. Even the wild game that you love so much will quickly strip every blade of grass. I have a better idea. The Linndee Valley has already begun to turn green again, and it can support the domestic herd. That land can be our land if we act now. Trust me once more, Grandfather. If I fail, you will still have all the wild game that you can eat. I will be leaving for Asgard at midday. Please, my lord, select four men to escort your messenger."

"Send you? No, I will not allow it. We just got you back. I will not risk your loss again."

His words caused her to become apprehensive as an overwhelming feeling of dread took hold of Hannah. She had faced her enemies fearlessly. She had faced the flames of death and had not been afraid. Now, in an instant, terror gripped her. She thought, *Oh dear, wait until he finds out that I do not intend to stay here. Lord, what am I going to do if he forbids me to leave?*

She took a long, deep breath before continuing. "Grandfather, who else would you trust with your plan? Yes, send me, lord. I must find out why so many of our fellow Celts had to die.

"All your forces must leave for Asgard as quickly as possible, driving the cattle and the prisoners ahead of them. First, send enough of our people to drive and protect the cattle. Feed the fire survivors. If they ask for one head of cattle, give them two.

"Second, send the heavily guarded prisoners following after the cattle.

PART 2—THE WRITTEN WORD

"Finally, send out the majority of your forces. This rear guard is to stay out of sight as they follow behind the prisoners. It is important to keep the prisoners well fed, naked, and drunk. And please, return only their sandals to them for the long journey to Asgard.

"Expect two of my escorts to return to you along the south side of the river, with directions and strategic information. If they do not find you for some reason, you will locate the hill-fort of Asgard on the south side of the aberdon.[12] An Asgard soldier told me that the hill-fort sits on the edge of the palisade.

"Master Warrior, Aunt Makcurr, tell your warriors not to show their fighting skills unless you command them to fight. After you have delivered the prisoners, grandfather will command you and your warriors to return with the cattlemen to bring the second herd of cattle and prisoners to Asgard. Of course, this is obviously a bluff. There will be no more cattle or slaves to deliver.

"One of two things will happen. The chieftain of Asgard will or will not send his men to assist you. If he does send his soldiers, kill them all once you are out of sight from the hill-fort. In either event, quietly return to our encampment after dark along with our rear guard to reinforce our position.

"One last thing; do you have any hemlock poison?"

"Yes, we keep it to poison rat bait. Do you plan to poison the prisoners as well?"

"I plan to kill our enemies any way imaginable for killing so many innocent people. Just make certain that our people do not drink anything from inside the Asgard hill-fort unless I have cleared it. Now, where is that hemlock?"

Makcurr could no longer remain silent. "Who do you think you are giving commands? You, you, you—it has always been about you ever since the night you were born. You are my sister's daughter. She was the same way—talk, talk, talk! Well, I say kill, kill, kill these prisoners at once! Who are you to come in here and give orders? Your plan will leave Currcroft unprotected."

Curr interjected and said, "Both of your positions have merit, my children. Hannah, in advance of making my decision, let me ask why we should not go to Asgard with a full showing of our warriors?"

---

[12] Aberdon: mouth of a river.

"I want the king to underestimate our numbers," Hannah said. "We will use his arrogance, pride, and overconfidence against him to gain a new Currcroft for the clan."

Curr made his decision. "Hannah, yours is a complicated and bold plan. It is a plan that would risk the lives of our people and the loss of Currcroft. I am a simple man and Makcurr's plan is simple. We will take the heads and horses of the thieves and be done with them."

"Grandfather, this cannot be what happens. There is something that you should know about me. I often dream, but I remember only a few of my dreams. Those that I remember actually take place in the future, and I had such a dream last night."

Hannah's words sent a chill through Curr. "Your great-grandfather also had the gift of divination. Tell me about your dream."

"Sire, the one thing that I remember clearly is seeing the colors of your plaid flying above a foreign hill-fort."

"Say no more. We are going to Asgard. "Respecting Makcurr's position as Master Warrior, Curr gave the order to invade the hill-fort at Asgard. "All right, this is what we are going to do. Makcurr, you will announce the plan to our people, and then order Princess Hannah to deliver my message to the hill-fort at Asgard. Send your twelve best warriors with her."

Makcurr was furious over her father's approval of Hannah's invasion plan. "What are we going to do if Hannah's bluff fails?"

"Calm yourself daughter. I hear not Hannah. I hear only the voice of destiny calling us to victory."

Within the hour, the clan gave Hannah a hero's send-off with strict instructions from her grandparents to "keep her head." Downward along the mountain stream to the river, and then along the riverside, they traveled eastward to a new land that was waiting for them. She became excited every time they met wildfire survivors with the hope of finding David and Jonathan. Alas, she was disappointed every time, especially when they reached a place where Glenn Morrah Inn once stood.

Hannah offered hope, encouragement, and relief to the survivors. "Our people are coming with food. You are invited to feast and join our clan." The promise of food could not arrive quickly enough for the fire survivors of Belmar Village. They allowed the emissary detail to enter their territory unchallenged,

PART 2—THE WRITTEN WORD

while planning to surround, rob, and kill the messengers during the night. It was an excellent plan except that Hannah and her many cur dogs were vigilantly waiting along the camp perimeter. Instead of eating dog meat, many dog bites added to the misery of the surviving Belmar clan members during the night.

Hannah kept her composure and addressed the subdued thieves of Belmar with a tempered voice. "I remember this place. Your tribe raided our village years ago, and my grandfather forgave your transgression. Once again, your clan has come against my people as thieves in the night. Now once again, we answer your crime with mercy, peace, and forgiveness. You may keep and eat the dogs that you have killed. As for compensation, follow us and help protect us, and we will feed you. Attack us a third time and you will surely die."

One week later, Hannah and her escort arrived in the hill-fort area expecting to see its watchtowers from miles away. Confused and feeling lost, Hannah questioned a young man along the road.

"Excuse me, sir. Would you please tell us how to find the Asgard hill-fort?"

"It is just straight on through the grove; straight on, it is."

"Sir, how far might straight on be?"

Pointing beyond a knoll he answered, "Oh, it is just there."

"Where? The sea is right there without a hill-fort to see."

"Keep going. It sits on the edge of the palisades."

Hannah replied, "It is a good thing that we are not invaders. We would have to ask for local assistance to find the place." She was joking on the outside, but frustrated on the inside.

She kept thinking, *Asgard, where are you? I am here to siege your walls—if I can only find them.* The mountain Celts continued "straight on" and rounded a knoll where the entire hill-fort estate came into view. Hannah pulled back on the reins to stop because she could scarcely breathe as her eyes filled with tears of joy. "Asgard, your banner will soon fall because God has already delivered you into my hands."[13]

Tomcurr was a frightened and doubtful escort. "Hannah, look at her. She is more formidable than Currcroft Village. How could you or anyone take her by storm?"

"We will take her by calm, in the same way that Deborah conquered the Canaanites."

"What are you talking about? Are you mad? What goddess is this whose name you speak? We will die in the name of this unknown god! Stop crying and let us go home."

"Tomcurr, we are home, and our new home is even more beautiful than it was in my dream or I could have imagined it to be. I believe I have been here before. I cannot say why, and yet I know that this is where we belong. We have always belonged here. My tears are not tears of fear; they are tears of joy in the

---

[13] The Dunnottar Castle pictured in this chapter is located about twenty miles south of Aberdeen, Scotland. The Dunnottar location was inhabited by Picts and others from 5,000 BC to 700 AD. Saint Ninian is said to have converted the Picts to Christianity and built a church at Dunnottar in the fifth century. Even in ruin, its beauty is only surpassed today by the gracious people of Scotland.

Lord that is my God. There is only one god, and The One has promised this land to our people."

"Well, I doubt that. Save your tears to weep over our graves in this place. I doubt that we will survive even if we retreat now."

They continued on and stopped beneath the guard tower. "We are here to deliver an important message from Chieftain Curr of the mountain territory to your great king." After a lengthy wait, a fort guard confiscated Hannah's obvious weapons. "King Lars will see you now. Address him as Sire, but do not look directly into his eyes."

Hannah could hardly speak to deliver the message from the shock of realizing that this dour king and all his clan were not Celts. She had to use extreme control to keep her thoughts of rage suppressed. *Who is this invader to rule this land and its Celtic people? Where did he come from? Calm down; don't attack him too soon. Be nice, and remember that you are Nova, Daughter of the Light. Remember that Abraham taught you to be patient and to trust in the Lord.*

"You may speak, woman!"

"Sire, I have come from Chief Curr of the Highland Territory with a message to his good neighbor King Lars. First, he sends his condolences and the condolences of his people over the tragic fire that has scorched your people and land."

"First? Is there a second?"

"Yes, Sire. The fire flushed many types of vermin, including human. He is pleased to say that he has captured the band of murdering thieves that have been raiding your coastal plains. Furthermore, he has filled a treasure chest with items stolen from your many subjects."

"Treasure to spend is of use. Prisoners to feed are of no use. Tell your chief that he has my permission to execute them."

"Might Chief Curr have the king's permission to enslave them? Some of the older ones would be useful as sacrificial gifts to our gods."

King Lars immediately realized their value as slaves and quickly reclaimed the prisoners. "Yes, slaves, I like that. I will keep them to rebuild and farm my territory. Is there anything else?"

"Yes, Sire, there is more. Chief Curr wishes to return thousands of your cattle that were driven into his territory by the fire."

After listening to the messages, King Lars addressed his courtiers. "You see, our mountain neighbor Chief Curr is a great chief because he understands justice. He understands what is right and what is wrong unlike those people of Linndee Valley. They did not understand that I receive the first fruits, and they receive what remains. Those agrarian swine would be alive today had they obeyed my laws of ownership and tribute. Today, they have nothing except their graves, and I will have what is mine. That is justice! Let the gods be praised."

Hannah thought, *His guards did set the fire.* She released her pent up rage toward these invaders in one deceptive lie. "How could they have dared to do such a criminal thing as to withhold tribute from their king? How did you ever bear such people?"

"I could not bear them, and thus, I destroyed them!"

"Sire, may I suggest that you send some men with my escort to assist in the return of your cattle and prisoners? They can relay your instructions about where to deliver the cattle. They can also carry out your wishes concerning the prisoners."

"The prisoners will be brought here to me. Everyone will see exactly what happens to those who steal from me or even from my neighboring kingdoms."

"We have also captured more outlaws on our way here. They have a history of raiding your villages, and they also attacked our diplomatic mission to your court. Might we have permission to kill them?"

"No! I will deal with them for committing crimes in my territory. Guards arrest and imprison these criminals in the hole!"

"My chieftain, Curr, directed me to stay here to be at your service until his arrival if that pleases you, my lord."

"Yes, of course. You are my diplomatic guest."

The king stared at Hannah openly for a moment and said, "You remind me of someone. Have we met?"

Hannah thought, *Yes, I remember seeing you with the Queen of Asbury during my hearing.* However, she answered the king with a lie. "No, my lord, we have not met before. It is possible that I only appear familiar. As you know, all Celts look alike."

"Yes, I have said as much. However, you, my dear, are quite pleasant to the eye."

PART 2—THE WRITTEN WORD

"Oh, thank you, Sire."

Hannah's appearance had changed since the Asbury hearing. It was as though her boyish body had suddenly changed into a beautiful, young woman, known in Albion as a bonnie lassie.

Everything was going according to the plan, including the time and freedom to study the strengths and weaknesses of the fort. The cattle arrived in a stockyard miles from the hill-fort by midmorning. Early afternoon found the Currcroft prisoners joining the Belmar prisoners in a large holding dungeon, known as *the hole* buried deep in the hill-fort ground.

King Lars was pleased with the cattle and the treasure that his captives had stolen throughout the land. He had a special dinner prepared for Hannah and, Envoy Elymas. to express his gratitude and hospitality toward his forthright mountain neighbors. Hannah sat with her Uncle Elymas during the banquet and whispered all that she had learned about the massacre. She began with a warning. "Be on your guard. This fine meal could be our last if it is poisoned. We are the guests of the king of tertiary." She thought that her uncle's barely contained rage would kill him that same night as he sat there with forced laughter and smiles. A great alliance would have formed if it had all ended at that dinner—an alliance with a foreign rat.

After many hours of food and entertainment, the feast was over, and it was time for Envoy Elymas to return to the Curr encampment west of the hill-fort.

"I'll be spending the night here, Uncle." Lowering her voice, she added, "Is Makcurr back yet?"

"Yes, a message arrived saying so. Otherwise, Hannah, you need to come with me back to camp. You have already spent too much time here."

"My work is not finished here. Tell Makcurr not to allow any prisoners to escape from the fort. They are to be killed or driven back into the fort to kill and to be killed. Those who remain standing inside the hill-fort should be thirsty after the fray is over. A bit of hemlock in the water should finish most of the battle survivors."

"What battle?"

"The battle that is going to begin once I set the captives free. We have three enemies here that think nothing of killing our innocent people. Let them kill one another if they love killing so much."

Hannah placed her hand on her uncle's arm. "Our host is coming this way. Do not fear. I was shown our colors flying over this hill-fort in a dream."

Raising her voice, Hannah called out, "Goodbye, Uncle! I will see you in the morning!"

"You are coming with me!" Elymas demanded, and he took his niece by the hand and looked deep into her eyes and spoke softly. "I believe what you said about the dream because my father, Jacurr the Elder also had the gift of dream divination."

"Yes, I know. Dream divination is my inheritance from Great-grandfather."

"It is not exactly an inheritance. You are—"

From the hand of her uncle to a king, Lars interrupted with, "Don't worry about your niece. We will take good care of her. Thank you for coming this evening. This will be a night for everyone to remember. My fortress is always open to you and your people."

Leading Hannah away and speaking softly, King Lars murmured into her ear, "How delightful you look tonight, my dear. Let me show you a part of the fort that you have not seen."

Hannah smiled and affectionately squeezed the king's hand as she planned to take advantage of the wee lamb. She disarmed him with passion to learn more about the motive behind the fire and to eliminate him. After several glasses of wine, she learned about the Queen of Asbury's connection to the great fire. Later that night, she gladly bludgeoned the king while he lay exhausted in a deep sleep. Then she bound, gagged, and stuffed the king into a cedar chest. From there, she covered herself with a robe and stepped out of his chambers, pretending to call back to the king. "I will be right back. Do not go to sleep, my king," she said in a teasing voice, and she closed the door and walked by the king's guards with a secretive, flirtatious smile.

One of the guards broke his stance and turned to the other guard. "Is that not the girl that we escorted to Glenn Morrah?"

The second guard said, "We burned a girl in Glenn Morrah. That was a woman that just walked by me."

From there, Hannah poisoned the drinking water and and deliver some banquet leftovers to the prison guards. They never expected that a small woman with a sheepish smile would dispatch them.

She called down into the prison hole and announced her presence. "My fellow Celts, how are you doing in there?"

PART 2—THE WRITTEN WORD

"Who is there?"

"I have been sent by the other servants with a message. The message is that we are Celts being forced to work here by foreigners. We will help you escape if you promise to help us escape. I am sad to say that King Lars has decided to put you all to death, and we do not think that is fair."

The alternating voices of Faolan and Latharn emanated from the pit. "What happened to the guards?"

Hannah answered with a lie. "I prepared a special late-night meal laced with hemlock for them." The truth was that she killed both guards quickly by hand and not ladylike by poison.

"Now listen: When you get out of the hole, there is a stash of weapons in the structure directly east of here. Just follow the sound of the sea and it will lead you to what you will need. Do you understand?"

"Yes, we understand. Now, get us out of this stinking mud hole."

"Be patient, I am trying my best. Also, be sure to take your time. You have all night to kill. The more foreigners you kill in their sleep, the fewer of them will remain to hunt us down later. Do not leave any witnesses except for us servants, of course."

"Why haven't you people killed them already?"

"Sir, we are simple and weak domestic servants. We are not big, strong men such as you. Will you please help set us free?"

"Yes, sure, we got it: You help us, and we help you. Now, what are you waiting for? Get us out of here!"

"All right, fine, I will try to lower the ladder."

"Hurry, woman!"

"I am trying to hurry. This ladder is too heavy for a small woman such as me."

"What about our clothes? We have been naked for days!"

"Select your new clothes from those who are about to die."

Hannah gave the ladder a good downward shove into the hole. The intended target replied, "Oh, you stupid woman! You just killed one of my best men. Are you trying to help us or kill us?"

There was no reply because Hannah was already gone. Moments later, she was back in the king's chambers with the door locked tight. She had finished tying the bedding together end-to-end when the escapees began to ram the chamber door. It finally crashed open as her feet touched the ground outside.

The full force of the Curr clan had surrounded the fort and killed or driven many of the escapees back into the fray during the night. Periodic sounds of screams and clashes emanated from behind the earthen walls even as the sun rose out of the sea. Later, the Curr clan and its dogs entered the fort with the sun directly overhead to claim victory without the loss of one clan member. The victorious highlanders thoroughly searched the hill-fort compound until the dogs uncovered several foreigners hiding with the Celtic servants.

Once all was secure, the members of the new royal family of Asgard gathered around their champion. "Well, Grandfather, how do you like your new croft?"

"Well, we certainly think highly of you, young lady. Hannah, I believe that any queen would have reason to be jealous and fearful of you, indeed. Go on with you, Warrior Princess Hannah."

Soon, the victors were growing uneasy as the people from the surrounding area gathered outside of the hill-fort. Makcurr and her exhausted guards took a defensive position at the gate.

"Sir, what has happened here?"

Makcurr's strongest guard, a man named Peatcurr, stepped forward and announced, "King Lars no longer lives here. The mountain Celtic chieftain, Curr, has taken up with the place now."

"What has happened to the king and all the king's men?"

Peatcurr gripped the hilt of his sword as he answered. "Oh, they will be in need of a sin-eater."

To his relief, the Celtic people of Asgard rejoiced. "We are free Celts once more!" It was with great pleasure that the local people escorted the few surviving foreign invaders and Celtic bandits to the hole. Every Asgard hill-fort slave agreed to continue their duties as new and free clan members. Bless their hearts. The fort would have quickly become a new Currcroft bat-cave without their help.

Many of the Curr clan warriors complained that it was a "victory without honor," and Curr told them that they "would be of no further use to the clan as dead heroes. Every man, woman, and child is needed to build and protect the new kingdom."

PART 2—THE WRITTEN WORD

The victory over the Asgard hill-fort ensured the survival of the Curr clan in a larger and healthier environment than they had existing in a mountain cave. The combined forces of three enemies would have massacred Makcurr and her royal guards in an all-out frontal assault, and the Makcurrie linage would have ended on that day in Asgard. As it turned out, however, future generations would exist because Hannah had murdered the enemy to avenge her people and to ensure their earthly survival in a healthier environment. God had answered her prayer.

Therein was her curse. What would have happened if she had fully trusted in the Lord? He had clearly told her that vengeance was His, and yet she had insisted on making it her own. She had prayed for mercy to be given to her brothers, and no sooner had she finished that prayer had she shown no mercy to her enemies. Likewise, it is probable that God temporarily used Hannah as a knight for His plan of vengeance. In either case, she realized that justice had prevailed without mercy, compassion, or love, and so she offered a contrite prayer. "Lord, my ways only lead to death and destruction. Teach me your ways of righteousness. Your word tells me that it is yours to avenge" (Deuteronomy 32:35).

The Princess Warrior side of Hannah wanted to confirm the deaths of her childhood friends from Asbury with the proof of their heads. The more she searched the more frantic she became.

"Hannah, what are you looking for?"

"Peatcurr, I am looking for their heads—I can't find their heads. Everyone, please listen to me. Are these all the heads?"[14]

"Calm down, Hannah, and tell us who you are looking for."

"I must find the two bandit leaders, Faolan and Latharn."

"The village people tell us that the king's head is also missing."

"Peatcurr, we do not need to worry about him. I know exactly where he is."

Hannah finally laughed when she realized that her two old friends had made their escape probably by following her down that bedcover rope. Perhaps

---

[14] Metempsychosis is a Druidic belief that a loose eternal being (soul) may enter and take over a living person. However, this was not always a good thing in the Druid mind. In addition to the obvious fear of this happening to a host, it also opens the possibility that a victor may not see the approach of a slain-reincarnated enemy. Any Druid would have understood that David's decapitation of Goliath was the only way to stop the endless reincarnation of the killer giant.

they would sail together once more on Loch Arbor and talk about the old days when they were the young Asbury prodigals.

The real identity of the warrior princess had to remain a secret to protect her two families from the Queen of Asbury. Prince Conan stepped up to the task. "I have summoned the right man to discreetly deliver our news to Midian."

Thus, the prince immediately dispatched a message addressed to Marsha of Midian along with Nova's horse as proof of her life. "Tell Marsha that I will be home soon. You are to return here as quickly as possible while avoiding the Monmouthshire territory. We just erased the Queen of Asbury's closest ally and his clan. So be careful. We will expect you back here in ten days."

The warrior princess stood with her grandfather on a rocky outcropping that formed a natural balcony, and together they watched as the messenger crossed the south bridge from Asgard. She wished to be that messenger. However, there were more pressing matters for her to resolve. "Grandfather, we need to place guards along our borders and prepare for a possible retaliatory attack from the Queen of Asbury. I have a plan to make sure that she understands that you are her new formidable neighbor of the north. I will return in two days."

"Tell me that you are not going to Asbury."

"I leave immediately."

"Please, Hannah, be reasonable. You are finally safe. Why run off and lose your head for nothing? It remains uncertain that the queen was behind the massacre."

"No, I am now certain of her involvement."

Makcurr was standing close by, and before she could say a word, Hannah asked, "What do you think, Stag Slayer?"

"By all means, little princess, I think you ought to attack the Asbury Palace all by yourself."

"She is not going by herself," Curr cut in impatiently. "I must see my granddaughter Star and have a few words with Madad."

"Grandfather, you promised me that no harm would come to my father."

"Yes, that is true, Hannah. It is also true that I will have my say and my granddaughter."

Druid Elymas sat listening quietly in the room by the fire until they finalized their bold plans and retreated from the balcony to join him. "Please hear

PART 2—THE WRITTEN WORD

my counsel. There is a time for war and a time for peace. This is a time to return to peace. Nothing good will come from seeking further revenge. Both of you need to go to Asbury with peace and forgiveness in your hearts. The moment of a minor victory of revenge can have long-term destructive consequences. Do not go as thieves sneaking in the night. Instead, go as peacemakers in the light of day."

"Thank you for your concern, brother. Just the same, we will do what needs to be done."

"It is true that you have suddenly become a powerful king, but I liked you more when you were a simple mountain chieftain. Do you remember how proud your people were when you showed mercy to the Belmar clan? Be that man now and go to Asbury in peace."

"Be our Druid as you were then and stand with us at Asbury."

"Not unless you both have a change of heart. My king, I implore you to stop and think about the consequences of what you are about to do."

"We do not seek revenge; we demand justice and freedom. It is this queen that caused the Glenn Morrah devastation and attempted to murder our princess."

"Brother, I will not give my blessing on this endeavor. In the name of Brigit, rethink your next step. If your positions were reversed, how would you want to answer to these charges?"

"Ah, Druids, there is a time and place for them too. The queen will answer for these charges. Hannah, how soon can you be ready to leave for Asbury?"

"I am ready and await my king."

Hannah, King Curr, and a four-man escort arrived on the outskirts of Asbury by the following evening and found everything to be normal. They were the first to arrive in Asbury knowing what had happened in Asgard.

"We will meet back here at this loch," Hannah said, and from there, she led them to the inn. "This is the place. You will find Star and Madad inside. I will not be going inside with you. It is best that everyone in Asbury believes that I am dead."

"How are we to protect you if we separate?"

"Grandfather, you have seen me safely through the wilderness. Look about you. You are already drawing unwanted attention. I have only one serious enemy here in Asbury. I will secretly deal with her while everyone is watching you: the dangerous looking stranger and his men."

"It is too dangerous. I will not allow it. You will wait here for us."

The travelers entered the inn without Hannah and ordered a meal. The time was growing late when an inn servant announced that their meal was ready and waiting for them. It was a fine meal of stuffed cabbage, a dark bread, and wine.

A hooded King Curr asked the servant girl to tell the manservant to join them. "Please be seated, sir. I wish to speak to both you and the girl."

Two guards gave up their seats and stood behind the pair as the king removed his hood. Madad was immediately terrified at the sight of his father-in-law. Star had never seen her father so frightened and turned toward Curr to find its source. "Star, I am your grandfather."

Curr spoke with his granddaughter at length without saying a word to his son-in-law. "Please know that you will always be welcome to take your rightful place as a princess in my kingdom. It is your decision. I will not force you to leave Asbury. Now that I know where you are, your grandmother and I will be watching over you. She longs to see the woman that you have become."

Star had only one question. "Grandfather, did Nova find you?"

"Nova is no more. Forgive me, Princess, it is time for us to go.

As for you, Madad, seeing you here doing the work of a servant girl gives me great pleasure. You would have been the succeeding clan leader if you were half the man that my daughter saw in you. Keep up the fine work that you are doing here. You may clear the table now, boy."

In the meantime, Hannah headed directly to the palace shortly after Curr commanded her to wait. She could not just sit there and wait. *It is easier to gain forgiveness than permission. Grandfather will forgive me even if I am killed. There is only one palace enemy, and I am sure to defeat her.*

From there, she found Asbury Palace to be ominously quiet as she worked her way through the shadows toward the queen's chambers only to find a locked door. Retracing her steps, she made her way to the roof and lowered herself onto the queen's bedroom balcony. It was a relief to find the outer door ajar. Inside, the queen and her overnight guests were sound asleep. First, Hannah stuffed all their clothing into a large sack and dropped it to the ground from the balcony.

PART 2—THE WRITTEN WORD

With the greatest stealth, she returned to the dimly lit room where she could see the form of her prey. The queen's head tilted back invitingly exposing her throat. There it was; the most beautiful of faces surrounded by its radiant amber hair. With heart racing, Hannah carefully cut an arm's length of the queen's locks, and stuffed it inside a pouch as a trophy for retelling the story. Finally, she left the bedroom door unlocked to make it appear that the intruder had unlocked the door and gained access to the room from the hallway.

She began second-guessing her actions and inactions. Hannah knew that she should have taken the queen's head instead of her hair and clothing. The Celts believed that, once decapitated, a person could not return as a human or a spirit. However, she could not bring herself to commit the murder. As planned, Hannah, clothes, pouch, and her escort were well on their way home when the royal screaming began in the palace.

The entire Curr clan was waiting for Hannah and King Curr to return from the south. Makcurr and the royal guards rode out to meet them with the greeting of, "Once more we thought you were lost, and here you are found again. Welcome home everyone! Come, a meal has been prepared for your arrival. Come tell us of your adventure."

Hannah's grandfather called out to her as the feast was about to begin. "Come sit between your grandparents at our table. This feast has been prepared in honor of your victory over Asbury Palace."

She smiled, thinking, *I knew that he would forgive my disobedience.* Once seated, Hannah proclaimed, "Grandmother, we return bearing gifts. I hope that the royal clothes will fit you." Hannah then told of how she had selected the gifts from Asbury Palace. "Can you imagine them running around the palace without any clothes?"

"Are you saying that you did not kill them in their sleep?"

"Yes, I did not kill them, Grandfather."

Makcurr seized the opportunity and yelled, "You stupid little coward. All that you have accomplished is to incite the queen's rage and bring destruction down on us."

The tone of Curr's voice favored Makcurr, while his words sided with Hannah. "Not the smartest thing that she has done. At the same time, everyone—including you, Makcurr—knows that she is certainly not a coward. Please let us speak and act kindly to one another."

"Thank you, Grandfather, but I am not finished. There is more to the tale."

"Do continue with your story. It can only improve."

Hannah reenacted how she cut the queen's beautiful amber-colored hair, and again Makcurr was on the attack. "You did no such thing. Prove it, you little coward!"

The king locked his eyes on Makcurr and spoke through tight lips. "That will be enough! I command you to speak respectfully! You do not know to whom you are speaking!"

Hannah rose from her chair and found her pouch. She opened it, saying, "I can prove it."

For a moment, everyone thought that she and Makcurr were about to have one of those rare family moments of one clan member raising a hand to another. Facing Makcurr, Hannah reached into the pouch and pulled out a handful of hair, which she raised above her head in a triumphal stance. There was a pause of silence until riotous laughter broke out after King Curr asked, "Didn't you say that the queen's hair was amber? I was wrong. Your tale is much worse than I thought."

Lowering her hand and looking at the black hair, Hannah prayed inwardly, *Oh, dear Lord, what have I done? Whose hair is this? Lord, tell me, am I trying to win the approval of my clan or of you? I did not murder, and, in not doing so, I failed my clan. I went as a thief in the night and stole your joy in me. Have mercy on me, Lord, for I am a sinner that wanted to embarrass and warn my enemy only to have made new enemies among my people. Elymas was right. I should have gone to Asbury in the light of day with peace and forgiveness.*

In the weeks that followed, it seemed as though the people of Asgard recognized Hannah more for her folly than for her victory. In time, they judged her palace invasion to be brilliantly cunning. Everyone knew that she had the queen's life for the taking. Instead of a life, Hannah chose to steal only the queen's pride and joy. She obeyed God's commandment not to murder. In doing so, this one action marked the beginning of the queen's downfall without the loss of one Curr clan member. The queen's reaction to the invasion was the second step toward the end of her Monmouthshire regime.

PART 2—THE WRITTEN WORD

The Queen of Asbury had been in tenuous negotiations with Celtic representatives of Gaul. She graciously provided her own chambers for her guests as the best accommodation available in the shire. Later, the visitors saw the boudoir invasion as an outrageous way of humiliating them and swore that there would be severe consequences for what they assumed to be the queen's spiteful actions. Fearing those consequences, the queen had the couple and their entourage killed in a tragic channel crossing accident. Their disappearance rightfully created suspicion and tension that demanded all of the queen's attention.

Nightmares of an innocent child burning and the screams of her drowning friends filled the queen's nights. She was heard saying, "It is the ghost of Nova that has caused all this trouble." She summoned her messengers repeatedly and asked, "Are you certain that there have been no communications from King Lars since the fire?"

"Your Majesty, I have just returned from attempting to deliver your message to King Lars and was again turned away at all points of entry. They said that King Lars no longer lives there."

"Did they say where he lives now?"

"Yes, my queen. They said that he and his entire clan now reside in the underworld." With that, the queen knew that her last ally was lost, and Monmouthshire became silent.

In Asgard, positions of authority under King Curr needed to be established. Of course, the king awarded the five highest positions to his children Makcurr, Hancurr, Conan, and his granddaughters Hannah and Star.

Curr's three children had always played and worked well together as compared with most siblings. As adult leaders, it would be their responsibility to maintain harmony throughout the kingdom. Princess Makcurr was to continue as master warrior, Princess Hancurr would serve as the diplomatic counselor, and Prince Conan would be senior advisor to the king. The sibling squabbling began with the public announcement of these positions of honor. They argued about who would be the greatest in the kingdom. A banquet of honor and celebration turned into a royal embarrassment as the king's adult children squabbled openly throughout the meal.

"As Makcurr the master warrior, I am the greatest power in the greatest kingdom of all the warrior clans of the Picts. We Picts are the greatest Celtic warriors, and, therefore, I am the greatest Pict warrior. My sons and I will rule all Albion. Everyone will kneel at my feet."

"As Hancurr the diplomatic counselor, I will avoid wars with words instead of spending the precious lives of our dear people on your stupid conquests."

"As Prince Conan, senior counselor to the king, and as king-in-training, someday I will be the greatest in the kingdom, and you both will do as I say or lose your ugly heads."

Invited guests suddenly remembered previous engagements and made their polite but embarrassed exits as King Curr stood and raised his hands for silence. "Please, everyone, be seated, and forgive my children for acting as though they were children. It would seem that both the wine and higher offices have gone to their heads. Be seated and wait. I have two more children to recognize.

As you all know, Hannah's Champion's Portion gives her the right of choice to the spoils of war. Hannah—Nova, Daughter of the Light, daughter of the king's daughter Elcurr, stand and state your claim in the matter of dominion within the Curr kingdom."

"Sire, I prefer to call it our *kindom* instead of kingdom.[15] I wish only four things, my king. First, I wish to serve my God and kindom. I am only a humble servant of the Lord, and of the clan that has given me life. Secondly, if it would please my king, make it so that Currcroft is renamed Elcurrest and made the estate of the children of Elcurr. And finally, decree that everything named Asgard be renamed Aberdon."

"Let me understand. First, you wish only to be servant of all and the master of none. Second, you want the small plot of Currcroft for the heirs of my daughter Elcurr. Thirdly, you request that Currcroft be renamed for her as Elcurrest. And finally, that everything bearing the name Asgard be renamed Aberdon."

"Yes, my grandfather and king, that is all."

King Curr was relieved to hear these modest demands because he had come to fear Hannah's popularity throughout Albion. He remembered the Torah story that Hannah told of King Saul's envy of David and echoed Saul as he thought, *What more can she get but the kingdom? I will keep a jealous eye on*

---

[15] Kinrick: Gaelic for kingdom.

PART 2—THE WRITTEN WORD

her from this moment on. Therefore, he gladly announced, "From this day forward, Currcroft shall be the estate of Hannah, also known as Nova, Daughter of the Light, and her twin sister, Star. Further, Currcroft is renamed Elcurrest in remembrance of my first-born child. And finally, everything bearing the name Asgard is hereby renamed Aberdon."

Hannah remained standing and turned to address the entire banquet. "Dear kinsmen, you are all invited to the sacred mountain home of our ancestors."

A heckler yelled, "No, thanks, we have been there."

Hannah waited for the laughter to die down before continuing. "Leave instructions to have your body brought home to the mountain for an eternal rest with our ancestors in Elcurrest."

The silence in the banquet hall was broken when the heckler stood to speak. "Princess, forgive my attempt at humor a moment ago.

Curr, you know better than anyone that I love and serve my king. Might you forgive me for saying that, on this day, Hannah is the greatest in the kindom."

Curr's fears came rushing back when he realized that his kingdom had just become Hannah's for the taking. Her humility had won the hearts of the people. He chose his answer wisely. "There is no forgiveness needed for speaking the truth, Leocurr. You have spoken well."

Curr then turned and faced Hannah. "Princess Hannah, would you honor an old man with a dance?" Everyone watched as the couple danced together, and, as was the custom, the dance ended with Curr giving a gentle bow to his granddaughter. He whispered jokingly to Hannah, "Should I be worried about my crown?"

"You do not have anything to worry about, Grandfather. It is much too large for me. I am only interested in serving my God, king, and country, in that order."

Speaking in quiet anger, Makcurr told Conan that his first command as king ought to be, "Off with her head!"

"Yes, and soak it in cedar oil, mount it on my trophy wall, and grant her wish of having her body buried in her precious Elcurrest."

Hancurr chimed in with, "Oh, you two stop it, and let me talk some diplomatic sense into her. She just needs to learn her place around here and remember that we were here first."

A few days later, Makcurr thought that she had Hannah's head twice in the same day. Hannah had the nerve to criticize the fighting skills of Makcurr's guards. When Makcurr was informed of this egregious insult, she found Hannah and warned, "Careful, little princess, or I will have my youngest man teach you a lesson that you will never forget."

"Dear Aunt, I watched their awkwardly savage way of fighting. They would never stand a chance against a real warrior."

"How dare you! You are your mother's brat! My guards are real warriors!"

"Aunt Makcurr, I am just trying to help."

"Prove it. Come meet my men, and pick any of them to prove your point."

Makcurr grabbed Hannah's arm and marched her to where her warriors were practicing next to the livery stable. Makcurr signaled for them to stop and gather around, as she announced, "Lads, your cousin here thinks that she can teach you how to fight. Who will give her a chance to prove herself?"

"Never, Master Warrior; this shall never happen. What sort of joke is this?"

"This is not a joke, Barthcurr. She says you are awkward savages."

When Makcurr was met only by silent stares of disapproval, she blurted, "And you, Joncurr?"

"No! The people and I love Hannah too much to even think of doing such a thing."

"You love everyone, Joncurr; that is your weakness.

What about you, Judcurr? Will you give this child a whipping for your commander?"

"I would be crazy to do such a thing to her. After the miracles of Aberdonshire and Monmouthshire, she is the most popular Celt in all Albion. You could not pay me to betray our national treasure."

Hannah walked over to the largest guard and asked, "What about you, Peatcurr? You would not mind fighting a girl."

"Cousin, you are not going to bait me into having a fight with you."

"Why are you such a coward? Is it because you fight as a girl fights?" That insult did it. Peatcurr raised his hand to strike her, and the next moment he raised his other hand for Hannah to help him up off the ground.

Cousin Tomcurr was the most shocked at the scene. "Now that I have seen it, I believe that the warrior princess has something to teach us about fighting."

The arrival of an equestrian interrupted the contest with urgent news that two naked escapees were seen breaking into a home just south of Aberdon.

PART 2—THE WRITTEN WORD

Makcurr mounted her horse and was back in command. "All right, lads, the fun is over. Let's mount up and track down these thieves."

Her tone became more contemptuous toward Hannah. "I suppose that you will want to come along, little princess?"

"No, Makcurr, I will stay here. Would you please go arrest them and bring them before your father. And remember his command that the prisoners are not to be killed."

"I am your superior. You do not give me orders."

"Once more, please believe that I only wish to help. Bring the bandits here, and the champion of Aberdonshire will fight both men at one time. You win if I die. You gain a teacher if I live."

"So you really think that you, a small woman, are the champion of Aberdonshire? Do you really think that you are going to fight two men at one time? It would please me to see the end of that fight."

Makcurr turned her horse in one swift move and called out, "Men, let's go get those murderers for your cousin, the so-called champion of Aberdonshire!"

"Makcurr the Stag Slayer, wait!" Standing close to horse and rider, Hannah spoke softly to her aunt. "Why are you so angry with me?"

"Why? It is because you made fools of Hancurr, Conan, and me during the honors banquet. You also keep forgetting that I am the master warrior of Aberdonshire. Don't think that you are going to come in here and usurp the order of succession. I will kill you before I let that happen."

"Dear Aunt, think about it. That joust is already lost. You made fools of yourselves. And my rightful place of honor waits for me in Elcurrest."

Digging her spurs and words deeply, Makcurr replied, "You being buried in Elcurrest cannot happen soon enough for me. You have troubled me since the night you were born."

A few days later, King Curr sent three messages throughout the kindom. The first message stated that the last two murdering bandits were imprisoned. The second stated that they would receive a fair public trial. The third message announced that Aberdon hill-fort would host the First Annual Albion Games during the summer solstice celebration.

As expected, the two fugitives were Faolan and Latharn. King Curr and Elymas decided the outcome of the charges against the accused before the trial began. The trial was simply an Albion game sideshow to demonstrate the fairness of the new justice in Aberdonshire. Finally, Hannah would have her day in King Curr's court.

Judge Druid Elymas presided over the prosecution and opened the trial by announcing the charges. "These men are charged with the murders of countless Celts including their latest murder of a family here in Aberdon. They killed the family for food and clothes. That is, these two men killed a generous family for what they would have freely given to anyone in need. These men standing here on trial were first captured in Currcroft, but then they escaped and were recaptured again here in Aberdon."

Druid Elymas turned his attention to the accused and asked, "What say you men to these charges?"

Faolan answered. "Oh, your worship, it was not us. The bandits had captured us and were going to sell us as slaves. That is our only crime, my lord. Someone else must have killed that man and woman here in Aberdon. Please, is there anyone who can step forward and say that he has ever seen us kill anyone?"

Druid Elymas stepped closer to the two men and replied, "There are two witnesses. First, you, sir, the accused, are a witness for the prosecution. You have just testified against yourself. Until now, the murder victims have only been described as a family—a family that you alone have described as a man and woman. I am the second witness against you. The man that you killed was my friend, and you are wearing his clothes. I thereby declare that you men are guilty, and I sentence you to a duel. In fairness, you will have first choice of weapons. Win and you regain your freedom. It is the hope of this court that you both will lose your heads, and we will be done with you forever."

The day of the First Annual Albion Games arrived, and the strong men of Albion matched their skills and strength against one another as everyone waited for the main event. It began as guards led Faolan and Latharn to the center of the jousting field where a hooded warrior was standing near an assortment of weapons. Soon, the other Celtic and foreign prisoners arrived on the field. King Curr's archers lined the perimeter as Master Warrior Makcurr gave two commands. First, to the delight of the audience, she ordered the hooded prisoner to be unmasked, thereby revealing the crowned and now sun-blinded King Lars. Then she commanded the prisoners, "Choose your weapons and let

PART 2—THE WRITTEN WORD

the contest begin!" Cheers immediately went up as the still sun-blinded King Lars lost his crown along with his head.

Criminals are brave only when they have an advantage of size or weapon or in some way catch their victim off guard. Pitting such people against one another resulted in a comic spectacle as the cowardly chased the more cowardly around the arena. Faolan and Latharn stood back to back in the center and waited for the attack of the remaining weary combatants. Sadly, in the end, Faolan and Latharn were the last to remain standing.

Once again, Makcurr addressed the crowd. "It is only fair to allow these traitors time to rest, eat, and drink before their final match. That event will be held here tomorrow morning."

> Greek and Roman historical records are the basis of the following scene. They report that the Celtic warrior broke the norms of warfare. Presented here are just six characteristics of Celtic warfare. Fully painted naked bodies of men and women would continuously circle their enemy to the frantic beat of drum and pipe while chiding their foe with insults. These were just a few of the psychological guerrilla tactics that set the Celtic warrior apart from the classic head-on-fighting of their Roman enemy.

Makcurr and Hannah argued privately that next morning while Hannah prepared for the challenge. The young Pretani gladiator stripped naked and painted her body an aqua color made from a woad mustard plant. "I did not have these breasts when I left Midian."[16]

Hannah began to pray aloud. "Lord the Mighty One, fill me with your strength and with your courage. Surround me with your armor of truth and justice to face these Philistines. Thank you, Lord."

---

[16] Pretani, or the painted people, was the name the Celtic people called themselves. The word *Pretani* was first translated into Greek, then to Latin, and finally to English as *Britannia* (the land of the painted people). From the Gaelic *Pretani*, the word was translated to the Greek as *Pretannike*, to the Latin *Pretannia*, and finally to *Britannia*. Another less likely source for Britannia is the name of the Celtic goddess Brigit.

Naked bodies were painted with the aqua dye extracted from the woad mustard plant and a red dye made from a moss plant. This practice appears to be savage without an understanding of the antiseptic qualities of these plants. The natural antiseptic in the dye entered their wounds during battle, thereby reducing the Celtic mortality rate.

After finishing her prayer, Hannah crossed the room to Makcurr and said, "Dear Aunt, would you please paint my back?"

"First of all, my father will never allow you to do this," nonetheless she applied the paint to her niece, albeit with a bit too much force. "And you are not going out there alone and naked. He would be in a rage for days. Let Peatcurr finish the death sentence."

"That is enough paint. I do not want my face painted except for a big smile. The paint burns my eyes. Thank you."

Hannah continued dressing herself in sandals, her special belt, the Celtic torc, her necklace, and her dagger. Finally, she covered herself with a light-blue robe with black embroidery. "This is something I must do alone. All the bloodshed here in Aberdon will be on my hands. As far as Grandfather is concerned, I will not tell him if you won't."

"I love your robe, Hannah," Makcurr conceded."

"Oh, it is just a little something I picked up in Asbury. All right, fine, I am ready and dressed to kill."

Out on the jousting field, the two criminals chose broadswords and shields. Soon they were trembling with anticipation as they waited to face the unnamed savage champion of Aberdonshire. Everyone waited to see which one of Makcurr's guards would step forward, while the musicians played a continuous and unnerving rhythm.

There was little notice as tiny Hannah took her place beside her aunt. Makcurr announced, "Bandits of Aberdonshire! You are hereby sentenced to die as you have lived. The survivor of this round will face our champion. Let the contest begin!"

Faolan viciously attacked his best, life-long friend without hesitation, and the fight was on. Latharn was fighting brilliantly by repeatedly taking advantage of Faolan's crushed foot. At the same time, Hannah disrobed and ran directly toward the fray, and the unexpected sight silenced the roar of the crowd. At first, they could not believe that they were seeing a beautiful, green, naked princess rushing toward two armed men. Some spectators fell to their knees in laughter. Others shouted proposals of marriage, while the wives shouted obscenities at the totally focused warrior who had come to slay her giants.

The sudden change in crowd noise distracted Latharn, and in turn caused the loss of his head. Now aware of her presence, Faolan postured to fight again

PART 2—THE WRITTEN WORD

as Hannah circled around him saying, "Top of the morning to you, coward! Are you prepared to die on this day? I hardly recognize you in clothes. How is that headache? Have you been swimming in the firth lately?"

Faolan screamed, "It is the ghost of the demon Nova raised from the grave. We killed her at Rocky Point Bluff. I know that we killed her and her demon horse Goblin!"

This shocking Rocky Point revelation struck Hannah harder than any broad sword could. Without knowing, Faolan had her life for the taking at that most vulnerable of moments. Her sudden stop appeared to be intentional as she continued to wear a big painted smile. "Yes, it is true. You did kill me. And being already dead, what are your chances of killing me today? I have returned for our fourth and final battle to drag your body to the underworld."

"Wrong; it is our fifth battle. We attempted to kill you after the hearing in Asbury."

Hannah raised her voice in anger so that everyone could hear. "This man has defiled all Albion since his youth. He has raised his hand not to invading foreigners. He has raised his sword against his Celtic neighbors. He is a thief and a widow maker." She slipped the necklace from around her neck as she continued circling, and then she placed a smooth river stone into its pouch and let it fly from the sling. Faolan fell facedown a moment later. Only stunned, he was quickly up and on the attack again before she could reload. Faolan attacked with both hands raised high and holding tightly to his broadsword. His raging war cry suddenly ceased as a dagger pierced his throat. His death made a dramatic conclusion of the First Annual Albion Games. It ended with the deaths of Faolan and Latharn along with their crimes against the people of Albion.[17]

Hannah won the contest and the hearts of her people. A proud and now loving aunt wrapped Hannah in the light-blue cloak. "Thank you, aunt; please, take me away from here quickly."

Hannah had won a great and justified victory, and yet she did not feel victorious. "Tell me, Stag Slayer, why do I feel so bad about killing him? Are my tears a sign of emotional weakness, or is it because God gave me mercy and I

---

[17] I Samuel 17:40-47—Then David chose five smooth stones from the stream, put them in his shepherd's bag, and with his sling in his hand, approached the Philistine. David said to the Philistine, "You come against me with sword, spear, and javelin, but I come against you in the name of the Lord Almighty, the God of the armies of Israel, whom you have defiled. This day the Lord will hand you over to me, and I'll strike you down and cut off your head.

returned it with death? How is the victory over my enemies just when I feel the sting of death so acutely? This sweet taste of a just victory is overcome by the bitterness of my anger and revenge."

"Taking a life is not easy, even for a warrior princess. You have won your challenge and my respect. You did what needed to be done in the name of justice."

In an attempt to lighten the mood, Makcurr said, "Now, tomorrow you can come and teach my men how to be better warriors. They want you to begin by teaching them how to wrestle."

"Oh, dear Aunt, can they wait a few days?"

"Hardly; here comes one of them rushing toward you now."

"Master Warrior, the king wants to speak to both of you back at the hillfort immediately. He is really angry about what you did today."

Both women replied in unison, "Oh, dear, can he wait a few days?"

"No! He demanded that you both come right now! The king is waiting for you."

Her grandfather's wrath was brief and tempered by the pride he felt for Hannah that he tried desperately to hide. This was similar to the rising confliction within Hannah that would prove to be lasting. The warrior within her spent a lifetime combating her spiritual side that sought peace and harmony with nature and man. One craved blood, while the other strove to understand the higher meaning of human existence. Her clan survived generation after generation by doing anything necessary for its survival, even if it meant resorting to cannibalism. The Celtic religion of Druidism offered answers that satisfied both the saint and warrior sides of the human character. It condoned extreme behavior when it was necessary for the perpetuation of its race.[18] Every Celt agreed that these Druidic beliefs were correct, and accordingly, their lives were in harmony with man and nature. However, Hannah would never be able to enjoy this sense of Celtic contentment because of her conversion to Judaism.

---

[18] There is strong archeological evidence of widespread cannibalism in Great Britain even before the arrival of the Celts.

The nation of Israel also resorted to cannibalism in desperate times, such as during the siege of the first Temple. Isaiah 9:19—They snatched on the right, but remained hungry, and consumed on the left without being sated. Each devoured the flesh of his own kindred.

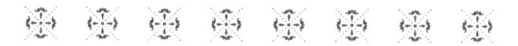

PART 1—THE WORD

PART 2—THE WRITTEN WORD

PART 3—LIVING THE WORD

PART 4—THE LIVING WORD

PART 5—SPREADING THE WORD

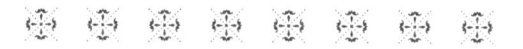

HERETIC PRINCESS

Nova's Age: Seventeen

King Curr gave a victory celebration to the people of Aberdonshire. A new nation of people now had freedom and direct access to its royal family for the first time that anyone could remember. The king, queen, and family actually came to serve their people in what became known as the Curr Kindom and not the Curr Kingdom. A princess running and playing games with the village children was previously unknown. As the day ended, some of the mothers gathered around Hannah with questions.

Hannah welcomed them with open arms. "I hope everyone has had as wonderful a day as I've had!"

"Princess Hannah, we love you. You really are one of us!"

"Aren't you Maggan's mother?"

"Yes, I am."

"She is so good at games. That clever little fox always knows exactly where to find me when we play hide-and-seek."

Another villager shouted, "Princess, is it true? Did you prepare this bread and soup yourself?"

Then there was a second question before Hannah could answer the first. "Is it true that you are the reincarnation of Nova, Daughter of the Light?"

Hannah thought, *Yes, in a way that is true. How do I answer that question?*

Another even more confusing question rose from the crowd. "Dear princess, tell us; are you excited about being Beltane blessed?"

PART 3—LIVING THE WORD

Puzzled by the question, Hannah paused and thought. *How does this woman know about the Beltane celebrations in Midian and Asbury?* She answered pretentiously, "Yes, the Beltane blessing is great indeed."

"Princess Hannah, where are you going?"

"Please, everyone, you must excuse me. I have been feeling ill this past fortnight."

"Yes, Princess, this is to be expected, even when expecting a sacred child of the Beltane blessing."

"What? Expecting a sacred child? I am not with child! What are you saying?"

"Oh, forgive me, Your Majesty. On the contrary, I know when someone is with child, as you are. Everyone is talking about how Cernunnos, the god of fertility, and Nantosuelta, the goddess of fertility chose you to bear their Beltane child. The fact that everyone in the kindom knows of your blessing, except for you, bears proof that it is true. Because you do not even suspect that you are in-waiting proves beyond a doubt that you have been Beltane blessed."

Hannah's thoughts were reeling. *David, what have you done to me? My sacred vow to God—Samuel, my son, my first-born son, is coming.*

"Thank you, everyone, for coming today. Please excuse me. I must leave you now."

The final words of Maggan's mother were of little comfort. "Yes, I knew it. The little princess is going to have a little prince."

Hannah was on her way back to the hill-fort when she met her uncle Elymas and his apprentice Phymas. "Hannah, when are you going to come and visit your old uncle? I have missed you."

"Uncle Eli, I am sorry. I have been avoiding you because there are many deep spiritual and ethical issues that we should discuss. Could we spend a day together soon?"

"It cannot be too soon for me. Visit me tomorrow. I will give Phymas the day off, and we can spend the whole day together at my place."

"I will bring breakfast if you will make something hot to drink."

"Speaking of drink, you do not look well my dear."

"I am not drunk, although I wish that were the truth of it. We will talk about the it of it tomorrow."

Hannah continued on to the fort as Phymas asked, "Master, why do you allow her to be disrespectful by addressing you as Eli?"

"She has called me Uncle Eli ever since she was a little girl. I always thought it was because she could not pronounce my name."

As promised, Hannah arrived at her uncle's tree-home that sat on a hill overlooking the village of Aberdon and the river. "Eli, I love what you have done with the place. It is so Druid. It is so you. And, of course, what Druid home would be complete without a giant oak tree growing right up through the roof? Where did you find all these interesting things?"

"I collected them during my travels. Most of it is just for fun to give the place a mysterious atmosphere. Other things hold great mysteries to ponder, and still others were gifts from friends. Most of the birds and animals just come and go as they please. Pay no attention to Raven Tom, or he will ramble on for hours. The hedgehog's name is Kerpee, and the owl is Solomon." Elymas turned to the bird and said, "Solomon, say hello to Hannah."

"Solomon? Uncle, do you mean King Solomon, the son of the Hebrew King David?"

"Yes, but where have you heard of him?"

"Oh, uncle, we really need to talk. But please tell me where you heard of Solomon, and I will tell you how I came to know of him."

The days passed with Hannah learning about Druid wisdom as her waist size expanded. Anger inside the displaced Bard Phymas also continued to

PART 3—LIVING THE WORD

expand against Hannah. "I have heard the blasphemy that she has spoken about her one true god. Master, how can you of all people tolerate her?"

"Hannah and I are searching for the truth. We can find truth through meditation and dialog. She makes me think about my beliefs, and then examine and test them. Although, it is true, she does worry me. However, if she is here every day, she is not out talking to our people about God. Thank you for your concern. I will speak to her about this."

"You see! There it is right there. You said, "She is not talking to our people about God." You should have said, 'She is not talking to our people about **her** god.'"

The Druid paused and rolled his eyes in annoyance. "Thank you, Phymas. You are correct. I will be more careful of my words around you, and as I already said, I will speak to her about this. Would you ask her to come in here? And you may have the rest of the day to yourself."

"Nova—Hannah, please come and sit with me. There is something that we need to have a serious conversation about."

"Is it that I am spending too much time here? Am I in the way?"

"Goodness no, you are always welcome here! There is no other person that I rather spend my time with. However, I do need to ask you not to be so outspoken about your god."

"How would that be possible after all that the Eternal One has done for me?"

The discussion lasted through the night until Hannah said, "The irony about my becoming a Jew is that it would not have happened without my being taken away from our clan. While Madad went to great lengths to take me from the clan, he did nothing to fill my loss or to answer my questions. At first, I tried to fill that void with riotous living. In the end, it was a clan's lingering Druid love for the truth, other people, and nature that made evil repugnant to me. However, the void in my eternal being remained until it was filled by the Hebrew God. I searched for the truth and found God because my father caused me to become lonely and disheartened.

It is only in these late days, that you have been able to so kindly teach me to appreciate the earthy wisdom of Druidism. Judaism would never have had a chance to enter my mind if you were my father. It is by grace and good fortune that Judaism has entered my heart because Druidism falls short of what it seeks the most: the truth. Don't you see? Your sacred trees, our people, the land, the sky, the sea—all that is good and real, is evidence of the existence of a creator. The truth and love that you seek are gifts that He freely offers to His people. I love you, uncle, but my heart belongs to the giver of these gifts—the One True God. He is the Creator of heaven and earth and all things within them. As Creator, He is not part of His creation. He transcends His creation, whereas Druidism seeks to define the indefinable. You are so caught up in the gifts of this life that you are blinded to the giver of those gifts. I appreciate the wonders that you have shared. In gratitude, I urge you to look beyond those wonders and reach for an unimaginable Creator who is without earthly limitations."

Elymas listened to Hannah's testimony and was very impressed with her. *What a powerful Druid she would have made*, he mused. *Instead, I am stuck with the mean-spirited Phymas.*

When Hannah was finished speaking, Elymas said, "I will think and pray about what you have said about your god. I will also pray for both of our eternal beings. Whatever is the truth, I do not wish to face eternity without you."

"Druid Elymas, thank you for your prayers. I have never told you how important you are to me."

"Don't say that. I remember what happened the last time you said that to me."

"What time are you referring to? When have I ever said that or called you Elymas before?"

"Oh, I'm sorry Hannah. Your inspiring Judaic words are very upsetting. I am so upset that I do not know what I am saying anymore. Please go in peace, and allow me to think about the things you have said."

Autumn turned to winter, and as foretold, the sacred child named Samuel was born on the Feast of Brigit.[19] It surely was the coldest of mornings that saw the birth of a healthy boy with his father's black hair, eyes, and the same family birthmark on his chest. Samuel's name and ethnic features were constant reminders that mother and son were to return to Midian once he was weaned.

Interestingly, the presence of this child did not cause any tension within the hill-fort, because everyone knew him to be the son of the gods Cernunnos

---

[19] The goddess Brigit or Brigid has been demoted to *saint*. The Feast of Saint Brigit is celebrated on February 1.

PART 3—LIVING THE WORD

and Nantosuelta. Hence, there was no question concerning Samuel's parentage. However, there was growing contention over Hannah's heresy against the established Druidic belief system. It was becoming increasingly intolerable for many Celts and especially their Druids.

Druid Elymas spent months trying to convert Hannah back into the natural order only to find himself questioning his beliefs. This young woman could harm the Druidic society, and that was a frightening thought. He could not let that happen—not in his territory. Hannah had to be silenced before everything that held the Celtic people together was lost. In the end, her uncle threatened to place a geasa on Aberdonshire if Hannah did not repent of her heretical ways and proselytizing.

A servant announced the arrival of Elymas to the royal chambers. "Sire, High Druid Elymas is here to speak with you."

"Show my dear brother in. He does not need an invitation."

Druid Elymas was ushered in. "Welcome, brother," Curr said, motioning to him to take a seat. "You seem upset. Tell me what is on your mind."

"It is about your granddaughter Hannah. I have just returned from the annual gathering of the Wise Men of the Oak. Word of her has spread far and wide. They are saying that she is making up stories of horses, queens, and Hebrew holy men to influence our people. Of the greatest concern to us is the story about the one true god. Can you imagine just one god to do everything? Everyone knows that there are sixty-nine major male gods alone, as well as countless goddesses and minor gods. Even with that great number of deities, bless their divine names, their work is never done. Who does she think she is coming in here and saying that there is only one god? Others are saying that she is a war goddess who has come to take us all to the underworld. Still another said, 'I know who she is. She is a witch. Without sorcery, how else could one wee lass conquer an entire kingdom?' Curr, what good will it do if she gains the whole earth and loses her eternal being to this heresy?"

"I will speak to her about it. Don't worry so much. You know that you are my Druid and always my brother."

"See that you do, Curr. Otherwise, the Supreme Council of Wise Men has sworn to place a geasa on your 'kindom.' We do not want her filling our children's heads with any of her foolishness. Our beliefs are what hold us together as a people. Take them away and we will all be lost."

"I said that I would speak to her about it and I will. Thank you for bringing this problem to my attention. After all that has been said, I must say that there seems to be more behind your obvious interest in this matter."

Elymas got up to leave without permission. "On your way out, brother, please tell my servant to find Princess Hannah and ask her to come to me. And it is King Curr to you, Elymas."

Elymas spun on his heel. "Don't ask her to come to you; command her! What sort of name is Hannah for a Pictish princess?"

Curr took a deep breath and maintained his composure. "That will be all for now, my Druid."

Hannah was already on her way to see her grandfather when she met her uncle. "The great King Curr wishes to speak with you," he said with obvious sarcasm.

"Uncle, are you well?" Elymas did not answer and kept walking away in a huff.

The young mother went directly to her grandfather with trepidation.

"Ah, Hannah, thank you for coming so quickly. We have a problem, my dear."

"Am I the problem? Or is it the baby?"

"The baby? No! I must speak to you of a serious problem that your uncle Elymas has brought to my attention. It is about you telling people of your god. You need to stop talking about him immediately."

"Grandfather, as I told Uncle Eli, I cannot do that."

"Hannah, Druid Elymas makes the judgments and punishments for our people, especially the spiritual judgments. He has the power to excommunicate you, our family, our clan, and even Aberdonshire and the mountain territory with a geasa if you do not repent of your blasphemy against our beliefs. Everyone believes the tenets of our faith; thus, they are true. Why can't you understand that? You are the only one who says that our beliefs are false."

"I already have an answer that will satisfy everyone. I must return to Midian." Curr listened carefully as she told him everything that happened the day of the Linndee Valley fire and the reason that this was the appointed time for her to deliver the sacred child Samuel to Midian.

Surprisingly, King Curr understood, and his reply was more surprising. "I do not care what people are saying. I believe you because of everything you

PART 3—LIVING THE WORD

have told me. Moreover, I have seen how your god has worked powerfully in your life. It is because of these things that I have also come to believe in your one true god. You must keep this sacred vow, but I wish you had never made it. Nevertheless, you did make the vow. Therefore, you must keep it. First Madad took you from me, and now your God is taking both you and Samuel. You will always be our Nova, and things will be very dim around here without you both. Still, I believe that it was through God that you have blessed and enriched all our lives. Subsequently, it does not seem right that you must be the one to leave because of the truth. And yet, leave you must. Perhaps you returned home only to plant a seed of faith, and now you must go to keep your vow. You will have a royal escort to Midian. However, there will be no going-away-celebration; you will have to forgive me for that."

"Thank you, Grandfather. Knowing that you are giving your heart to God is the best going-away-celebration I could ever have."

Hannah and baby Samuel were packed and ready to leave before morning. They would make the journey by horse and cart. Their military escort stood by as those closest to her said their goodbyes. Curr was having second thoughts. "Hannah, I am concerned that the messenger to Midian never returned. Perhaps you will not be welcomed there. It is also worrisome that we have not heard anything, good or bad, from Asbury. What is the queen planning? You are embarking on a long and dangerous journey. It is too risky. Don't go. Wait until we know more. Damn the Druids—stay here!"

"As you said last night, Grandfather, regardless of everything else, my sacred vow must be kept. I will leave here and arrive in Midian unannounced because the fewer people that know of my journey the safer we all will be. I am dreading my return to Midian more than looking forward to it. However, with Samuel weaned, the time for our departure is now. How ironic it is that I, the champion of Aberdonshire, should have to be the one to leave. Instead of blocking my return to Midian, Druidism is hastening the fulfillment of my Judaic vow."

"At the moment, I am not very fond of the Druids, Madad, or God," Curr said. "It is hard to see them as loving when they have taken you and now Samuel from us."

"My vow was that I would give my first-born son to God. I know within my heart that if our roles were reversed, the Almighty One would suffer and do the same for me. Pray with me, Grandfather, that I would have the patience and faith needed for God's will to be done in my life. Grandfather, would you please give us your blessing and pray for us?"

Two carts and the royal escort left the Curr Kindom that morning, casting a spell over the land. The general mood was mournful.

"Excuse me, Prince Conan," Hannah said tentatively.

"Yes, cousin, what is it?"

"Why are there two carts?"

"The second cart is packed with your belongings and supplies for the journey, thus giving you more room in this cart."

"That was very thoughtful of you, cousin. Thank you."

Hannah's departure from Aberdon reminded her of the time when she had to leave Asbury. Two years earlier, the slave Nova had escaped from Asbury with only the clothes on her back. Her emotions were conflicted at the time because part of her was frightened while another part was excited by the realization of gaining her freedom. In contrast, on this day, Princess Hannah and her son were escorted from Aberdon as royalty, but she was consumed with a feeling of dreadful anticipation.

King Curr's messenger never reached Midian where Abraham was sleeping restlessly. He was dreaming that he left the synagogue by the backdoor one morning and found that fire had scorched all the western land. Many frightened people were peering out from behind burnt tree stumps, and Abraham cried out to them, "Fear not, the Messiah is coming to save us from our sins."

Then from the fire he heard four voices calling to him, "Father, have mercy on your children!"

He called back, "David, Jonathan, my sons, is that you?"

"Yes, Father, we are here with your son Samuel and your daughter Hannah!"

Soaked with perspiration, Abraham sat straight up in bed.

"Abe, my darling, what is it?" Sarah asked with concern, having been jolted out of her sleep.

Abraham told Sarah about his dream while the dream remained fresh in his mind. "What could it mean, Sarah? As Yah is my witness, I promise you that you are the only woman I have ever been with."

PART 3—LIVING THE WORD

"Abraham, my dear, it was only a dream. Here, put on this dry nightgown, and let's go back to sleep. You will feel better in the morning."

"No, Sarah, I tell you—the Holy One is trying to speak to me."

"Well, go back to sleep, and if He calls again, ask Him to be more clear."

A short time later, Abraham was awake again. "Sarah, wake up! I need another nightgown, and you are going to need one, too."

"Why, Abraham? What is your problem?"

"It's not my problem, but our problem, Sarah. The One Who Reveals has shown me that we are going to have another son named Samuel and a daughter named Hannah."

"Please, it is the middle of the night. Go back to sleep. I am an old woman who needs her sleep. Now is not a good time to make me laugh."[20]

On the Sabbath, Abraham described the dreams to the congregation. "I had an unimaginable dream last night. It must have been those herbs Sarah puts in her soup."

After hearing about Abraham's dream, one man jokingly asked, "So, Teacher, when this dream of yours comes true, could Sarah share her soup recipe with our wives?"

"Her soup is wonderful, but we can only pray for such an elixir."

For Hannah, the journey back to Midian was going by too quickly. There was so much to think and pray about. Everyone would want to know what happened to David and Jonathan and how only Hannah had managed to escape the fire. How could she possibly tell the exact truth without adding to the sorrow of her parents and friends, or even worse, to have her words held in doubt? Sometimes honesty seemed to be overrated, and this was such a time. What was she to say? Oh, I'm sorry; David was burned to death just hours after he raped me. Or should she lie and create a story where David and Jonathan gave their lives to save her life? Nevertheless, what would happen if she became confused later on and was called out in the lie? Everything was simpler in Aberdonshire where the people knew Samuel as the son of the gods.

Her Jewish faith complimented her Druid heritage as an equal tormentor by saying that a person should have truth in the heart, strength in the arm, and honesty in speech. That is, both Druidism and Judaism sought the light

---

[20] Genesis 18:10-15—Then the Lord said to Abraham, "Why did Sarah laugh and say, 'Will I really have a child, now that I am old?'"

of truth. Both faiths were demanding that she ought to be honest in all things even if the truth brought pain to the ones she loved.

Then she remembered that the last thing David said to her was to "come, sit, stay, play, and have some fun. What my parents don't know will not hurt us." Proverbs states, "A trustworthy man keeps a secret." So, she changed her mind and decided to lie. She reasoned that everyone in Aberdonshire agreed that it was good to have destroyed an enemy through dishonesty. This time, dishonesty was also good because it would save Sarah and Abraham from learning the truth about what happen to her in Glenn Morrah. *Yes, I will not tell my parents the truth.*

Then her mind changed once more as she thought, *Wait! I never agreed to keep David's secret. I disagreed with him and even begged him to leave Glenn Morrah. Only a deceptive person would not trust me with a dark secret again. Wait! I have been a deceptive person. El Shaddai, Almighty God, please keep me from madness. Show me the answer that will bring glory to your holy name.*

A week passed before Hannah's entourage crossed the bridge into Midian. When she saw that familiar landscape, she felt anticipation mixed with dread. She loved her son more than she could express, and being here meant that she had to fulfill her vow to give him to the Lord. Hannah looked down at baby Samuel as she held him in her arms. "Well, Samuel, our lives are about to change, and I'm afraid that we will be forever separated in this lifetime."

Looking heavenward, she prayed, "My ever present Lord, I need you now. Please give me your strength, courage, and love. Could there be any greater torment than parting with an only child? Please, dear God, if there is any other way, release me from this bitter vow. Otherwise, it is for your will that I pray."

She looked at the horseman riding alongside of the cart. "It is the first house on the right."

The royal escort stopped on Prince Conan's command. He dismounted and gave Hannah his hand to step from the cart. Abraham was standing in front of the house, and the dreaded moment was here. He saw Samuel in her arms, and then he looked deeply into her eyes. She could tell in an instant that he knew everything there was to know. "Nova, you have returned home to us." The old man and young woman stood there holding each other weeping bittersweet tears. "Give me a moment to announce your arrival to Sarah."

PART 3—LIVING THE WORD

As he walked away, Hannah thought, *He called me Nova. The messenger never made it here. They do not know anything about what has happened. God, this is going to be more difficult than I imagined. Please help me to be strong and honest.*

Sarah was already walking toward them. "Thank you, Eternal One, for bringing our daughter home!" Stopping abruptly just short of Hannah she asked, "And who is this?"

"This is Samuel."

Four souls instantly bonded together in sorrow and joy. The moment of dread turned joyful when those two old people danced and sang with happiness. "Our daughter was dead and now is alive. Everyone, come and meet our Samuel!" In a moment, it seemed as though all their friends were in the front yard singing and praising God. It also seemed strange to Hannah and her escort that some kind of universal awakening was happening that they failed to understand. How strange and yet how fitting it was to see Sarah holding her grandson and laughing with joy. Even so, there was that moment when Sarah's questioning eyes met Hannah's eyes with, "Are Jonathan and David alive?"

Hannah's eyes answered with, "No, Mother."

Then Abraham eased the pain of the moment. "We knew months ago that the Lord took our David and Jonathan, and we thought you as well. The Lord took our children, and the Lord gave us our children. You and Samuel have arrived safely to us. Please let me hold this most precious of gifts. Let me hold my grandson."

"Grandson? So you did receive my message."

"No, we have not received any message from you."

"Tell me, then, how you could know that he is your grandson? Mother, Father, there is something I need to tell you. After The One Who Redeems saved me from the wildfire, I made a vow."

Abraham stopped her from having to say anything more. "We know. The One Who Reveals has already told us. Are you sure that this is what you want to do, Hannah?"

"Hannah? I have not said anything about my name. How did you…?"

"That is true. We should listen to what you have to say."

Then Abraham drew everyone's attention with an announcement. "Everyone, listen to Nova! She has something to tell us."

"Go ahead, dear, we are listening," Sarah said.

"My name is Hannah. I have been known as Hannah for the past year."

Again, with that announcement, there was dancing, singing, and praises, that served to add to Hannah's confusion and frustration. She had prepared herself for mourning, tears, and even people wearing sackcloth and pouring ashes over themselves.[21] Instead, there was only rejoicing.

"Why is everyone so happy? Listen to me! I made a vow to the One Who Is Holy. I vowed to dedicate my first-born son to be raised in His house as His servant here in Midian."

Again, Abraham asked if she was certain about keeping her sacred vow.

"Yes, it is what I must do. It makes it easier knowing that Samuel will have the best parents that I know. Calling me Hannah would be a constant reminder of Immanuel, the Lord's reassuring presence in our lives, and of course, calling the boy Samuel would be a reminder that I was *heard of God* when he saved me from the flames of a great fire."[22]

Sarah wrapped her arms around Hannah. "Yes, my love. We know. The Lord has told us everything. You may relax and enjoy this moment. You are welcome here. This is your home and family. Shalom, my darling."

"I love you, too, Mother, but please help me understand what has happened here today. I dreaded the anguish of this reunion, and yet you seem so happy. I do not understand how you could know that Samuel is your grandson and that you already know me as Hannah. And yet, it is obvious that you did not receive my message that was sent months ago from Aberdon. I thought that you were angry with me when you did not answer my message. To be sure, much remains for us to talk about after everyone leaves."

"Go enjoy this day. Your friends are waiting."

Hannah began working her way over to where Marsha was waiting for her. When the two embraced, Hannah felt truly at home once more. Marsha was the one person to whom she could tell everything.

"I'm not calling you Hannah," Marsha said. "You will always be Nova to me. Now, come meet my husband."

---

[21] Esther 4:1—When Mordecai learned of all that had been done, he tore his clothes, put on sackcloth and ashes, and went out into the city, wailing loudly and bitterly.

[22] The name Samuel sounds like the word for *heard of God* when spoken in Hebrew.

PART 3—LIVING THE WORD

"Hello, Hannah! Marsha never stops talking about you. Look behind you. I believe there is someone else she wants you to meet."

Hannah turned around to find Marsha holding a baby. "Marsha! Who is this fine-looking young man?"

"This is Moses. Look how he reaches for you! He has always been shy of strangers until seeing you."

Then another familiar voice asked, "Hannah, darling, why the tears?"

"Haggai, Leah, I have missed you both so much! Come see the beautiful Prince Moses."

The entire reunion party became silent when everyone turned their attention to the arrival of a Celtic woman. Hannah ran, embraced the woman, and announced, "Everyone, please welcome my friend Caoimhe, who cared for me when I was cast down and beaten."

The two women exchanged the usual pleasantries, and then Caoimhe's demeanor turned serious. "At first I was worried about you, then I grieved for you, and now I rejoice to see that you are alive. Please promise that you will visit me and tell me all that has happened to you."

For the first time, Hannah sensed that there was much more to know about this woman. "Caoimhe, I promise I will do that."

Hannah looked around at her friends and thought, *This is home. I am finally home.* Waiting for her with open arms was the nation of Israel to lift her out of her darkness and into the loving light of God. They knew her for who she was and loved her anyway. They showed her God's love when it was needed the most, and it was already time to leave them far too soon. It was a privilege for her to have glimpsed into their exclusive God-centered world of Midian.

Thereafter, Abraham performed the circumcision followed by the dedication ceremony of Samuel into the service of God. "The One Who Creates gave me a son, a son that I hereby return for His Glory." From that moment, Samuel grew to become an outstanding teacher for his people. His future was full of promise that the loving spirit of God would shine brightly through his life giving hope and peace to an otherwise darkened world.

Hannah spent the next day telling her Midian parents everything that had happened in the previous year without dwelling heavily on her last moments with David. "Once more I need your wisdom and help. First, I cannot be true to my vow and stay here stealing little moments with Samuel and dying a thousand deaths. Secondly, my presence once again endangers the people of Midian. The Druids have driven me from my native home as a heretic, and I know that there are enemies lurking about who want to do me harm. I know that the Queen of Asbury would die to know that I live. All in all, I need to find a safe place to live away from here."

"Druids, highwaymen, kings, queens, fire, a new name, and a baby; did we miss anything?"

Hannah buried her face with both hands. "Father, even I would not believe all that has happened if it hadn't happened to me."

"Try us."

"As Deborah conquered the Canaanites, I vanquished the enemies of my people, tripled the size of my clan's territory, and captured a hill-fort without the loss of one clan member. The men and horses that you see outside waiting are my royal escort. My grandfather is the king of this new territory, and I am his warrior princess."

"Such a story, and yet coming from you, we can believe it. Are you sure that you need the help of a humble old man? Really, what may I do for Your Highness?"

"Please, I really do need your help. First, pray with me and for me. Secondly, help me understand what to do. Humble old man indeed; you are the wisest man in Albion."

Sarah joined the conversation with spiritual encouragement. "Do not worry about your life. The One has already prepared everything for you. Do not worry about your enemies, or about where you will live. Have you come so far and witnessed El Shaddai's presence in your life only to lose heart now?"

"My faith is in crisis. The winter was spent comparing theologies with my Druid Granduncle Elymas."

"I would think that to be a dangerous thing to do with a Druid. What was the result?"

"I thought that it was going well until it suddenly caused me to be here. Mother, can you believe it? Druidism banished me from my clan and forced me to keep my Judaic vow."

"Have you forgotten that you are the great Nova, Daughter of the Light? Be that woman, and have faith. Be strong in the Lord," Sarah said encouragingly. "I have a suggestion. As you know, I always travel with Abraham on his visits

PART 3—LIVING THE WORD

south to Avon for the Sabbath of the new moon. It is almost that time. Come with us this time, and give your mind a rest. Besides, it is well past time that you meet the rest of your family."

Sarah and Abraham were originally from Avon. Their two older sons remained there when Abraham and Sarah moved to Midian as a central location for his itinerate ministry between Asbury and Avon. The thought of meeting their other sons lifted Hannah's spirits. Little did she know that the village of Avon was to be her new home and a source of a continued relationship with Abraham and Sarah. Living in Avon would bring her a step closer to her destiny.

With safety and acceptance secured, it was time to release the royal escort of Aberdonshire. Hannah never suspected the animosity that Conan held toward her. The prince planned to kill his interloper cousin during the journey to Midian. Otherwise, Hannah would surely come to her senses and trade her god for a comfortable place within the Curr Kindom where she was not wanted. First, he had sent the messenger directly to his friend King Cumobelius of the Britons instead of sending him to Midian. Conan rewarded the messenger handsomely not to return to Aberdon. Then he made several failed attempts to kill Hannah on the way to Midian. It was as though she had a guardian spirit protecting her. He would have another chance at murder if she would return to Aberdon.

When Hannah told Prince Conan that he would be returning home without her, he said, "Are you really going to stay in this hamlet? Give up this god of yours and the entire Curr Kindom will be yours. What is there of any worth in this place? Come home to Aberdon with us. It will not be the same without you."

"Thank you, Prince, and please thank your men for looking after me. I will pray that you have a safe journey home. You will soon be the king of the Aberdonshire territories. I know that you will reign with love, dear uncle."

"If not to Aberdon, we should see you safely to and from Avon, my lady."

"I am in safe hands here in Midian. Please, I have kept you too long. Go in peace."

"By your leave, princess," Conan said, and then he and the royal escort rode off from Midian along with Hannah's title of Warrior Princess. Suddenly, she became just plain Hannah, the one who was heard of God.

Avon was located as far south from Midian as Asbury was to the north. Coincidentally, her Celtic friend Caoimhe and her people lived in the territory between Midian and Avon. Hannah looked for her friend in vain as they traveled to Avon. Still, just knowing that Caoimhe was close by gave her a sense of a Celtic connection as well as a link between the two villages. It started her thinking. *Caoimhe invited me to visit her. Perhaps I could live with her people; but then again, rejection would follow once I told them about God.*

Soon the trio arrived in the delightful village of Avon. Hannah did not expect that this coastal village would be her home for the next thirteen years. It was a wonderful time in her life that began with a family dinner and meeting the "boys," Esau and Israel, who were twice her age.

Sarah had a question for Hannah once they were alone again in Midian. "So, what do you think?"

"Think about what?"

"My son Israel."

"Mother Matchmaker, what are you saying?"

"It is a match made in heaven. Do you need a sign from the Divine Master of the Universe himself? Here is a sign. Israel is from Avon."

"How is Avon a sign that I ought to marry your son?"

"My dear, it is because Abraham tells me that Avon is Nova spelled backward."

"Mother, slow down; it could just as easily be a coincidence."

"You have met him and talked with him. So, what do you think? I know that Israel is the perfect man for you. Did you see the way he kept looking at you? So, what do you think about him?"

Hannah's face flushed when she thought about the prospect of marriage and her answer. "His name being Israel is a greater sign from The One Who Reveals than the coincidence of Nova and Avon. All right, fine, I will agree to him courting me later in the year."

"Hannah, the longer you wait, the harder it will be to let go. From now on, Samuel lives here in Midian where the face of Nova is well known."

"Of course you are right, Mother. My vow requires me to surrender Samuel to the Lord. It is time to take the next step in the Lord's plan for my life. Tell Israel that I agree to a short betrothal period."

"Wonderful! I will send a messenger to Israel tomorrow."

PART 3—LIVING THE WORD

Sarah paused and then asked somewhat cautiously, "Hannah, darling, why is the name Israel a sign from the Lord for your marriage?"

"Because, just as the Torah tells us that Israel wrestled with the Lord, I have been wrestling with Him a great deal lately. If your Israel is true to his namesake, then we are a match that I hope was made in heaven."[23]

"Oh, yes, I see your point. In any case, it would be a heavenly match for me by any sign from the Almighty One."

Sarah's voice turned playful. "Hannah, my dear valiant daughter, we are having a feast this evening. Perhaps you could simply be the teacher's calm daughter for once and try not to vanquish any of our guests."

"Nice, I love you too, Mother, but forgive me. I am not in a festive mood. I will spend the evening in my room,"

Hannah found it ironic to have been rejected by her clan for telling the truth about God and accepted in Midian before she could have told a lie about David and Jonathan. Her combined Druid and Torah-based integrity culminated in a sacrificial trust in God that demonstrated a quantum leap of faith. From that point on, she was determined to tell the truth at all times.

In Aberdon, Conan and his men were welcomed home, where the clan listened to tales of his adventure. He saved the details of his plot against Hannah for when he was alone with his sisters. Makcurr the Stag Slayer did not receive this revelation as he expected. "So, you are the reason that the messenger to Midian never returned. You are wasting your time. Hannah has no interest in succeeding Father's throne."

"How do you know? Have you become Makcurr the Mind Reader?"

"I know Hannah, understand her, respect her, and even love her. You will answer to me if anything suspicious happens to her."

"Sister, it is unwise for you to threaten your future king."

The Slayer quipped in returned, "Said the sheath to the saber. Therein is the difference between the two of us. Hannah would not have survived the journey if I had escorted her with your hatred for her in my heart. You talk, talk, and talk. I execute."

---

[23] Genesis 32:22-32—Jacob wrestled with God and was renamed Israel afterward. Israel: who wrestles with God.

Diplomatic Counselor Hancurr finally intervened. "Will you two ever stop your bickering? Forget her. Banishment has renounced her claims to royalty. She has chosen to be the humble servant of her god. In doing so, she has become a common peasant."

MADE IN HEAVEN

Nova's Age: Seventeen to Twenty-One

Israel was a pleasant looking man with a slight build and a slight limp to go with it. He was the owner of the Neptune Trading Company. This captain of the shipping industry was captivated the first time he saw his bride-to-be at half his age. His only thought was, *There really is a God in heaven.* Israel was always ready to seize an opportunity, and here was an opportunity to marry a younger woman to match his tenacity.

Once again, a pauper married for wealth and a more secure life. Hannah's family history repeated when she sold her youth and beauty for a more secure life for herself. However, time would prove that this marriage was made in heaven and born in truth. The face of Nova was unknown in Avon. However, there was one person in Avon who needed to know the truth in order for the marriage to succeed. Israel was told everything, beginning with Hannah saying, "Israel, we have to talk. You must know everything about me."

Afterward, he teasingly said, "You cannot be Nova. Everyone knows that she is tall and keeps bears as pets. You will be wife and bodyguard all in one. Seriously, Hannah, your life story has made you even more endearing to me. Everything about you is attractive: your openness, your experiences, and your faith. Please say that you will share your life with me."

"Yes, I will!"

Finally, here was someone who knew everything about her without being even a little frightened. Yes, Israel knew everything about Hannah in one day. In contrast, it would take decades of learning before Hannah would know the depth of Israel. They were married several months later with an introductive reception into Avon society and beyond. The celebration was held in their home. It was the grandest home for many miles.

Hannah thought that her heart would stop when one wedding guest greeted her. "You look familiar. Have we met in the past?"

Hannah remembered delivering a message to the woman's home in the north. "Oh, thank you. That is so kind. I have heard it said that everyone has a twin somewhere. Tell me, do you have children?"

"Yes. I have two boys and a girl."

"Oh, dear, come sit with me and tell me all about them."

Israel lived in an inclusive world where almost everyone was welcome. He seemed to know everyone, from business magnates and community leaders to the poorest of the poor. Surely, all his friends from many nations attended the wedding, meeting and greeting the bride's most trusted guests from Midian and Aberdon. They all came to share in a joyous and proud moment. One very special guest named Abraham performed the sacred kiddushin wedding ceremony.[24]

Israel's business enterprises lifted the lives of many people. Neptune Trading Company's boats and ships were already moving people and products between Albion and all known ports. He continuously added new ports and avenues of trade as the business and fleet grew. The company flag was respected both on land and at sea. It seemed strange that even the coastal pirates

---

[24] Kiddushin: sanctification, is the name of a sacred Jewish wedding.

PART 3—LIVING THE WORD

often left Israel's ships unmolested. Much later, Hannah came to understand that Israel owned a second fleet that displayed the flag of his Manawyddan Utility Company.[25] The utility company made good use of Israel's older vessels, employing them for fishing, training, local transportation, and protecting the Neptune fleet.

While Israel was a captain of twin industries, his twin brother, Esau, was the senior ship captain of a Neptune Trading Company. Of course, he was a tall and robust outdoorsman. Everyone knew Esau as unpretentiously honest, fair, and hardworking.

Life in Avon quickly returned to normal except for a bride in search of her place. "Well, here I am, Lord: your married woman in Avon, and far from the sacred dwelling place of my ancestral spirits. I transformed into a person of deeper faith and commitment to you, Lord. My life has been one of great earthly loss and greater eternal gain in you. The past and present are fading. There is only the future in you, Lord. Upon what path will you lead me? How might I serve you in Avon?"

Once settled, Hannah's first four married years in Avon were wonderful. She often helped at the shipping company while continuing to learn, teaching children, and managing her home. One year she was a young girl, and the year after she was the mother of Samuel, the wife of a man twice her age, and instantly the stepmother of two children half her age. Israel's first wife had died several years earlier of a fever. Hannah's personal experiences with grief and her compassion eased the transition of such a marriage. She came as a friend to share in their grief and lighten their loneliness.

As part of the normal routine, there was always the week of the new moon when Sarah traveled with Abraham during his three-day monthly visits to Avon. During those visits, they stayed with Israel and Hannah in rooms kept specifically for them. Abraham did not have to rehearse in a horse stable while staying in Avon. As he prepared, the teacher could depend on one person to be there. The rehearsal began with teacher and student exchanging smiles that expressed their love for each other. In his mind, he could still see little Nova sitting up in the hayloft watching and listening for the message to be repeated

---

[25] Manawyddan was the king of the oceans and the son of the Celtic sea god Llyr. The Roman sea god was Neptune, the Greek sea god was Poseidon, the Norse sea god was Aegir, and the Hebrew sea god was, is, and forever will be God.

in her native Gaelic language. As always, he made the message so simple that even an uneducated Celtic stable girl could understand it.

Around the time when Abraham was to visit Avon again, Hannah noticed a young sailor praying in Hebrew at the end of the company dock. The familiar words of his prayer drew Hannah's attention. "Listen Israel: The Eternal is our Lord, the Eternal is One." He stood up as he finished and faced her. She greeted him with welcoming gestures and by saying, "Shalom. Welcome to Avon. Where are you from?" She was stunned by his answer.

"Shalom. I have just arrived from Jerusalem."

Until that moment, Jerusalem was only a name of a place mentioned in the sacred scroll stories. She repeated it, "Jerusalem...Jerusalem..." and began to weep because the truth of God's written word suddenly came rushing over her. Her emotion pushed his homesick heart to join her as they wept together over the city dedicated to the Eternal God.

Meeting that sailor made all scripture more real to her, and Hannah became determined to learn more about God and His people. However, literary educational resources were almost nonexistent in Albion. Hannah only knew of her stepchildren's Greek tutor and a teacher who visited three days each month.

Hannah began to attend the tutoring sessions with her stepsons. Israel paid the poor tutor extra to encourage him to teach what the tutor claimed to be the "slowest student that ever lived. I agreed to teach your boys. Teaching your wife is an entirely different matter. Israel, I hardly know where to begin teaching her. And why does a woman need an education? Excuse me for saying that she wants to learn, but she does not know how to learn."

"Stephen, she has always seemed very quick-witted to me. Perhaps you could begin by teaching her just that. Teach her how to learn, and then introduce her to philosophy, geography, history, mathematics, languages, and drama. I know that she would enjoy the theater."

"Yes, I agree. This is already a Greek tragedy."

"Would you agree to allowing her to attend the lessons in silence?"

"Yes, I suppose that would be acceptable."

Later that evening, Israel discussed the problem with Hannah. Her feelings were hurt without knowing the full extent of Stephen's complaint. "Israel, I do not think that my questions and comments are without reason."

PART 3—LIVING THE WORD

Israel's face clearly expressed agreement. "Could you do a favor for me and just listen during the lesson and discuss your questions and ideas with me later?"

"All right, fine, I can do that. My silence is a small price for knowledge."

Israel allowed Stephen to present the lessons in his business office where he and Hannah could listen. Once alone, Israel found most of Hannah's comments and questions to be highly academic and thought provoking. "Hannah, you are not the problem. For now, I am uncertain of the reason for Stephen's objection to your education. For the future, let us continue to attend the sessions in silence and later, the boys can discuss the day's lesson with us. I have come to enjoy our family discussions."

Philosophy, the love of wisdom, was closest to her first love of theology. She found the teachings of Socrates, Plato, and Aristotle to be fascinating. The thing that she loved most about Socrates was that he never wrote anything down because he knew that people would twist his words to mean something other than what he intended. The Druids gave the same reason for their spiritual oral tradition. At last, she had an apologetic defense for this particular Druidic wisdom. If a great philosopher such as Socrates did not believe in recording his thoughts, then perhaps the Druidic safeguard over their sacred beliefs was reasonable.

She also learned that Plato recorded some of Socrates's thoughts, and it was Plato's analogy in his thesis *Justice and the Shadow People* that struck very close to the mindset in Currcroft. He presented the story of a group of people who lived their entire lives among the shadows of a cave. It was a cave where sacred spirit shadows danced on the cavern walls. These shadows were obviously real and were all that these cave dwellers knew and worshiped for as long as anyone could remember. One day, a member of the group left the cave and stepped outside and into the light of the world. Later, he returned and told the others that their beliefs were wrong and disproved simply by stepping out of the dark and into the light. The cave dwellers knew that this could not be true because they all agreed that the shadows were real. Only one troublemaker said that their beliefs were wrong. Consequently, they did the only thing that they could do to maintain their traditional social order. They killed the heretic, and tranquility returned to the depths of darkness. Hannah thought, *I guess there **is** something worse that being banished as a heretic.*

At first, she showed little interest in history until Stephen taught about how the Keltoi invaded the Apennine Peninsula and sacked a city called Rome four hundred years earlier. After weeks of silence, Hannah could no longer contain her frustration. "Teacher, forgive me. May I ask why we care about what happened someplace far away, four hundred years ago?"

"Why? There are several reasons why. First, as a Keltoi, I think you would agree that history has a way of repeating. Secondly, the Romans and the Keltoi are still fighting today. And finally, you of all people ought to be interested in these facts because you are one of the Keltoi."

"No, I'm not. I am a Celt."

"Hannah, Keltoi is the Greek name for the word Celt, as is Gaul in the Latin language. Your people and the Romans have been, still are, and forever will be enemies. Julius Caesar's army stood where we are standing. He invaded this land twice just to prove that it could be done. They will do it again. Soon, they will stand where we are standing now."

"How can you know that the Romans will return?"

"I know because they did the same thing to my people, the Greeks."

"Most of the people of Albion have no idea about this. Please continue, teacher. I will be quiet. You have my full attention."

"Our historians have recorded that your people the Celts are not from here. Your ancestors were driven here from far away in the east, leaving Celtic names such as Galatia all across the land. East of here, just across the water, is the Celtic territory known as Gaul. The people of Gaul speak a dialect of your Gaelic language. The Romans forced your once mighty nation to migrate here to the end of the earth in Albion. They know the southern part of Albion as Britannia and the northern part as Caledonia. The Romans also caused me to be here far from my homeland. They have conquered Gaul, and Albion is next. It is not something that happened four hundred years ago in a land far away. It is happening to you right now. Your people must decide to fight or to take flight, but never agree to unite with anything Roman. Otherwise, only tribute, misery, and lies will follow you all your days."

PART 3—LIVING THE WORD

"Stephen, finally we have found a common ground in a common enemy."

"Not really. We Greeks have not forgotten the Celtic invasion of Greece three hundred years ago."

"Ah, yes, I understand everything now. Thank you for allowing me to participate in the lesson. Please forgive the interruption."[26]

That evening during dinner, Israel said, "Well, I guess we have finally arrived at the bottom of why you are supposedly the slowest student that ever lived."

"He said that about me?"

"It was said without merit. You are even able to detect the lesson behind the lesson. What he did not say was that he is a Greek who does not like Celts because of something that happened in Greece three hundred years ago. However, I think that you have changed his mind just a little bit. Besides, your silence in class is less threatening than your thought-provoking comments that were making him feel as though he were the student."

"Yes, he does seem to be more pleasant toward me."

A few years later, Israel returned home one evening from "Druid-land up north" and swept Hannah into his arms. "I have great news from your grandfather!"

"You went to see Grandfather and you did not take me with you? You have met my entire clan? You were in Aberdon? How is he? How are they? You went without me?"

"Calm down. Listen to what I have to say. Remember that the Druids drove you out as a heretic and the danger that you were in. Well, after I spent some time talking with your grandfather, he called a meeting of your clan leaders, including the Druids. Your grandfather made a decree saying that each person in his kindom could worship as he or she wished without fear of retribution. Hannah, you should have heard him declare to the entire kindom that as for him and his household there was only one true God. And, oh yes, everyone including your uncle Eli sends their love to you."

---

[26] Stephen's accusation against the Celts was not fair because a Greek ruler had hired them as mercenaries. According to ancient historians, in 275 BC, the ruler of Troy, a man named Nicomedes, hired a Celtic army and paid them with land that became Galatia (within modern Turkey). Nicomedes paid them with land that he did not own.

Israel paused to catch his breath. "Well, say something, Hannah! Say something!"

His words left her awestruck and speechless. God had answered her grandfather's prayer. Inwardly, she prayed, *Blessed are You, Eternal One our God, Universal Presence Who is Good and Who bestows Goodness.*

Then she asked Israel, "Who will lead my people? Who will teach them about the One Who Is Holy?"

"That is how I got to Aberdon in the first place. Esau and I have been visiting the villages up and down the coast looking for new business opportunities. I purchased Haggai's messenger service in Midian. Haggai asked Esau and me to take him and Leah to Aberdon because The One Who Reveals has called him there to teach and lead our people. He and Leah moved there and became instant friends with your grandparents. They are now living in the hill-fort compound. Haggai is our first teacher in Aberdon. Oh, and there is one other thing. Your grandfather has changed his name to King David Curr."

Again, Israel's words left her awestruck in silent prayer. *Our God is an awesome God. Thank you for Israel, Haggai, Leah, and my dear Curr. They are mighty in you, Lord. Great are your ways, oh merciful God, the Great I AM.*

She still had no idea how great He was. God used Israel to remove the Druidic threat through commerce and business relationships. In doing so, Israel expanded his trading business from Avon to Aberdon in cooperation with Hannah's grandfather, King David Curr. They cleaned God's house in Aberdonshire together without Hannah.

In all, Hannah's first four years in Avon were wonderful. She delighted in helping at the trading company where she specialized in preparing fragile items for shipping or carefully handling them when received. For her, these days were waterfront adventures of seeing new things and meeting people from the savory to the noble. Her days were filled with questions and the fascinating answers they evoked: "What is in these boxes?" "Where are these hounds going?" "Where did this wine come from?" "Where is your home?"

Her housekeeping was easy because Israel had staffed their home with servants. In time, Hannah came to realize that housekeeping was second to their central task of providing household security. That explained why they often lacked the delicate touch for housekeeping. They were there largely to protect the family from an enemy foolish enough to invade Israel's home. Scheduling, planning, and hosting social gatherings were Hannah's household chores. Yes, in all, life was good in Avon without having to fight for survival, and then the four-year honeymoon was suddenly over.

THE ENEMY WITHIN

Nova's Age: Twenty-One to Twenty-Nine

Do not trust a neighbor; put no confidence in a friend. Even with her who lies in your embrace be careful of your words. For a son dishonors his father, a daughter rises up against her mother, a daughter-in-law against her mother-in-law—a man's enemies are the members of his own household. But as for me, I watch in hope for the Lord. I wait for God my Savior; my God will hear me (Micah 7:5-6).

Approximately seven hundred years before Hannah's time, the prophet Micah wrote the above words to tell her that people like Faolan are largely looking after their own interests. That basic animal instinct for self-survival is what preserves us yet often demeans us as human. An animal has no reservation about putting itself first even at the destruction of others. This is often the inhumane behavior of the nonbeliever.

In contrast, humane people have the will to work in harmony with others, even at the risk of their own destruction. They are the type of people who define us as human. They are the children of God. A believer in God often blindly takes a step higher as he lives by faith and not by the values of a nonbelieving world. The vulnerability that this creates for the believer is seen by the nonbeliever as an open invitation to destroy the believer with wicked and deceptive ploys. Such nonbelievers are as smiling wolves wearing garments of lamb's wool while stalking, pacing, drooling, and pouncing on their next opportunity to exist and survive. To them, believers are forgiving fools who go around talking to an imaginary friend in the sky. The lowest of this breed are family members who watch and wait to seize an opportunity to exploit their advantage. Nonbelieving family members easily abuse the believer because they do not fear retribution from a believing earthly father or from a heavenly God. Caring only for the moment and themselves, they are only fearful of life and death. What they do not see is the divine boundary of protection that surrounds the believer. The unbeliever is unaware that it is eternally unwise to victimize one of God's own.

Even as a believer in God, Hannah often harbored desires of revenge. Her father, stepfamily, and adopted brothers all betrayed her for their self-interests. As a Druid Celt, she desired to seek revenge instead of relenting to God's will. The way of the Celtic warrior was to sever an enemy's head from his body and therein be finished with him. Hannah had to remind herself constantly of who she had become in God. As a believer, she held out eternal hope for everyone, especially for her family. She prayed that each member would come to enjoy a personal relationship with God. Everyone is naturally self-willed, whereas the believer obediently chooses God's will to replace justification and punishment with His mercy and forgiveness. The world perceives this choice as a sign of weakness, when it is actually spiritual strength. The believer's deep level of self-control requires real strength as he or she counts all things to the glory of God, including suffering, and leaves vengeance to Him. God's kingdom is eternal, while this world and everything in it is temporal.

Although strangers may scar us, we die a thousand deaths when the enemy is one of our own household. This scarring can cause deep-seated anger, and that is exactly what had entered the heart of Hannah's home in Avon. The only problem was in determining the mysterious source of this evil.

The household servants in Avon were extended family members. It was a mystery where Israel found so many fierce-looking men and woman. In the end, Hannah would come to learn that Israel was a very good judge of character. Those dear people had simply lived hard lives that had forged them into guardian angels that placed an armed ward around the family. There was no enemy among them.

Abraham, Sarah, and Esau were the personification of God's chosen people. They were trusted and loyal mentors, and in some ways, they seemed as angels sent from God.

Israel's two sons were of no problem almost to a fault. They related to Hannah as though they were close friends more than parent and child. It did not seem right for two boys not to have bragging rights to some sort of mischief. They were more apt to help Hannah with her studies and chores than to cause any harm. Those two dear innocent people were not the enemy within.

Israel was an outstanding businessman, a loving husband, and a good father. He never raised his voice or hand, and he granted every wish requested by his family. Hannah asked to sail with him, and they sailed. He peaceably silenced her enemies; he brought religious freedom to her people of Aberdonshire; and he was missed terribly whenever he was away on business. Then one day he was heard saying, "Hannah, you don't have to bite my head off! What is wrong with you?"

The boys were less kind to her and insulted her daily with a litany of barbs:

"You are not our mother!" "You don't tell us what to do."
"She never did that." "She always did this."
"She was very pretty." "She was a good cook."
"She was our teacher." "She was a musician and singer."

Such comments were both expected and minor in comparison to the psychological and physiological abuse that Hannah had suffered in Asbury. She understood that they were cries from her stepsons' great loss. And yet, she could not understand why there was so much arguing after four congenial years. Finally, Hannah took a long look within herself and wondered, *Are all marriages this difficult, or is it just this type of marriage where the newcomer must compete with a ghost? Why is the honeymoon over? Ah, there you are. I see you. You are the enemy within this home.*

It is I, Lord! I have become the enemy within my family and community. Lord, your Hannah is a mean, irritable woman. Save me from myself. Have you brought me all this way just to let me be thrown down again in Avon? Dear God, do I dare ask what you have planned for my life?

Nova, Daughter of the Light, had become the enemy within her family. Even the romance between Hannah and Israel ended because of an illness. Hannah's last regular period did not completely stop. Very small amounts of blood continued to flow. She prayed and prayed and prayed again for God to

PART 3—LIVING THE WORD

remove this thorn from her flesh, but the bleeding would not stop. This was regarded as a genuine physical weakness that requires real spiritual strength to live with and teach her that God's power is made perfect in weakness. It eventually led her into a ministry for discarded women and children, something she never would have become involved in when she was well.

One must know Levitical Law to understand how a sudden physical illness could become a socially life-changing condition. Leviticus is the third book of the *Torah*. These laws were written to protect the Hebrew nation over the rights of the individual, and they worked well for over a thousand years for the majority at the suffering and guilt of the individual. Leviticus 15:19-31 states that a woman with a bleeding discharge was unclean.

"Lord, please remove this tamay (disease) from me, for your law is harsh," Hannah prayed.

Hannah clearly had a physical, religious, and social problem that could lead to a moral problem. It was such a small discharge, and it was her body, so why did it have to be anyone else's business? Why not keep it her personal secret? She had done nothing that required atonement for sins committed. Nevertheless, keeping the secret would have been living a lie, and she had promised to live in the truth. However, this truth could transform her from a treasured daughter, wife, mother, and teacher into a social outcast. The social isolation that could follow the truth would be a harsh sentence for a twenty-one-year-old woman. Socially, she did the only thing that a good Jewish woman could do. She declared herself unclean and withdrew from her people. Over time, the resulting isolation turned from anguish into spiritual purification. There was only one thing she could do, and that was to fully depend on God again. Her self-imposed solitude gave her the opportunity to study languages and the scriptures in depth. She pondered each Psalm and Proverb until they guided her every thought.

It was about that time that she began to notice street people during her brief ventures outdoors. It was there that she discovered an entire society of unclean people in need of someone to love them. Their lives seemed to be enriched and their burden lightened simply by Hannah's presence and touch. Because she was already unclean, she was not afraid to touch any of them. After all, she had had a great teacher of compassion in Sarah, who had once held an unclean Celtic girl in her arms.

THE ENEMY WITHIN

One day, a homeless person said to her, "Hannah, your faith and encouraging words give us hope." Those words from the least of the least gave her confirmation that ministering to the unclean was God's will for her life.

Israel invited her to go for a walk one morning. "Come with me, Hannah," he said. "There is something I want to show you."

Hannah began to feel uncomfortable as a great reception of friends greeted them while they walked together. People began cheering, "Hannah! Hannah!" They came to celebrate the opening of two baths where ceremonial cleansing rituals would take place. There was a bath for women and a bath for men. Above the entrance to the women's bath were inscribed the words Hannah's Pool.[27] Everyone gathered around Hannah to hug her and kiss her, or just to reach out and touch her. It would seem that she had overestimated the severity of the Levitical law and underestimated the compassion of her friends. In the following years, Israel built a medical clinic called Caoimhe and a homeless shelter with the name The Sarah House written above the entrance.

Thirteen years passed, her stepchildren matured, and Hannah had become satisfied with her life in the Lord. Many disenfranchised souls returned to spiritually productive lives through her ministries, and others retired to a peaceful, eternal rest. Some of the healed continued to work with the sick and the poor while many others went back into society. Israel stayed faithfully at Hannah's side as the blood continued to flow for nine more years. Even though her condition gave him the right to divorce her, he lovingly kept her as his "bodyguard wife."

Through it all, she matured into a Celtic-Jew who displayed many admirable character traits, including love, kindness, and gentleness. There are no laws against such behavior. Hannah emerged from this period of her life with a deeper understanding of God and a greater dependence on His grace. Her spiritual bond with the One True God seemed to surpass even her earthly relationships.

---

[27] Mikvah: a ceremonial building for cleansing Jewish women after childbirth, menstruation, or when recovering from certain diseases.

TRUTH IN ALL THINGS

Nova's Age: Thirty

Abraham and Sarah arrived in Avon with another new moon. This time Sarah was helping Abraham with simple tasks and finishing his sentences. He would begin speaking and just stop in midsentence.

"Israel, how old is Father?" Hannah asked her husband one day.

"I believe that he is over eighty-years-old. As I am to you, he was twice the age of his bride when they were married. As you can see, he is now only slightly older than my mother after fifty years together."[28]

Abraham managed to pull himself together during dinner when he announced, "My dear children, Sarah and I want you both to come to Midian next month to help celebrate Samuel's coming-of-age."[29]

"Father, have you forgotten my vow?"

"Certainly not, I remember your vow. How could I forget such a thing? The term of your vow is near completion. Samuel is now a man prepared to serve El Shaddai. Everyone in Midian wants you to come to the celebration. You must be there."

Israel answered, "We can leave straight away. Isn't that right, Hannah?"

Hannah just sat stone-faced and silent.

Israel redirected his attention toward his parents. "She did not speak for days the last time she had that expression on her face. We will be there, Father."

---

[28] Abraham was 100 percent older than Sarah when they were married and only 20 percent older than Sarah fifty years later.

[29] The term BAR MITZVAH means *son of the commandment*. Today, Jewish boys have their Bar Mitzvah at thirteen years of age. The Bar Mitzvah ceremony did not exist until over thirteen hundred years after the period of this story.

"The feast will be in one month. In addition to your coming to Midian, there is something else we wish to ask of you both."

"Father, you know that Hannah and I would do anything for you and Mother. What may we do for you?"

"Samuel dreams of continuing his studies in Jerusalem. Could we ask you to make that dream come true? Would it be possible?"

"Yes, Father, we will do all that we can do to make his dream come true! Merchant ships frequently arrive in Albion from the Great Sea. Hannah, what do you think? Do you want to make a journey to Judea?"

Between sobs of joy, Hannah managed to say, "Samuel....Midian.... Jerusalem!"

Israel translated Hannah's babble: "Yes, Hannah would love to go. We will do as you have asked!

"It just so happens that I have been communicating with Rome on some business matters," he continued. "They want to talk about expanding and formalizing our shipping agreements. Mostly, they need more Albion tin for the manufacture of bronze. I will send my positive reply immediately to Rome and have Esau organize our adventure. Three new ships are near completion. Once ready, we can leave for Rome in time for the best sailing weather. I am sure that the Romans will allow us to continue on to Jerusalem once our meeting with them concludes. I hope other business opportunities await us in Judea!"

Hannah was finally able to join the conversation. "Israel, did you say 'our adventure'? So then you will allow me to go with you?"

"Yes, of course you will come with me. How could I bear to be away from you for so long? This journey could take more than a year. Soon after, it would be time to go again to bring Samuel home."

"Oh, Israel, this is going to be a great family adventure with Samuel. If it is possible, I think that you are more excited about this than I am."

"Excited? Yes, I am excited. I will arrange for our transport to Midian, and then afterward, off to Rome we go. This is very exciting. I cannot wait to tell Esau about this! Can you believe it? We are going to Rome and Jerusalem!"

Israel was excited about the adventure and the possibility of achieving his objective of obtaining a Roman shipping contract. On the other side of the contract, the Romans were mainly interested in gaining strategic information from Israel in preparation for their invasion of Albion. Several decades earlier,

PART 3—LIVING THE WORD

Julius Caesar succeeded in leading the way by invading the island twice with little to show for his effort other than proving it possible. What he started was only the beginning of more than three hundred years of Roman domination in Albion affairs.

The month passed, and Hannah and Israel sailed up the coast to Midian. It was hard to believe that thirteen years had passed, and it was time to celebrate Samuel's passage into manhood. Hannah could finally reunite with old friends without worrying about a mean queen, king, or highwaymen. A morning fog moved across the inlet water and broke away from the dock just as they arrived in Midian. Years of longing for her child and suddenly there he was. Hannah could see him standing right before her on the dock between Abraham and Sarah. Clinging tightly to Israel's arm, she said, "Israel, hold me up."

He could feel her whole body trembling. "I've got you. Now, don't you go and faint on me. Remember, you are Nova. Be strong, but not so strong that you become a warrior princess again. You don't want to frighten him!"

When Hannah took Samuel into her arms, she heard Sarah say, "Samuel, this is your sister, Hannah." There was little that Hannah could say after that awkward moment. She always assumed that Samuel knew about her vow and the events that led up to that significant moment.

Marsha's son, Moses had also grown into a handsome young man, and he was Samuel's lifelong friend. During the ceremony, Hannah and Marsha sat together clutching each other's hands as their boys stepped into manhood together.

Later, an aging Abraham called Hannah to sit and talk with him once calm returned to their Midian home. "I have been waiting for this day. Yes, today marks Samuel's beginning of manhood, and yet he is still very much a boy. Let me tell you about his dream to study in Jerusalem."

"Yes, Father, we know about his dream. Samuel is going to Jerusalem. It is being arranged as we speak. Esau is in charge of the project, and you know that he will see to every detail. Remember, Israel and I, are going with him. We will look after him."

"Hallelujah! Praise be to the One Who Is Holy! Can you see him studying there in the land of the prophets?"

"No, I cannot even see myself there without you. It makes me remember when we first walked in Midian together. Samuel and I will be walking the streets of Jerusalem. He will begin to live his dream in a month with a brief stop in Avon. From there, we will be sailing in Israel's three finest new ships in the best sailing weather. Father, guess what he has named the ships?"

"Tell me."

"Israel has named them the *Nova*, the *Avon*, and the *Hannah*."

"So, Sarah made a good match for you."

"The best match ever."

"Hannah, did you know that I knew Nova when she was a little girl?"

Hannah wiped the tears from her eyes, took a deep breath and compassionately replied, "Yes father, she loved you very much."

Several dinners later, Hannah said that she wanted to ride up to Asbury and Aberdon. Surprisingly, Abraham, Sarah, and even Israel were against the visit.

Sarah was first to object. "What if someone recognizes you?"

Abraham joined in with a moment of clarity. "There could still be highwaymen out there looking for you!"

It was unlike Sarah to use guilt to gain her way. Therefore, Hannah was startled to hear her argue the point with, "If you love us, you will stay here."

She went from startled to shocked when Israel sided with his parents' objections. "Hannah, be reasonable. We will miss leaving for Rome on time if we go to Aberdon."

Hannah knew these people well and could tell by their behavior that they were trying to hide something from her. "What is going on? Israel, what are you not telling me?"

"Nothing, everything is fine. We just want you to be safe. Have you forgotten how the Druids drove you away from Aberdon?"

"Have you forgotten my grandfather, King David Curr's Edict of Religious Freedom? How about this plan: We will stay here an extra week, and then our guards can escort us to and from Aberdon. As far as someone recognizing me is concerned, where on this pudgy body do you see anything recognizable as that wild fourteen-year-old girl last seen in Asbury? This is important to me. And Israel, this is the first time that you have ever said no to me. The three of you are not telling me something, and I want to know what it is. What is wrong?"

PART 3—LIVING THE WORD

They all shook their heads and said nothing. Two days later, Hannah and Israel entered the place that once was Asbury. It was all gone save a few battered landmarks. The inn and stables were gone. Asbury Palace was gone. Everything was laid to waste. *A curse has been placed on this village. All my friends and family are gone. Did I cause this devastation? Has an evil spell been cast over this once magical paradise known as Asbury?*

In a sense, the single answer to her thoughts was yes. She did not know that her actions and inactions had contributed to the misdeeds of many others who had destroyed something once so beautiful. Self-interest, greed, civil inequality, and the weather had turned against a city once founded on faith. Finally, commerce spiraled downward along with the physical decline of Asbury. Despite its destruction, when people asked Hannah where she was from, she still proudly replied, "Asbury." Yes, she was proud of a place that once was, and she was honored to have known such wonderful people who knew her as the person she used to be and loved her anyway.

Israel had no desire to stay long in Asbury. "All right, you have seen it," he said with barely suppressed impatience. "May we continue on to Aberdon?"

"Israel, what happened to all the people who once lived here?"

"Some have died, and others have moved away. Still others have stayed, clinging to a memory and reaching for a future with hope."

"How did they die? Where did they move? If it is this bad here, what is going on in Aberdon?"

"Hannah, everything is fine in Aberdon! Nobody was killed here if that is what you are thinking."

"Then what happened here?"

"Who knows what happened. Leave it alone, and let us continue to Aberdon."

Israel was not being honest. He knew that the consequences of Hannah's midnight raid against Asbury Palace along with other factors were what had happened. Abraham, and Sarah also knew this, and they were trying to protect Hannah from learning the truth. Her own clandestine actions had chipped away at the foundation of Asbury. Her family had previously agreed that Hannah did not have to know the consequences of her actions. What good would come from telling her the whole truth? What she did not know would not hurt her.

"Are you saying that it was I who conjured the Asbury Curse that caused this devastation?"

"I must admit that your midnight assault upon the palace is legendary. However, not even my amazing wife could take down an entire village."

"Sneaking into the palace is an act that I have regretted ever since that night. Israel, I must see that my clan is safe and say good-bye to them before we leave for Judea. Yes, Israel, to answer your question—we can leave for Aberdonshire. You remember Aberdonshire. You might remember it as Asgardshire, before the Lord used me to bring it down."

"All right, I see your point. On to Aberdon we ride to see **our** northern clan."

Upon arriving in Aberdon, everything seemed fine until they were greeted with the news of Curr's death. King David Curr was gone, and his son King Conan was already working with Hancurr and Makcurr in leading the kingdom. Yes, the 'Curr Kindom' was over.

"We must have a celebration in honor of our visitors," King Conan said to Hannah.

"Thank you, dear uncle, but that can wait for another time. Instead, I want to hold a celebration to honor King David Curr's life."

"The Druids and the sin eater have laid him to rest on the mountain. It is time to go on with life."

"His death is new to me, as is my grief. Allow me this visit to honor his memory. He still lives here among us in our hearts.

What has become of Haggai and Leah? Where are they?"

"Oh, they found a comfortable little cottage just outside town. Rest here tonight, and you can visit them in the morning."

The next morning, Hannah and Israel found the elderly couple living in the squalor of an abandoned shack. Haggai greeted them with tears. "Israel, Yah has sent you here to Leah and me. The new king and his Druid told us to leave Aberdonshire. We cannot afford for passage by ship, and there was no way that we would have felt safe returning to Midian by walking alone on the country roads. Furthermore, there is the question of what we would do in Midian."

"Haggai, if nothing else, I will return the Alpha One Messenger Service to you. However, I believe that The One Who Reveals wants you in Midian as its teacher. Soon, you will be holding a shomer ceremony for my father. Be at peace, my friend. You are going where Yah wants you to be."

PART 3—LIVING THE WORD

Israel thoughtfully paused and continued. "Listen to me, giving a rabbi spiritual advice."

Haggai led the second memorial celebration for King David Curr with prayers of thanksgiving and recollections of happy memories of the king's life. "Glorious is the Lord's great name. Lord, you have given and taken away the life of this great man that we knew as our King David Curr. After all is said and done, only you, the Eternal One, will reign forever. Amen."

Hannah ended the memorial by thanking everyone and reminding them that their king had often asked them to love one another. "Do an act of kindness for someone in loving memory of our king. Ask yourself what the king would do for that person. Perform that act of kindness in his name and memory." The memorial was a bittersweet occasion filled with prayers, hope, and praise for everyone including the king's brother, Uncle Eli.

Hannah was on her way back to the hill-fort when Elymas called to her. "Hannah, when are you going to come and visit your old uncle? I have missed you."

"I am sorry, Uncle Eli. It has been a long day, and I am tired. I have been avoiding you because it is a bit awkward seeing you after our last meeting. In a way, I have missed you the most. You are the only one who really understands the deep spiritual issues in my heart and mind. Could we spend a day together before I leave?"

"It cannot be too soon for me, Hannah. How about coming tomorrow?"

"I will bring breakfast. It will be as it was years ago," she said with a warm smile.

"Wonderful."

As promised, Hannah arrived at her uncle's home that sat on a hill overlooking the village of Aberdon and the river. "Eli, I love what you have not done with the place since I was here last. The owl is new. The place is still so Druid. It is so you."

"Oh, the owl's name is Flowerface." Elymas knew that they were spending too much time with light talk and went straight to his concerns. "I have missed you terribly, especially because of the terms of your exile. My dearest friends and family are gone, and you are about to leave again. This time before you go, I want you to know that your friendship has been my most precious gift."

"Uncle, that means so much to me. It is extra special because I know how close you were to my great-grandfather. I promise to find you as soon as I return from Rome, and possibly a place called Jerusalem."

"Will I still be on this side of eternity is the question. However, that is not my main concern at the moment," Elymas said. "Israel is internationally known as a great businessman. I do not understand how he can afford to be away for so long. The people of Albion have come to depend on his leadership."

"Oh, don't worry about that. We will be returning once Samuel is settled in Jerusalem. Israel's sons and his brother Esau will be looking after the business. Israel says that the journey will give Samuel and me a chance to make up for lost time. It will be all right. Don't worry so much."

"Hannah, this is a mistake that violates your sacred vow. You are taking back what you totally surrendered to God. Your place is not with God's child. You are about to make a mistake that you will regret."

"I understand what you are saying. I can assure you that it will be all right because we have Abraham and Sarah's blessings on the decision. It was their idea because of their advanced years. Israel and I are the only two people who can look after Samuel now."

Hannah paused for a moment when she realized the unique choice of words her uncle had made. "Uncle, you just referred to my Lord as God, and not as my god. Does this mean you believe in Him now?"

"This is important. Don't try to change the subject. You know that I am right. Hannah, please do not do this. I warned you not to seek your personal revenge on the Queen of Asbury, and look what followed your selfish action."

"You are blaming the destruction of Asbury on me?"

"You caused the queen to fall and her dominion followed. Who else do you think is to blame? However, taking the greater view, this should not concern you. Your valiant actions have doubled both the Novian saga and the size of Conan's kingdom. In addition to the mountain territory, our clan has gained control over Aberdonshire and Monmouthshire because of you. You made that happen."

"Druid rule number one: tell the truth in all things. My family knew this, and yet they lied to me. They know that Samuel is my son, and they lied to him."

PART 3—LIVING THE WORD

"Again, Samuel does not belong to you. Samuel is not your son. He belongs to God. The one thing everyone agrees on is that Samuel is a sacred child. It is obvious that they did not tell the whole truth about Asbury or Samuel because they wanted to protect both you and Samuel from the painful truth. Learn from this. Learn that even a small lie can have great consequences. From now on, you will question everything they say because of their misguided good intentions."

Elymas crossed the room and clasped Hannah's shoulders in his hands. "My dearest friend, do you think a time will ever come when we can part in agreement?"

"Eli, we may not always part in agreement, but we will always part in love and truth. Again, thank you for your concern and for the truth. Please try to be here when I return from Jerusalem."

"I will pray to whatever god will listen to me for your safe return."

Druid Phylmas and King Conan spent the time conspiring instead of attending what they called the "pagan god memorial service."

"Relax yourself, my sage," King Conan said with smug reassurance. "They say that she is only visiting and will be gone soon."

Phylmas pondered the possibility that Hannah might return to Aberdon. "She better be gone very soon. I cannot stand her presence for one moment. The people have almost forgotten her, and here she is back again. Why has she returned? She and that teacher, has everyone—even Elymas—talking about their one true god."

To the pleasure of Phylmas and Conan, Israel's people left soon after the shomer. The three villages of Avon. Midian and Aberdon had advanced because of the influence of Israel, Hannah, Esau, and Abraham. The future of these villages was full of promise as Asbury and Abraham were following King David Curr into history.

From Aberdon, Hannah and Israel resumed their visit in Midian as promised. "I am not looking forward to seeing my brother," Israel said. "He is going to be furious with me by now for returning so late."

After another week, Hannah, Israel, and Samuel arrived safely in Avon only to find that the ships were still not ready. By this time, they were already two months behind schedule for a safe departure from Albion. However, now the missed schedule blame shifted to Captain Esau.

"Esau, why are the ships not ready?" Israel demanded to know.

"I'm sorry, Israel. There were complications with that new oil that I am using to treat the timbers, and it put us behind schedule. We will have to wait out the winter weather."

"We are leaving now!"

"Israel, be reasonable. Leaving at this time of year would be extremely risky. The voyage could take months to reach Rome in good weather. If you make it at all, there is no way of predicting how long it will take in bad weather. My men and ships have not experienced the fall and winter weather of the Great Sea. Another captain told me that those winter waters are very dangerous. It would be best to wait until the Beltane returns with smooth sailing weather."

"How could the Great Sea be more dangerous than our winter waters between here and Gaul? Are the ships almost ready?"[30]

"Yes, Israel they are almost ready, but...."

"Esau, you know how urgent it is for us to gain free access to Roman waters. Quickly finish the preparations, and let us sail out of here!"

"You are risking precious lives and everything that we have worked for!"

"I am aware of the possible consequences of my actions. We must take many risks if we are to save Albion. We will all lose our lives if we let the Romans take control of this land. Make ready, my brother, and may The One Who Is Merciful have mercy on our souls."

"As you wish, brother."

Everything that Hannah had learned over the past thirty years was about to expand exponentially in just a few years. Even beyond the world and its knowledge, she would gain a glimpse of the enormity that is God. Her future would unveil the might of Rome, the hypocrisy of Jerusalem, and the majesty of the Divine Presence of God.

---

[30] The Great Sea or the Inner Sea is the Mediterranean Sea of today. Israel was correct in thinking that water between Albion and Gaul, (English Channel) is more dangerous than the Mediterranean Sea. What he did not know was that his ships were more seaworthy than Roman ships of that time. This was because the Atlantic waters demanded more skill of Celtic shipbuilders than the Great Sea demanded of Roman shipbuilders. As a result, the Celtic ships proved to be seaworthy, while their passengers favored solid ground.

THE VOYAGE TO ROME

Nova's Age: Thirty

The *Hannah*, the *Nova*, and the *Avon* towered over the other vessels harbored at Avon. Each one was made from Albion oak and was a masterpiece of Celtic craftsmanship. Many of the crewmembers were Hebrews who shared Samuel's dream to visit Jerusalem. Others, planned to stay in the Promised Land. Hannah asked one of the craftsmen, "How did the Druids ever allow you to build these ships from their sacred oaks?"[31]

"Surely you know that Master Israel does not bow to Druids in his territories."

"His territories? Sir, what is your name?"

"I am the ship's carpenter, so everyone calls me Carpenter."

"Carpenter, I would watch your words if I were you. My husband is the kindest, gentlest man that I know. He has no quarrel with the Druids."

"Yes, ma'am, please forgive me."

"I'll say no more of this for your sake. I suggest that you do the same. My husband is coming this way. Just go about your business."

Raising her voice in a playful greeting, she called out, "Israel, my darling, I love them. And how did you ever think of such wonderful names? May a wife have a guided tour?"

"Why, yes, my dear. Please follow me. Below the main deck, we have the crews' quarters and cargo storage. Above the main deck, as you can see, there

---

[31] The Promised Land is the land promised by God to Abraham and his descendants. "To your offspring I will give this land" (Genesis 12:7).

are three masts and thirty oaring portals. Follow me to the stern. There is something special back here."

"It is the first thing that I saw. It is a house."

Opening the door for his wife, Israel said, "It is our home. Normally, these would be the captain's quarters. But on the *Hannah*, half of the space is our quarters."

"Israel, this is a castle."

"Then that is what we will call it: Hannah's Castle."

The three ships finally sailed down the Albion coast until the shoreline rose to form white cliffs, and the shores of Gaul appeared in the east. Captain Noah gave the command to come about, and the three ships turned in unison toward Gaul. Samuel, Israel, and Hannah were standing on the castle deck together when Samuel made a startling observation. "Look at these waters. Even the Warrior Princess Nova could not swim across this channel."

Hannah was delighted to hear him speak so proudly about her Celtic identity. The thought occurred to her that he might actually know the whole truth about their relationship.

"And what do you know of Nova?" Samuel dashed her hopes by telling of Novian deeds, many of which were news to Israel and Hannah, without any mention of what was most important. "Who told you these things?" Hannah asked her son.

"Oh, the people of Midian often speak of her. Many say that they knew her. Mostly I have learned about her from my best friend's mother. You know her, Hannah. She's Moses's mother, Marsha."

"Oh, I see, so close and yet so far away."

The Neptune Trading Company ships often traveled in threes. Normally, two lesser vessels flanked a third greater ship or the mother ship, as it was on this voyage. This was a security policy to protect against pirates or ships from competing countries. There was no threat of being attacked at this time because the Neptune Trading Company controlled these waters as the *Hannah* sailed with the *Avon* and the *Nova* at her sides.

Hannah commented to Israel that many other boats and ships in the channel were too close and that they were making her a bit uneasy. He calmed her fear by saying, "Oh, don't worry, my dear. They are just a few friends giving us a safe send-off. Just smile and wave. These other vessels represent the bulk of

PART 3—LIVING THE WORD

our Manawyddan Utility Company fleet. There is no danger while this flotilla is nearby." As the days passed, Israel's other ships returned home as the Israeli voyagers of Caledonia approached the entrance to the Great Sea.

It was a clear day as they passed through the Pillars of Hercules, known later as the Strait of Gibraltar. With the other vessels gone, the *Nova* and the *Avon* were not the only protection around the *Hannah* from this point in the voyage. Pax Romana protected the Great Sea from the Pillars of Hercules to Jerusalem. The imposed peace showed no mercy to any misconduct within the Roman Empire. These three Celtic ships were licensed to sail to and from Rome under its protection. At the same time, there was still cause for concern because the western end of the Great Sea was the fringe of the Roman Empire. It was on these open waters that they were more likely to encounter the pirates of the Great Sea instead of their Roman protectors.

Because these were new waters for them, they sailed only in the daylight hours and always kept the south shore in sight.[32] They spent their nights in safe harbors, or they dropped anchor safely offshore. When possible, they made for port early on the sixth day of the week to allow the crew to rest on the seventh day. These moments gave everyone time to rest and worship as a community.

Other travelers and native people were always greeted and engaged in conversation about the local area and its people, language, and commerce; how much farther it was to Rome; and most importantly, about sailing conditions, such as areas to avoid for fear of running aground or into pirates. At first, everyone assumed that Hannah was fluent in Latin. However, her Latin often resulted in laughter instead of local business and nautical information. Still, she made herself understood most of the time to keep them on the right course. A few times, Samuel's excellent Hebrew led them to Rome.

Signs of a great civilization became increasingly apparent as they slowly approached the Apennine Peninsula and Rome. The three Celtic merchant ships continued to be impressive, even against the standard Roman ship. One morning, a single raindrop struck Captain Noah's face as the *Hannah* was first away from port and broke through heavy surf. He called down from the castle deck, "Israel, I do not like the looks of this sky or the sea. We are going to return to port."

---

[32] Following the heavily populated and jagged north shore would double the distance to Rome as compared to following the south shore of the Great Sea.

THE VOYAGE TO ROME

"We must be close to Rome. Keep going."

"Sir, it is better to be safe. I am captain of this ship, and I say that we are making for a safe harbor."

"I said to keep going. I am the owner of these three ships, and I am ordering you to keep going or else you will never sail again as a captain!"

Captain Noah mused, *You stupid man. I am the master of this ship, and you will regret that you ever questioned my orders*, but all he said was, "All right, all right, as you wish, sir; clear the deck and let me go to work."

Captain Noah knew that Israel was unaware of semaphore code.[33] His first order of business was to signal the *Avon* and the *Nova* to wait out the coming storm in port. Then they were to search for and possibly rescue the *Hannah* and her crew once calm weather returned.

"Men, we have prepared for this day. Today we are great seamen. You know the task set before us. Everyone do your task, and we will come out of this storm alive. Let's ride the coming tempest all the way to Rome. Rig the sails to quarter mast!"

Before long, a powerful wind came out of the west, and they were in the teeth of the storm. Noah was on the castle deck, controlling the side-rudder when the bow dove beneath the sea surface the first time. "Come on, my lady, rise, *Hannah*, rise!" And rise she did with her bow faithfully snapping back upward and racing to the top of a swell only to race down the other side to greet one ensuing swell after another. The seamen harnessed themselves to their stations and stood there fast on seasoned sea legs. "We are sailing now, men! This is who we are! These are the moments we live for!"

The *Hannah* sailed blindly through nights so dark that the passengers and crew feared running aground. Fortunately, Noah was an experienced captain who knew how to read the sea as he held a deep-water course away from shore, reef, and sandbar. In addition to the danger of running aground, there was still the chance of ramming or being rammed by another ship in the night. On the morning of the third day, they remained in the grip of the storm. Everyone was bailing water or throwing cargo overboard as the *Hannah* began taking on water. Israel finally lost all courage and crawled from inside the castle to order Noah to run the mother ship aground.

---

[33] Alexander the Great used semaphore code centuries before the period of this story.

PART 3—LIVING THE WORD

"Damn it, Israel, I'm the sailor here. We would not be in this mess if you had listened to me in the first place. Listen to me now. It would be safer to weather the storm."

"Now you listen to me. Give the order to run aground if you wish to continue giving orders."

"You are a fool, Israel. I cautioned you to return to port, and again I am strongly cautioning you that it would be suicide for ship and crew to run aground in this storm. The Lord only knows the fate of our other ships. Wait, Israel! The storm has to end soon."

"You and the crew are the only ones that have been able to keep anything in your stomachs for the past three days. This has become the ship from Sheol, except that Sheol probably smells better. Look at your crew.[34] They no longer have the strength to work. Give the orders to run aground, and prepare to abandon ship. Now!"

Noah pretended to relent and gave the order to run-aground. "Everyone prepare to abandon ship."

The rage of the storm drowned out the rage of his vow. "That is the last time that you will ever disrespect me on this ship or any other. I am going to kill you."

Almost too quickly, the *Hannah* ripped across a reef, tearing a gash in the hull as everyone prepared to go overboard even though the ship was still fifty meters from shore. And where was the magnificent warrior princess while all this was happening? She was so seasick that all she could do was to beg people to kill her. They would have gladly done the deed had they not been sicker than she was. They all agreed that seasickness is the worst of all feelings. The order to abandon ship was a welcomed sound. With Samuel at her side, Hannah stripped out of her clothes and yelled to him to do the same. "Hannah, what are you doing! You are naked and your hair – your hair is red!"

Hannah stood on the deck wearing only sandals and a golden torc around her neck. "Samuel, get out of those clothes or drown in them. This is no time for modesty. You must remove all that will hinder you except for your sandals. Can you swim?"

"Not very well."

---

[34] Sheol: the home of the spirits of the dead in Jewish theology.

"Don't jump into the water. Slowly follow me into the water. We will hold on to the ship and lower ourselves into the water. Then hold on to me."

"No! You are naked. I am not touching you!"

"All right, fine, then I will hold on tightly to you." Then, nose to nose, she yelled at him. "Strip or drown!"

With the thin veil of modesty now torn, outer clothes were flying off everyone just as the ship listed slightly to one side. There was a final command to abandon ship, and soon fifty weary souls were splashing around in the water. Fortunately, the autumn water still held the warmth of summer.

Israel and Noah were the only two people who remained aboard. "Come on, Noah. We need to get off this ship."

"No! A captain must remain with his ship."

"A ship I can replace. You are not replaceable. Let's go!"

"No! You go. I am staying."

"I am not leaving without you, Captain. Give me one good reason why you must stay aboard the ship."

"I do not know how to swim."

"This cannot be true. How is it possible for a sea captain not to know how to swim? Well, Noah, it is past time for you to learn. Hold on to me once we are in the water."

Moments later Noah cried out in panic. "Israel, save me! I cannot make it! Save me!"

"Oh, shut up before the crew hears you! Grab hold of me. I said to hold on to me! I did not say to drown me. Calm down, I've got you. Noah, stop it, you are going to drown both of us!" It took a powerful breaker to break them apart. Israel resurfaced a safe distance from Noah and yelled back to him to grab hold of a large piece of the hull floating close to Noah.

Villagers raced to the shore as the sea gave up its victims. At least one stranger helped each voyager out of the water and into a shelter. Then they handed out dry clothes while hot food and drink were being prepared over a fire. The seawater, a desperate swim, and solid ground under their feet drove the vertigo from their heads and starving bodies. Hannah stood naked in front of the fire, stuffing her face with the best tasting food and drink one could ever eat. Someone put a cape over Hannah's shivering body, and she thanked the woman, who acknowledged her in Latin.

PART 3—LIVING THE WORD

"I have to learn how to make such manna from heaven." The villagers appeared to be puzzled as she obviously missed the language translation and tried again. "I have to learn how to make this wonderful food and drink. Thank you!" With that, the host replied that she was welcome.[35]

Then Samuel whispered to Hannah, "These clothes and people stink. This food is not clean. We do not eat shellfish. I want to get out of here."

"Stink? On this very night, you reeked of your own vomit. What will you wear without these clothes? What will you eat without this wonderful food?"

Israel interrupted by saying, "And wherefore will you run, my son?"

"I'm not your son!"

"More than you know."

Hannah cut him off from saying anything further. "Israel, Samuel! Both of you, please stop it. We are guests here. Give these people respect."

"Do not tell me what to do, sister. Respect these Gentiles? They will probably eat us before it is over!"

"Samuel. That will be enough!"

"Don't talk to me that way, woman. They are unclean swine and unworthy of respect. You are not my mother, so shut up, woman!"

Israel could not let the moment pass without saying, "Oh, yes she is! Abraham and Sarah are my parents and your grandparents, so you ought to shut up!"

"Drat!" Hannah directed her attention to their gracious hosts as the family tension continued to simmer. Perhaps it was fortuitous that they had landed in a place without a name—the kind of place that big ships always passed on the way to somewhere else. For Hannah, it was as though she had stepped back into her Stone Age element. These people were willing to share everything with love, and they put more value on people than on things. How could she and Israel ever thank them enough for sharing the little they had with strangers who had crashed nakedly onto their shore?

These dear people lived with the sea on one side and a mosquito-infested marsh on the other. It was then that Hannah realized that God had delivered them to Nineveh. She cried out, "El Shaddai, God Almighty, finally, I understand! You have prepared me for this day. Our once glorious ship has ended

---

[35] Exodus 16:15—Manna was the food miraculously supplied by God for the Israelites in the desert.

its voyage broken, scattered, and capsized. This scene is not unlike a giant beached whale; the belly that I spent three days and nights covered with a blanket of digestive juices. This is Nineveh, I am Jonah, and you have delivered me here to deliver your message. Place your words on my lips, and let's do this together. Amen."

Wanting to make sure her hunch was correct, Hannah asked, "Please, someone tell me. What is the name of this place?"

The villagers spoke among themselves, and one man answered. "This place does not have a name. We have thought about calling it Mosquito Haven because they torment us day and night."

"Yes, I have never seen such hungry insects. Please gather around, for my God has sent me to deliver a message to you. First, I am going to pray right now for His blessing on each of you, and then I will ask Him to rid us of these terrible mosquitoes."

The voices of children prayed along with her to protect them from the bloodthirsty insects. "Please help us! You are the Great I AM." The word "amen" was a cue to the entrance of hundreds of dragonflies. A swarm of the darning-needle-shaped insects suddenly invaded the prayer circle. Hannah thought, *Oh, great, first mosquitoes, and now dragonflies. How badly do they bite?* The audience sat waiting for her to continue speaking when she noticed that everyone had stopped slapping themselves free of mosquitoes.

The obvious insect disappearance caused Hannah to ask, "What just happened?"

There was a questioning pause before a villager answered her question. "Your god has sent the dragonflies to eat the mosquitoes."

"Dragonflies eat mosquitoes? I did not know that." Everyone continued to sit waiting to hear the message from the visitor's god. "Wait, let me understand this. We prayed that the mosquitoes would be gone, and they disappeared as soon as I said amen."

"Yes! Is there a problem?"

"Excuse me while I pray once more," Hannah said. Looking heavenward, she prayed, "Dear Lord of lords, I want to thank you for opening the hearts of these dear people through this blessing and for teaching me to have as much faith in you as they have. You sent me here to teach them about you, and in

PART 3—LIVING THE WORD

return, they have taught me about unquestioning faith in you. Thank you, Lord. I needed that lesson. Amen."

The villagers listened to the message of repentance, and learned how the people of Nineveh turned from their evil ways. "When God saw what they did and how they turned from their evil ways, he had compassion and did not bring upon them the destruction he had threatened" (Jonah 3:10).

Two days later, a cheer went up as the *Nova* and the *Avon* appeared offshore, and the castaways lit a signal fire on the strand. Everyone gathered at the edge of the water, and Hannah prayed aloud, "Dear Ever Present God, thank you for delivering us from the storm and into the arms of these people. Thank you for their hospitality and for including me in your work. Please use me again. In your Holy name I pray."

A young girl took Hannah's hand as she prayed, and after the prayer, she walked with her to the rescue launch. The child would not release her hand and said that they ought to go together. "Please take me with you," she begged. Hannah's confused expression prompted a more desperate plea from the little girl. It was as an echo from the past. In Avon and Aberdon, she had helped many women and girls who had the dreadful appearance of this child. One look into her eyes told a story of abuse and neglect. This would be the child's only chance to escape from a real living Hades.

Hannah clasped her hand tighter and led her onto the launch with everyone watching. When they were aboard, Hannah turned and called out to the gathered crowd. "This girl has asked to go with me. Whose child is this? What child is this? We are not coming back to this place. Does anyone object to her leaving with us?"

Surprisingly, Israel's voice rose from behind her. "Yes, we will love and take care of her. Look at her. She needs people who will take care of her. She is just one little girl. What harm can one little girl cause? Then again...." Israel began coughing and looking pointedly at Hannah the former warrior princess.

Hannah just shook her head and smiled, responding to his compassion and not to his tease, as they left the shore. A villager shouted across the water, "We have named our village Dragonfly. Thank you." From that day forward, whenever a Caledonian voyager had a crisis of faith, another would say, "Remember the day of the dragonflies?" The question was always a source of spiritual encouragement.

Hannah spoke to God as she looked back toward the shore at the smiling faces of the people who were waving goodbye. "We did it, Lord. Look at them. They are so happy. You prepared me to give your message, and you prepared them to receive it. Dear God, I miss my mountain people of Currcroft so much. This visit was a reminder of my home village. Thank you for the people of Dragonfly; thank you for allowing me to share your message with them."

Noah was the first to notice that Israel had not recovered along with his fellow castaways. "Israel, are you all right?"

"Yes—why?"

"You do not look well. Are you sure that you are all right?"

"Yes, let us go, Captain; cast off. I will be better once we are under way."

Hannah touched Israel's face and also asked if he was all right. "You do not look well. Israel, you have a fever. How do you feel?"

"All that has happened in the last few days has been difficult for me. I lost my best ship, almost drowned my family, divulged your secret, and along with everyone, I was awed by your prayer and message to the people of Dragonfly. Can you ever forgive me for all the times that I have been unkind to you?"

"Israel, you have never been unkind to me. Is there anything about you that I don't know?"

"For one thing, what about your secret of being Samuel's mother?"

"Ah yes, that is true, but it was my vow, not my secret. It was our parents' secret of protection, I suppose. We would not be in this difficult family situation if they had told Samuel the truth from the beginning. Did they not recall the commandment to be a 'truthful witness and give an honest testimony? The cause of this situation is not unlike the three of you not telling the whole truth about my part in the destruction of Asbury. From this time on, let us promise to be completely honest with each other in all things.

Speaking of honesty, there is a certain young man who I hope will forgive us and learn to trust us again. First, let me get the girl settled, and then we will face the little rabbi together."

Three crews and passengers were crowded into two small ships. Of course, conditions onboard were more cramped and confusing for everyone, and they must have been overwhelming for the newest family member. Noah was calling out orders to secure the launch, host full sails, raise the anchor, and set the course for Rome. The waif was still clinging so hard that she was crushing Hannah's hand. "Ouch, that is a strong grip you have for a little girl," Hannah said. She reached out her arms, and the girl let Hannah hold her. "For now, the safest place for you is in my arms. Well, come on, little one; I guess this is going to be our first family meeting."

God spiritually or physically rescued almost everyone in Dragonfly except for Samuel. The illusion of his life was lost in a storm that raged within him after learning that his life was a lie. One moment he was a Hebrew prince and the next moment a Gentile bastard. His whole life was upside down. With just a few words of truth, the righteous one transformed into the unrighteous; the clean became the unclean. They found Samuel sitting alone in the bow of the ship.

"Samuel, my son, we can tell you the truth about everything if you will let us."

"Who is my mother? Who is my father? Who are my brothers? Who are my sisters?"

"I am your mother." From there, Hannah gave an almost accurate family history without betraying his father's weakest life moment. There was no point in telling the whole truth, Hannah reasoned.

"Samuel, do you understand?"

"Yes, I understand that my whole life has been a lie! I hate you if you are my mother, and I hate you if you are not my mother. Each of you conspired to make my life a lie. I have become the riddle of what is not a nephew, whose mother is not his mother, whose brother was his father, whose sister was his mother?"

"Samuel, please...."

"I do not want to hear it. Sarah is my mother. If you are my mother and a Celt, then I am at least half Gentile and just as easily fully Gentile. Mixed or fully Gentile, it does not make any difference. The mother's ancestry determines Hebrew lineage and not the father's ancestry. Going to Jerusalem is a waste of time. They will never allow me in the school. They might not even allow me in the outer court of the Temple."

"Think about it, son. Think of Sarah's age. She is the mother of Esau and Israel. Israel is old enough to be my father and your grandfather. I gave you fully to Yah as I promised. That was kept a secret to protect you from my enemies. Today you are safe from those people, especially way out here—wherever way out here is."

"That just shows that you do not know anything. The sacred scrolls tell us that Abraham was one hundred and Sarah was ninety-years-old when Isaac was born."

"Samuel, you know that our Lord performed that miracle two thousand years ago. Have you seen any ninety-year-old expectant mothers lately? Put your hand on this rail beside mine and tell me what you see?"

"They are the same. Your middle fingers are bent just as mine are bent."

"Now put your foot beside mine, and tell me what you see."

"Our small toes are twisted exactly the same."

"Look at my nose and chin."

Samuel put an arm around Hannah's neck and looked into her blue eyes. "I believe you, Mother." Then he paused and whispered, "That girl needs a bath."

His mother whispered back into his ear, "I used to be that little girl, and yes, we both need a long bath."

"Should I call you Hannah or Mother?"

"I like it when you call me Sister. It makes me feel young, but it would be best to call me Hannah. It will remind us of my sacrifice to Yah and my devotion to you, for like Hannah of old, I was heard of God, and thus I named you Samuel."

"Yes, there is a strong connection between our names. I never really gave it any thought before. Besides, you are obviously much too old to be my sister."

PART 3—LIVING THE WORD

Hannah playfully returned, "Ouch, that really hurt. Go ahead; let it all out on your poor old mother."

"And you, Israel, what should I call you: Father, Brother, or Uncle?"

"I am both your uncle and your stepfather, but how about calling me Friend?"

Turning back to his mother, Samuel continued to ease the tension by saying, "Well, I will never believe that you are the great warrior Nova."

Later in port, a bath and new clothes for the little one were the first orders of business. While scrubbing the girl, Hannah asked, "What is your name?"

And the girl answered, "Morona."

"Sweetheart, Morona cannot be your name."

"Everyone calls me Morona. I am Morona."

It was an upsetting answer. *Moron* is a Greek root word used to insult a person's intelligence. *Morona* would be a stupid, foolish, or dull girl. Hannah prayed silently, *Dear Elohim, who would do such a thing to a little girl?*

Hannah smiled as she picked up the only decent clothes that she could find. "I am sorry, but these will have to do until we arrive in Rome."

"I like them!"

"But they are boy clothes. Will you not mind wearing them?"

"Hannah, I have never had clothes this nice. Thank you."

"Why are you crying Hannah?"

Now Hannah fully understood how she had once appeared in Asbury and Midian. She just wiped away her tears and answered with a smile. "I am going to tell you a story before we join the others for dinner."

"All right."

"Once long ago, a woman by the name of Naomi had two daughters-in-law named Ruth and Orpah. The husbands of all three women had died, and Naomi told the younger women to return to the homes of their mothers where they could find new husbands to care for them. Then she kissed them and wept. Both women wanted to stay with their mother-in-law. Naomi insisted that they leave as the three women wept bitterly, and Naomi kissed them goodbye again. Orpah returned to her family, while Ruth insisted on staying with her mother-in-law. Ruth clung to Naomi and pleaded, 'Don't urge me to leave you or turn back from you. Where you go, I will go, and where you stay, I will stay. Your people will be my people, and your God my God.'[36] Did you enjoy that story?"

The girl was fast to respond with a positive, "Yes!"

"How would you like to be called Ruth?"

"Will you be my Naomi?"

"My name is Hannah, but only you may call me Naomi. Come, Ruth. Let us join the others for dinner."

This Sabbath eve was extra special because they made port in a Hebrew village, and the smell of fresh baked bread filled the air. All crewmembers and passengers were down on the beach talking, praying, and singing. People indigenous to the area told the voyagers that they should reach Rome by the next evening. They also warned them not to make port on any island near the main coast because Emperor Tiberius resided on the island Capri, and uninvited visitors often disappeared.

Hannah gathered Israel, Samuel, and Ruth to a place overlooking the other people. "Israel, I have an introduction to make."

"Quiet, everyone," Israel called out. "Hannah has an announcement!"

"Friends and fellow travelers—everyone, I want you to meet our new daughter and Samuel's sister, Ruth. Please make her welcome!"

Everyone came to greet Ruth as she stood between Israel and Hannah with Samuel behind her. Samuel asked, "How do I tell her that she is welcome?"

"Offer to pick her up and hold her."

The moment that Samuel held Ruth high for everyone to see his new sister, calm returned to his heart, and he knew he belonged right where he was—with his family.

The table was set with fresh bread, poured wine, and lit candles. People of different nations and of one God joined hands, and the village rabbi prayed. "Blessed are you, Eternal One our Lord, Ruling Presence of the Universe, Who makes us holy with commandments, and gives us this blessing of kindling the Sabbath lights. Amen."

---

[36] Ruth 1:3-16 This is a story retold each year fifty days after the second day of Passover as spring gives way to summer with the festival of Shavuot. In Old and New Testament times, the first fruits were taken to the Temple during Shavuot.

ROMANS

Nova's Age: Thirty-One

Excitement and renewed energy filled the air as a new day began. By midmorning, they could see their destination in the distance with tempered joy. Israel's health was fading. Hannah felt her husband's forehead and said, "Captain Noah, he is burning with fever."

"You will have to look after your husband. I am very busy. The Romans are about to come aboard."

A Roman seaport agent checked the cargo and entry papers. Fortunately, each ship carried a complete set of documents for all passengers and crews except for Ruth, which turned out not to be a problem because women and children did not need papers. The Romans considered them incidental cargo. The problem was that they were missing an entire ship, and even that was quickly resolved. Everything seemed to be in order until the seaport agent withheld permission for them to disembark. As an extra measure of precaution, the seaport agent purposefully separated the *Avon* and the *Nova* to divide the number of crewmembers. He also demanded that the foreigners remain aboard the ships until further notice.

Noah went to Israel once everything was in order. "All right, Israel, let's take a look at you." Noah took one look at Israel and prayed silently. *Dear precious and holy Elohim, please be merciful. Lord, forgive my evil thoughts and murderous heart against Israel. Please do not take this man. We need him here with us.*

From there, Noah easily lifted Israel and carried him to the top of the castle deck. "A bit of fresh air, sunshine, and some really great wine, and you will be better soon, my friend."

Several days later, Israel was not any better when a messenger came with documents granting permission for the visitors to disembark. The documents contained information about temporary housing and meeting schedules as well.

The Israeli voyagers of Caledonia found Rome to be spectacular, even from a distance. On the inside, the city was beyond the imaginations of the Albion villagers. This was an entirely different world in every way. Their previous existence consisted of a village of a hundred people. Most of the buildings in their village were only one floor high. In sharp contrast, they were now experiencing Rome at the height of its Golden Age.

"Noah, I am too sick to leave the ship," Israel said in a weak voice. "Take Hannah with you in my place to meet with the Council of Commerce."

Reluctantly, Hannah and Noah went to the meeting in Israel's place. It did not take long to learn one great difference between Romans and Celts. Celts accepted the participation of women in business and leadership roles, but that was not part of the Roman culture. Their men revered women while treating them as property. It would have been beneath the dignity of a man to strike a woman or to regard her as an equal. Those things were outside normal Roman behavior. In contrast, Celts often considered women and men as equals, and a man might just as easily strike a woman. Furthermore, unlike the Romans, it was normal for a Celtic estate to be in a woman's name.

Noah and Hannah were there as Caledonia's two finest available emissaries being carted through the center of everything Roman. Little seven-year-old Nova's culture shock of Asbury was slight in comparison with thirty-year-old Hannah's impression of Rome. The splendor of Rome was simply unimaginable and magnificent. She erupted with laughter as though she had heard something funny.

"Are you all right? What is so funny?"

"Noah, can you imagine if my mountain clan could see me now?"

"I am here with you, and it is still hard to believe."

Equally shocked were the Roman negotiators when a tiny "Hebrew" woman appeared before them to discuss business. They were insulted by her presence and by the lack of her language skills while describing Israel's sickness. There could not have been a more disarming emissary to stand before the Roman Intelligence Committee (RIC) fronting as the Council of Commerce.

PART 3—LIVING THE WORD

"Ah, we are disappointed. We were looking forward to meeting Israel. Tell him that we wish him well."

"I will do that...."

"Silence, woman! Let us not make your presence any more unbearable than it already is."

Reflecting their culture, the committeemen greatly underestimated the value of women. Therefore, they directed most of their questions to Noah. Hannah translated their questions and his answers except that she edited many of the answers to the committee. The RIC never suspected that they had a sharp strategic military mind standing in front of them. It is possible that Caledonia remained free because of such a moment in time. Certainly, Caledonia has stood fast because Caledonian women stood side-by-side with their men as equals.

The commerce chairman named Gaius continued. "Israel, Noah, and Hannah—are these not Hebrew names? We were unaware that there were any Jews in Caledonia until we received a communication from a certain sea merchant named Israel. How do you account for Hebrews living so far from Judea?"

"Moses and the Hebrew prophets Nehemiah, Jeremiah, and Ezekiel all predicted that the people of Israel would be 'scattered among the nations.'"

"You said 'they' and not 'we.' Are you not a Jew?"

"I am a Jew by choice and not by birth. Even so, I would be proud and happy to have Hebrew blood flowing through my veins."

The entire committee broke into laughter just when they could not possibly have thought any less of her. "Why would you ever say such a thing?"

"I would be proud to have their blood flowing through my veins because the coming Messiah is from the House of King David, and everyone knows that blood is thicker than water."

"Well, whatever that means, you will find plenty of Jews in Rome. You should be very happy during your visit. Did you know that they only have one god? Is that also true in Caledonia?"

"It is equally true there as it is here."

"So, if you are not a Hebrew, what are you?"

Hannah took a deep breath, and in quickly recalling her Celtic/Roman history class, she considered lying about her Celtic identity. Instead, she chose honesty. "I am a Highland Pict Galatian of Aberdonshire."[37]

That provoked dismay and more laughter until Gaius explained their reaction. "Forgive us. You see, Julius Caesar reported Gauls to be tall warriors. We have been trying to exterminate your kind for over four hundred years, and here you stand brazenly before us. I would be very careful of your words, woman! Being a barbarian Galatian, a small woman, and someone who disrespects our gods leaves you with little reason to be alive within these chambers. We have not forgotten the several times that your people attacked Rome. It is only out of respect for your husband, Israel, and our goddess, Minerva, that we suffer your presence. Have I made myself clear?"

"Yes, sir."

Chairman Gaius turned his attention to the committee members and made his plea. "Romans, my fellow countrymen, look at her! This is the best that Britannia could send to speak for them. Their best is a female Galatian dwarf, and a Jewish convert at that. Men of Rome, what more do we need to know? Julius Caesar misled us years ago, and now we have these exaggerated accounts of Nova, the giant goddess warrior of Caledonia. The truth is this tiny excuse for a human standing before us. This being the case, we can confidently proceed with our plans. We will reconvene in three days. Everyone is dismissed."

The two Caledonian emissaries were relieved to be walking away from such a degrading interrogation when a voice called out to them. "Noah, Hannah, wait!" A man named Joseph came chasing after them as they were leaving the building. They would learn that he was a Hebrew translator, and he knew that Hannah had altered many translations.

Captain Noah placed himself between the stranger and Hannah. "Sir, how may we help you?"

"Shalom. My name is Joseph, one of the many Jews in Rome who want to meet you. We will be interested to hear about our brothers and sisters of the dispersion that have been living so far away. Please, it would mean so much to us."

---

[37] Galatian and Gaul are the Latin words for Celt and Celtic. Caledonia is Latin for northern Albion (Scotland).

PART 3—LIVING THE WORD

Hannah's pent-up emotions erupted into tears as Noah continued. "It would mean so much to you?" Gesturing toward Hannah, he said, "As you can see, our people would weep with joy and praise Yah for the blessing of meeting their brother tribe members. Go tell them that the lost have been found and are running to meet them."

"After that commerce meeting, it is a relief for us to finally meet a friendly Roman."

"Noah, how many of you are there?" Joseph asked.

"There are over one hundred and fifty Hebrew crew members and passengers from Caledonia."

"Hallelujah! Praise be to Yah!"

About a hundred crewmembers and passengers from Albion united with hundreds of their brothers and sisters of Rome. The boundaries of time and space fell before the eternal bonds of kinship and love that they had for one another. Hannah prayed. "Dear Ever Present God, how I wish that Abraham, Sarah, Haggai, Leah, Marsha, and all of Midian could be here to experience this love," Everyone there knew about the Galatian woman who had come from the ends of the earth to proclaim the one true God before the Roman government. They knew about Hannah and loved her as a sister in faith.

There was a moment when Hannah became the center of attention when Joseph asked, "So, Hannah, everyone here knows what a beautiful thing you have done and are doing with Samuel. We are curious to know your name before you made your sacred vow and became Hannah."

"I rather not say."

"Please tell us. We are your friends."

"It was Nova, Daughter of the Light."

"How great is the Mighty One that He would take a girl named for a pagan goddess, purify her, and bring her to Himself!"

Of all the people there, only Samuel knew Hannah's full identity, and they kept her secret from their new friends. Once they were alone, Samuel looked at his mother and said, "Goddess—really?" The two of them broke into laughter.

"All right, fine, we had our laugh. You can let it go now."

"Are you kidding? This is the best Nova story ever. I am never going to let you live this down."

"Samuel, please let this end here."

"Yes, of course, not another word, Goddess Nova."

Later, Samuel could not wait to tell Israel about the Celtic goddess named Nova. More as a brother than a husband, Israel smiled and said, "Nova, my darling, you have always been my goddess. I adore and worship only you."

Going along with their teasing seemed to be Hannah's only defense. "Both of you, not another word, or I will tell Mother and Father when we get home, and then you will be sorry."

Making so many new friends was a much-needed break before returning to the Council of Commerce and facing Chairman Gaius. The fact-finding inquiry lasted two days until the council had drained what they thought to be the last measure of information from the two Celtic emissaries. In exchange, the Neptune Trading Company was granted continued access to Pax Romana waters and ports. Equally important, the "barbarians" gained military information about the Romans.

Chairman Gaius made the adjournment. "These meetings are concluded."

"Sir, if I may; I have a request of the committee."

"What is it, woman?"

"Sir, we have traveled here from the very ends of the earth. Would you allow our ships to continue to Judea?"

"You mean intentionally? You choose Jerusalem over Rome?"

"Our son wishes to attend school in Jerusalem."

"Even after King Herod's restoration projects, Jerusalem is still a dung-heap in comparison to Rome. Am I to understand that you want to travel to that dung-heap rather than enjoy an extended stay in our paradise on earth? What could possibly be of any value in Judea? We send our troops there when they are in need of penitence. But if you insist, I grant your request. Now leave before I change my mind."

Not everything about the Roman visit was unpleasant. The presence of God was evident in their new friends, in their freedom to travel to Jerusalem, and in the healing of Hannah's family. The Roman healers seemed to improve Israel's health, but he would never fully recover from the Dragonfly ordeal. However, he did become spiritually stronger through his physical weakness. The Nineveh message, the miracle of the dragonflies, and his illness all worked to awaken a greater sense of spirituality within him. Israel was not alone in

PART 3—LIVING THE WORD

this awakening. A revival spread through the crewmembers, too. Most affected was Captain Noah.

It would take time before Ruth would become the person that God made her to be. Little by little, a very bright child emerged from a very dark place. Hannah spent years encouraging the real Ruth to come forward through games, play, drama, reading, writing, music, and worship. Then one day Ruth and Hannah were playing a Celtic board game and Ruth won. They played repeatedly with the same result. A little girl was reborn as Ruth through acceptance and love, while Hannah finally came to realize that between the two of them, she was the intellectual Morona.

The truth freed Samuel. Henceforth, they could travel peaceably together as God's family because the storm within Samuel was over. Ruth, Israel, and Samuel were healed, while Hannah still bled. "God, I thank you for allowing me to help Ruth out of her darkness. Thank you for bringing Israel and Samuel back to me. Lord, you are the only one who can heal me, for I cannot do it myself. Once more, I beg you to please remove this curse from me."

Sometimes the disease caused Hannah to be so tired that she could only sit, pray, and talk quietly with Ruth. In spite of everything, the hope that Roman advancements in medicine would have a cure for Hannah's decade-long disease went unanswered. Neither God nor the Roman physicians cured her ailment of bleeding at that time. As a great equalizer, the disease had caused Hannah and Israel to appear to be of the same age.

The set departure date came, and about one hundred and twenty-five people assembled at the dock. Captain Noah delayed, and only two more people arrived two days later. Many of their shipmates decided to live out their lives in Roman opulence. At first, the remaining crewmembers were sad over the loss of shipmates until Noah commanded that the course be set for the Promised Land. As a bonus, Noah had already made a new business contract with cargo bays full of Roman goods bound for Judea. It was time to raise the anchor and to make sail.

Looking back across the open sea, Hannah saw a Rome that sparkled as a diamond on the outside, but was as dark as coal on the inside. Their advancements in medicine, architecture, literature, math, science, and government defined them as civilized, while their technology in warfare and thirst for world domination proved them to be world-class barbarians. She was intellectually aware of the Roman hatred against her Celtic people, and now she had experienced it while being examined by the Council of Commerce of Rome. She had suffered a deep level of hurt and humiliation as a Celt and as a Jew in the Roman Empire. Hatred begets hatred. Hannah went to Rome with a bouquet of Caledonian heather and left with a wreath of Roman thistle. "Romans," she muttered under her breath, as the city grew faint in the distance. "I hate Romans!"

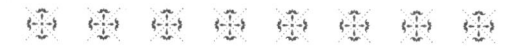

PART 1—THE WORD

PART 2—THE WRITTEN WORD

PART 3—LIVING THE WORD

PART 4—THE LIVING WORD

PART 5—SPREADING THE WORD

A BRIDGE IN TIME

Nova's Age: Thirty-One to Thirty-Three

The remaining Israeli Voyagers of Caledonia were no longer emissaries in a foreign land. Many of them were now pilgrims on a sacred journey, while others were coming home to the land of their ancestors. "Can you believe that we are walking where the prophets once walked?" Once again, Hannah was the fourteen-year-old Nova taking that first walk through Midian with a man of God. Now, years later, she was walking through Jerusalem with her family. Sacred words written over a thousand years earlier became alive. This was Jerusalem.

PART 4—THE LIVING WORD

Israel and Samuel went to the Temple, where Samuel made their introductions to the priests. Surprisingly, their welcome was not as pleasant as it was in Rome. A chief priest named Caiaphas greeted them in Hebrew, "Shalom, Samuel, to you and your father. We have heard of Caledonia and thought it only a place of legendary tales. We are glad that you have come home. Then again, you must understand that many others come to Jerusalem from all over the earth to stand where you are standing. Soon it will be the Passover, and our streets will be filled with other foreigners. With all that in mind, what may I do for you?"

"Sir, I have come from the end of the earth to sit and learn at the feet of the Masters of the Law in Jerusalem. After finishing school, I intend to return to Albion fully prepared to teach our people about the One Who Is Holy."

Light laughter broke out among the other priests and law students. "Oh, don't let them bother you. It is good that you have such a desire. We interview young men every day with the same dream. I will tell you what we will do. Some of our people will speak with you, and we will decide how to proceed from there. However, let me save time by being honest. Living so far from the Temple, how will it be possible for you and the people of Caledonia to achieve salvation? Without the Temple and its priests, how will they be able to do what is necessary to please Ha-Shem (The Name)?"

As anticipated, the acceptance interview did not last very long once Samuel told them that his mother was a Galatian. Most importantly, only his paternal grandparents were descendants of the Tribe of Levi, and even that was questionable in their minds. Their hasty summation was that Samuel worked very hard and was surprisingly educated for someone from the regions. However, he still lacked the proper qualifications and adequate preparation for training at the Temple in Jerusalem. Many other young men from solid Hebrew families wanted to study at the Temple. His background fell short of being good enough.[38]

Samuel sat by himself deep in thought. *It was stupid to tell them the truth. My parentage is no one's business. All my life I was taught to tell the truth while everyone was making my life a lie. I understand everything now. The truth is*

---

[38] The priests of the Temple were descendants of the first Israel's son Levi.

only for children. He struggled with that angry thought for a moment. *I believe it to be true that The Holy One honors honesty in all things.* As soon as he had that thought, a wave of doubt came over him. *Well, if they lied about my life, perhaps they also lied about The One Who shall not be named. Do I know the truth about anything?*

Israel told Hannah what happened during the interview. Hannah was filled with dismay. She said to Israel, "He has worked so hard. We have traveled so far for him to be here. It just is not fair. I will talk to him."

"Hannah, perhaps we should just give him some time. The good news is that we will stay together as a family, and good sailing weather is almost here again. Our first port-of-call is Alexandria and the land of the pyramids. It is where Joseph served in pharaoh's court before there was a Jerusalem. He will be coming with us to the land where Abraham and Moses once stood."

"Thank you for lifting my spirit, but what about you dear husband? You do not look well. I think that we ought to stay here until you have fully recovered."

A young man stepped forward and interrupted their conversation. "Excuse me. My name is Gamaliel. I am a student of the law. I overheard what the teachers said to you, sir. They did not tell you the whole story behind their laughter and rejection. These priests of the Lord are Sadducees, who can only see what they consider the right kind of people serving Him through the sacrificial services of the Temple. Foremost, they are few in number, yet greatest in influence because they are in control of the Temple. They are honestly seeking to do what is right, nonetheless, in their zeal, they can be a bit inflexible. They have a very narrow view in a very large creation where they see themselves as the only bridge between man and El Shaddai."

"Gamaliel, I am Israel, this is my wife Hannah, and you know Samuel sitting over there by himself. This information is helpful in understanding the Sadducees. At the same time, there seems to be another option in your voice. Is there another way that Samuel may continue his education in Jerusalem?"

"Yes, I do have an alternative suggestion for Samuel. There are many other Hebrew religious groups, and two of them are very strong. They are the Essenes and the Pharisees, both pure and separated. There are also divisions within the Pharisees. Among them, only the Pharisees of the Hillel School would be understanding and appreciative of Samuel's quest. I can assure you

PART 4—THE LIVING WORD

that they would welcome Samuel as a student. I could introduce you to them if you are interested."[39]

"We are very interested. But Gamaliel, what sets the Hillel Pharisees apart from the other sects?"

"They are more flexible in their interpretation of the law. That is, they live by the spirit of the law instead of the letter of the law. While they hold the *Torah* as sacred, they rely more heavily on its oral tradition. They believe that each man is responsible for his relationship with Eloah. The Pharisees do not believe the Temple cult and its sacrificial system as centrally important to Judaism as do the Sadducees. Further, they encourage Jews to worship Yah in synagogues far beyond the geographical limits of our holy Temple. They believe that Yah is everywhere and is not just hiding behind a curtain in the Holy of Holies. Most importantly, the Hillel Pharisees are open to Gentile converts. Thereupon, they are already appreciative of Samuel's calling to serve Eloah in Caledonia far from the holy Temple."

"You said 'of the Hillel School.' Are there other pharisaical schools?"

"Yes, sir. There is the School of Shammai Pharisees. These Pharisees exceed even the Sadducees in matters of purity. They will not have anything to do with Samuel because of his mixed parentage alone. They are so fundamental that they make the Sadducees seem liberal."

"Gamaliel, what can you tell Hannah and me about these Essenes?"

"They have become so disgusted with the religious politics and society in general that they live in remote places. They live predominately as a male group of hermits and have become a bit strange in their search for the truth."

"How soon can you introduce us to the Hillel people?"

"I can do it right now."

Once again, Samuel answered all questions honestly only because the whole truth was already publically known. The interviewers concluded the meeting by telling Samuel to return with his parents. He did so later that day, and they were escorted to the school chancellor, where they were told that Samuel's application was accepted. "We are impressed with how far you have come, the extent of your knowledge, and your dedicated preparation. However,

---

[39] The Essenes were a Jewish ascetic men's group that flourished between the second century BC and the second century AD.

the course of study will require a contribution of ten thousand shekels paid in advance."

Samuel's frustration was beginning to show at this point. "We were told that it would require a contribution of five thousand shekels."

"Be careful of your tone when you speak to me," the chancellor warned Samuel.

"Yes, sir," Samuel replied with the right amount of contrition in his tone.

"Now, about the contribution: It is true that families with a long unbroken connection to this land and its people are required to make a contribution of only five thousand shekels. It has been our experience, however, that students from the outlying regions require special tutoring, and they often quit before completing their education. That is unfair and disruptive to the teachers and the other students. Because you are one of those students, your special contribution of ten thousand shekels will be an incentive for you to consider your application with serious commitment. Five thousand shekels will be refunded if and when you complete your studies."

It was Israel who replied, "That is both fair and understandable. I further pledge that it will be deducted from his inheritance." Samuel and Hannah were shocked and could not imagine that amount of money equal in weight to three hundred pounds of silver.

"Samuel, excuse us while we settle the payment for your education."

"All right, Father. Mother and I will wait for you outside."

After they left the acceptance interview, a puzzled Samuel said, "Israel, I did not know that I had an inheritance."

"Yes, it is true, albeit an awkward way for you to have found out about it during your interview. Someday you will receive an inheritance equal to that of our other two sons, minus the value of ten thousand shekels if you do not finish school."

Outside, Gamaliel was waiting to speak with his new friend. "Shalom, Samuel. How did the interview go?"

"Shalom, Gamaliel! Guess what! Hillel School has accepted my application. It would not have been possible without your help. Thank you for helping me."

"Congratulations, Samuel. It was no problem, and I am looking forward to studying with you. Your story is my grandfather's story. He returned to

PART 4—THE LIVING WORD

Jerusalem from Babylon ninety-eight years ago. He suffered great hardships before and after being accepted by the school of Sh'maya and Abtalion.[40] In a very real sense, he made your acceptance possible here at Hillel. He was the forerunner of many men of the Lord, including you, Samuel."

"I can tell that you are very proud of your grandfather as I am of my grandfather Abraham. What was your grandfather's name?"

"His name was…."

Israel interrupted their conversation before Gamaliel could finish. "Samuel, we have to go. Captain Noah is waiting for us."

Samuel began walking away from his new friend, but he turned to say, "Sorry, Gamaliel, I must go now. I will see you soon. I want to hear more about your grandfather, and thank you again."

Their next order of business was to find a place for Samuel to live while in school. Israel gave that task to Noah, who found a place close to the school. It was dark by the time they concluded their business. Therefore, Samuel had his first houseguests spend the first night with him. Hannah rose early, shopped for breakfast, and returned to awaken everyone with a joyful, "Arise, everyone, and rejoice in the day that the Lord has made."

She came to an abrupt stop at the shocking sight of a tearful Captain Noah standing in the doorway. "Noah, what is it? What is wrong? What has happened?"

"He is gone, Hannah. Israel is gone, and it is my fault."

Placed in the ground that same day, Israel had returned from the Diaspora for his final rest in the Promised Land.[41] Two weeks passed, and Hannah still was not ready to return to Avon, for she knew that it meant leaving Samuel and Israel. Noah told her that he could not wait for her any longer. It was past time for the crew to return home.

"Noah, I have decided what I must do. Samuel, Ruth, and I will stay together and return to Albion when Samuel finishes school. Please tell my brother-in-law to arrange for our return in three years."

"If that's what you want, Hannah, then consider it done."

"Noah, could I ask you to do one more thing before you leave?"

---

[40] Also written as Shemaia and Abtalion. See the previous page and reference to the Shammai Pharisee.

[41] Diaspora was the scattering of the Jews outside of Judea after the Babylonian captivity.

"Of course, Hannah, but I assumed that you changed your mind and would be returning to Albion. You have my word that you will be safe returning home with me. Besides, Esau would have my head if anything were to happen to you or if you remain here unprotected. Because you are Israel's widow, it is your brother-in-law's responsibility to marry you. It falls on me to unite both of you as quickly as possible."[42]

"Esau will understand that our childbearing years are beyond both of us. No, my place is here with my children. Would you find a larger place for us to stay here in Jerusalem?"

Several days later, Noah had several homes ready for Hannah to see. He saved an outstanding home for the last stop. "How many families live here?" Hannah asked. "This house is much too nice and large for us. I wish to live in the first house you showed us. That house would be perfect for us."

"Hannah, that one is also a large home, and from what I have heard about you, it is one that I am certain you will fill with stray women and children in no time. My concern is the location. You should also know that arrangements have been made with a local merchant to see to your food and household needs during your stay."

Upon returning to the first house, Ruth asked, "Mother, where will I sleep?"

"Ruth, honey, you can sleep wherever you would like to sleep."

"You mean that I will have my own place to sleep?"

"Yes, dear, you are part of our family, and this is your home, too."

Noah announced, "Well then, our house-hunting business is settled. Please, everyone, come and eat. The house girl has prepared a meal for us in the eating area."

During the meal, Noah asked, "Hannah, what made you decide on this place and not the last house that we visited?"

"This location is closest to Samuel's school."

"A school on one side and a Roman garrison on the other. Yes, it will be convenient for Samuel and noisy for you."

Hannah did not think she would mind the noise. The way she saw it, living near the Roman garrison would give her a vantage point from which to

---

[42] Deuteronomy 25:5-11—Her husband's brother shall take her and marry her and fulfill the duty of a brother-in-law to her.

observe the Roman soldiers. She wanted to know how they trained for battle. One day the Roman legions would return to Albion, and she wanted to be ready to meet them.

"Hannah, if there is nothing else, the crew and I really do need to return to Albion. Where are Samuel and Ruth? I would like to say goodbye."

"I saw them going toward the market. I think they want to find something special for you, Noah, as a goodbye gift. I will find them, and we will meet you at the dock. Don't sail away."

Later, Hannah felt confused when she saw only the *Nova* moored at the dock. "Captain Noah, where is the *Avon*?"

"Oh, more of the crew members have come home to Jerusalem from the Diaspora and are going to remain in Judea. Consequently, there is hardly enough men to sail one ship back to Albion. So Israel sold the *Avon*."

"That was a fast sale. When did he have the time and how much was my husband paid for her?"

"Didn't Israel tell you that he sold it to the Hillel School to pay for Samuel's education?"

Noah could see that Hannah was unhappy to find out about the sale of the *Avon* after the fact. "Samuel, I don't think your mother is in a prayerful mood. Come over here and pray for our safe journey!"

Time proved Noah correct about Hannah and Ruth ministering to the needs of discarded women. Prostitutes, divorced women, and sick women clung to life in the shadow of the Temple. Some women survived being stoned for committing adultery. It was always the women and never the men. Hannah never understood this double standard and was afraid to say what she thought. *With whom did they commit adultery? Did they do it by themselves?* Hannah had seen the women and children of Avon endure similar difficulties. Therefore, she was willing and prepared to continue her ministry of mercy in Judea.

Samuel was not completely isolated from the misery of Judea while studying at the Hillel School. His classes were preparing him for life outside the school and far from the Temple. When awake, the students were in study, in prayer, or involved in a community or school project. The objective of the Hillel School was to send well-prepared rabbis into a suffering world. Their mandate was to love God and to lovingly treat others as they would want to be treated. Their purpose was to make the world a better place through moral and ethical actions.

One day, Samuel rushed home with exciting news about his friend Gamaliel. "Mother, I am home."

"Samuel, Ruth and I are in here. How is school?"

"Hello, Ruth!" Samuel said, giving his little sister a quick hug. "Mother, school is nothing as I expected it to be. Our school time is divided between prayer, study, and good works. They have us out serving the poor, teaching, and playing with children. I did not know that school could be so much fun."

"I'm glad that you are enjoying it, Samuel."

"Mother, remember Gamaliel and how easily we found a school after meeting him?"

"Yes, he was the answer to our prayers."

"We are probably the only people in all Judea that did not know who he is. He is the grandson of the school's founder. My friend Gamaliel is the grandson of Hillel the Elder."

"Samuel, we are so happy for you. Tell us something that you learned in school today."

"All right, here is something that you would find interesting. In any situation—say for example, someone has wronged you, and you have the right to demand justice—you should ask yourself, *If our roles were reversed, how would I want to be treated?* In other words, we should do to others as we would want them to do to us."

"They are good words to live by. I like your school."

"Something else is different from what I expected. The Hillel School does not emphasize reading and writing. Their method of study is the Mishnah. It is an oral tradition, and the word Mishnah means 'teachings that are repeated'."

"Reading and writing have held our people together. We can and must work on those important subjects together."

During that time, Hannah had little time for study or prayer as she immersed herself in the filth of the forgotten and helpless victims of Judean society. She worked with the Hillel School administrators to aid those who sought refuge and assistance from the nation of Israel. Some Hebrew people provided financial assistance specifically for widows, orphans, and converts. People

PART 4—THE LIVING WORD

including Tobin, who pledged, "A third tenth I would give to the orphans and widows and to the converts who attached themselves to Israel."[43]

Hannah's ministry for women gave her a purpose to be in many places within the city that would otherwise be off-limits, such as the Roman garrison. She came to know some of the Roman soldiers while checking on women who often visited the garrison. One of these women came to repentance during the Jewish celebration of Rosh Hashanah and asked Hannah to help her return to her home in Capernaum. She was afraid that her family would reject and possibly kill her if she went home alone. Of course, Hannah and Ruth agreed and traveled with her until a daughter was safe in her mother's arms. The following morning, Hannah and Ruth woke early to the smell of a special hot breakfast prepared especially for them. The supposed redeemed daughter greeted them with, "My mother has prepared a parting meal to thank you for all that you have done for me."

With farewells exchanged after breakfast, Hannah was pleased to have been able to return a lost daughter to her home. It was a pleasant surprise to see the daughter walking away from the house with them. "Oh, I see you are going to walk with us to the city gates and see us off."

"No, Hannah. My mother thanked me for letting her know that I am well, and she was thankful to you for bringing me here for a visit. My parents say that they must live here among these people. I have brought shame on my parents, my home, my neighbors, and my town that can never be forgiven. I am not welcome to stay in Capernaum."

"Then come with us. You are part of our family now, and we shall call you Orpha, because you are without parents."

"Thank you, Hannah. What should I call you: Mother or Hannah?"

"Always call me Hannah."

Hannah, Ruth, and Orpha began their homeward journey, when Hannah recognized a soldier as they were leaving Capernaum. He walked over to a Nazarene and spoke to him with his head bowed. It was very strange to see a Roman speaking to a Jew in such a manner. He said, "Lord, my servant lies at home paralyzed and in terrible suffering."

The rabbi answered him saying, "I will go and heal him."

---

[43] Tobin is a book found in the *Septuagint* and the Catholic Bible, but not in the Jewish Tanakh.

The centurion stopped him and replied, "Lord, I do not deserve to have you come under my roof. But just say the word, and my servant will be healed. For, I myself am a man under authority, with soldiers under me. I tell this one, 'Go,' and he goes; and that one, 'Come,' and he comes. I say to my servant, 'Do this,' and he does it."

When the teacher, Jesus, heard this, he was astonished and said to those following him, "I tell you the truth; I have not found anyone in Israel with such faith. I say to you that many will come from the east and the west, and will take their place at the feast with Abraham, Isaac, and Israel in the kingdom of heaven. But the subjects of the kingdom will be thrown outside, into the darkness, where there will be weeping and gnashing of teeth."

Then Jesus said to the centurion, "Go! It will be done just as you believed it would" (Matthew 8:5-13).

Hannah expressed her amazement to Ruth and Orpha. "Wasn't that strange? Marcus called a Jew 'Lord.' And the Nazarene offered to go to the man's home. As you know, it is illegal for a Jew to enter the home of a Gentile. Look, Marcus is coming this way. We will ask him the meaning of this. Hail, Marcus!"[44]

Marcus was both confused and embarrassed when he heard a woman greet him in such a way, and then he recognized them. "Hello, ladies. What are you doing all the way up here on the north shore of Galilee?"

"I was wondering the same thing about you. I have not seen you for a while."

"I am sorry, Hannah, but I must go. My servant has been ill, and now he is well. I must hurry to him. Good day, ladies. Please excuse me! I am in a hurry and must go."

Hannah spoke to the centurion's back as he hurried to his servant. "How can you say that? You have not seen your servant to know that he is well. Marcus, how do you know?"

Even if Marcus had time, he could not comment on his peacekeeping assignment. The Roman governor had noticed a growing subversive movement in Judea. The Nazarene was "rebellious against Rome and the peace in Judea." Marcus and his men were assigned to keep the peace and report on the

---

[44] The powerful influence of the Shammai Pharisees caused laws to be placed upon laws until visiting, eating, or doing anything with Gentiles was strictly forbidden.

subversive activities of this rebel named Jesus. Instead of subversion, however, he and his men were daily witnesses to the ministry of the Prince of Peace.

From Capernaum, the three women returned home to their normal daily activities, and Samuel continued to be busy with his studies, prayers, and good works. One morning he placed a note on the table for his mother before leaving early to school. "See you this evening, Mother. After the Lord, you are the Nova of my life."

Hannah read and then left the note on the table in plain sight. "Ruth, Orpha, I am going out for fresh bread, eggs, and cheese. Do you want to go with me?"

Ruth, who had a surprise celebration to organize, answered, "No, we will wait for you here."

Hannah thought, *Whatever happened to I'll go wherever you go?* Instead, she answered, "All right, fine, shalom, my dears. I will be back soon with breakfast."

It was a short walk from her home to the market, where most of the vendors were just beginning to open their shops. Each one greeted his or her prospective customers cheerfully, eager to make a sale. Hannah always answered back, "Good morning. This is the day the Lord has made; let us rejoice and be glad in it!" (Psalm 118:24)

"Hannah, try these fresh apricots!"

"They are as large as a pomegranate. Are you sure that they are not pulpy?"

The vendor cut the fruit and handed her a piece. "Try it."

"Oh, my dear, every other apricot wants to be this apricot. I will take eight, and thank you."

Even at a distance from the fruit stand, Hannah noticed a large, restless man standing in line at the bakery. He was worried that too many people would discover that Jesus was there, and when they did, they would all want something from him, or they would find fault with him. His anxious thoughts were disrupted when he noticed Hannah standing behind him. "Dear woman, you may take my place in line if you promise to save thirteen loaves for me."

"Why, thank you, kind sir."

Peter was curious. "Your accent is interesting. Where are you from?"

"I am a Galatian from Northern Albion where the earth ends in the west. The Romans call my homeland, Caledonia."

The baker interrupted their conversation. "Here is your bread, Hannah."

Peter questioned her name. "Now I am all the more curious. Did I hear him call you Hannah? You are a Galatian named Hannah?"

"My given name Nova was changed to Hannah when The Holy One did as I pleaded for Him to do." Hannah paused and looked perplexed at the expression on the man's face.

"Sir, are you all right?"

"Might I ask? Did you name your first-born son Samuel and give him to our Father in heaven?"[45]

"Our what? No, I gave him to Elohim. Samuel has come here to continue his study of the law."[46]

"Which school is he attending?"

"The Hillel School. Have you heard of it?"

"Yes, I have heard that it is a good school."

Peter's manner became more relaxed, and he was no longer restless. "It has been a blessing to meet you this morning, Hannah. My name is Simon Peter. My friends call me Peter."

"That will be easy for me to remember because you remind me of my cousin Peatcurr. Shalom, Peter. Enjoy that bread. You will love it. It is so rich and good that you could live on it alone. I call it the king's bread."

"I am sure that I will. Have a great day Hannah of Caledonia."

Peter returned to where his friends were patiently waiting by the lake for breakfast. They prayed together, broke bread, and ate it with honey, grilled fish, and hot saffron tea. Meanwhile, a large crowd gathered around them. A leader from the local synagogue came through the crowd and fell to his knees before Jesus. "Please come with me and heal my dying daughter!" Jesus and his followers left immediately for the home of Jairus (Mark 5:21).

Back at the market, Hannah was still looking for special things to buy for her friends and family when a searing pain struck low in her abdomen. Until then, Hannah's small issue of blood was just that—a small issue in comparison with a dying little girl. Every heart is saddened to learn that a child's life is ending soon after it has begun. Jairus and the others were coming toward Hannah

---

[45] Matthew 5:16 is the first time that God is referred to as our Father in heaven.

[46] Jesus addressed God as Our Father. This is a huge change from Elohim, Eloch, El Shaddai, or the One that shall not be named.

PART 4—THE LIVING WORD

as her life was draining away. She was almost to her home when the few drops surged into a life-threatening hemorrhage.

Hannah said to herself, *Well, I will just sit here until the crowd passes by, and then I will continue home to die. I do not want to be seen in this condition.* She sat a few moments, and her thoughts turned into a heartfelt prayer. *Lord, why did you bring me to this distant land to die? My purpose must have been to bring Samuel here, or was it to minister to the women? Thank you for each of them. You have been so kind and generous to your servant. I wish to die and rest in my motherland to be among the spirits of my ancestors. Lord, allow me to live so that I may return to Albion with your good news that the Messiah is coming. Please don't let me die here. Let me rest at the side of King David Curr. Please grant this one last request before I die.*

She turned away from the oncoming crowd to see her bedridden friend Rachel standing in front of her. "Hannah, they say that Jesus the Nazarene is coming this way. Hannah, the Messiah is coming. Jesus touched me since our last meeting. He told me not to tell anyone, but I must tell you. He placed his hands on me yesterday and said, 'Rise and walk!' And here I am, walking on my way to see you."

"Rachel, look at you. You are so tall. I cannot believe that it is you standing there. Did you say his name is Jesus? That is the second time that I have heard that name. This time, I felt his name vibrate through my entire body as you spoke it. Did I understand you correctly? Do you mean that Jesus is the Messiah and that He is coming this way right now?"

Rachel could see that her friend was weak, so she asked, "Hannah, what is wrong?"

Pulling back her garment, Hannah answered, "Look!"

"Hannah, there is so much blood!"

"Please, I beg of you, Rachel. Help me up. I must go to him before I die. If I can just touch his clothes, I will be healed."

Then she heard and knew the voice of Jesus as she pushed her way through the crowd just in time to reach out and touch the hem of his robe. An instant later he was gone, as was her pain. Jesus suddenly stopped and turned back and demanded to know who had touched him. Peter replied, "Master, the people are crowding and pressing against you."

"Someone touched me. I know that power has gone out from me."

The crowd drew back leaving Hannah exposed in his sight, so she went to him and fell at his feet. "I was healed the moment I touched your robe."

"Daughter, your faith has healed you. Go in peace and be freed from your suffering" (Mark 5:25-35).

He was gone as quickly as He had appeared before her, leaving Hannah stunned. *Jesus called me daughter. When did I become His daughter?* And in a trice, her life flashed through her mind. Was it the night that she refused to attack helpless people? Was it her kindness to animals? Was it when she defended Abraham, when she showed mercy to her enemies, or when she dedicated Samuel to God? Perhaps it was when she taught others about God. Then, instead of the face of Jesus, she could only see the faces of every destitute woman, child, and man that she had helped in God's name. At last, she could clearly see the one face that the child Nova wished so desperately to see once more. She saw her mother's face again. So long ago, she begged to see that dear face again, and God had not forgotten. Everything that had happened in Hannah's life had led her to this moment. It was the fulcrum point of her life. In that twinkling of time, she recognized Jesus as the Christ—the one who knew her as daughter even before the beginning of time.[47]

"Rachel, this Jesus is my Good Spirit incarnate who spoke to me directly to go in peace, not to follow along after Him about the countryside. Instead, He told me to go in peace. I have been given new strength to return to Albion with your good news that the Messiah has come!"

Hannah suddenly remembered her family waiting at home. "Ruth, oh dear, poor Ruth and Orpha are still waiting for their breakfast."

Hannah was already walking toward her home as Rachel called out behind her. "Hannah, he is the one I told you about. That was Jesus who healed you, but are you sure you're all right? Can I help you home?"

Hannah called back to her friend. "Thank you, Rachel. I am fine. Sorry that I cannot stay and talk. I have to run. My girls are waiting for breakfast. Come to the Great Garden this evening and meet Ruth and Orpha."

"Run? So I guess that means that you no longer need my help."

Still learning to walk and taking baby steps, Rachel thought, *I will see you tonight, but it might take me a while to arrive there.*

---

[47] There is an indication here that Jesus knew that the woman was a Gentile in what he did not say. See Luke 17:14.

PART 4—THE LIVING WORD

Back at the house, Ruth and Orpha were not home. Hannah knew that her neighbor would know where they were. Inquiring about them would have to wait while Hannah made herself presentable. To knock on her neighbor's door would initiate the tea ritual, and that would require more time than she had this morning. "I really need to teach those girls how to read and write," she muttered. "A simple note telling me where they are would have made the rest of my day much easier."

Despite her reluctance, she went to her neighbor's house and knocked on the door. "Good morning! Are you home?"

"Yes, Hannah, come in! Sit and have some tea with me. I have been expecting you."

"How are you? Oh, I love that dress. Have you heard from your cousin? Does your back still ache? Here, I have fresh bread, cheese, and some wonderful apricots to go with our tea."

"Hannah, you are too kind. You should not have brought all this food. You are my guest. Would you want another apricot? They are wonderful."

"No, thank you. They are so large that I could hardly eat just one."

"Well, all right. I will take a moment to put this food away, and we can talk."

"By the way, have you seen Ruth or Orpha?"

"Oh, did I not tell you? They could not wait any longer for you. They went to meet some of their friends for breakfast. They said you were not to forget to meet them this evening in the Great Garden so that you might pray together."

Eventually Hannah managed to slip away from her neighbor's home by evening and arrived at the garden to find many of her friends waiting for her. They had come to wish their friend well without knowing that it was her rebirthday.

Samuel left school early and went straight to the garden to join the celebration, and for the first time someone asked him, "Is Hannah your older sister?"[48]

---

[48] Birthdays are not celebrated in Hannah's story because they were considered a pagan holiday that was closely associated with astrology. The Tanakh reports one birthday. It takes place in the *Bereshith* scroll during the story of Joseph. "Now the third day was the Pharaoh's birthday. And he gave a feast for all of his officials" (Genesis 40:20). The New Testament also reports only one birthday where John the Baptist lost his head.

Samuel grimaced and answered, "No, she is not my sister. But, that is what I was always told as a child."

Days passed, and Hannah could not stop thinking about the miracle of Jesus healing the servant of Centurion Marcus. She knew that she had witnessed a faith greater than her own. The centurion knew that Jesus could heal the servant without being in the presence of the servant. He had unconditional faith in the Nazarene who answered his faith by saying, "Go! It will be done just as you believed it would." In witnessing that miracle, she came to realize that God was also the god of her enemy, the Romans. There being only one god, God is God of all, even the Romans.

Surely, this was the saddest of all mornings for Marcus and his men as they mourned for their beloved general. The soldiers were standing respectfully at attention as Marcus and the other centurions laid the general's body to rest in the pantheon. The outward structure of the Judean pantheon was not as magnificent as the one in Rome, while the illustrious remains of their general gave the place splendor from his inner character and strength. At day's end, Marcus stood alone, staring at the graven image of Mars looming over the tomb of his fallen commander. His voice echoed through the chambers in anger. "What kind of god are you that can only stand there and do nothing? You are a god created by human hands. You stand there doing nothing because that is all you can do. You are the god of death, destruction, and of every Roman soldier. Countless men of war have been baptized by immersion in the blood of countless bulls in your name. Even our Mars-red uniforms speak more loudly than you have ever spoken. I have seen great miracles each day while you, Apollo, Neptune, Jupiter, and other gods stand here in the shadows doing what you do best—nothing. Jesus does not take lives. Instead, he gives life and gives it more abundantly. His words are of life, faith, hope, and love. Tell me, you god of war, what do you have to say?" The final light of day faded, and the silence of a tomb was his answer.[49]

His servant finally broke the silence. "Master?"

"Yes, what is it?"

"Your men are troubled because the number of Nazarene followers is growing among the people and among many of our numbers, including myself. We

---

[49] Jesus spoke the following: "The thief comes only to steal and kill and destroy; I have come that they may have life and have it to the full" (John 10:10).

PART 4—THE LIVING WORD

are afraid that Rome will command us to crush the source of this tension before it grows any further. How are we to kill our brothers and sisters of faith?"

"Have the men assemble on the drill field!"

One hundred soldiers came prepared for a night combat drill and instead heard Centurion Marcus deliver a proposal. "Soldiers, comrades, and brothers: On his death bed, our dear general approved my request for a transfer to western Gaul. From that vantage point, there are only Britannic barbari to kill just across the water within sight of Gaul. All volunteers are welcome to join me in leaving this sheep pasture for a western wolf hunt."

His one hundred men answered, "Hail Marcus!"

Both Marcus and Hannah had personally experienced the physical and spiritual power of Jesus through their faith. Marcus fully trusted and knew that Jesus had healed his servant even before he saw it with his own eyes. Hannah felt the ambient power of Jesus by simply touching his robe, and in doing so, her faith had healed her of a twelve-year-long illness. Still, she had her doubts and wanted to be certain that Jesus was the Messiah."

In the months following her personal encounter with Jesus, Hannah obeyed Jesus' directive to go in peace. He did not tell her to follow him. However, she did keep a journal of his words and actions to retell in Albion. Her personal testimony was that He answered her prayer of healing so that she could return to Albion with His good news. Hannah doubted many of the reported accounts of Jesus, and she wanted to be sure of the truth. She wanted to know without any doubt that He was the One to come. She knew from personal experience that people often exaggerate and even create a story about someone or something. Therefore, she kept two journals about Jesus: a thin journal of confirmed reports and a thick journal of the unconfirmed reports of His miracles and His teachings. At this point, the thin journal only recorded the healings of the people she knew, such as her friend Rachel and herself. She prayed over each report and eliminated those that did not ring true with a loving God. Still, there were many other reports to verify.[50]

The time for Hannah and Samuel to return to Albion with Ruth and Orpha was drawing near, and she still had many questions about Jesus. According to the travel plans, in just one month, a local transport would take them to Rome

---

[50] 1 John 4:16—God is love.

and from there a Neptune Trading Company vessel would carry them home. One evening she went to the garden to pray for greater discernment about Jesus so that she could confidently separate fact and doctrine from fiction. Upon arriving at the garden, instead of peace and solitude, she found a group of Galilean women preparing a meal. Farther along the way, a group of men was talking and laughing together with Simon Peter. There they all were on holy ground in the garden—Jesus and His closest friends. Overcome with excitement, Hannah walked directly over to Peter.

"Peter, do you remember me?"

"Hannah of Caledonia, yes, I remember you! We met twice in one day, first while waiting for bread and again later that same morning when you were healed. I hardly recognized the new you."

"Yes, thank you, Peter. I often hear that from my friends and family."

One of the men from the group called out to Peter in a slightly piqued voice because Hannah had intruded upon the inner circle of men. "Peter, who is that woman you are talking with? Come, I want you to meet our dinner guest."

"It is all right, Andrew. I will be right there."

Peter quickly returned to his attention on Hannah. "Peter, I have many questions to ask of the Nazarene."

"Ah, I understand. Do you see those women preparing a meal over there? You can trust them to give you the answers to your questions."

"Thank you, Peter, and may the Lord bless you."

"He does, Hannah, He really does, and the Nazarene, as you call him, is the Christ, the Son of the living God. I must rejoin my friends now, but please go and meet the other women. Tell them that Peter sent you to them. It was good to have seen you again. Shalom, Hannah"[51]

A few steps later, Hannah approached the women, and surprisingly, one of them greeted her by name and met her halfway. "Ladies, this is my friend Hannah. Remember, I told you about her. She is the first person who really loved me and gave me hope."

Hannah's mind was racing. *Who is this person? Where did I know her?*

---

[51] Matthew 16:13-17—When Jesus came to the region of Caesarea Philippi, he asked his disciples, **"Who do people say the Son of Man is?"** They replied, some say John the Baptist; others say Elijah; and still others, Jeremiah or one of the prophets." **"But what about you?"** he asked. **"Who do you say I am?"** Simon Peter answered, "You are the Christ, the Son of the Living God."

PART 4—THE LIVING WORD

Saved from total embarrassment, one of the other women invitingly called, "Mary Magdalene, don't be selfish. Bring your friend over here, and put her to work."

"Mary? It cannot be you. You are...."

"Yes, I know, and look at you! I can tell that you have met Jesus. Now, come—come and meet Martha and the other women." (See Luke 8:2.)

Hannah spent several days hanging on to every word of the Galilean women. She was learning so much that soon she would need more writing vellum. At that time, information was recorded on bronze, stone, wood, papyrus, or vellum. She preferred the smooth, strong, and expensive vellum made from sheepskin instead of the course papyrus paper made from the Egyptian aquatic papyrus plant. However, most Jewish people preferred using paper instead of touching the skin of a dead animal.

Simon the Tanner was always glad to see his best vellum customer walk through his door. Not only was she making him rich, but she also treated him with great respect, even though his profession made him unclean. "Good morning, Hannah! What may I do for you today?"

"Shalom, Simon. I thank the Lord for you, and I have another large vellum order."

Simon enjoyed Hannah's company and decided to have some fun at her expense. "Tell me what the problem is? Is my vellum so poor that you need so much?"

"No, it is not you. I am the problem. I write and rewrite the same story, and I repeatedly make the same mistakes. Not only do I make mistakes, but I am writing about Jesus, and I want it to be as perfect and conclusive as possible."

"Well, that is all right for you, but you are making all the Judean sheep very nervous."

"Oh, really? Then perhaps I should use papyrus instead."

"Hannah, do not worry about what those dumb sheep say. Give your order to me."

Several weeks later, Hannah was still making corrections and updates to her journals when her guests arrived. It was to be her bittersweet going-away, open house event where all were welcome. The gathering turned into a feast of plenty as friends arrived with baskets of food and drink to share. While she was busily scurrying about, she turned and came face to face with Jesus.

"Hannah, I have been told that you have been a true and faithful servant to the least of those in Judea and in Albion. Salvation has come to many who have entered this house because of your faith. Well done, my daughter."

Hannah was speechlessly at peace as she catered to and observed her friends gathered in and around her home. She specifically kept her eye on Jesus and his closest friends. There was one young disciple in particular who caught her attention. "More wine, sir?"

"Oh, yes. Thank you, Hannah. And thank you for having us here tonight. My name is John."

"John, may I ask you a question?"

"You just did, and yes, you may ask me anything."

"Has anyone made a written record of him? Of Jesus, I mean."

"No. Some of us have talked about it. The problem is that we move around so much. We do not have the time or place to begin. So far, Matthew is the most qualified, and he has given it some thought. None of us is a scribe. Most of us are average men following a carpenter who has said, 'With man, these things are impossible. But with God, all things are possible.'"

"Would you call Matthew over here, please?"

"Matthew, come over here and meet our hostess."

Matthew set down his handful of food, looked for something to wipe his hands on, and came over to where John stood with Hannah.

PART 4—THE LIVING WORD

"Matthew, this is Hannah," John said, making introductions.

"Shalom, Hannah."

"Shalom, Matthew. Forgive my insistence, but you must record what you have heard and witnessed of Jesus. I want to give you my journals, as they might help you begin this important work."

"We agree that it must be done," Matthew said, and then he began leafing through Hannah's journals. "John, look at this book!"

The two heads bent over the writing as Matthew turned a few pages, and then he looked up and said, "Hannah, this is too much; we cannot accept such a priceless gift. Did you write all this?"

"I am certain that it is only a simple draft that does not belong to me. It belongs to its author and not to His scribe. Please take it in His name. Please take them. They are only journals, God gave me His son."

"Hannah, come sit with us at our table. A great feast has been prepared in your honor. A feast is made for laughter. So let us eat, drink, and be merry." (See Ecclesiastes 10:19.)

ONE HANNAH – TWO MASTERS

Nova's Age: Thirty-One to Thirty-Three

Dear brother Joseph and friends in Rome who love the Lord,
The time to return to my homeland is rapidly approaching. We plan to visit you in Rome, and from there we will travel to and possibly through Gaul on our way back to Albion. It will be a joy to see each of you again. With favorable winds, our ship should arrive in Rome one month before Passover.

Your sister in the Lord, Hannah of Aberdonshire
Traveling with Samuel, Ruth, and Orpha

Much of what Hannah learned about the teachings of Jesus put her mind to rest concerning her previous spiritual struggles of living under the domination of the law. Nevertheless, some of His other teachings were more troubling. Hannah was the Warrior Princess as well as Nova, Daughter of the Light. Now, the Light of the World was telling her that the warrior princess must die within her.[52]

One day Hannah heard Jesus give the following admonition when he was teaching to a crowd that had gathered around him: "I tell you who hear me: Love your enemies, do good to those who hate you, bless those who curse you. If someone strikes you on the cheek, turn to him the other also. If someone takes your cloak, do not stop him from taking your tunic. Give to everyone who asks you, and if anyone takes what belongs to you, do not

---

[52] John 9:4-5—Jesus is speaking: "As long as it is day, we must do the work of him who sent me. Night is coming, when no one can work. While I am in the world, I am the light of the world."

demand it back. Do to others as you would have them do to you" (Luke 6:27-31).

His words caused Hannah to become conflicted. While she knew that his loving words were true, she also knew her passion for the field of battle. She favored the lies of the dark side. Knowing this, she fell to her knees and prayed, "My Father, who is in heaven, Jesus has proclaimed a death sentence on your warrior princess. You are going to have to teach me how to obey this command. How do I love an enemy that desires to kill and subjugate my innocent people? Was it wrongful for me to have vanquished four evil forces for the greater good of Aberdonshire? Was King Saul wrong in killing his thousands and David wrong in killing his ten thousands? You sanctioned Deborah to lead Israel to victory over the Canaanites, and Gideon to be victorious over the Midianites. You are the God of Abraham who stood behind Moses and Joshua as they fought the Amalekites. These and others are my heroes, and now that it is my turn, Jesus has commanded me to love my enemy. This command is confusing. Please teach me how to love my enemies. When new battles come, help me to place the eternal ahead of the earthly victory. This teaching is the very opposite of everything a Celtic warrior princess believes and lives by. She would not hesitate to take the head of anyone who threatened the survival of her children, clan, or nation. This is a bitter command for me to follow. Your Son would ask, 'Hannah, what good would it do for you to gain the whole earth and lose your soul?' Lord, you know that I would give both my body and soul to save my people from harm. Saving their bodies is my tangible and practical course of action. To ignore the growing Roman threat would be an act of treason against the blood of my blood. To ignore your command to love my enemies would cast an everlasting shadow over the souls of both enemy and friend. Saving their souls is up to you, Lord. Smashing their heads was to be my destiny and pleasure. How could you place this command against everything opposite of who I am? My will is to see their blood and bone cultivate the earth of Albion and not have their culture contaminate the innocent Celtic body and mind. I cannot understand this command of love. How do you expect to force me to love what I hate? You have placed this curse upon me, and consequently, it is for you to teach me how to obey you willingly. Until then, it is by sight that I wish to vanquish, and it is by faith that I wait for you, Lord, to teach me how to love those I detest. Forgive me, Father, for I cannot honestly say amen."[53]

A greater obstacle to her faith in Jesus was that same nagging question that John the Baptist asked his cousin: "Are you the One to come?" An imprisoned John sent his disciples to ask Jesus this direct question. Jesus replied indirectly. "Go back and report to John what you hear and see: The blind receive sight, the lame walk, those who have leprosy are cured, the deaf hear, the dead are raised, and the good news is preached to the poor. Blessed is the man who does not fall away on account of me" (Matthew 11:4-6).

Although John knew the Isaiah prophecy, he could very well have thought, *Jesus, you are forever unchanging. You were the same way when we were children. Thank you, cousin. I understand the meaning of your answer. However, a simple direct answer of, 'Yes, I Am the One to Come.' is all I wanted to know.*[54]

Just a few days later, it was time for Hannah to leave Judea, which she would do alone. First, Orpha and Ruth insisted that they wanted to stay in Jerusalem to continue Hannah's ministry for outcast women. Orpha's true nature began to surface when she played upon Hannah's struggles over leaving the Judean ministry. "Yes, you and Ruth could look after our flock so that they would not be scattered and lost again. I do not know which is greater; my pride in both of you or the anguish I feel at the thought of never seeing your faces in this life again."

The subsequent revelation was a life-changing sentence. It meant that Hannah might not ever be able to return to Albion. Samuel announced that he was going to stay where he had made a life for himself in Jerusalem. Hannah reminded him that he had told everyone, including the high priest Caiaphas, that his dream was to study in Jerusalem and return to Albion to preach God's

---

[53] Matthew 16:24-27—Then Jesus said to his disciples, "If anyone would come after me, he must deny himself and take up his cross and follow me. For whoever loses his life for me will find it. What good will it be for a man if he gains the whole world, yet forfeits his soul? Or what can a man give in exchange for his soul? For the Son of Man is going to come in his Father's glory with his angels, and then he will reward each person according to what he has done."

[54] Isaiah 35:2-6—They will see the glory of the Lord, the splendor of God. Strengthen their feeble hands, steady the knees that give way; say to those with fearful hearts, "Be strong, do not fear; your God will come, He will come with vengeance; with divine retribution he will come to save you." Then will the eyes of the blind be opened and ears of the deaf unstopped. Then will the lame leap like a deer and the mute tongue shout for joy.

message to the Celts. Samuel insisted that God needed him more in Jerusalem, because that was where his betrothed wanted to stay and live.

He adored a sweet girl who could not possibly leave her family to live among Gentiles so far from the Temple. He made the point that it was for this purpose "that God made them male and female. And for this reason a man will leave his father and mother and be united with his wife, and the two will become one flesh." These were justifiable words for Samuel's decision to stay in Jerusalem. Hannah could not force her family to leave Judea with her. (See Mark 10:6-7.)

She came to realize that she had not been waiting to take Samuel home after he finished school. Instead, she was waiting for Samuel to escort her home. Samuel could travel alone, but it would have been unsafe and unheard of for a woman to travel such a long distance without a male escort. She would certainly have become the property of a stranger during such a foolish misadventure.

Several more weeks passed, and Hannah began to think that her changed plans did not matter. The arrival of her ship was weeks behind schedule when her prayers were answered in an instant. Ruth called to her from outside the house. "Mother, someone is here to see you. He says that he is your brother-in-law!"

"**Esau!**" This was the first word that anyone had ever heard Hannah scream.

Hannah dropped what she was doing, fussed with her hair and clothes, and ran down the stairs and outside to greet Esau with open arms. "Hannah? Who are you? You cannot be my sister-in-law."

"Esau, it is so good to see you too! Yes, it is me. Ask me anything."

"I see you, but I do not understand. What has happened to you? It is seventeen years later, and you are as you were the day I met you. Who are you? I must sit down."

Hannah also sat down and put her arm around him. "I can prove that I am Hannah. Go ahead, ask me anything."

"Let me think...all right, what is the color of Asbury Castle?"

"First, it was Asbury Palace and not Asbury Castle. Second, it was made from red stone to match the hair of its resident, the Queen of Asbury."

Esau was now convinced that the young woman was his sister-in-law. "I was not prepared for this. You appear to be the same age as my granddaughter. What has happened to you? Did you die and then were born again?"

"Yes, that is exactly what has happened. I have been born again in body, mind, and eternally in spirit."[55]

Old Esau and the youthful thirty-three-year-old Hannah talked as much about Albion as they did about Judea for several days. She told him all that had happened, and then she explained that her children would not be returning to Albion with her. There were two reasons why she had to return. First, she wanted to fulfill her promise to deliver God's message of love to her people, and secondly, she must prepare her nation for the Roman invasion. Through an endless conversation, Esau continued to wear a frown while Hannah was smiling once again.

"Esau, my brother, what is troubling you?"

"I am ashamed to say that I rejoiced over the prospect of obeying the law to marry my brother's widow even while grieving over his death. I have always been jealous for you. It breaks my heart to see you as the youthful beauty that you have become once more, while I have grown old. Fear not. I will not claim my right of marriage, and you may return home safely under my protection.

Still, I cannot imagine how you can return home without Samuel and the girls" Hannah would have remained in Judea if she had known the sad future that was waiting for her children. Samuel divorced his barren object of adoration several years later. In the years after the divorce, his ex-wife had two children with her second husband. Samuel cried out to the Lord for forgiveness when he heard the news of the birth of the second girl-child named Hannah.[56]

Orpha was also on the path of destruction even before the day of Hannah's separation arrived. Orpha would deserve to have burning coals poured over her head for attempting to take Ruth into the darkness of Orpha's old ways. In the end, she died without notice along with countless other destitute women. Hannah never would have left Jerusalem if she had foreknowledge of Orpha's tragic end. Leaving her family and Judean ministry was difficult enough

---

[55] Jesus answered, "I tell you the truth, no one can see the Kingdom of God unless he is born again of water and the Spirit. Flesh gives birth to flesh, but the Spirit gives birth to spirit" (John 3:5).

[56] Jesus replied, "Moses permitted you to divorce your wives because your hearts were hard. But it was not this way from the beginning. I tell you that anyone who divorces his wife, except for marital unfaithfulness, and marries another woman commits adultery" (Matthew 19:8-9).

without suspecting how far two of her children would fall from the grace of God.[57]

Only Ruth stayed on the straight and narrow path, while Samuel and Orpha strayed. She greeted each day with a joyful heart in the service of God. He had placed Hannah in her life to lead Ruth out of the darkness, and accordingly, it was time for Ruth to lead others into God's light. As a young Jewish woman, she made a vow to God that she would never leave or forsake Him. Her ministry touched the lives of thousands of women throughout Judea and the world. The coming tragic Diaspora of AD 70 would scatter many of them to many nations as seeds are scattered in the wind. They were the seeds of the Word of God that caused synagogues to be planted throughout the earth.

Jesus spoke these words to encourage His followers whenever they felt the sorrow of parting for His sake. "And everyone who has left houses or brothers or sisters or father or mother or children or fields for my sake will receive a hundred times as much and will inherit eternal life" (Matthew 19:29).

That alone can be a tumultuous motivation without being totally committed to Christ. Therein was Hannah's dilemma: She knew that the message of Christ was not her single motivation for returning to Albion. Her primary motivation was to prepare her nation for war. Could anyone have a greater internal conflict?

Nova, the Daughter of the Light, was torn between leaving her enlightened family in Judea and returning to her unenlightened nation of Albion. On one side were her children and the Judean ministry for women. She had taught her children to know and love the Lord. They were spiritually equipped with the armor of God and prepared to continue the women's ministry she had built through the years.

On the other side of this conflict was the tug of her home nation, that was spiritually lost in the darkness of polytheism. To Hannah, it was obvious that her urgent heavenly mission was to pick up the banner of taking God's Holy Word to Albion since Samuel had dropped it. Her return to Albion was urgent for the eternal salvation of its people. She believed that she was the only Celtic saint, or perhaps the most prepared one, to carry the light of God's Word into

---

[57] Jesus said, "And whoever welcomes a little child like this in my name welcomes me. But if anyone causes one of these little ones who believes in me to sin, it would be better for him to have a large millstone hung around his neck and to be drowned in the depths of the sea" (Matthew 18:5-6).

the darkness of her warrior nation. However, she might have stayed in Judea if she had known that God had already won the spiritual battle between the light and the dark. It never occurred to her that God does not need anyone to accomplish His will. He only allows us the privilege of participation.[58]

Hannah the Warrior Princess was more certain of the urgency of her return for the national security of Albion. To her way of thinking, she was the one person who was prepared to stand against the military evils of the Roman Empire. As a patriot, she saw it as her responsibility to alert every Albion Celt of the crimson tidal wave that was rising to flood their shores. Again, if she had known the future, she would have remained in Judea, because God had also won that battle without her interference. Still, in her mind, she alone had to return home to save Albion from the Roman sword.

Even as deeply as she believed these things, there was nothing sweet about her sorrow in leaving. Hannah's family had to take over the travel preparations because the parting drove her into a deep depression. They had to assist her onto the *Hannah II*, bound for Rome. She continued to weep and pray throughout the voyage that seemed to last for an eternity. Fasting was a given because of the sea swells, the closet-like quarters, the sea rations, and her overwhelming grief. Hour after hour, the cadence of the oars kept rhythm with the pounding in Hannah's head. The seemingly unending voyage between Jerusalem and Rome gave her time to fast, pray, reflect, and focus on God between her waves of nausea. The Gospel message and the women's ministry were all that she had to show for her time in Judea, and she still had not made her final decision about Jesus. In agony, she cried out, "Lord, I am not there yet!" Then her thoughts turned to Ruth, and in her illness and despair, she remembered her promise: "Wherever you go, I will go, and wherever you stay, I will stay." Those words repeated over and over in her mind, and finally, through her weakness, she fell peacefully asleep hearing the voice of the Lord in her heart: "Nova, Daughter of My Light, I am with you always."

The *Hannah II* finally made port and rejoined the *Nova II* and the *Avon II*. Joseph, Julia, Aquila, and his wife Priscilla gathered on the Roman dock to

---

[58] Ephesians 6:10-13—Be strong in the Lord and in his mighty power. Put on the full armor of God so that you can take your stand against the devil's' schemes. For our struggle is not against flesh and blood, but against the rulers, against the authorities, against the powers of this dark world and against the spiritual forces of evil in the heavenly realms. Therefore, put on the full armor of God, so that when the day of evil comes, you may be able to stand your ground.

welcome their friends from Jerusalem. They waited longer than expected until Julia finally said, "Everyone has left the ship. I guess they did not make it."

They were about to leave when a seaman called to them. "Are you here to meet a woman named Hannah?"

"Yes, we are. Do you know what has happened to her?"

"Yes, she is on board. I am her brother-in-law, Captain Esau. I'll bring her and her things. You should prepare yourselves for a shock."

"Are her children not with her?"

"No, they stayed in Jerusalem."

First, he placed a small bag with a large odor on the dock. Then he produced a half living creature that had not seen daylight in days. It seemed to be a young, frail, extremely bedraggled woman. Even the normally calm Joseph was becoming aggravated with waiting. "Sir, where is our friend Hannah?"

Bursting into tears, this horrible excuse of a human creature, blinded by the light, spoke out toward the voices on the dock. "Joseph?"

"Quiet, the young woman is saying something."

"Yes, I am, Joseph."

"It is I, Nova."

"Who?"

"I'm sorry. I'm Hannah."

Confused and even more annoyed, they were slow to respond when Aquila said, "When did you steal that choker? That is Hannah's choker."

"Aquila, I am Hannah."

Feeling as though she was about to faint, Hannah turned to her brother-in-law and said, "Esau, my head is spinning. You tell them that I am Hannah."

Before Esau could answer, Priscilla said, "That is a lie. Hannah is a heavy woman twice your age. Who are you, and what have you done with our Hannah? And how do you know our names?"

"My dear friends—Joseph, Julia, Priscilla, and Aquila—I am telling the truth. I am Hannah. Please believe me."

Julia and Priscilla wanted to leave her there on the dock, but Joseph took pity on her. "She must be Hannah. How else would she know our names?"

Joseph walked over to where Hannah and Esau were standing. "Hannah, listen to me. What was the Roman Commerce Committee chairman's name?"

"Gaius."

"Julia, wait! I don't know how, but this is Hannah. You women need to clean and bring her back to good health."

Esau supported his sister-in-law as they walked slowly with Joseph. "I told you that you were in for a shock," Esau murmured in his ear.

Once back on land, Hannah quickly blossomed under the nurturing of her friends. She shared her Judean experiences and spiritual struggles with them. Seeing her physical transformation, some immediately believed her miraculous stories and the teachings of Jesus that she shared with them. Many believed that he was the One to Come. Others believed that for some unknown reason, she was an impostor pretending to be a much older Hannah of Albion. These things threatened the religious leaders, and they were the happiest to learn that she was leaving. Her last evening in Rome was made special with a farewell dinner prepared by Joseph, and Julia.

Joseph knew that he would never again see this messenger from God. "Hannah, why not stay here until after Passover?"

"Thank you, Joseph, but I have learned that everything has its time, and it is the beginning of good sailing weather. The season, my ships, and their captain are waiting. It is time to go back to my homeland with very good news. I want to thank you again, Joseph, for your kindness and persistence. I would probably be dead if it were not for Julia and Priscilla nursing me back to health. This is the second time that a godly person has rescued me. I will never forget you."

Just days after her arrival, Hannah was back on a Roman dock looking at the three Celtic cargo ships that would take her home to Albion. The *Hannah II*, *Nova II*, and *Avon II* were longer and more sleek than the first. Remembering the reason that they ran aground at Dragonfly and her recent experience with seasickness, Hannah asked, "Esau, is there any way that I could walk back home?"

"May I suggest that you stay out on the upper deck and look out across the sea as much as you can? Sunlight, fresh air, and nourishment will keep you healthy during the voyage. Try to stay active."

It was about that time that a stranger approached Hannah on the dock. One could tell by his dress and manner that he would be a misfit in any social group. "Hannah, may I speak with you?"

PART 4—THE LIVING WORD

"Yes, of course. What is it that you wish to speak to me about?"

"My name is Patricius. I have been listening to everything that you have said, and I have decided to accept Jesus as the Messiah. I want to go to Caledonia with you and tell people about him."

"So, you have already told your neighbors and all of Rome about Him."

"No, you are the first person that knows about my decision."

"Sir, first I would suggest that you find others here in Rome who believe. Learn from them and become a new person in Christ. Then, when you are ready, look about you. Are there not people in Rome who you can share your faith with?"

"Forget them. I do not like any of my neighbors. They are terrible people who would never listen to me."

"Sir, why would your personal relationships be better in Albion than they are in Rome?"

"The barbarians would have to respect me because as a Roman, I am better than they are."

"Patricius, as an Albion Celt, I can assure you that you would be much happier if you were to stay in Rome."

"What would you suggest that I do here in Rome that would make me more respectable?"

"Sir, have you thought about becoming a tax collector?"

Even the misfit understood her sarcasm and sadly walked away leaving Hannah and Esau to continue their conversation. "Esau, these ships declare that they are all about me. I want them to be all about the Lord. How hard would it be to rename these ships?"

"It can be done, of course. But as you know, Hannah, it is considered bad luck to change the name of a ship, and you are asking fate to curse us three times."

"Captain, would you allow me to address the crew about the ship names?"

"Yes," Esau replied as he turned to call out to his crew, "Attention, men: Israel's widow, my sister-in-law and our newest crewmember, has a few words to say!"

"This can't be the entire crew."

"Yes, I am afraid that once again, many have returned home from the Diaspora and will not be going back with us."

"Esau, what are we going to do? Can you find enough men in Rome who are willing to sail to the edge of the earth?"

"Don't worry about it. Help is coming."

Addressing what remained of the Celtic crew, Hannah made her plea. "I am happy to see some familiar faces here today, and I am looking forward to meeting the new crewmembers. I am excited to be going home to Albion because I have wonderful news to share about the Messiah. I am trying desperately to live my life in a way that is pleasing to the Lord and that gives Him glory. However, the names of these ships oppose that quest. As you may know, their names are all about me. I am asking each of you to allow these three ships to be renamed for the Lord. Captain Esau has cautioned me that renaming the ships would place three curses on us. However, if the new names praise Him Who Is Holy, what is there to fear if the Lord is with us?"

The crew answered Hannah's question with silence. "Please tell me. If your answer is no, then no it is, and the names will remain unchanged."

Finally, a crewmember raised his hand.

"Shalom, Carpenter. It is good to see you again. Do you have a question?"

The ship's carpenter turned to the other crewmembers. "You see, it is Hannah. She even knows my name."

Then Carpenter turned back toward Hannah and asked, "Tell us how it is possible that a woman has become a child?"

"I know many of your names, and others are new crewmembers. To answer your question, I was very ill when you last saw me, and since that time, I have been healed by the Messiah."

"Did you say the Messiah? I know that I am just a simple carpenter. Who am I to question such a great lady? Look about you. Can you not see that Albion has come to you, and yet you have not shared this great message of the Messiah with anyone aboard these ships? Are we not the people of Albion? Are we not worthy of hearing the Good News?"

Esau interrupted Carpenter. "You will watch your words when you speak to my sister-in-law!"

PART 4—THE LIVING WORD

Gently touching Esau's arm, Hannah stopped any further escalation as her face became a deeper shade of red than her hair. "Please, Captain, he has spoken the truth. I am the one who is at fault."

She took a deep breath and prayed to herself. *Lord, please forgive your blind and stupid daughter. I am no more prepared to share your message than the Roman Patricius is. Perhaps I ought to consider becoming a tax collector.*

Although she should have known better, she and the crew realized that she had discounted them as people because she thought of them as being simple. Despite the fact that these were the brothers in faith that she had prayed with, she had thoughtlessly treated them as common deckhands. She had discounted them as an unsavory lot. Hannah had not seen them through God's eyes.

From there, she did go on to share the great message, and the spirit gave birth to the spirit even though the message was delivered through an imperfect messenger.

"Once more, please forgive me. As you know, I really am trying desperately to live for the Lord. I am asking each of you to allow these three ships to be renamed for the Lord."

With no objection raised from the crew about renaming the ships, Esau went directly to the maritime registration office. "Captain, it is a fearful thing to rename a ship," the clerk warned. "When disaster strikes, they will be asking why I let such a terrible thing happen. No, I won't do it. It is not possible."

Experience had taught Esau of the venal character of Roman officials, and therefore he had prepared for such an answer. "I am sorry to hear that. Oh look! I found this purse here on the floor, and it contains twenty shekels. Is it your purse?"

"Oh no, Captain, that is not my purse. Yes, it is true that I have lost a much larger purse containing fifty shekels."

"How foolish of me; you are correct! This is your lost purse. It does contain fifty shekels."

A few days later, the ships were still moored in Rome, and waiting for their cargo to arrive when Hannah asked, "Esau, the arrangements of the storage compartment and deck are very strange. What is going on?"

"Look there on the road, coming this way. We have contracted to transport over two hundred Roman troops to the western coast of Gaul. Now we have a crew."

"Why would you allow Roman troops aboard ship? I hate the Romans! Tell me that we are not complicit in delivering our enemy to Albion's doorstep. In my opinion, that would make us traitors and worthy of death."

"How can you of all people say such a thing? Have you become so Jewish that you have forgotten that you, too, are really a Gentile?"

"That has nothing to do with it, and you know it. This is not a case of Gentile against Gentile. It is pitting an elephant against a mouse. It is sacrificing our nation for a few pieces of silver."

"Hannah! That will be enough! I am asking you to trust that Israel's sons and I are doing what is in the best interest of Albion. Please be patient; everything will be explained to you once the four of us are together again."

"But...."

"Enough!"

"Might I ask one question?"

"What?"

"Wouldn't the Romans reach Gaul more quickly on foot or by horse and chariot?"

"I would think so. All the more confusing is that for this voyage, they are paying more than what is required under our contractual agreements."

"I did not need to hear about the fortune that we are making for betrayal."

"Hannah, please do not make me raise my voice in anger again. Go stay in the castle."

A furious warrior princess retreated to the castle as seventy soldiers boarded the first ship and about thirty soldiers boarded the second ship while another one hundred stood their ground staring up at the names of the three ships. Esau went down to the officer in charge.

"Good morning, sir. We are ready to sail. You and your men are welcome to board."

Still they did not move, and Esau thought, *I will have Hannah come down here to translate. He obviously does not understand a word I am saying.*

At that exact moment, the warrior princess was strategizing. *I can score a great victory by striking first. I am sure that I can persuade Esau and the others to see it. We could abandon the ships off the coast of Dragonfly during the second watch and simultaneously set all three ships ablaze. Then we can safely sit back in our dinghies and enjoy watching them burn and drown as the rats* they are. That will be another huge victory without the loss of one Celt. Everyone will speak of this for a thousand years. Step back, Makcurr, for I am the master warrior! I will show the Stag Slayer how to kill, kill, kill.

Wait, I am also Nova, Daughter of the Light. God, something tells me that you and your love are behind this. My will is to kill, but love is your will. All right, fine, I surrender. I will do it your way this time. Show me how I am to love my enemy.

Esau called out. "Hannah, come down here on the dock and speak to this chief. He does not understand anything that I am saying to him."

"I'm coming, Captain." Hannah prayed silently while she walked down the gangplank. *Please, God, give me your strength, your peace, and your love. Help me to stay calm in the face of my enemy.*

Her life took a new direction as Hannah stepped from the gangplank onto the dock. She immediately recognized someone she had not seen in a long time. "I know that face—Marcus!"

"Hannah?"

Esau was surprised. He expected clarification and received confusion. "Not only does he speak, but he knows you?"

"Captain Esau, this is Centurion Marcus and his men from Judea.

Marcus, I cannot tell you how happy I am to see you." Hannah could not hold back her tears knowing that God had immediately showed her how she could love her enemy. Because of this event, she had blessed assurance that with God, all things are possible. She walked boldly toward Marcus and embraced him. "Marcus and my brothers, this moment was set forth by our Lord. Fear not; you are welcome aboard these ships!"[59]

"Hannah, what are you doing here, and what are these ships? We were told that we would be transported on Galatian ships. These cannot be Galatian ships!"

"Why not?"

"Their names identify them with our people of the Way. How can this be?"

"My family owns these ships, and I am a Galatian."

"I thought you were a Hebrew. Dear woman, are there many of the Way in Britannia?"

---

[59] Mark 9:23 and 10:27: Jesus looked at them and said, "With man this is impossible, but not with God; all things are possible with God."

"Who is and who is not is known only to God. I for one am a Galatian Jew who has decided to place my faith in Jesus as the Messiah."[60]

Her answer was not what Marcus wanted to hear. "Gaul and the shores beyond were to be our escape from ever being faced with marching against others of the Way. We have heard stories of the savage warriors of Britannia. It is only now that we find out that one of the most humane people that we have had the privilege of knowing is from Britannia. Hannah, what are we to do?"

"As His followers, we are to first seek His will in our lives. For now, please, everyone come aboard lest we lose the day. We will have the entire voyage to pray together and to figure out just how we are going to love one another."

"With you, that's a given. Everyone here is honored to know you as their sister Hannah of Judea. We know you as the one Jesus called, Daughter."

"Then say no more. This is my home at sea, and you and your men are my guests. Welcome aboard."

Esau walked up the gangplank alongside Hannah. He spoke softly in a girlish voice, "Romans! I hate Romans!"

Equally softly, Hannah replied, "Oh, hush up, Captain Esau—sir!"

Shortly afterward, *The Truth*, *The Way*, and *The Life* sailed from Rome carrying the first Christian missionaries to the western end of the earth.[61]

"Esau, it looks as though there will be a storm. The sky is as dark as night."

"Yes, I have never seen conditions turn so badly so quickly. It is too late to make port, so we will have to weather the storm. Tell everyone to tie everything down, including themselves."

The skies brightened once more on the fourth day of Passover in Rome as Aquila was looking for Hannah. "Joseph, is Hannah gone?"

---

[60] Galatians 2:11-21 where Paul opposes Peter as one Jew to another in explaining that they no longer receive justification by the law, but by faith. For them, Jesus came to fulfill the law and not to abolish the law. The name Christian did not exist until the distinction between Jew and followers of the Way was made later in Antioch.

Romans 3:29—Is God the God of the Jews only? Is He not the God of the Gentiles too? Yes, the Gentiles too, since there is only one God.

Romans 3:22—This righteousness from God comes through faith in Jesus Christ to all who believe. There is no difference, for all have sinned and fall short of the glory of God, and are justified freely by his grace through the redemption that came by Christ Jesus.

[61] John 14:6—Jesus answered: "I am the way and the truth and the life."

PART 4—THE LIVING WORD

"Oh, yes, she left days ago. Why?"

"Terrible news has arrived from Jerusalem about her Jesus."

The prevailing winds of the Great Sea blew from west to east as though to bid Hannah to return to Judea. Instead, her three ships tacked back and forth in a jagged path westward with long intervals of rowing. Esau was now a confident navigator of the Great Sea, able them to sail both day and night. During that time, Hannah learned to love every bloody and calloused hand that pushed and pulled her ever closer to home with every stroke of the oars. While in port, instead of resting, she was out gathering enough food and drink to fuel an army until it reached the next port. They responded to her efforts and kindness by pulling increasingly harder on their oars to deliver her home. Wind, confident seamanship, kindness, physical strength, and even a bit of competition between the ship crews all worked together to deliver Hannah safely home in record time.

With two hundred and sixty crewmembers, there were enough men to allow each oarsman to rest two-thirds of the time on windless days. The Roman crewmembers rested below deck, and most of them remained below deck while in port. Hannah kept encouraging them to get out into the fresh air. Instead, they insisted on staying below deck, as though they were hiding. They only came up on deck at night when the ship was offshore. It was strange to see them rise up in the night as though from a mass grave.

While in a safe harbor, they inquired about the latest area news. Increasingly, there were warnings of pirate activity on the western end of the Great Sea. The warrior princess rose up within Hannah once more as she began to plan and strategize. *A successful pirate attack would be a great way to kill so many Romans at one time.* Then she thought about those haunting words to love her enemies. *Do I help the pirates of the Great Sea or the greater bandits of the Apennine Peninsula? Life was so much simpler before Jesus. I knew exactly who I was back then, and I always knew what to do. I was the Warrior Princess.*

"Esau, could I speak with you about the pirates?"

"Don't worry about the pirates, Hannah. I know that we can out sail them."

"I have a better idea. Let us bait them into attacking."

"What? Are you crazy?"

"Will our ships and crews ever be coming this way again?"

"Yes, of course we will."

"Will you always have two hundred Roman warriors aboard?"

"Hannah, I am beginning to see your point."

"All right, fine, I'm going to tell you my plan, and you can present it to the Romans, because you know how condescending they are toward women and children."

"Yes, they always say that women and children are to be seen and not heard. But it was my impression that these men knew you, so surely they must respect you, too."

"A girl has got to have a few secrets, Esau. They only know me as their sweet sister Hannah. They don't know that Warrior Princess Nova lurks beneath the surface."

Esau replied teasingly, "What is your plan, sweet sister Hannah?"

"First, disable one of the three ships and put it in tow of the other two. Perhaps you could move the cargo and passengers to the stern so that it would appear that the ship is taking on water. Second, the lame ship would appear not to have anyone aboard while the soldiers hide below deck. The other two merchant ships would seem to have a minimal number of crewmembers. Third, allow the pirates to begin boarding all three ships before swarming the decks with Romans. Finally, but do this beforehand, order our people to retreat below deck where they are to remain in safety while our enemies kill one another. They are not to stand in the way of the mighty warriors of Rome."

"That sounds good to me. Are you sure that you were not a pirate in a former life?"

"Not that I can recall! Now, we need the Romans to agree to the plan, and we need some pirates to pay us a call."

Esau presented Hannah's plan to Centurion Marcus. There was a long pause until Esau said, "Please Marcus, I know that you understood what I said."

"Captain Esau, I think that is an excellent plan. Could we begin tomorrow?"

Hannah was impatiently waiting on the castle-deck for Esau's return. "What did he say?"

"Hannah, he thinks it is a great idea. We will start tomorrow."

Below the main-deck, Marcus met with the other two centurions and asked, "Well, men, what do you think of Captain Esau's plan?"

PART 4—THE LIVING WORD

Anthony answered, "It is an excellent plan considering that it matches perfectly with our orders from Rome, although the lame ship is a clever touch."

Soon, more than a few pirates took the bait. They seemed to be coming from everywhere at once while the Caledonian battle plan unfolded with one flaw. Hannah's hiding place was the castle of the *Truth*. It came under heavy attack and quickly breached, where the poorly prepared pirates met the warrior princess in her favorite battle uniform. Hannah and the Romans sent all the pirates into the depths of the Great Sea. The victors seized the pirate vessels and added them to the original trio of ships to become a small fleet. Pax Romana reigned supreme without the loss of one Celtic crewmember.

Their destination was just two weeks away as the fleet continued on with the victorious Roman soldiers. The Caledonians treated each Roman as an honored guest all the way to the mustering point in Gaul. Esau had their respect for his cooperative efforts in giving them the victory that all Rome was waiting for. More importantly, in return, it gave the Neptune Trading Company a new level of Roman acceptance and prestige. The company flag received unquestioned passage throughout the empire as a reward for Neptune's loyalty to Rome.

Hannah was also treated differently. Previously, she was everyone's little sister, and very sorry was anyone who disrespected her. They had always greeted her as they would their own mother. Now, after the sea battle, they were unsure of their mixed feelings of seeing her naked body covered in the blood of those who sought her blood. The intensity of her lethal combat skills caused the sea battle to stall as pirate and soldier became spellbound at the sight. Several days of silence were broken when Marcus found her standing at the castle deck railing.

"Hannah, may I speak with you?"

Hannah glanced over at her brother-in-law for permission. "Yes, what is it?"

"I just wanted to say that you are one surprise after another. My men and I never really knew you, did we?"

"You did. You just did not know everything about me."

"Who are you?" Marcus asked.

"I don't know who I am," Hannah said, letting out a heavy sigh. "I only know who I want to be. I want everyone to love and respect one another. I want to be the person that you and the others thought me to be. Instead, everyone has seen me for who I really am. Marcus, I do not want to be that person. Even worse, this time I realized that I love being in the fight, and it is only afterward that I am now remorseful."

"Look out over there at the men," Marcus said, sweeping his arm toward his soldiers. "You are one of them. You are a warrior, and they all know that you are their better. There was nothing savage about your fighting skills. They were a thing of military beauty. It makes us wonder how we are to face and survive the men of Britannia. Excuse me for laughing at your words, 'everyone has seen me.' Yes, we have, and fortunately, the voyage has run most of its course. Hannah, my sister in Jesus, we have to decide which camp we belong. The choice is between being of this world, or being a visitor from the Kingdom of God. It is one or the other, but not both."

"Whoever would have thought that a Roman would be giving me spiritual advice?" Hannah said, giving Marcus a friendly nudge. "Speaking of strange events, I noticed that your men prefer to be above deck ever since the sea battle. The pirates were the real reason behind your being aboard these ships. You and your men must have had a good laugh over Esau's advice to bait the pirates."

"Now that I know you better, I would say that we found Hannah's plan to be boldly interesting," Marcus said with a smile.

Hannah's voice turned playful. "Sir, I will have you know that I am just a simple mountain girl from Caledonia."

Two more weeks passed and Marcus organized a parting ceremony to honor Captain Esau, Hannah, and their crew. "Hannah, my men and I had something made for you that symbolizes the Hannah we love and admire most." Marcus then presented her with a beautifully embroidered, full-length white cape. He placed it over her shoulders as a symbolic cape of peace. This time she had many brothers wishing her farewell as the *Truth* and its skeleton crew left its mooring for a final stop in Avon. At that moment, Marcus commanded, "Soldiers of Rome, salute!"

Two hundred voices responded, "Hail Hannah of God's truth, way, and life!"

Then she heard a soft girlish voice behind her murmur, "Romans! I hate Romans."

PART 4—THE LIVING WORD

Equally soft, Hannah turned her head slightly and said out of the corner of her mouth, "Oh, hush up and take us home, Captain Esau, sir."

✣ ✣ ✣ ✣ ✣ ✣ ✣

PART 1—THE WORD

PART 2—THE WRITTEN WORD

PART 3—LIVING THE WORD

PART 4—THE LIVING WORD

PART 5—SPREADING THE WORD

✣ ✣ ✣ ✣ ✣ ✣ ✣

THE FIRST MISSIONARIES

Nova's Age: Thirty-Four to Forty

More than a hundred missionaries of the Way landed in Gaul, and a small crew of believers was bound for Caledonia on an early morning high tide. The channel proved to be a challenge for the crew of *The Truth*. How easily they had forgotten its powerful Atlantic tidal waters. Seasick or not, every hand, including Hannah's, was needed to stay on course. The damp air was much colder than they were used to. At least the work kept them from suffering from hypothermia. Finally, after endless rowing, Esau called out, "Home firth ahead!"

Avon—home at last, Hannah thought. *More than anything, I have missed the mountains and their oak groves. For now, I will settle for some food and sleep. A bath will have to wait until tomorrow morning.*

The Port of Avon was peaceful that evening. Even the company dock was vacant. "Esau, have my things delivered to the house. I just want to go home and sleep," Hannah instructed.

"Before you go, let me look at those hands. Yes, they are just as I thought—a bloody mess. Sit down, and let's get you cleaned up. Even with your hands bandaged, my nephews will think that I have mistreated you."

As the captain cleaned and dressed her wounds, he said, "I am very proud to be your brother-in-law and to have a friend such as you. I will be making some changes in my life because of the faith that you have shown. Now I understand what Captain Noah meant when he said that you had changed his life."

"How is the captain?"

PART 5—SPREADING THE WORD

"He has become our most trustworthy seaman and has been promoted to my former rank of senior ship captain of the Neptune Trading Company ships."

After a pause, Esau said, "Hannah, I am sorry about our argument. Israel and I should have included you in our business plans years ago. Please forgive us. It is just not our tradition to burden a wife with such details. However, we were equally aware that you were not the average Jewish wife. Tell my nephews that I am coming to dinner tomorrow, and afterward we will discuss the Neptune Trading Company objectives. Until then, just be patient and trust us."

Hannah simply smiled in response.

"What are you smiling about?"

"This moment reminds me of something that happened years ago when I was a girl in Asbury. I could use a horse by the name of Black Thunder to carry me home this evening.

Esau, back to what you were saying—the apology is mine to make. You were correct. I said some terrible things about you. Please do not repeat them."

"Apology accepted," Esau said, as he tied a knot in the bandage to secure it. "There you go. Your hands should be fine in a few days. You know, you can always have a job as my shipmate if you become the bored widow."

"Thank you, kind sir, for the job offer, but no, I have fought my final sea battle. My plan is to retire as the Lady of Avon."

"Can you make it to the house on your own?"

"Yes, I can make it home just fine. As you know, it is not a long walk. Please come to dinner on the day after tomorrow. I will need at least one day of rest to feel human again. See you then, Captain. And by the way, I am proud to be your sister-in-law."

Arriving in Avon, she was an unsightly mess and odorous, even by barbarian standards. One cannot imagine her appearance after traveling for weeks in the same clothes while accompanied by over two hundred sweaty men. Walking alone was enjoyable without anyone recognizing or acknowledging her. She stopped at a street vendor for some sweet cider and offered him a Roman coin. With one glance, the vendor assumed that Hannah was a person of the street. Refusing to accept her money, he said, "That's all right, dear. I've been there, too."

"Do I look that bad?"

The street vendor responded by covering his nose and mouth with his hand.

"Oh, I'm that bad. Please forgive me. I have just returned from a long journey. This cider is wonderful. Thank you for your kindness."[62]

Once home, she knocked on the front door, and no one answered. She started around the side of the house, and a house servant stopped her, saying, "Leave here before you get hurt!"

"It is all right. I am Israel's widow."

A moment later, she found herself escorted back onto the street by several house servants. "And make sure that you do not come back! We do not want your kind around here."

Hannah realized that nobody in Albion expected her to return home so early. Furthermore, Samuel and Esau were not with her, and she returned appearing to be a younger-looking tramp in contrast to the well-groomed woman who had left Avon years earlier. It was an understandable mistake, and it did not worry her. It could wait for Esau to correct. Therefore, she resigned herself to returning to the ship as a lone tramp in the night. Once there, she found that everyone was gone, and the gangplank was not in place. Then she remembered the Sarah House for the homeless and finally found a safe place to bathe, to eat, and to spend her first night home in Avon. Sleep, finally a deep well-earned sleep until an older woman with two guards woke her abruptly.

"Good morning. What is happening? What are these men doing in the Sarah House?"

The old woman answered with a question of her own. "Where did you get that torc?"

"I'm sorry, what?"

"That torc belonged to my son Maon.[63] What have you done with him?"

"Has Maon been missing for about seventeen years?"

"Yes, he has been gone for a long time. Did you murder him for his golden torc?"

---

[62] Coinage was used at that time in the southern parts of Albion as the Roman influence spread northward. Not only were there Roman coins, but King Cunobelinus of Britain also minted coins during this time.

[63] Maon (Moon) is a Gaelic name that means *hero*.

PART 5—SPREADING THE WORD

"What? No! On the contrary, I was the only one to weep over his grave. I am alive today because he died in my place."

A crowd of onlookers grew as Hannah explained what happened to the woman's lost son and how honored she was to finally meet the mother of the boy who gave his life to save hers.

Then a guard said, "You are coming with us. Who are you trying to fool? You are not much older than seventeen years of age now."

"Go with you where? I'm not going anywhere with you!"

The house-servant from the previous evening came along just as they were dragging her into the street and said, "That thief tried to break into the Israel House last night!"

When she proclaimed that she was Israel's widow, the response was laughter, ridicule, the loss of her treasured torc, and sudden incarceration. "My brother-in-law will have your heads for this."

"Shut up and get in there."

Hannah found herself in a room with another woman as the door closed behind her. "What crimes have you been accused of?"

The woman spoke up and said, "My only crime was that I sought shelter in a place they called the Sarah House, and then I was brought here."

As the day passed, Hannah thought that Noah or Esau would rescue her any moment. More hours passed, and finally the door swung open to disappointment. The guard had returned to take the captives to an old transport ship that was bearing the colors of the Manawyddan Utility Company. It was bound for Gaul and a life of prostitution for the women. Hannah angrily protested. "You cannot do this to Celtic women. Only slaves and foreign women can be treated and sold this way."

"Well, young lady, you be sure to tell that imaginary brother-in-law of yours. Now shut up lest we shut you up."

Then Hannah heard the guards talking among themselves. "Do you know what I think? Some new soldiers have just arrived on the other side. I'll bet they will pay a small fortune for that one."

"Wait, I am not a head of cattle to be sold at market. Even if you do not believe that I am who I say I am, you cannot sell a Celt into slavery. Our laws only allow foreigners be sold as slaves. The Druids will place a curse on all of you for this."

"Yes, Druids, we will warn your Esau about them. Now shut up before you are a dead piece of Celtic trash.

The guard then said, "Can you imagine the poor Roman that buys her? Have mercy on him—she will talk him to death."

Hannah always knew that Israel and Esau had business secrets, but she never suspected them to be so sinister. Suddenly faced with a future of prostitution simply to survive exceeded anything that she could have imagined about their business dealings. It was then that she realized the fate of the rehabilitated women of Avon. The Sarah House was nothing more than a staging place to clean up young, marketable women. The only women that Hannah ever knew from the Sarah House were old, physically impaired, or very ugly. The more she thought about it, the angrier she became.

She thought about the argument that she had with Esau over the Neptune Company's contract to transport Roman troops to Albion's doorstep. For the first time, Esau raised his voice in anger and told her to be patient and trust him. Esau finally considered Hannah mature enough to be able to understand the company business. *So this is the family business that needed explaining. Did he think that this slave trade would somehow make me forget that we are aiding the enemy? Esau said that I should be patient and trust. Does he not understand that one crime is no less tolerable than the other? I have been a fool all these years. Rome is not Albion's greatest enemy. My family is the greatest enemy within Albion.*

The other woman disrupted Hannah's thoughts. She managed to break free and jump overboard during the channel crossing. She chose death by drowning over slavery. This dramatic display of Celtic courage and pride lifted Hannah's spirits.

The ship docked in a remote area of Gaul where Hannah was loaded into a cattle cart. She caught a glimpse of the ship's faded name as the cart door closed her in. A once grand sea craft had come to a dreadful end in despicable servitude. The warrior princess had refused to cry until that instant. Not one tear for herself, yet a thousand were shed for the other woman, and for her lady-of-the-sea, the *Nova*.

The cattle cart bumped along for a short distance to the slave market where Hannah lost her clothing and gained chains to wear. It did not take long before someone bought Hannah, and less time for her to be shoved into a Roman

PART 5—SPREADING THE WORD

chariot. She thought, *Marcus has come to my rescue.* Instead of Marcus, her tall dark master cracked his whip and the chariot left the market behind. Once out of sight he pulled over, released the chains, and handed her a full set of clothing. They continued on their way after she dressed and had some food and drink.

"You do not need to be afraid. My name is Cornelius. Do you understand me?"

"Yes, I understand. Thank you, Cornelius. Where are you taking me?"

"We are going to my home to meet my family. They are waiting for us. I know that they are going to like you because you are obviously a woman of quality. We will be interested to learn what happened to you."

A few miles later, the family greeted Hannah as though she were a long lost family member. It was reminiscent of her Currcroft homecoming years before. "Cornelius, you cannot imagine how happy I am to meet you and your family."

"Oh yes, we do know how happy you are. First, let us remove that iron band from around your neck, and then we will see how we can help you."

"I don't know why you are helping me, but I am not happy to learn that free Celtic women are being kidnapped and sold by my family's business."

Hannah was momentarily silenced as the neck shackle was released, but not without giving her a painful pinch. "Ouch! Thank you. I feel much better now that that thing is off. Why are you and your family helping me?"

"We are helping you because we have personally experienced the injustice of slavery. Both my wife and I were slaves. As a Roman military conscript, I was awarded my freedom for extreme valor in the face of the enemy. Later, I saw my future wife at the slave market, and it was love at first sight. I bought her, freed her, married her, and I have been her slave ever since. We buy slaves whenever we can and release them when they are ready. Many of them live here in Corneli Village."

"Cor-nel-i-us; that is an interesting name. I have never met a Cornelius before."

"I was named after the Roman dictator Cornelius Sulla who preceded Julius Caesar a century ago. His one humanitarian act in life was that he emancipated ten thousand slaves as a reward for murdering their masters, who

THE FIRST MISSIONARIES

were the enemies of Sulla. My ambition in life is to unconditionally free more than Sulla's ten thousand slaves."

"And for that, I am in your debt. I will see that you are repaid one hundred fold. For now, can you help me go home? I am ready."

"Yes, we have a way to do that. Where do you want to go?"

"I wish to go back to Caledonia to the small coastal village of Midian north of Avon."

"We will make the arrangements and see you off as soon as possible. I can promise to deliver you to some place in Caledonia. You will have to find your way to Midian from there."

"I can do that. Where is your home, Cornelius? Your accent is familiar to me."

"It is a place far from here called Caesarea."

"Oh yes, just one day by horseback north of Joppa on the coast. Would you please take some messages back there for me?"

"Hannah, have you been to Judea? Can you read and write? Who are you?"

"I am Princess Hannah of Aberdonshire."

"As I said earlier, you are obviously a woman of quality."

The promised boat was ready and waiting a few days later. "Thank you for rescuing me, Cornelius, and please thank your family for me."

Hannah was beaming with happiness, and she began laughing with joy.

"It is good to see that you are so happy," Cornelius said. "What has made you laugh?"

"I feel as though I have forgotten something important. The only things that I had when you bought me were a shackle and chain. You may keep those rusty old things."

"Yes, you are leaving with more than you had when you came to Gaul, including a smile. We miss you already, Princess Hannah of Aberdonshire. Come back when you can and tell us more."

Hannah talked to God as she boarded the small craft. *Father in heaven, you promised to be with me always. Why did you forsake me when I needed you? Why have you let this happen to me, your daughter? Why did I have to come all the way back to Gaul only to return to Albion? Ah, I see, it was so that I could learn about the slave trade. Thank you, Lord, but I rather not have known this truth.*

PART 5—SPREADING THE WORD

She settled into her seat and turned to wave goodbye. Cornelius, his family, and many of the villagers lined the shore waving back to her. She smiled as she recalled the same scene on the shore of Dragonfly, and she said another prayer, this time aloud. "Thank you, Lord, for these dear people and the people of Dragonfly where you sent me to share your message."

No sooner had she uttered those words than she knew what she needed to do.

"Boatman, turn around—I must go back!"

"Sorry, ma'am, but I am expected on the other side by evening. The wind is in our favor, and we will miss riding the tide if we turn around. Time and tide do not respect anyone. Did you forget something?"

"Yes, I forgot who I am."

The boatman looked at her as though she was crazy but said nothing. Hannah prayed, *Dear almighty and powerful Father, how will you ever forgive me for not seeing or listening? I did not tell the other enslaved woman about you, or the guards, or the auctioneer, and I especially failed to tell Cornelius and his people about you. That is why you sent me here. I forgot who I am in you because of my anger. I could have already repaid Cornelius a thousand times over with the greatest gift of all gifts: you. The other woman would be alive today if she knew the joy and hope that you bring. How could I have been so blind as not to see your hand in this?*

Later that week, when she arrived in Midian, it appeared to be just as she had left it four years earlier. This time, Hannah made her entrance in the daylight as she waited for the message center to open, except, it did not open that day. Then she realized that it was the Sabbath, and immediately she headed east toward the synagogue. Everyone was already inside, so she decided to wait at her family's home instead of disrupting the worship service.

Later, a young boy ran to Haggai and said, "Rabbi, come quickly! There is a strange-looking Gentile woman sitting on your stoop!" Everyone followed closely behind the rabbi.

"Hello, there. May I help you?"

"Shalom, Haggai! Where is Leah?"

"Hannah? Is that you? No, it cannot be you."

"It is I, Hannah, previously known as Nova. Do you have a horse that I might borrow?"

"Hannah! When and how did you arrive here? Look at you; what has happened? Where is Samuel? If it is you, where is you torc?"

"I do not want to talk about it right now. Allow me to rest before telling you everything."

After resting, she called Haggai, Leah, and Marsha to meet with her for a private conversation. "Before I begin, please tell me about yourselves since our last time together."

She listened to the stories of their lives, hoping in vain to hear of dreams that would have prepared them for what she was about to say. "You are my three dearest friends, and I pray that will be true after I tell you everything."

Hours later, Haggai said, "For now, let us keep these things between us. Give me time to think and pray about what you have told us, Hannah. I am not willing to believe that Esau is the man you've described him to be."

Five days earlier and south of there, Esau had stopped by the Israel House for dinner and for their family business meeting. There was a great deal of company business for the four of them to discuss. It was long past the time for Hannah to learn of their global plans.

A house servant answered the door. "Please let my nephews know that I am here," Esau said.

"Captain Esau, they are not at home, sir. They are not expected back for several days from now."

"Oh, then please tell my sister-in-law that I am here."

"Sir?"

"My sister-in-law Hannah, Israel's widow. What is wrong with you, man?"

"Sir, I think that a terrible mistake has been made. Hannah has not been in this house for years."

"What?"

Esau immediately organized a search and reward for the recovery of Hannah. Shortly afterward, the accusing elderly woman from the Sarah House quickly came forward and explained everything that had happened mornings earlier at the Sarah House. "Sir, what she said about my son being killed in a horseback riding accident; it was true, then?"

"Yes, it was."

"Sir, how will she ever forgive me?"

PART 5—SPREADING THE WORD

"Knowing Hannah, she already has forgiven you. Because of your son's sacrifice, you are no longer destitute. Where is your home?"

"I had a croft north of here, but I lost it because I no longer have a husband or children to help me."

"You may stay here until I find something more comfortable for you. In exchange, I want to return the torc to Hannah."

The two guards and household servant were also quickly sorted out, standing before Esau and giving their sides of the story. The house servant was simply doing his duty. The guards, the ship's captain, and the crew were a different story. "All right, I need you two guards to come with me to Gaul so that we can correct this travesty. I will have all your heads if any harm has come to my sister-in-law."

Of course, Esau knew that something unforgivable had already happened. The slave market auctioneer remembered the sale of a woman matching Hannah's description. He told Esau that a Roman soldier had bought her. From there, Esau continued searching in vain. His thoughts were plagued with fear. *If Marcus or one of his men finds out about this, they will kill me. Why did I not walk her home that evening? Perhaps I will save everyone the trouble and kill myself.*

In Midian, Hannah was preparing to leave for Asbury. After collecting some travelling money, she selected an amber-colored stallion from the messenger service stable. "Haggai, would you please have a message sent to Esau saying that I will pay him back." Haggai and the others naturally thought that she was speaking of the horse, tack, and money. Instead, she was speaking of the untold number of Celtic women who had been sold into prostitution through the Sarah House. She mounted her horse saying, "I will return as soon as I can, and we will talk more then."

Addressing the crowd that had gathered to see her off, she said, "Thank you, everyone! Shalom, everyone. May the Lord bless each of you. I will come back to you soon."

While holding her horse's mane and looking up at her, Haggai spoke softly. "You must admit that everything that you have told us about your Jesus is hard to believe. You returned without Esau or Samuel when we were looking forward to Samuel and his mother's return. You are confusing us by claiming to be the mother of a man that is older than you appear to be. Even the things that you have said about Israel and Esau are not believable. It all brings back the memory of your returning to Midian without our David and Jonathan. Please, give us a little time to adjust."

"Who do you say that I am?"

"You are little Nova and our Hannah, of course. I have known you since you were fourteen, and look at you. It is eighteen years later, and you are as you were back then. Your appearance and stories are frightening to us. Everything will change if there is any truth to what you have said."

"Then brace yourself, because everything is about to change, and I long for the innocence of Aberdonshire before it does. Shalom, Haggai."

"How can you say shalom and then go away angry? Please, I beg you to stay. Hannah, please stay. Stay until at least the Shavuot is over and you have spoken to Esau. I am sure there must be another explanation for what has happened to you."

"Thank you, Haggai. No explanation is required. I am finished talking."

Soon after, she found a man mounted on a white mare and an older woman waiting for her at the bridge. "Well, Moses, I guess there is no talking you into staying here?"

"I am not going to miss an opportunity to ride with Samuel's mother, otherwise known as Nova. Besides, he would want me to look after your safety."

The two women exchanged polite smiles because they knew that Moses would be safe while traveling with Hannah. "And Marsha, my friend, what do you have to say about this?"

"You are the two people that I love most. Will you promise to come back if I let my two favorite people go?"

"We will if it is the Lord's will."

As they rode together, Hannah asked Moses, "What will you give me if I can guess the name of your white mare?"

"I am sure that you will say that it is Epona. And what is the name of your red horse?"

"I am uncertain. It is either Mars or Aht."

"Aht?"

"Aht means horse in a land far away."

PART 5—SPREADING THE WORD

"Choose Mars. Horse is not much of a name for such a noble beast in any language, and Mars is a better match to the red-haired Warrior Princess who rides him."

They entered Asbury later in the day to find that it had decayed even further. The couple rode and walked freely throughout the Asbury area without seeing one person. "Well, Moses, our destination was to be Aberdon, but on second thought, I want to visit my property in the mountains. I need some calming solitude among the spirits of my ancestors. What do you say? Would you like to see the mysterious birthplace of Nova, Daughter of the Light?"

"Lead the way, Warrior Princess."

"This is going to be a new adventure for me, too. I have never gone directly from Asbury to my mountain birthplace of Elcurrest.

Hannah sighed as she gazed around at the desolation of Asbury. "I would like to return here someday to take part in its restoration. I wish that you could have known it and its people years ago. It was a magical place."

Over in Gaul, Esau was still frantically looking for Hannah when her message arrived in Avon. As time passed, the message remained unopened. Eventually, it was lost in a pile of other messages.

During the journey, Hannah brought Moses up to date on everything that she knew about Samuel, Judea, and Jerusalem. Then she told him about Ruth, Orpha, and the Romans. "You heard everything that I said about Jesus. What did you think?"

"I am just about as lost for words about him as I am in this wilderness," Moses admitted. "Are you certain that you know where you are going?"

"I am as sure of where I am going as I am about what I am saying."

"Princess, was that intended to comfort me or frighten me?"

"It was these same waters that led me to Aberdon and from there to the ends of the earth. Don't worry, Moses, you will not be lost and wandering about in this wilderness for forty years."

In the evening, Hannah and her escort made camp in the foothills below her mountain home. The following morning began with a breakfast of oatcakes and goat's milk in preparation for another ride. "Rest here today, Moses. I will be going on alone from here, but I will be back before nightfall."

"Hannah, you are my charge. I cannot leave you, and besides, you promised to show me your birthplace."

"You are right. Just remember that this is the home of my ancestral spirits. The spirits of these trees will not allow any harm to come to me. However, they do not know you. So, stay close to me, and do not touch the mountain or anything on it lest you be struck dead. You are my charge from this point on. We are in the pinewoods, and we should reach the Cairngorm Plateau by midday."

"Just lead the way, and stop trying to scare me. I will not be afraid."

Hannah and Moses did arrive in Elcurrest later that day, expecting to find it overgrown. Instead, it was obvious that someone had transformed the old village into a beautiful apple orchard where the deceased clan members could rest in peace. In the center of the orchard stood a large dolmen that protected the graves of King David Curr, his Queen Jucurr, and their daughter Elcurr.[64] Living relatives could sit there and reflect on the endless cycle of life. The only sounds came from the birds of the air and a gardener pruning trees close by.

"Hannah, would it be all right if I went exploring while you visit your family grave?"

"I don't see why not. The spirits seem to like you. Nevertheless, for my sake, please don't leave the orchard. Let us agree to meet back here halfway

---

[64] Dolmen: a structure regarded as a tomb, consisting of two or more large, upright stones capped by a horizontal slab of stone.

PART 5—SPREADING THE WORD

between now and dark. The entrance to my family cavern is directly across the orchard from here. See if you can find it."

Hannah sat on the grass beside her family's dolmen. "Grandfather, you have a peaceful place here to rest. I promise to have a new engraving made. It will read King David Curr, Servant of the One True God. Grandmother, I am planting your favorite flower, the blue hydrangea, the one I call the snowball flower. Hello, Mother. To the best of my ability, I have kept my promise to become the woman who would make you proud. I suppose that you already know that this place bears your name: Elcurrest. I have missed the three of you. Rest here in peace until we meet again, my dear family."

Hearing a noise, Hannah looked up to see that the gardener was seated on the dolmen for a meal of bread and wine. "Hello, sir. I want to thank you for this place that you have made for my family, but please do not eat your meal on my family's grave. It is disrespectful of the dead."

"I know your mother and grandparents well. If Curr were standing here right now, what would he say to you?"

"Surely, you intended to say, 'I **knew** your mother and grandparents.' To answer your question, King Curr would say, 'Nova, come sit at our table and eat with us. A great feast has been prepared in your honor'."

"Then come and join us, for a great feast has been prepared for you."

"You are right. That is what all three of them would want. I'm baffled about something, though. You say that you knew them well, but I do not remember you or recognize you."

The gardener made no reply because he was rubbing his hands and wincing in pain.

"Oh dear," Hannah said, "I see that you have cut your hands. Let me look after them for you. How did you do this?"

"That old tree over there never did bear good fruit, so I took it down and threw it into the fire. I suffered and bled because of it, and now it is finished.

Now daughter, come to me and find rest. Share my bread and wine."

Hannah's eyes expressed culinary delight as she bit into the bread. "I once had bread exactly like this bread in a place called Judea. It too was so good that I called it the king's bread. Have you ever heard of Judea and Jerusalem?"

"Yes, I have even wept over Jerusalem. Look over there. See how that hen gathers her chicks under her wing? That is how I feel when I think of Jerusalem."

Hannah could only see the large gap between his teeth, his dirty clothes, his bleeding hands, and the messy hair on his head. She had become too angry and filled with hate to recognize him or to listen when he spoke. "Oh, really? **You**, a gardener, have been to Jerusalem? That seems hard to believe. Would you excuse me? I am worried about my friend and must go look for him. He does not know the way. Thank you for your bread and wine."

"Wait! Do not turn your back on me. Don't be angry or anxious about anything. Hannah, come back to me."

"Yes, sure, I'll see you later, gardener. Would you please tell my friend to wait with you if he shows up here?" *He called me Hannah. I really am getting old. I do not remember telling him my name.*

She continued walking and made her way to the family cave while Moses found his way back to the dolmen in the apple orchard. She called out. "Moses, where are you?" No response to her plea gave her a frightening thought. Surely, he would not have ventured into the cave alone.

At the dolmen, Moses was just as perplexed at Hannah's absence. When he saw the gardener, he approached him and said, "Hello, sir; have you seen a young woman around here?"

"Why, yes, Moses. Hannah wants you to stay with me until she returns. Come sit, and have some of my bread and wine."

"That sounds good to me. I am hungry. I just realized that today is Shavuot. It is an annual day of remembrance for my people. Would you allow me to tell you about it?"

"Moses, I would love for you to tell it."

Moses did not see the gap between the gardener's front teeth, the dirty clothes, or the blood on his hands. He only looked into the gardener's eyes of peaceful purity and heard only sweet music in the gardener's voice. "Give me just a few moments until I have some more of your bread and wine."

After eating his fill, Moses said, "Ah, that bread and wine was so rich and good that a person could live on it alone. It is fit for a king. Now for the Shavuot story. It is a story that encourages the believer in the One Who Is

PART 5—SPREADING THE WORD

Holy to accept the temporal and the eternal as a relationship with the human condition and to find harmony between the two in one's life. In other words, we as the temporal should be at peace with The One Who Is Eternal, who without any need of us, chose to share His living Word and kingdom with us. Shavuot is celebrated on the fifty-second day after the start of another celebration known as Passover. These celebrations originated over fourteen hundred years ago."

Time seemed to stand still as Moses recited the Scroll of Ruth from memory and told of the presence of God and the giving of the *Torah* to the Hebrew nation through the first Moses. "And then Moses came down from the mountain top, and his face was radiant because he had been with the Lord. Ever since then our people recall these things and then pray for the Creator's spirit to rest on each of them" (Exodus 30-34 & Joel 2:28-32).

"Oh, excuse me, Moses. I take pleasure in the Shavuot tradition, but it reminds me that I must return to my father's house. After I leave, then the Spirit of my Father can rest on you." The gardener stood and placed his hands on Moses's head and prayed. While Moses drifted off into deep Shavuot meditation, the gardener slipped away to the Eye. He met Hannah as she was nearing the Eye.

"Oh, there you are, Hannah."

"Sir, have you seen the young man who was with me earlier?"

"Moses? Yes, he is waiting for you at the king's table. First, come walk with me to the gateway." They walked and talked together all the way through the narrow gateway as though they were old friends.

"This place is my home and treasure," Hannah said. "It is where my heart is. It was this place that gave my people life, and it is here that they come for their final rest."

"Yes, I can tell. Your heart is here with your people. How quickly you have departed from me. I have given you an abundant life, and it is only within me that you will find rest. Your anger has made you so blind that you cannot see and so deaf that you can no longer hear."

"I'm sure that you are right, gardener. Thank you for looking after my land and my family. Oh, sir, don't go that way. That is the Road to Nowhere. Many lost people have gone that way."

"Yes, I think I have lost one of my lambs around here."

THE FIRST MISSIONARIES

"Be careful. That is a dangerous road. One lamb is not worth losing your life."

Hannah turned and began walking back toward the orchard. She heard the gardener bid her farewell with unexpected words. "Nova, Daughter of My Light, remember: Do not be anxious about anything, and know that I am with you always, to the very end of the age."

She turned sharply back toward the gardener. "What did you say? Sir, where are you? Where did you go? Did Moses tell you my names?" She was still confused as she returned to the dolmen, where she found Moses meditating in the presence of the Lord.

"Moses, I am so glad I found you!"

She stopped suddenly in front of Moses. "Oh, Marsha is going to kill me for this. Moses, what has happened to you? Moses, speak to me! What has happened to your face? Your eyes are as fire! What has that man done to you? Moses, please speak to me, and tell me what has happened here?"

"While you were lost, I received the Shavuot blessing. The Holy Spirit of God the Father has come over me."

At first, Hannah was jealous of the blessing that Moses received, and then she was filled with grief over her neglect and rebellion against God. "Forgive me, Father, for my anger and hatred has blinded me and separated me from you. I have placed the things of this life first and you second. I am your lost lamb on the Road to Nowhere. Each day, Esau sells my people. Each day the Romans gather at Albion's gate in preparation to plunder, destroy, and kill my people. Each day, I try to forgive them, and each day I fail. You have shown me how to love my enemies, and still I seek their destruction. Each moment of every day, I fall short of your glory. I have taken pride in openly proclaiming your Holy Name and have defamed it with the hate and anger of a hardened heart. Please forgive me, Lord, for you know that I am sinful. Continue to teach me your ways; let your Holy Word light my path. Open my eyes that I may see you. Open my ears that I may hear you. Soften my heart with your love once more. Elohim, have mercy on me, for I am a sinner. Lord, I have fought my final battle against your will. I surrender to your purpose for my life. Amen."

"Excuse me for interrupting your prayers, Hannah, but it has grown late. Where are we going to spend the night?"

PART 5—SPREADING THE WORD

"Come with me, and I will show you that birthplace of mine. We will sleep there."

"Are we to spend the night in a graveyard?"

"No, we are going to spend the night in my family cavern. It is the safest place on earth."

"How is sleeping in the ground better than sleeping on the ground of a graveyard?"

At the cave entrance, Hannah found and lit two torches. "We will enter through a narrow passage that will lead to the grand chamber. Here, take this torch."

Upon entering the darkened depths, Moses said, "This cave has a forbidding odor. It is as though we have entered the Gates of Sheol."

"Hardly, this is my birthplace within Mother Earth. For me, that odor is the aroma of home."

"Even our dancing shadows on the walls are eerie," Moses said, hesitant to go deeper into the cavern.

"Oh, they will not harm you as long as you are with me."

"On second thought, that graveyard has become inviting. Did I tell you how much I love to sleep outside in the fresh air?"

"Listen to you. What happened to 'I will not be afraid'? Be not afraid, for God's Holy Spirit dwells inside you. The shadows that you see dancing on these walls are only shadows of the past. Know that God is always with you. We are here. Everything we need should be hidden up here out of the reach of mice and rats. It is high on this rock that we will find rest."

"I hear what you are saying Hannah, and yet this 'safest place on earth' still frightens me. I am ready to listen. This would be a good time to tell me more about God the Comforter and the Christ."

Hannah spoke God's message of a king who left his throne in heaven to be with his people so that they might have life and have it more abundantly in him. Finally, she slipped into a dream where she and Moses stood in a great light surrounded by darkness. Voices cried out from the darkness. "Why have you come here?" "What is that great light that you have brought to us?"

Hannah's mouth was closed, and Moses answered, "We have come with the Light of the World."

Moses woke the next morning to find Hannah preparing to leave Elcurrest. "Good morning, Moses. See, I told you that you would be safe."

"What are you doing, Hannah?"

"I'm restocking the supplies that we used so that they will be here for future visitors."

"No, I meant what are you waving at, and who are you talking to?"

"Oh, it is an old family tradition. It is the way we say goodbye to our ancestral spirits that haunt this cavern."

Moses looked all the more skeptical. "You are really scaring me. Could we leave this place now?"

"Speaking of scary, there is something you should know about me. I often dream, but rarely remember my dreams. Those that I remember actually occur in the future, and I had such a dream last night."

"What was your dream about?"

"I dreamt that you are going to share the good news of God to souls living in darkness."

"All right, then, no more wine for you, Warrior Princess."

To Moses's relief, they reached the end of the cave within minutes and stepped outside into the sunlight. "Finally, it is good to be back outside in the fresh air and sunshine again. I have never been happier to see a graveyard.

It is cold up here, especially in the morning. It feels as though autumn is already in the air. The horses have enjoyed the orchard. Have you decided on the name of your horse?"

"Yes I have," Hannah said. "Epona, meet Phoenix."

Hannah wanted to visit Fort Aberdon, but that would have to wait until Moses was safely at home in Midian. The shortest distance between the two points was a straight line that carried them through the hearts of the Albion people. It was a slow ride back to Midian. It seemed as though every door opened to an obvious pair of "white Druids." The pair had a regal appearance, with Hannah's beautiful, long red hair and Moses's radiant face and youthful hair that was already beginning to show streaks of white. Staying in some places for weeks, they told the story of how God found them, and many of the lost listeners believed and were found. Faith, hope, and love enriched their lives. Burdens were removed, and life was bright and no longer a drudgery. With changed hearts, they toiled with joy as they worked for the glory of God.

PART 5—SPREADING THE WORD

Leaving the highlands behind, they were halfway home, and it was already the time of the Samhain celebration when they reached an area that centuries later would be known as Stirling. Druids gathered there from as far away as Gaul to celebrate this magical time of year. They formed a circle on a sacred meadow as music specifically arranged for this occasion played. Many omens and dreams foretold of a great spiritual event that would occur in that place at dawn of the Samhain full moon.

Villagers along the way had told Moses and Hannah that the Druids were gathering directly south of them. "It is the annual gathering of the Wise Men of the Oaks." This was something that the couple was so interested in observing that they traveled through the night and reached the gathering point just as the first light brightened the sky, and the full moon was setting. "Moses, there they are." The two riders approached the outer circle in hopes of gaining a vantage point to observe the pagan ceremony. At that magical moment, both circle and dawn broke, spotlighting the messengers of God.

"Moses, we have ridden straight into my darkest dream."

"Hold fast, Hannah, and have a little faith. Dismount here and walk into their sacred circle directly to where that old Druid is standing. Remember that our Lord is an omnipresent God and that He will never leave us or forsake us. He is standing right here beside us. The evil in this place will not prevail against us."

The old, blind Master Druid stood facing the rising sun with his arms outstretched to welcome the new day of the Samhain as the intruders walked toward him from the west. Still walking, Hannah whispered, "You know that we have left no way to escape. This will be the day that we die once they find out who we are."

"Warrior Princess, after all that we have been through, how could your faith be so small?" The old Druid turned to face the couple coming up behind him, and Hannah broke her stride into a run toward the Druid.

"Hannah, don't harm him!" Moses called out, afraid that she was about to attack.

Hannah threw her arms around the old Druid's neck and exclaimed, "Uncle Eli, I found you! I have missed you so much!"

"Little Nova, you have returned again! I am blind, and it is only now that I see that my brother King David Curr was right. Your god is God!"

THE FIRST MISSIONARIES

Raising his voice, he proclaimed. "My fellow brothers of the oak, I have known this eternal being even before her birth. This is Nova, Daughter of the Light!"

Some of the Druids and bards gathered around Moses and asked, "Why have you come here?"

"We have come to learn about your religion and culture. Afterward, if you are interested, we will tell you about our spiritual beliefs." Even there, Moses shared the good news of God. A few believed, many doubted, and most people refused to listen.

Druid Elymas also asked Hannah why they had come to the Samhain gathering.

"I have important information to share about the enemies of Albion," she said, speaking quietly.

Elymas summoned all the senior Druids together in response to Hannah's news. She shared everything she knew about the Romans' plans to invade, and she told of how the Celtic people of Albion were being enslaved. She also told of how the Neptune Trading Company was actively making a fortune transporting Roman troops to Albion's front door. "Every chieftain must know of these things and of the Roman crimes across the earth."

"What do you propose that we do about these invaders and your brother-in-law?" Druid Elymas asked.

"We must prepare to defend ourselves. To do that, we will need Esau's ships and money to fight the coming invasion. A delegation of noblemen must appeal to his patriotism. Awaken and arise, Albion! The enemy is at our door! Over the past four hundred years, we have allowed these Romans and others to drive us westward across the earth until our backs are to the sea. Where are we to go westward from here? Are we to drown in the sea or stand and fight? I say that we take our stand here and give death to Roman tyranny, death to Caesar, and death to Celtic enslavement. Long live freedom! How say you all?"

Elymas responded for everyone. "It is an excellent military plan. Remind me never to make you angry. Nova, may I speak with you in private for a moment?"

Uncle and niece sat by themselves as the others discussed everything that Hannah had reported to the Druids. Elymas began their conversation with a

PART 5—SPREADING THE WORD

sharp tone in his voice. "I introduced you as Nova because One-God Hannah would not be welcome here."

"Your apprentice, Phymas, knows who I am."

"Don't worry about him. Druid Phymas was not able to attend this gathering because of urgent family matters. Hannah, where is your God in everything that you have told us? You have always said that He is love. I did not hear any love for Esau or the Romans in your words. You have defiled this sacred ground by coming here with murder in your heart."

"As always, uncle, you have come right to the point of my torment. How can I remain silent and allow these Roman barbarians to sweep unencumbered across our land? How do I love those people that seek to destroy what I love?"

"It is a dilemma, especially if you do not stay centered on the eternal. In truth, we Druids seek harmony between the gods, nature, and humankind. Our creed is to respect all living things. That includes those who make themselves our enemies. They, too, were born of Father Sun and Mother Earth. You learned of this Druid love in Currcroft and again in Aberdon. Everything that you have said about the Romans is true. They will not rest until every nation bows at their feet. Accordingly, we have been expecting and preparing for the Romans to invade Albion for years. What surprises us, however, are the two serious charges that you have made against Esau and your stepchildren. You reported that they are enslaving Celtic women and assisting our enemy for profit. What did Esau have to say when you accused him of these things?"

"Esau promised that the four of us would sit down to discuss all the details of the company and its objectives, but I was captured and taken to Gaul before that meeting could take place. God rescued me out of slavery, and I ran home to Elcurrest and now to you."

"We Druids hardly know what to say about the enslavement of Celtic women," Elymas said with a look of deep concern on his face. "We believe you because it happened to you, and our women have been disappearing from the Avon area. However, it is difficult to believe that Esau is capable of such a thing. There must be some other explanation. Still, your enslavement testimony also gives creditability to your report about the selling of Albion for silver and gold. Finally, your husband should have confided in you about the company business and the destruction of Asbury years ago. Not telling you everything was as good as a lie. Instead of protecting you, he planted seeds of deceit by not telling you the whole truth."

"Of course Uncle, they would not dare tell what I found out on my own. What else do you know? Tell me the whole truth."

"I warned you years ago to keep your sacred vow of totally surrendering your only son to God. You reclaimed the child that you gave to God. Your vow is not the only thing that you have destroyed. Israel and Esau spent years strengthening the unity of Albion. Your arranged marriage to Israel formed a close relationship between him and the Celtic leaders of Albion. Israel and Esau have been our greatest and most reliable source of information about the Romans. Everyone here knew them as their friends until your arrival today. It was a strong Albion alliance until you alone brought it into question. Finally and most importantly, you have destroyed your personal testimony of God. You spent years convincing me that your god is God, and now you have forced yourself on this assembly and thrown away your sacred testimony in one angry moment. You seek harmony between man and God on your terms with a sword in hand. Put your hatred aside and be the person he has made you to be. Give him what is his. Your god is not about you. You are to be about him and his love. You have forgotten everything that you have learned."

"Uncle Eli, everything is turned around. I did not expect to have so many Roman friends. I did not expect to be the enemy of my family. I did not know these things about Israel and Esau. Nor did I expect to be the ally and disciple of the Master Druid of Albion and Gaul. Moses and I left Elcurrest on the same path, and I keep straying from it. I am supposed to be the mature spiritual leader, and yet, a child is leading me. He easily takes the high road of righteousness, while I take the low road of destruction. I am the child who wants to learn but does not know how to learn. Uncle, you are correct. I have become the enemy within the Kingdom of God."

Elymas blindly reached out for her hand. "This may sound strange coming from an old, blind Druid, but might I suggest that you seek first the will of your god and learn what he wants you to do? You must rid yourself of this evil. Leave here and go stand beside your family where you belong instead of roaming the countryside with a single man half your age."

PART 5—SPREADING THE WORD

"Thank you, Uncle Eli. I needed to hear these words. I feel much better. You have put my mind to rest except for one thing. What did you mean when you said that my marriage to Israel was arranged?"

"I do not understand why you would ask this question. You must already know that King Curr sent Prince Conan to Abraham of Midian as an ambassador. He presented you to Abraham as an authentic Pictish princess, along with your Grant of Elcurrest and your Champion's Portion dowry. Abraham held your dowry in trust until you were married. We were all surprised by how quickly your marriage to Israel followed your return to Midian."

"All? Everyone knew about my dowry except for me?"

"There it is again: anger. Please keep your voice down. How quickly you become angry. Wait until Esau can answer your latest charge against his family before you become so hot-headed."

"I disagree. It would seem that my anger is long overdue. What more proof do you need of their lies? What a fool I was to believe that Israel loved me for me. What was the value of the dowry?"

"Hannah, calm down. Your anger will cause the end of you!"

"What was the value of the dowry?"

"I cannot say the exact value. However, my brother and I struggled to lift the treasure chest of gold and silver into your baggage cart."

"Its value was probably enough to build a fleet of ships. Eli, I am a fool. Grandfather had to bribe Israel to take me as his wife. That is worse than Cornelius buying me as a slave."

"I must admit that it all sounds criminal. Then again, I think that you must be patient until you have all the facts. Would you please do that for me?"

Hannah did not answer.

"All right, then, let us just sit here quietly and try to calm ourselves," Elymas said.

Meanwhile, several Druids plotted to use the two intruders as a ritual human sacrifice. In response, Elymas embraced Hannah and whispered that she was to leave the gathering immediately. "Save yourself and go now!"

He released her as he called the gathering back into assembly. "My friends, we have had such wonderful blessings during this gathering. It is with great pleasure that I adjourn this year's annual Wise Men Oak Gathering with a human sacrifice. Therein, as the sun sets on our Samhain week of worship, I hereby willingly give up my spirit to join our ancestors. Live in peace, and love one another always."

The sudden departure of the Druid's eternal being stunned everyone including Hannah. She could still feel the breath of his whisper upon her ear, "Save yourself and go now!"

"Moses, Eli is gone. His soul has left his earthly body. Come, we must go now while everyone is distracted by his sudden departure."

"I am right behind you, Hannah. This pagan place of sorcery and golden idols has stressed the limits of my faith. Stay here long enough and anyone would shatter the commandments. So far, your dream has come true. I have shared the light of God's message in a dark place. Please tell me that we escaped from here in your dream."

"Truly, I don't know. I woke before the dream ended. Fear not. I am sure that we are safe. We were led here for me to be reminded of my roots in Druid love and wisdom." The thought caused Hannah to pray. "Dear precious Almighty One of the Universe, thank you for placing Eli in my path and making it bright and straight."

The ending of Hannah's dream must have been good because they went on to teach in the first village that they came to. It was much easier for Moses to share God's message after surviving what he referred to as "that dark place." More villages and weeks passed when Moses said, "Hannah, is it my imagination, or has that same owl been following us since the Druid gathering?"

"Yes, I have noticed her. Hello Flowerface! We see you up there, you crafty old bird."

"Hannah, I want to be home for the winter solstice."

"Midian is not far from here, but I wish it were far away, because I do not relish the idea of facing your mother. You only have a few traces of black remaining in your hair. Could you at least cover your head until she and everyone in Midian recovers from the excitement of your return?"

"They are just going to have to accept who I have become."

"Marsha is going to kill me. I have taken her Moses to the mountain and returned with a stranger in the land."

The people of Midian lit the first menorah candle and prayed, "Lord, please return our son Moses." The next day they lit the second menorah candle

PART 5—SPREADING THE WORD

and prayed, "Lord please return our son Moses." Finally, they lit the seventh candle as the synagogue door opened. Then someone cried out, "Thank you, Almighty One, for Moses has returned from the mountaintop!"[65]

Hannah sat to the side while Moses eloquently gave God center stage. She listened as he described their experiences to the congregation and told what the Lord had done during their journey. He was giving his testimony of how God had touched his life when a thin man with curly, orange-red hair and wearing a light blue cotton shirt burst forward and screamed, "What do you want?"

"What I want is for everyone to know that the Messiah has come. A Jew of the house of David named Jesus has come not to condemn the world but to save the world from sin. We can confidently place our faith in Him and follow His commandment to love one another. That is what I want."

Haggai tapped Hannah on the shoulder and beckoned her to follow him to a private room. "Please come in, Hannah. Sit and listen to what I have to say. My dear, you must leave immediately for Avon. Before you go, you should know that Esau has been here several times searching for you. We told him that you were going to Aberdon when you left here."

"Thank you, Haggai. I plan to leave for Avon in the morning. Perhaps I will confront him there."

"Hannah, stop and listen to me. Don't go away angry. Yes, you must go home right away, but go in the way of the Almighty One. Sit and listen to what I must tell you. Remember that I am your friend, and I have always spoken the truth to you. Esau told me everything. He conducted an investigation into your abduction, and you were correct. The Sarah House was used to find and enslave Celtic women. Esau then enlisted the aid of the Druids to test everyone involved. The Druids, tried, convicted and executed those that were found guilty. The Druid court also exonerated the house servant, Esau, your stepsons, and Israel of any knowledge of this heinous crime. The people they trusted betrayed them. That includes you. Above all, you are the greatest

---

[65] Chanukkah of today was unknown two thousand years ago, and it is unlikely that the nine candle menorah existed at that time. Josephus was first to record the wonderful Chanukkah story in the first century. Historian Josephus wrote about the Maccabees War of 164 BCE in his books *Jewish Antiquities* and *The Jewish War*. Furthermore, the Tanakh does not contain the two Maccabee books (the Jewish Bible). The Maccabee story was later included in the Septuagint and the Jewish writings.

criminal among them. You were and are wrong about the people who love you very much."

Hannah sat listening stone-faced in silence. This was almost more than she could bear. "Hannah, have you been listening to me? Do you understand what I have been telling you? Hannah? Do you understand that you are the one to be confronted?"

Haggai called to his wife. "Leah, would you come in here please?"

Leah came quickly and stopped in the doorway. "Yes, what is it? Oh, I see. You have told her. Haggai, we must take her to Avon in the morning."

Haggai, Leah, and Hannah arrived in Avon on the following evening. Esau's servant greeted them at the door and told them to wait in the courtyard. He went to Esau and said, "Sir, Haggai and Leah are here, and they say that your sister-in-law is with them. Forgive me if I am being too bold, sir, but I didn't recognize that woman as Hannah."

"That will be all for now; thank you. Have the cook prepare a light meal for four then bring it to the great room. I will see to our visitors."

Esau walked to the door and said, "Haggai, Leah, welcome to my home. Please come in, and bring her with you." He gestured toward Hannah with a curt nod of his head.

"You have come a long way, and you must be hungry. Haggai, please bless this food, and then we can talk after we have eaten."

Afterward, Esau began the conversation by saying, "Hannah, first of all, I have something that belongs to you."

"My torc! I have been a different person ever since it was taken from me. I always wore it to remind me of the Lord's protection and of the one who died in my place. His name was Maon.

Haggai told me about the enslavement investigation and the findings of the Druid court. Oh, Esau, how will you ever forgive me? How will the boys forgive me?"

"At the moment, I am the only one you need to be concerned about. The boys, as you call them, do not know the whole story. The greater question is how will Albion forgive you? You accused the boys and me of being traitors of Albion when you said that we were complicit in delivering our enemy to Albion's doorstep and that we were worthy of death because we were sacrificing our nation for a few pieces of silver.

PART 5—SPREADING THE WORD

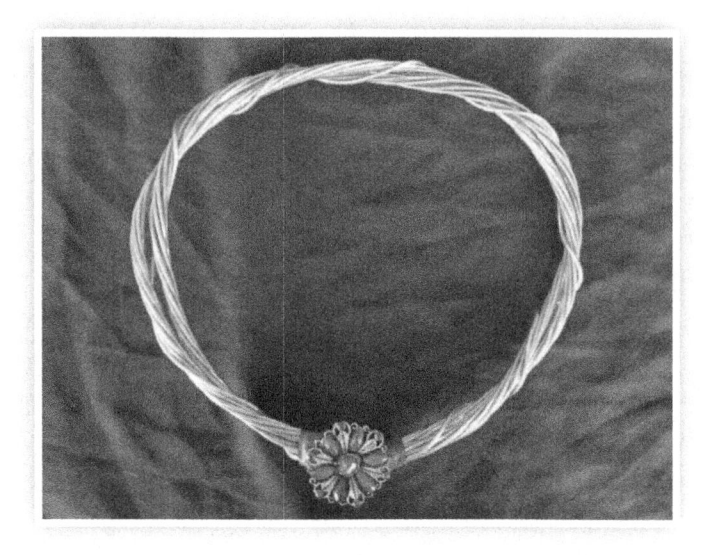

I asked you to trust that what we were doing was in the best interest of Albion. I pleaded for your patience, and I assured you that we would explain everything once the four of us were together again. Then later here in Avon, I apologized that we did not tell you about the details of the Neptune Trading Company objectives. You and I agreed to wait until the four of us could discuss those details together. Unfortunately, you were kidnapped before knowing everything about the company's objectives. I am sorry that happened to you.

With all that said, let me tell you about some of the business details. For your information, we spent years building a fleet and a relationship with Rome. They trust us even if you do not. So great is their trust in us that we have been granted free access to all Roman ports. The irony is that we were waiting for the right time to use that trust against the Romans in a preemptive strike against their homeland seaports and Alexandria. Now, those plans are in turmoil because of your accusations against us.

Your transgressions do not end there. Hannah, my parents adopted you out of slavery and shared their home and family with you. They educated you and stood by you during your Asbury Palace hearing. My brother spared nothing for your sake. He treated you as a spoiled child. He gave and did whatever you asked for two decades, and you betrayed my family the first moment that we needed and deserved your faithfulness and trust. I expected you to share the great message of your Jesus throughout Albion. Instead, you went out and spread a great message of slander against the same people who loved you. You rushed home to tell everyone about your Messiah. Well, someone needs to tell you about him. Your Jesus has been tried, convicted, and crucified as a common criminal.

If you decide to stay in Avon, you will be welcome and safe at the Sarah House. You are no longer welcome to stay here in the Israel House. Indeed, how will you ever be forgiven?"

Haggai answered the charges in Hannah's defense. She was too overwhelmed to speak. "Esau, seeing that you have included Leah and me in these revelations, let me ask you a question in Hannah's defense. Why didn't you and Israel include her in your plans years ago? Why were they hidden from her?"

"First of all, you know that it is not our tradition to burden our wives with business details. Haggai, you need to understand that we did not tell her everything to protect her from the truth and the coming war."

Haggai had a ready answer to that weak claim. "In responding to your first point, you and Israel knew that it is a Celtic tradition for men and women to fight and work as equals. She can never stop being a Celt. It is who she is. Furthermore, you did not trust her with the truth, and now you want to know why she did not trust you. You both kept her in the dark about important business matters. What did you and Israel think the result would be? A half lie is still a lie. What was she to think when she was alone, stripped naked, and sold as cattle in a foreign land by Manawyddan company agents? You must forgive her as she has forgiven you of that atrocity!"

"Although there is truth in what you have said Haggai, I am not ready to forgive her. I am too angry."

"Anger is what brought you both to this impasse. Both of you need to let go of your anger!"

"Esau?"

"What do you want, Hannah?"

"Jesus has been tried, convicted, and crucified as a common criminal?"

Esau snorted in disgust. "You have betrayed your family, and your only concern is for some foreign criminal? Yes, Hannah. Your friend, Centurion Marcus, sent this message to you saying that it is true." He handed the message to Hannah, who read it in one sweep of her eyes.

PART 5—SPREADING THE WORD

Once again, Haggai intervened. "Hannah will be staying with us for a while. Come to Midian to see her if you have a change of heart, Esau, but I am telling both of you: Do not allow this anger and hatred to continue."

Hannah fought through her anguish to ask one more question. "Esau, is there anything left of my dowry?"

"What dowry?"

"Somehow, that is what I thought you would say."

Haggai turned toward the door and took Hannah by the arm. "All right, that is enough anger. Come with me. I will see you to the Sarah House for the night."

How the first followers of Jesus coped with the news of His crucifixion is unimaginable until one experiences an indwelling of God's Holy Spirit. The shepherd was struck, and His flock was confused, heartbroken, and scattered. At the time of this story, the Jewish people expected to be rescued by the Messiah; especially from the Romans. A fair conclusion would have been that Jesus was not the Messiah because, instead of delivering His people, the Romans crucified him. Believers such as Hannah had their memories of Jesus and the promises of God to carry them through a predictable crisis of faith, and they had one other source of encouragement—one that surpasses all other spiritual experiences. They were filled with God's Holy Spirit. It happened to the followers of Christ on the first Shavuot that followed the crucifixion. God's Holy Spirit rested on the apostles and empowered them to preach and do miracles as Jesus had done in His earthly ministry. This Shavuot experience has blessed believers for more than three thousand years since Moses led the nation of Israel to Mount Sinai. Today it is widely known as Pentecost. (See Exodus 19 and Acts 2.)

Hannah approached the gates of Fort Aberdon months after leaving Avon in despair.

"Who goes there?"

"Princess Hannah of Elcurrest has returned!"

It was Peatcurr that came greet Hannah. "I would say that you have not changed a bit, but then again, you look much younger than when I last saw you," he said jovially. "Come in, and give me a moment. I will tell everyone that there will be a special guest for dinner. They are not going to believe their eyes when they see you." Hannah reached up to put her arms around his huge neck, and he stepped back playfully saying, "Don't hurt me!" Then he embraced his tiny cousin.

"That owl looks familiar," Peatcurr said. "Does it belong to you?"

"I'm beginning to think that I belong to her."

"Where is Makcurr?" Hannah asked, but Peatcurr kept going to the banquet hall, where he prepared a place for Hannah at the table beside Makcurr. Then he returned to the entrance and whispered an announcement to a guard. Hannah waited patiently until Peatcurr returned and offered his arm to escort her. From there, the two cousins paused for the guard to announce, "Welcome home, Princess Hannah of Elcurrest."

Surprisingly, even Druid Phymas seemed happy for her return home. "Come and be seated," he said, "and tell us the secret of how you have remained young while the rest of us have aged so much."

Once all the greetings and dinner were over, a now more mature king asked, "We heard about your Samhain declarations against the Romans and your family of Avon. So Hannah, what are your plans?"

"I have gone out from the river of Aberdonshire to the ends of the earth and returned again to serve my God, king, and country against our foreign and domestic enemies. Please accept my apologies for the things I said against my Hebrew family. I have since learned that my accusations against them were false."

"We accept your apology and were sorry to hear of your loss when Israel died."

Already knowing most of what she was going to say, Phymas baited Hannah with, "Tell us about your god."

Hannah shared her testimony until Phymas rudely interrupted. "Let me understand. You came here years ago with the good news of your one true god. You persisted in this heretical behavior until you were expelled you from the kingdom. Now you return with the news of another one true god. Princess Hannah, you and your new true god are not welcome here."

"The Almighty One is understood in three manifestations or representations as God the Father, God the Holy Spirit that rests on believers, and God the Incarnate."

PART 5—SPREADING THE WORD

"Are you saying that your god is a triskelion?"

"No, God is not some manmade carving in stone. He is the creator of heaven, earth, and all living beings."

"Blasphemy! You gave false testimony against your family during the Samhain celebration, and now you come here bearing false testimony against our gods. You are a witch. You are of the lowest character. The best thing you could do for your god is to never bear witness to him again. To best serve your god, you ought to take up the cause of other gods that you do not worship and witness badly in their names."

Makcurr gently placed her hand over Hannah's hand and cut Phymas short by changing the subject. "Could we put religion aside for a moment? Our army needs her as does the king, clan, kingdom, and all of Albion. You Druids also need her unless you rather we face the Roman armies without her."

King Conan finally found his voice. "Please, sister, she is just one woman. What could she possibly have to offer in our defense against Rome?"

"My king, is your memory so short? Have you not learned anything from history? It was this one woman who conquered Asgard and subsequently placed you on a great throne."

"That was then; this is now, and you will watch your words when you speak to your king."

Conan redirected his attention toward Hannah. "Now, as your king, I command you not to speak of your gods while in my kingdom."

"God is one. If I may not worship freely here, will you deny my right to make my home in Elcurrest?"

"Aberdonshire, Monmouthshire, and the Mountain Territory, that includes Elcurrest, are all part of my kingdom, where your gods are not welcome," Conan said icily.

Hannah persisted undeterred. "God is already in Elcurrest and even in this room. God is everywhere and in every good deed. Even though you can banish or kill me, you will never banish my God. He has been, is, and forever will be in this place."

"Nova, the truth is that I have never liked you. You have never known your place since the instant you were born. Here it is thirty-five years later, and look at you. Have you been born again since then? Your youthful appearance was more shocking than the announcement of your arrival. The Druids of old once proclaimed you a witch. Others called you a shape-shifting demon. In response, your clan defended you against these accusations for years. Now I see that your accusers were correct. You are an old witch that has shape-shifted herself into a bonnie lassie. Years ago, the people of Aberdonshire agreed that your beliefs were heretical. I listen to you today and confirm that you are indeed a heretic. You will renounce these beliefs and your god if you are to remain anywhere in my kingdom."

There was no choice in the matter. Hannah put God first and chose banishment over luxury. "No. I will not renounce the God that I serve."

Her words only antagonized her uncle even more. "Do not even stay the night. Leave my kingdom, and take your heresy with you. I should have done everyone a favor and killed you years ago when I escorted you back to Midian."

For once, Makcurr attempted to be the peacemaker. "Brother, wait! Think about this for a moment. Allow her to stay long enough to tell us what she knows about the Romans."

"No, sister! A heretic or a witch cannot be trusted, and she is both. She has even admitted betraying her Hebrew family. She is the greatest domestic enemy we have ever had, and she is hereby banished from my kingdom forever!"

"Step lightly, brother. You are making a mistake."

Makcurr's intervention was enough to allow Hannah a last word. "My dear uncle and king, might I have one last request before leaving Aberdonshire once more in disgrace?"

PART 5—SPREADING THE WORD

"What is it?"

"In all our years together, I never suspected that you held me in such contempt. With your mouth, you have always blessed me. It is only now that I learn that you have always cursed me in your heart. Please tell me what happened to my dowry that you were to deliver to Abraham."

"I gave it to the old man along with your other belongings."

"Was that before or after you failed to kill me and my child? You never took it out of the baggage cart along with my other things. You kept it for yourself."

"Yes, it is true. I kept your dowry. I had the future of a clan and kingdom to think about. What did you need it for?"

"That is not the point. The point is that you violated the first law of Druidism, and yet now you use it to banish me."

"Get out of my kingdom before I have you killed!"

Several guards and Makcurr escorted Hannah away from the hill-fort. Hannah stopped to pray at the bridge south of Aberdon. "Father in heaven, sear my lips with a hot coal. Can you forgive me for falsely casting dispersions on the blood of your blood. I have done so with one insistence after another to prove that I could not be so wrong or so slanderous without just cause. I have been repeatedly guilty of this trespass, and yet you show me mercy. Why? I accused Israel and Esau of being traitors, and I was wrong. I accused them of being slave traders, and I was wrong. I accused them of stealing my dowry, and now I learn that, yet again, I was wrong. What else could your people be falsely accused of I cannot say.

Dear Lord of lords and King of kings, where do I go from here? I burned my bridges to Avon, Midian, and now Aberdon. The fox has his den, the bird its nest, but I have nowhere to lay down my head. Still, I am better off without a home than in chains or dead. I am free to rise up out of the ashes of my life. Asbury is the only other place that I have known as home. It is a place of ruin and ashes, just as I am. I will go to Asbury to seek my restoration in you, Lord. Amen."

Makcurr came alongside Hannah and put her arm around her. "I have collected some food and money for you."

"I will miss you, Stag Slayer. I will be in Asbury if you need me."

"Asbury is within Conan's kingdom."

"Yes, but you will know where to find me. Besides, Asbury is as I am: ruined. Nobody goes to Asbury anymore."

Hannah symbolically burned the bridge leading southward out of Aberdon behind her. Both women stood facing each other with Hannah on the south side and Makcurr on the north side as the flames leaped skyward between them. Hannah cried out her farewell. "I am proud of you, Makcurr the Stag Slayer! I will remember you forever!"

Peering through the heat wave distortions, Makcurr could clearly see through the snow-like ashes raining down over her kin, and then she was gone again in a smoky cloud. Makcurr stood there as though frozen in time. The wintry scene of Jacurr the Elder's death just replayed before her eyes. "Hannah?"

A week later, Hannah and her dog Caesar were walking Phoenix when they came to a place where a white rose rose up through the rubble of what once was the red-stone Asbury Palace, and she prayed, "Thank you, Father in heaven, for this sign that Asbury is the place for me to take root and blossom."

Later that day, she stood on the beach looking out over the sparkling blue waters with frothy waves washing gently across her feet as she prayed. "Here I am, Lord. I am your daughter in what was once the village of Asbury and far from the sacred dwelling place of my ancestral spirits. I have drifted far from you since Judea. I have been renewed again and again into a deeper faith and commitment to you, Lord, but as you know, it has not been without travail. My life has been one of great earthly loss and greater eternal gain in you. There is no past or present; there is only the future in serving you. What is your plan for my life? How may I serve you in Asbury?"

A crowd of children gathered around her as she prayed. It was a strange sight for them to see an adult with arms raised to the heavens and talking to the air. She turned to find them transfixed at the sight of her praying. "What are you playing?" one of the children asked.

"Could you teach us how to play this game?" asked another. "Where are you from? What is your name?"

With the beach as her classroom and the smooth, wet sand to write on, Hannah taught the children about God until the winter storms began. "Dear Almighty maker of the Universe, please help me find a schoolhouse for these children. You said that if I ask anything in your name, I shall receive it."

A familiar but now scratchy voice interrupted her prayer. "Excuse me, teacher. The summer is over, and you cannot be out here with our children during the winter. Nevertheless, there is a place where you could teach throughout the year. Would you like to see it?"

"Yes, I would. It's good to make your acquaintance. My name is Hannah."

"Yes, I know. That is all that we ever hear from the children: 'Hannah said this' and 'Hannah did that.' I am Atina. I think education is very important, and my grandchildren love you for it.

It has stopped raining. Come, I will show you your place around here."

There was a rainbow framing the ruined building when they arrived. Hannah felt that the rainbow was a sign from God that proclaimed, "I hereby make a new covenant with you. Your faith has healed you, my daughter. Go and teach in my name."

Atina apologized for the storm damage and for it being only one room. "As I said, winter is coming, and at least this building will allow the instruction to continue out of the weather. It will put a roof over your head."

"Thank you, Atina. This is perfect for my needs."

Atina stood silently for a moment, trying not to be rude in the way she was staring at Hannah openly. Finally, she said, "I must say that my sister Star and

THE FIRST MISSIONARIES

I agree that you remind us of someone we knew a long time ago. Her name was Nova."

Hannah continued to speak as though she did not hear what Atina had said. "Oh, thank you so much, Atina. This will make a fine school building. Excuse me, I want to pray and thank my God for you, the children, and this place."

She closed her eyes, lifted her arms, and prayed, "Dear powerful and awesome God, thank you for this beautiful Rainbow Room School and for all the brilliant students who will enter and leave here. Thank you for the challenges in my life that have made me strong in you, Lord. Amen."

Before long, the small community worked together cleaning and decorating the room in every color of the rainbow. One man promised to clean the room each evening, and Star volunteered as a teacher's helper. Out of scarcity, it was largely a school of the oral tradition. In its beginning, there were no books, paper, or pens. It did have a large sandbox and a teacher who spent hours drawing letters and numbers in wet sand. The whole community came together when Hannah told stories from the *Tanakh*, particularly the stories about the fulfillment of its prophecies of the Messiah. One day she was telling them that God sacrificed His son Jesus for the atonement of their sins.

Some of the people began to weep, and finally Atina said, "Forgive us, teacher. You see, this is a cursed land because of our cruelty toward an innocent little girl. How can we ever be forgiven?"

The mood suddenly changed because of Hannah's riveting response. "Go in peace. Your sins are forgiven."

Atina erupted in anger. "How dare you? As you have said, only God can forgive sins. How will God forgive your blasphemy? Who do you think you are to stand there and say that our sins are forgiven?"

"I also ask for your forgiveness for breaking your nose. Can you find it in your heart to forgive me?"

"What did you just say? Would you repeat what you just said?"

"I am Nova, Daughter of the Light. I did not die in the fire all those years ago."

Her words left everyone stunned until Star said, "This cannot be. Look at me. I am Nova's twin sister, and you are half my age. Where did you come from? Nova died in a fire years ago. Who are you?"

PART 5—SPREADING THE WORD

"I have come out of the ashes of my life to tell you about the love and forgiveness of God. I am your sister, Nova, the stable girl you once told to take a new direction for her life. I am the Hannah that God redeemed out of the ashes. On this day, I am gratefully standing here and asking everyone to forgive my sins against each of you."

With her mind totally centered on Christ, Hannah rose up out of the ashes and blossomed for God in Asbury. It was fitting, because Asbury was where she had first heard that she was to love her Lord with all her heart, strength, and mind, and that she was to love her neighbor as herself. From the blessings of a mountain orchard to the birthplace of her faith and back again, only God was with her each step of the way to Asbury. Nova, Daughter of the Light, had returned with the purpose of proclaiming the love and forgiveness of God. Redemption came to a fallen village once founded in faith. The Asbury ministry for children and women began with the sand, surf, and sky as its cathedral. From there, Hannah rose out of the ashes along with Asbury where she found her home, ministry, and redemption.

In another part of the world, the Judean women's ministry had outgrown Ruth and burgeoned into a large organization. Stronger and more dominate personalities had gained control and pushed her aside as a disenfranchised woman of Judea. The situation caused Ruth to pray in desperation. "Dear Lord, the ministry is all that I have ever known in Judea. I promised never to leave you or forsake you. Why have you forsaken me? I am lost without you and...."

"Ruth, are you home?"

"Samuel, is that you?"

"Yes, it is Samuel. I have come to say goodbye. I am returning to Caledonia, and I want you to know that having you as my sister is a happy part of my life. I will miss you."

Ruth answered him in a playful manner. "Samuel, come in here, and I will make us some tea."

They had just begun to talk when there was another knock at the door. "Well, I am the popular one today," Ruth said, and she stood to go to the door.

"Stay seated, Ruth. I will see to the door."

Samuel opened the door to the impressive sight of a massive Roman officer and about twenty of his men. The soldier spoke first. "I am looking for Ruth of Dragonfly or Samuel of Midian."

THE FIRST MISSIONARIES

"I am Samuel, and Ruth is here, too. This is her home. What have we done?"

"Done?" The officer laughed and said, "Yes, I suppose that we do look arresting. No, Samuel, we are not here to arrest you. I come bearing letters from your mother."

Just hearing the word mother brought Samuel to tears. "Ruth, we are going to need a lot more tea and your best wine!"

Ruth rushed to the door. "Samuel, what is it? What is happening? Who is this? Why is he here?"

Roman Centurion Cornelius spoke for a speechless Samuel. "I have come bearing letters from your mother."

Many tears and hours later Samuel turned directly to Cornelius. "Thank you for redeeming my mother and coming all this way from Caesarea. You could have easily had the letters delivered. I will go and find our mother with all haste."

Cornelius was pleased. "That is news worth coming all this way. I will make the arrangements for your safe passage all the way to Midian."

"Midian—my home. I have been gone so long that Midian remains only as a faint dream-like memory to me. Thank you, Cornelius."

"My men and I must return to our Italian regiment in Caesarea in the morning."

"Sir, I am ready to leave for my home in Caledonia as we speak!"

RUMORS OF WAR—CALIGULA

Nova's Age: Forty to Forty-Four

On March 16, AD 37, Roman Emperor Tiberius was murdered. His nephew, Gaius Caesar Germanicus, otherwise known as Caligula (Little Boots) was the chief suspect in the case. Tiberius had a relatively long reign from AD 14 to 37. There was great unrest in Rome as he ruled from his fortress on the island of Capri. During his reign, he had the entire family of Roman Governor Sejanus massacred because Sejanus had become too powerful and was suspected of being involved in a conspiracy against Tiberius. Tiberius also had members of his own family killed. The rich and powerful were in danger during his reign, while common people and barbarians lived in relative security. The death of any emperor was good news to the barbarians in the outlying regions. Even so, hearing that Caligula was the new emperor was very bad news, because Tiberius was sane when compared with his nephew Caligula.

There is a saying that only the paranoid survive. Many of the Caesars, including Tiberius, were not paranoid enough. While the royal family members were crazy to varying degrees, they were not stupid. In the end, the murder of Tiberius proved that his paranoia of the upper class was justified. Such assassinations were becoming traditional even before Julius Caesar was murdered. A half century later, Caligula was correct in thinking that almost everyone of power or influence wanted him dead including his own family. He was safer out killing barbarians than he was in the comfort of his Roman throne room.

Caligula's predecessor Tiberius and the senate left the Roman military in deplorable condition on the northwestern and western fronts. It was up to Caligula to bolster those fronts and expand them. Speaking to his general staff, Caligula said, "The situation with the Germanic and Britannic tribes is an embarrassment to my empire. Those fronts need a surprise inspection by their Caesar." He was correct in thinking that never inspected meant always neglected, as the saying goes. Historians have reported that the emperor gathered two hundred thousand of his closest friends and headed north for a surprise Germanic inspection. They arrived on the Rhine in November only to find the Roman forces stationed there to be more degraded than expected. Caligula found the same deplorable conditions on the western front in Gaul. He probably thought, *It will require several years just to rebuild the infrastructure on these fronts to ensure a successful conquest. The senate will know the edge of my sword over this travesty of neglect.*

There is a time to fight and a time not to fight. Everything has its season, and considering the early Germanic winters and his paper tiger army, this was the season to sow and not the one to reap the bounty of conquest. This was a time to reorganize and bolster the Roman military presence in the northern and western frontiers.

One of the emperor's first actions was to discharge many soldiers including high-ranking officers who had gained their rank through political influence instead of their military record. Caligula discharged them on the grounds of incompetence and failure of duty in the face of the enemy. This decisive action was one of many that served to increase an existing tension between Caligula and other leaders of Rome. He also staged several military drills that served to verify his original assessment. He concluded that his sorry excuse for a northern army was the barbarians' best weapon against Rome. With a hasty Germanic reorganization in place, he turned his attention southward to headquarter in Lyon, Gaul for the winter of AD 39-40.

Once again addressing his general staff, Caligula said, "It will require some time for our legions to be battle-ready along the Rhine. I will inspect our presence there again and expect them to be ready for the spring offensive of 41. In the meantime, while we are here in Gaul, Britannia is ripe for the taking. As you all know, we have been preparing for this invasion at great expense for years. Put your heads together and finalize the plans for the invasion. You have all winter to prepare our troops and material. Keep me informed of your progress. Until then, you are dismissed."

PART 5—SPREADING THE WORD

In Britannia, King Cunobelinus of the Britons was trying to organize his too-little-too-late military forces and his divided sons. Prince Adminius was educated in Rome and welcomed the prospect of a peaceable annexation into the empire. The other three men dealt strongly with anyone or anything they considered as a threat to their kingdom.

"Adminius, you cannot expect us to allow them to walk in here and take control of our land and lives."

"Father, I strongly urge you to send your ambassadors to negotiate and organize a peaceable union with the Romans while they are still abroad. There are many ways that they can enrich our lives only at the cost of tribute. You know that your meager forces are no match against the greatest military force on earth. Will you sacrifice the lives of our people simply to preserve yours?"

"You are no son of mine to surrender without a fight."

"That is what I am telling you. There does not have to be a fight. Welcome them with open arms. Join hands with them for a better future for our people."

"You are a sniveling little coward. Your brothers will be here soon, and I will not be able to stop them from killing you for this treason. Take your men and leave Albion while you can. Otherwise, I just might kill you myself."

"You are underestimating me and the Romans!"

"Get out of my kingdom, and stay out!"

"I will leave your kingdom only to return another day." Adminius did not dare finish his thought aloud. *And when I do return, I just might kill you myself.*

Prince Adminius arrived in Gaul a few days later to submit his strategic military information and soldiers to the service of the Roman Empire. Some Briton Celts wanted to believe that it was only a ploy to lure the Romans into a trap. Nonetheless, it was just as it appeared to be: treason. Caligula responded by exaggerating the Prince Adminius submission. His report to the Roman Senate stated, "All Britannia has been given over to me."

In Caledonia, the Curr clan gathered once more for the winter solstice celebration. Afterward, King Conan met with his advisors to discuss kingdom affairs and to share the latest news. All of Albion was aware of Caesar's proximity. Even so, impatience was growing against Makcurr's constant war cries. Her brother, the king, shook his head in frustration.

"Makcurr, the other leaders are growing tired of your relentless nagging, and I am too. For years, we have been ready for the attack that never comes. We have spent a fortune on an imaginary war instead of building for the future."

"They are coming! I know that they are coming!"

"Sister, your own spies have informed us that they are preparing for another major spring offensive against the Germanic tribes. The northern Roman legions have been heavily reinforced. I cannot even imagine how Rome is feeding them all. One estimate is that they have a force of five hundred thousand warriors. That number cannot possibly be correct. We do not have that many people in Albion. Whatever the real number is, are you suggesting that they are suddenly going to divide their forces and attack both north and west?"

Diplomatic Counselor Hancurr burst into the throne room. "Excuse me for being late, sire."

"Yes, Hancurr, what is it?"

"We have just received a message that there is a massive military build-up of men, material, and ships directly across from our white cliffs in the south."

Makcurr sat back in her chair and folded her arms across her chest. "I told you...."

"I'm warning you, Stag Slayer, don't say it. Right now, our friends in southern Albion are executing your battle plan to allow the Romans to come in without resistance, and then attack their supply lines. At this moment, everything that is immovable is being set ablaze. The question is: can we rely on Esau to do his part in blockading the Roman supply line."

Makcurr did not appear optimistic. "It is a vulnerable plan. There are probably as many Roman sympathizers living down there as there are freedom-loving Celts. It is hard to tell our friends from our enemies. We do not know who can be trusted."

"It is killing you, isn't it Stag Slayer? All right, go ahead and say it. Tell us that we were warned."

"I was only going to say that given the circumstances, I think we are as ready as we can be."

"For all our sakes, I hope that you are correct.

Is there still no word from Hannah?"

There was no positive response to the king's question except for reports of her seen here and there. Master Warrior Makcurr could not let the moment

PART 5—SPREADING THE WORD

go by without an attack. "If it is her help you desire, you should have thought about that before you banished her forever. Perhaps the Druid priests will defend your kingdom."

"Makcurr, you are still angry because the Druids disallowed some of your war plans such as the rejection of your Dirty Legion plan."

"They are great plans. When are you and your Druids going to learn that there is only one rule of war: to destroy the enemy by any means. It is a stupid law that forbids criminals and slaves to fight for Albion. Every one of their deaths could have saved the life of an honorable Celt. It is a righteous way to dispose of our human trash. Instead, when this war is over, criminals, slaves, foreigners, and the insane will be the only people left alive to govern Albion because of this stupid law. My way redeems the dregs of society with honorable deaths while the shires are relieved of their otherwise useless burden."

The older sister, Hancurr, offered her compromise. "Both of you stop your bickering and allow me to talk to the Romans. It is my understanding that the Romans are mainly interested in collecting a tribute from their conquests. Other kings have successfully negotiated with them to everyone's benefit. Send me as your ambassador to negotiate and organize a peaceable union with the Romans while they are still abroad. There are many ways that they can enrich our lives only at the cost of tribute."

Both the king and the master warrior glared at the diplomatic councilor in disbelief thinking, *She can only talk, talk, talk.* After all her preparations for war, Makcurr was prepared to go on the attack. "Hancurr, tell us that you do not expect freedom-loving Picts to allow these foreigners to walk into Albion without a fight."

"Have you thought about how our ten thousand men and women are going to oppose five hundred thousand? The answer is obvious even if there are only fifty thousand. You know that our meager forces are no match against the greatest military force on earth. Will you sacrifice the lives of our people simply to preserve your own? The answer to that question must be no if you love our people."

King Conan was not willing to abdicate his throne at any cost. "Thank you for sharing your insight with us today, Hancurr. Let me think about your diplomatic plan, and we will talk again. In the meantime, would you please find out what is taking so long for our tea to be served? Thank you, sister; please close the door on your way out."

Conan paused until she was gone. "Can you believe that she wants us to bow down and negotiate with the Romans?

"Yes, my king, I hear that there is one in every family."

"Now, back to my question: Is there still no word from Hannah?"

"Why? Have you decided to exonerate her in our time of need?"

"No, my dear master warrior, and one day you will go too far. Stop being the fighter for just one moment. We have received a message for her from her son Samuel. He has returned home from Jerusalem to Midian and wishes to reunite with his mother. Do you know where she is?"

"Yes I do, my king.

Druid Phymas, would you please read the message to me?"

A few days later in Asbury, Hannah was praying. "Dear Lord, I can sense the pressure of war building all around me. It is the quiet before the storm. First the Germanic tribes, then Gaul, and now the dogs of war are coming here to devour everyone they can find. Oh, dear God, save us! This Roman wrath brings war, famine, pestilence, and death to stunt the youth of Albion. Have you brought us this far only to allow us to die with your name on our lips? No! You are El Shaddai, the Almighty One. You have always been faithful to me, and I will be faithful to you. I will trust in you, my Lord. I will not be afraid." She looked out across the channel, expecting to see the sails of death's fleet. "In God I trust. I will not be afraid. Elohim, have mercy on my people and me. It is I, Hannah, Daughter of Your Light. This is your sea and your land, and these are your children; please spare our lives from the winds of war. Save our souls. You are the Great I AM."

"Excuse me, Hannah."

"Yes, Star, what is it?"

"There is a fierce-looking old woman outside with some soldiers. They are looking for you. She said to tell you that her name is...."

"Stag Slayer!" Hannah ran outside and almost knocked her aunt over with her embrace. "What has brought you to Asbury?"

Makcurr told Hannah of the huge military build-up across the channel.

PART 5—SPREADING THE WORD

"Say, that owl looks familiar. Isn't that Elymas's Flowerface?"\
"Yes, she was his owl, but now she's mine."

"Hannah, what would the Warrior Princess do in this situation?"

"The Warrior Princess is dead and thus unable to help you."

"Well, wake her from the dead. We need her now!"

"I cannot help you because of my faith, Aunt Makcurr."

"Please, Hannah, you must join us. Come with me to Avon and Aberdon."

"Those bridges have been burned to me. I can only pray that God will defeat the Romans for us."

"Putting religion aside, it is your patriotic duty as royalty to aid your nation. Tell me how I can prevail if your god favors Rome."

"Well, there is a passive way to defeat them. Allow them to enter our land, and defeat them through assimilation."

"Never! I was once wrong when I called you a coward. I know how much you love Albion. Do you really love your god more than Albion? Tell me: Am I wrong again thinking of you as a traitor?"

"My flesh is willing. It wants war. My spirit is not willing. It wants peace."

"There you go again talking as my sisters have talked. I will name you the Traitor of Albion if you do not take your rightful place and lead us to victory! Please Hannah, I am begging you. Come and join us."

"There is no way that I will put Albion before the command of Jesus to love my enemies."

"I would not be too sure about that if I were you. I think there is a way to persuade you to lead us into battle."

"There is nothing that you can say that would persuade me to disobey my Lord."

Makcurr rebuffed her flatly. "We have your son Samuel."

The tempered banter between dearest friends with differing agenda suddenly turned hostile. "Makcurr! That is a lie. Samuel is in Jerusalem."

Makcurr was ready with Samuel's message for her rebuttal. "Really? He told me to tell you that, "after the Lord, you are the Nova of his life"."

"How dare you use my son in this way? You will regret harming him."

"No harm will come to him. Just agree to help your nation – Warrior Princess."

"Do you mean the nation that banished me forever? What do you want, Master Warrior? What are your terms?"

"I will take you to your son if you promise to lead your nation against her enemy. Come with me to Avon and Aberdon. Once again, I ask you: What would the Warrior Princess do?"

With that, Hannah cast her religious beliefs aside and chose to redeem her son because she would give body and soul for him. "You can be certain that the Romans are coming if they have so many troops at our gate. However, there are advantages for us in their aggressive numbers. One advantage is that they will not cross the channel until spring. Their ships are not equipped to handle our winter waters, and their supply lines are always vulnerable. However, our ships can handle the driving western winds and the winter seas.

Another factor is in our favor. From what you just told me, there cannot be much of a military presence in the Roman heartland. In coming full force against Albion, they have left their back door wide open to Rome. A record time between here and the eastern Great Sea could be set with gale-force winds and the likes of Captains Esau and Noah at the helm."[66]

"You cannot be serious. Have you gone mad?" Makcurr demanded.

"Stop thinking defense, and start thinking offense as the master warrior you are. Think back. We were once a small mountain tribe. With nothing to lose, we attacked and won a kingdom. Now we are part of a small nation with comparably nothing to lose by attacking an empire. Albion must strike first for there to be any chance of surviving as a nation. Your target must be the Roman food source and its supply line. The Nile River Basin is the main source of their food supply. It is the Romans' breadbasket, and it only shuts down for two months in midwinter. Your mission would be to seek out and destroy any vessel large enough to ship Egyptian grain.

We must immediately contact Captain Esau of Avon and organize an invasion fleet. He already has made the invasion plan. It would be of great encouragement to him for us to join forces with his.

Do this and you will teach these Roman imperialists a lesson they will remember for the next three hundred years. Otherwise, only God will be able to save Albion. News of the naval invasion will quickly arrive in Gaul and cause the Roman forces to retract to Rome. That will be the signal for Esau's

---

[66] Ships used a side rudder at this time in history.

Manawyddan Utility Company fleet to attack every Roman ship anchored at Gaul and Albion."

"Hannah, it would be suicide to attack the Romans, especially in winter."

"Why? They will not expect to be invaded by little barbarian Albion at any time of year. Do you not see that our invasion of Asgardshire was only a precursor to this day? Esau has already made a Great Sea extraction plan. There are Jewish Zealots waiting for the invasion and ready to assist in our escape from Alexandria."

"You are the only person who could rally the nation behind such a bold plan. I have never even heard of Alexandria."

"I promise to do what I can to save Albion. Now take me to my son!"

"I have already sent a message to Esau and told him that we are coming. If you promise to ride with me to Avon to meet with Esau, you will have your son."

Makcurr, Hannah, and fifty horsemen crossed the bridge into Midian later that day. Hannah successfully risked a running dismount and charged forward into her family home. She burst through the doorway yelling, "Leah! Haggai! Are you home?"

Leah did not answer. It was another woman's questioning voice that answered from the kitchen. "Mother?"

A moment later, Hannah found Leah with a young mother holding an infant. "Ruth?"

"Mother!"

There was hugging followed by kisses and tears. "What are you doing here, and who is this beautiful baby girl?"

"Mother, meet your baby granddaughter Naomi. She was named in remembrance of you, my best friend, who rescued me with love."

Feelings of anxiety mixed with joy as four souls joined in celebration of reunion and new life. It took several minutes before Hannah refocused on her purpose for arriving in Midian. "Ruth, do you know where they have taken Samuel?"

"Taken? No one has taken my husband any place. Samuel is in the synagogue praying with the other men."

"Your what? He is where? Naomi really is my granddaughter?"

"Oh dear, you better sit down. Samuel is my husband, and this really is your granddaughter."

The mixed emotions became more intense as a red-faced Celtic warrior erupted with, "Excuse me, but I have an aunt to murder and a synagogue meeting to disrupt."

The synagogue meeting was already disrupted by the arrival of so many horsemen at the family home next door. Samuel and Hannah were on a joyous collision course that ended at the front door of the home. From there, Hannah had an issue to settle with her aunt. "Makcurr, you lied to me! Stop laughing! It is not funny."

"I told you that if you promised to ride with me to Avon to meet with Esau, you would have your son. Now you have your son and more. All I did was to show you the order of your priorities, and that is why you are angry with me. Keep your promise and ride with me to Avon. We have family, friends, and a nation to protect. Your god will have to wait."

Makcurr and Hannah arrived in Avon and found only old Esau waiting for them. "You are too late," he grumbled. "The invasion fleet has already gone. Now, all that we can do is wait until the Romans retreat to defend their homeland."

The retreat did not come when expected because the invasion fleet never reached the Great Sea. Instead, the Caledonian Armada sailed into an Atlantic winter storm where Captain Noah addressed the crew of the *Hannah III*. "Men, we have prepared for this day. Today we are great seamen. You know the task ahead of us. If you do your part, we will come out of this storm alive.

PART 5—SPREADING THE WORD

Let's ride the coming tempest all the way to the Pillars of Hercules. Rig the sails to quarter mast!"

The intensity of the storm increased while Noah was on the castle deck controlling the side rudder, and the bow dove beneath the sea for the first time. "Brace yourselves, men. The old king of the oceans, Manawyddan, is in an angry mood today. Come on, my lady—rise, *Hannah*, rise!" And rise she did not. Makcurr was correct this time. It was suicide to attack the Romans, especially in the winter. News of the naval invasion never arrived in Gaul, and the Romans seized Manawyddan Utility Company fleet.

In Gaul, Centurion Marcus led his men in prayer. "Dear Lord our God, we obey your command to love our enemies, and yet these innocent Celts are not our enemy. As a herd of sheep is to a pack of wolves, they are about to be our victims of slaughter. Rome says that they are just subhuman barbarians whose lives do not matter. They matter to you. Give each of us the faith, strength, and courage to do what is right in your eyes. You have always been faithful to us, and we will be faithful to you. We will trust in you, Lord. We will not be afraid. Dear Father in heaven, we pray for your protection to be placed around our sister Hannah and all her people."

Winter passed, warmth returned to the land, and calmer waters flowed in the great channel between the island and the continent. Caligula's mood was bursting into a rage as his invasion forces stood steadfast on the western shores of Gaul. "Commander, why have you not commanded the invasion force to board the ships?"

"My Caesar, the order has been given, and yet the men refuse to follow your command to board the ships."

"What, another mutiny? Do they think that we came all this way just to collect seashells? May Mars damn them all to Hades![67] If that is how they want it, then command the cowards to collect their seashells! I will have all their heads for this. Find out who the leaders are behind this conspiracy and mutiny. Why has this happened again?"

Later that day the commander returned saying, "My Caesar, everyone has confessed to being the leader of the mutiny."

---

[67] Hades is the home of the evil spirits of the dead in Greek mythology and the name of the Greek god ruling over the underworld.

"Kill every tenth centurion and make arrangements for our return to Rome," Caligula commanded, and then he muttered, "How am I going to explain this to the Senate?"

"Forgive me, my Caesar, for saying that your command begs the question: who is strong enough to go out there and decimate the centurions?"

"Perhaps commander, you are a traitor! Ah yes, there it is. You are the man behind this mutiny!"

Makcurr the Stag Slayer and her legion were still waiting on the frontline when word of the withdrawal came. "They are all gone except the Provincial Guard."

She was at once shocked, relieved, and disappointed. "What has happened? Why didn't they invade?" Then she paused as she realized that a disaster had been averted. "The old Druids were right. What would have happened if they had allowed my Dirty Legion plan? There would have been five thousand slaves, foreigners, and criminals trained, armed, and spoiling for a fight. They would have become a homegrown enemy within Albion. Thank you, Uncle Elymas, and all our Druid ancestors for Druid wisdom. Hannah, what do you think? Why didn't the Romans invade?"

"There are several reasons that I can think of. Roman historians will define Caligula as a military genius. I think this is because he has studied us and knows us better than we know ourselves. It is possible that he will return another day and just walk in on the little nation that fell back to sleep. In that case, we have greatly underestimated the pure genius of our enemy.

However, it is more likely that we have underestimated God. I believe that this decision to withdraw was God working through Marcus. His faith always was greater than mine. He and his men surrendered to the will of God instead of obeying the command of their Caesar. They put God first. I know that is what happened."

"What are you talking about, Hannah? In that case, they did nothing. They refused to follow Caesar's command to board the ships."

"That is exactly what happened. Instead of Caesar, they trusted in God and followed His command to love one another, including their enemy. Marcus led his men with the love of Jesus. Their bravery was in what they did not do."

"Who is this Marcus? Are you saying that you have Roman friends?"

"Centurion Marcus and his men are my brothers in Christ."

PART 5—SPREADING THE WORD

"No, you are wrong. I believe that Caligula is a military genius. Therefore, it is Caesar that I praise and not your god. It is also feasible that the invasion failed because the Roman supply line could not support such a huge military demand."

Hannah had to admit to being delightfully surprised to learn that the Lord had won the battle before it had begun. "Hallelujah! Praise be to God! You are a merciful God. On this day, you have spared the life of my nation. On this day, I surrender all to you. Thank you for my centurion friends Marcus and Cornelius and their brave men."

THE HUNGRY BEAR—CLAUDIUS

Nova's Age: Forty-Four to Eighty-Six

Great and mighty bear loves the honey of tiny busy bee.
Bright of day, works honey bee.
Stalks hungry bear, dark of night.
Worker bee, stalker bear,
Which is great, which is small, busy bee, lazy bear?
Oh life be fair, no Roman beast to bear.[68]

In the months that followed the failed invasion, repeated cries that the Romans were coming fell on deaf ears, and the Albion defense program was neglected. Counter to that, Emperor Gaius Caesar Germanicus, also known as Caligula, refortified the Roman presence on the north and western fronts before his assassination on January 24 AD 41, by his Praetorian Guard. The senior praetorian officers and their power brokers had Caligula killed because he was uncontrollable. They needed a controllable figurehead. The obvious choice from the royal line was Tiberius Claudius Drusus Nero.

Most people had never heard of Claudius because his unattractive physical appearance and defects were an embarrassment to his family. Romans held people with skin-deep beauty in adoration while holding defective people in contempt. Some historians credit Claudius with a high intelligence because of all that he said and did. However, those closest to him knew that he was

---

[68] J. J. McCurry originally wrote this satirical poem in the Azeri-Turk language in 1995. The bear, bee, and honey represented Russia, Azerbaijan and petroleum oil in that order. Bear = ayi (ah-yee) and bee = ari (ah-ree) in Azeri-Turk. Therein, ah-yee and ah-ree gave the poem a rhythmic sound.

PART 5—SPREADING THE WORD

only intelligent enough to parrot the lines and directions given to him by his Roman power brokers.

On the western front, the mutinous centurions of AD 41 and most of their men were no longer in Gaul. Caligula discharged some soldiers, transferred others, and still others died of both natural and unnatural causes. They were gone, but their Christian influence remained. They had successfully planted the seeds of the Gospel message in Gaul before their dispersion throughout the known world.

Life finally returned to normal in Albion except for the enormous debt of the war that never happened. The chieftains agreed to resolve this debt by cancelling the lives of their creditors. Israel's sons struck preemptively against their own assassinations by patriotically cancelling the war debt owed to them. When asked why the debt was cancelled, they said, "We have a responsibility to protect our country and its people." While that was true, it fell second to something that their Greek tutor once said: "History has a way of repeating," and they did not want to become part of that dark side of history.

Religious life in Midian was anything except normal. The community had split into several religious factions. Some people remained faithful to the Mosaic Law. Another group of people sought salvation only through faith in Jesus Christ, while others said that a person had to do both, and still others said that salvation came from being a good Christian Druid, and Jesus was their Druid.

Moses of the River Kirk proclaimed that it was all about Jesus. Not a day went by that he did not think about his hero, Nova/Hannah. His mother, Marsha, also thought often about her best friend.

One day Moses said, "Mother, what am I going to do? I cannot stop thinking about her day and night."

"I am tired of waiting to be a grandmother. Go to Asbury and find Nova. Then tell her that you love her."

"She is much older than I am. She is old enough to be my mother."

"Son, stop worrying so much about age. A man is as old as he feels, and a woman is as old as she looks. In that view, she may have already become too young for you. Stop worrying. You are perfect for each other. Now, go find her with my blessing, and make me a grandmother while I am living. And hurry!"

THE HUNGRY BEAR—CLAUDIUS

Moses knew that Hannah was in Asbury and remembered something that she once said to him. "I want to return here to Asbury someday and take part in its restoration. I wish that you could have known it and its people years ago. It is hard to believe that all this rubble was once a magical place."

In that rubble, he easily found the Rainbow Room School—one of the few remaining buildings in Asbury. He stood in its doorway and saw her, the Warrior Princess disguised as a teacher. "Excuse me, teacher, could you tell me the way to Elcurrest?"

Hannah did not look up from drawing a lesson in the wet sand. "What took you so long to find me?"

"Say, what are you doing the rest of your life?"

Hannah stood and walked deliberately to his lips and much later said, "Your mother is going to kill me. Oh, this is going to be awkward."

"You do not have anything to worry about. My mother already knows that I am in love with you, and she told me not to return home without her grandchild."

"Let us take one step at a time. At the moment, there is something more awkward than your mother becoming my mother-in-law."

"What could be more awkward than that?"

"You are the age of my children."

"Yes, I thought of that. It will be strange telling my best childhood friend that I intend to marry his mother."

"It is much more awkward than that. Can you imagine Samuel calling you Father?"

"That would be strange. Is there any chance that he would be interested in marrying my mother?"

"None. Not a chance."

"So, Nova, Daughter of the Light, will you marry me?"

Yes, most everything finally returned to normal in Albion and the empire, but then conquest was normal for the Roman Empire. Senator Cleverous pulled the Roman military Commander Aulus Plautius off to one side. "Placing Claudius on the throne was the smartest thing that we have ever done. Finally, we have been able to make some positive changes. However, the emperor's public image is wearing thin for everyone in the Senate and even for the average Roman citizen. How close are we to confidently invading Britannia?"

PART 5—SPREADING THE WORD

"Senator, we are ready to invade immediately. Since Caligula's withdrawal, we have found that he made all the right decisions. The Picts were ready for us, and the last thing we needed was another military fiasco."

"And how prepared are the barbarians now, Commander?"

"We are sure that they are not prepared. Our withdrawal caused them to drop their guard three years ago."

"Then proceed with the invasion. We will secure our position in Britannia, and then send Claudius there to claim the victory. That should keep him alive and us in power for decades. I will tell him to announce his approval for the invasion."

About twenty thousand (some reports say as many as forty thousand) Roman soldiers stood posed once more to invade Albion. These figures sound more manageable and realistic than those of Caligula's reorganizational campaign. Whatever the real numbers, it would have been reasonable for Caligula to return to Rome with many of the old guard while leaving the new behind. Three years later, however, the change of guard also refused to attack initially. Their Commander Aulus Plautius was determined that the invasion would proceed, and he went among the legions offering encouragement.

"Forget Caesar and even Rome! Follow me, and do this for the glory of our people. Do it for your people—your families! Do it for the future and honor of your children. These Gauls are just over there on the other side laughing at us. They are there making wagers on how fast we will retreat to Rome again as cowards. We can crush these barbarians! So what do you say? Who is with me?"

The imperialists launched their invasion fleet and landed in Britannia with surprisingly little resistance. As planned, Claudius arrived to claim the victory after the establishment of a stronghold in southeastern Britannia. He arrived from Rome to play his part and then quickly returned to Rome to receive all the credit. National propaganda informed the people of the empire that Emperor <u>Britannicus</u> Tiberius Claudius Drusus Nero personally led his armies to conquer Britannia for them. It was quite a show with a victory parade led by elephants through southeast Britannia. Britannicus had succeeded where even the great Gaius Julius Caesar had twice failed, and Gaius Caesar Germanicus (Caligula) had retreated from just three years earlier.

THE HUNGRY BEAR—CLAUDIUS

In albion, Prince Adminius replaced his father as King of the Britons. "I told him that I would be back!" he proclaimed. Adminius spent his years in exile educating the Romans of the strengths and weaknesses of his homeland. History proves that he sided with the prevailing world power. As a result, Rome rewarded Adminius for his treason by placing him on the throne as their man in Britannia.

Once established, the Romans pushed westward and northward in Britannia until they met resistance. Moving up along the coast, they came to a small village where they were welcomed and shocked to find a large wooden cross of the new religious sect known as Christians. Until this period, the Romans had treated foreign religions with a relative measure of toleration. However, the regime of Claudius was harsh on any religion that did not include the Roman gods. Druidic resistance to Roman occupation served to reinforce this Roman intolerant resolve. Consequently, the Romans did not hesitate to destroy anything Druid, Jewish, or Christian.

Centurion Decius looked up from his maps to see a young recruit standing in his doorway. "Yes, soldier, what is it?"

"Sir, we have a report that there is another coastal Christian community just north of here."

"It can wait."

"Sir, it is rumored that the Christian leader is a national hero to these people. Some say that her name is Hannah. Others say that it is Nova."

"I will put it in my report. Command can ask King Adminius about her. Thank you, soldier, you are dismissed."

Just north of there, the reconstruction of Asbury was showing real progress with people and commerce returning. Sadly, the success was to be short-lived. Even as she slept, Hannah knew that she would remember this dream because it foretold an important event. This time she recognized her spiritual dream guide. "Uncle Eli, why have you come to me?" Without speaking, he revealed an imagery of a second destruction of Asbury. The only sign of life was a fire consuming the Rainbow Room School. The image caused Hannah to cry in her sleep until she awoke to find the owl Flowerface sitting on her chest.

"Hello, you crafty old bird. It is time to leave, isn't it?" Flowerface answered her by flying out of the open window close to where Moses was standing. "Moses, I had a dream. We must leave Asbury and return to Elcurrest at once!"

PART 5—SPREADING THE WORD

"I know. We are waiting for you." Hannah was both surprised and reassured to find that Moses had already packed their possessions and was waiting for her with their infant Gideon and Samuel's family: Ruth and Naomi. They stayed in Asbury just long enough to warn their extended family and friends to evacuate. "Star, you, Atina, and the others must come with us."

"We have no desire to live in the ground," Star said. "Go without us. We will be fine."

Hannah removed her torc and fastened it around her twin sister's neck. "I am glad that we had these days together. I want to give you this torc as a symbol of our bond."

"Thank you, Hannah. I have always admired your torc. It is beautiful. I am going to miss you. Please, Hannah, let me warn you once more. I think you are headed for trouble, and I think you ought to change your mind and stay here in Asbury."

"Really?"

"It is up to you. It is your choice. Bye, Hannah."

Soon after Hannah's departure, refugees reached Asbury with the news of Midian's destruction and the torture of its people. Star was then convinced. "Hannah was correct this time. The Romans are coming here. I think it is finally time to reunite with my clan in Aberdon and claim my rightful inheritance. Atina, you, the children, and the others are welcome to come with me."

A few days later, the Roman Commander Aulus Plautius met with Rome's man in Britannia. "Adminius, do you know of a Celtic hero with the Jewish name of Hannah?"

"Hannah! Yes, I attended her wedding when I was a child. Her husband, Israel, was a close friend of my father. She is a legend to these people. My spies tell me that Hannah was not her real name. They informed me that her real name was Nova. Why do you ask?"

"We have a report that she is some kind of spiritual leader north of here."

"Did you say *is* some kind of spiritual leader?"

"Yes, in a place called Asbury."

"If this is true and she is still alive, she is the one person who could unite all the tribes against us. A bounty must be placed for her head immediately!"

It did not take long for the news of the bounty for the traitor Hannah's head to spread throughout Albion. A person could retire with that much wealth. It was too great a prize to ignore. It even drew the attention of some of those who knew Hannah as a friend.

Star and the others settled safely in Aberdon just ahead of the news of the reward offered by King Adminius. One evening, Star was alone in her room when there was a knock on her door.

"Yes, who is it?"

"I am a friend from long ago!"

Star opened the door to find a pleasant-looking woman standing there. "Please come in," she said, baffled about who this stranger might be.

"Hello, Princess, do you remember me?"

"No. Where do I know you from?"

"A great victory celebration was once held for the people of Aberdonshire when I was a child. I remember your torc from that day. You ran and played games with the village children. Later that day, you told my mother that I was good at games and the clever little fox who always knew exactly where to find you. Guess what? I have found you! I am Maggan."

"I'm sorry, but I don't know...." And before she could finish explaining, Star's body slumped to the floor, and Maggan went about the business of harvesting her trophies: a head and a torc. With proof in hand, she booked passage on a neutral merchant ship that carried her south to the white cliffs, and from there she made her way to claim her reward from King Adminius.

"State your business with the king."

"I have come to deliver the head of Hannah and collect my reward."

Two guards escorted Maggan to a courtyard to await her trial along with the other claimants.

"Sire, the real head of Hannah has arrived. I remember her face. The last time I saw her was the day that Prince Conan sent me to your father. Also as proof, the claimant is wearing a torc that belonged to Hannah. I remember seeing it worn by Hannah. Now that we have the real head of Hannah, what should I do with the other bounty hunters? Should I release them or charge them with murder?"

"There are many heads, and only one of them is Hannah's—if it's really her head. Wait until the criminals stop coming to my door. Afterward, hold a public trial before executing all them for murder. No, wait. On this day, I hereby convict and sentence them all to death. Such people do not deserve

PART 5—SPREADING THE WORD

a trial. Because of them, Albion has a sudden shortage of forty-five-year-old women. Our nation will be a better place to be rid of such people who could so easily take innocent lives." He continued thinking smugly. *There is only room for one such person in my kingdom, and that person is me.*

In the far north of Caledonia, Hannah safely returned to her Elcurrest home with her five favorite people, and life was good in the safest place on earth. The family sat outside the cave entrance talking one evening when Moses said, "Hannah, come in and rest now. It is getting cold out here."

"I will be there soon, and it is only cold if you are not wearing enough clothes."

"Was that intended to be funny?"

"Yes, I have always thought so."

Hannah sat alone for a while thinking about everything that had happened in her life. She was often amazed at how lucky and blessed she was. "Father, Ruling Presence of the Universe, I thank you for my life and family. Teaching about you here has been difficult because our time is spent trying to survive. Teach me how to teach about you even in this place. Amen."

The night mountain air finally sent her deep within the dimly lit cave until she found where her family was sleeping high on a cavern rock. "Move over, husband, and keep me warm and safe." Soon thereafter, she was asleep and entering dreamland, running and very cold. She was holding the lead with the other hunters close behind. Earlier, she had only wounded the deer, and now they must make the kill. Her family had only eaten gruel for the past two

THE HUNGRY BEAR—CLAUDIUS

days. This was a pivotal moment for the family's survival. Even the doe could sense their desperation as the hunters and death came ever closer. The runners were very high on the mountain in a place so cold that they did not dare stop.

The elder directed the hunt. "Samuel, you go left. Moses, you go right. Gideon, and Naomi wait here. Ruth, where I go, you go. Everyone remember, take the shot when you can, but not too soon. Take that extra moment then kill." Man and hound were closing in from three sides until Gideon's deadly aim scored one for the family's survival and for every generation to follow. Months of practice had just paid off. He had made his first kill.

The elder urged the others to hurry. "Quickly, let's hack off these legs. All right, that's it. Eat some of this hot liver, and let's get off this mountain before we freeze."

When they began running in one direction, the elder called out, "No, not that way—this way! We are leaving a blood-scented trail that wolves could be following. We will return home another way, but we must hurry. Watch every step you take."

Even while running, Moses could not ignore the bite of winter. "It is so cold here!"

"It is only cold if you are not wearing enough clothes."

"That old joke of yours never was funny, especially now."

"True, but it made you stop thinking about being cold for a moment."

The winter sun faded as each of them carried twenty pounds of meat over their shoulders. "Let me take the lead," said the elder hunter. "I can run this

PART 5—SPREADING THE WORD

trail with my eyes closed." At that very moment, the clouds parted and the moonlight lit the snow-covered landscape.

"Do not worry. Where you blindly go, I will go, but you can open your eyes now!" The six hunters laughed as the entrance to Elcurrest came into view.

Never one for enjoying being at the wrong end of a joke, the leader insincerely returned. "Thank you, Ruth. You are so kind to the elderly."

Gideon let the whole earth know that he was the new Deer Slayer. "Home—we are finally home. Can you believe it? I made my first kill!"

The clan elder stopped and turned to face the other five hunters and said, "I am so proud of you. I love each one of you so much. Keep going. I must do something alone. Now, go before you freeze!" Yelling after them, the leader shouted, "I love my family, and this is the best day ever! Gideon, the Deer Slayer, this is your day to remember!"

They were soon gone, and quiet returned to Elcurrest. "Eli, I knew that you would be waiting for me. Here, let me help you up off the cold ground. How have you been, Eli?"

"Eli? Why do you call me Eli? I am in good spirits as always. I knew that if anyone could save the clan, it would be you. Come, the others are here with me. They are waiting by the king's table."

"Hello, Jucurr, I'm home!"

"Welcome home, my dear. A stranger has been waiting for you."

"Lord, is that you?"

"Yes, I have come to take you to a mansion that I have prepared especially for you."

"Hey, did everyone hear that? The Lord has prepared a place especially for us! This is great! Elcurr, go and bring everyone here. Jesus is going to take us to a place that he has prepared especially for us!"

Jesus quickly responded to the misunderstood invitation. "No, I have prepared it only for you, my child."

"Am I to understand that my family and ancestors are going to stay here? Do you mean that my people who gave me life and loved me are not going with me?"

"Yes, of course. Don't be anxious about anything. Their day of judgment is yet to come."

"Lord, I do not wish to go without them. I want to stay here and wait with them."

"Don't you remember that you left houses, fields, brothers, sisters, father, mother, and children for my sake, and that you will receive a hundred times as much and will inherit eternal life?"

"But Lord, that would be selfish. I cannot forsake the place and people who gave me life and taught me how to love."

"I am the one who gave those things to you. They have all passed away. I have always been with you for eternity. Don't worry. Your family's day of judgment is yet to come. Until then, just be patient and trust in me. Why are you smiling my child?"

"This twinkling in time reminds me of the night I returned to Avon from Judea, and Esau said those words to me. Things would have been much different if I had listened to him. It all seems like a dream now. Still, what kind of soul would I be if I turned my back on my family? Please Lord, let's take them with us."

"Because of your disobedience, you deserve to spend some time with your clan. Remember this: We are going to leave this graveyard on the third day. Be ready to leave and not look back."

Jucurr drew closer to the new arrival. "Dear, who were you speaking to?"

"That was my new best friend, Jesus. I would be lost without Him."

"Oh, it will be all right dear. Come, everyone is waiting for you."

"Aren't we going to stay here at our family grave?"

"No, dear, that is where our bodies are buried. Our eternal souls dwell deep in our ancestral cave."

The Curr clan champion returned once more to the depths of the family cavern. "Hello, everyone! I did not know that so many of us had died. We are dead, aren't we?"

Makcurr answered, "Yes, we are dead, and I kept telling Conan that the Romans were coming, but he did not believe me."

"Good grief, I spent a lifetime listening to the tiresome 'I killed the stag' story, and now it is going to be hell listening to 'I told you so' for eternity. I should have cut off your ugly head when I had the chance."

"Yes, said the sheath to its sword. Talk, talk, talk—you are all words and no action."

PART 5—SPREADING THE WORD

The diplomat Hancurr chimed in. "Thank goodness you are here—finally, an eternal being I can have a real conversation with. Come with me. I will show you your place around here."

The Curr clan champion thought, *Some things never change. Even in death, the three of them are still bickering.*

"We heard that. There are no secrets here. There are only memories, and I remember the times that you cut off the head of your childhood friend."

"Oh, hello, Maggan. I was hoping to forget my transgressions."

"I recently arrived in time to make your stay here an eternal hell. Your twin and that damned torc got me killed."

Star's familiar voice interrupted Maggan. "Yes, well, you had it coming, stupid. You cut off the wrong head."

"Anyone can make a mistake. Really, Star, give it up."

The latest arrival attempted to change the subject to something more benign. "What are you all doing up there on the cavern walls?"

"Speaking of stupid, what do you think? We are the shadow people of the Chambered Cairn. Come up here and dance on the walls with us."

The night was spent reuniting with some and meeting many other family members for the first time. They took pleasure in pouring out a history of transgressions against one another. They savored each misdeed of others as though it would save them from drowning in their own pool of transgressions.

"I remember hearing many of you speak about Jacurr the Elder and how he died the moment that I was born. Jucurr, where is my great-grandfather Jacurr?"

"What do you mean, dear?"

"Where is my great-grandfather, Jacurr the Elder?"

No one knew what to say until Jucurr finally said, "You forget every time you return."

"What have I forgotten?"

"You are my husband. **You** are Jacurr the Elder!"

Hannah sat straight up and screamed, "Jesus come back! Take me home! I do not want to be Jacurr the Elder! I do not want the memory of my transgressions to torture me. I do not want to be here. I am ready to leave and not look back! Jesus, save me!"

"Hannah, Hannah, wake up!"

"Moses, what has happened?"

"You were screaming in your sleep."

"Yes, I remember now. It was a horrible dream!"

"Go back to sleep, and tell us about it in the morning."

When morning came, Hannah was the first one awake and preparing breakfast. "Good morning, my beautiful family," she said when breakfast was ready. "Wake up! The porridge is hot and ready to eat."

"Mother, what are you doing?"

"Oh, Gideon, it is an old family tradition of the way we used to say good morning to our ancestral spirits that haunt in this cave."

"Mother, sometimes you really scare me."

Moses joined the conversation. "Speaking of scary, you promised to tell us about the bad dream you had last night."

"I don't remember having a dream good or bad last night."

"You jumped out of my arms and sat straight up and yelled, 'I do not want to be Jacurr the Elder!'"

"Now who is being scary? Why would I say that I am my great-grandfather? Don't worry about it. I only remember the dreams that come true."

"All right, wife, there will be no more staying up late for you. And how do you know that your dreams do not come true if you do not remember them?"

"I just know. That is how."

The years passed in the safest place on earth as the relentless Roman advance continued. Hannah lived to see her great-grandchildren and tell them about her friend Jesus. She told how He once walked and talked with her in the orchard of Elcurrest. The sun finally set on her life when she went home to be with the Lord in AD 82 just ahead of the Roman advance. The advance stopped atop her mountain home known today as Ben Avon where Hannah was last heard praying.

PART 5—SPREADING THE WORD

El Shaddai, God Almighty
I am the cave born slave.
You are the deliverer.
I am the child of desperation.
You are the God of liberation.
I am the Warrior Princess of Aberdonshire.
You are the King of kings, the Prince of Peace.
I am the mother. I am the wife.
You are the Father, giver of life.
I am the traveler.
You are the journey.
I am the fallen.
You are the risen.
I am but the dust of Albion.
You were, are, and forever will be the Great I AM.

JERUSALEM

And did those feet in ancient time
Walk upon England's mountain green?
And was the Holy Lamb of God
On England's pleasant pastures seen?
Bring me my bow of burning gold!
Bring me my arrows of desire!
Bring me my spear! O clouds, unfold!
Bring me my chariot of fire!
I will not cease from mental fight,
Nor shall my sword sleep in my hand,
'Til we have built Jerusalem,
In England's green and pleasant land.

Poem written by William Blake in 1804 and put to music by Hubert Parry in 1916.

AGRICOLA

AD 81 to 85

The Ninth Roman Legion invaded southern Scotland under the command of Gnaeus Julius Agricola in AD 81. The Roman forces continued to drive northward until they claimed to have defeated the Celts who were under the command of Chieftain Calgacus in AD 83. Rome claimed victory, and yet the remainder of their troops suddenly withdrew to the safety of southern Caledonia, and the construction of the defensive Hadrian and Antonine Walls soon followed. What frightened these conquerors of nations remains a mystery. Some say that demons captured many of the invaders and threw them into the underworld. Seemingly, they just vanished without a trace.

Celtic Chief Calgacus assembled his Master Warriors together in the final days leading up to a valiant battle against the Romans. "Warriors of Albion, I have called you together to apologize. It was a mistake to place our people in a situation where a pitched battle was inevitable. We cannot win this type of battle against the Romans. Our backs are literally against the wall of these great mountains. Though this battle is already lost, we do not have to lose the war.

I am going to divide our forces so that Albion can fight another day. There is a stone for each master warrior in this pouch. Half are black and half are white. This is what will happen if you draw a black stone. You will take command of three hundred warriors over the age of twenty-five and take a stand against the Romans here in the mountains.

If you draw a white stone, you will take command of three hundred warriors under the age of twenty-five. Then you will immediately withdraw from the field of battle. You have standing orders to avoid head-on confrontations

PART 5—SPREADING THE WORD

with Roman forces. Instead, find ways to kill them in their sleep or while they eat or play in small numbers. Remember your clansmen who gave their lives so that you and your clan might live. In their memory, take the fight into the Roman home. Finally, it has been my honor to fight alongside each of you. Until we meet again, may the gods be with each of you. You are dismissed to the task set before you."

Calgacus motioned to Gideon to stay. "Gideon, I have a special assignment for you. We have received information that the Romans want you and every Makcurrie dead. Your raids against their supply lines have been both lethal and strategically effective. Our enemy has orders to hunt you down and exterminate your clan. Your orders are to pretend to desert your position and draw this enemy away from the coming engagement. Until we meet again, may your god be with you. You are dismissed to the task set before you."

Soon, the inevitable battle began. The fight was on, and the Makcurries threw down their colors and took flight across the great river away from the battle. The young warriors were halfway up the mountainside when Gideon first noticed that there were one hundred enemy Romans in pursuit of his force of thirty. "They have taken the bait. We are so close to safety, but they are gaining ground on us too fast."

Red uniforms covered the mountainside below and were driving upward after their prey. Celts could be seen in the distance running and losing ground to the equestrian horde. First, it was Britannia and Aberdon, and now they were coming to claim the remaining lives of the Makcurries.

"Oh, dear God, save us! Please help me think and to use what I know. Have you brought us this far only to die here in this wilderness? No! You are El Shaddai, the Almighty One. You have always been faithful to me, and I will be faithful to you. I will trust in you, my Lord. I will not be afraid."

Gideon looked once more toward the river below, and his whole body turned as cold as ice even though salty sweat poured down his face, and again he cried out to God in desperation. "In God I trust. I will not be afraid," he declared, and warmth returned to his body. "Elohim, have mercy on me and my people. It is I, Gideon. This is your land, your mountain, your wind, your sky; please spare our lives. Save our souls."

It should not have come as a surprise, but he had to admit being delightfully surprised when the wind drove a raincloud between the opposing forces. Heavy hailstones pummeled the advancing dragoons below while Gideon's warriors were bathed in sunlight above the storm cloud.

"Hallelujah! Praise be to God! You are a merciful God. On this day, you have spared my life and the lives of my people. From the ends of the earth, I call to you as my strength fails me. Lead me to the rock of my ancestors. Give our dear horses the strength to rise up this mountain as though on eagle wings. Take us home, Lord; take us home. Deliver us safely home to Elcurrest. Deliver my people, oh Lord. Amen."

I remember that old spiral tree. What did mother always say about it? Yes, thank you my God. See the tree, Eye is nigh.

"Come!" Gideon called out to his people. "Elcurrest is this way through those trees. The cloud will not protect us much longer."

Throughout the day, sounds of raging warfare rose from the valley below in a place where unclaimed stones of their memorial cairn remain to this day. The heather grows brightly there as a testimony to those who willingly paid the ultimate price in blood for freedom and survival as a nation.

Gideon prayed as he guided his people to higher ground. "Lord, there has been too much sacrifice for one day. Each life is precious to me. I easily love my brothers and sisters, but how can I love an enemy that thirsts for the blood of my innocent people? Help me not to lead this band into a field of battle. Instead, help me shepherd them to peaceful green pastures. My heart cries out to you, Lord, as I lead these lambs away from slaughter. I am afraid of what awaits them in the hour of their death. Please, Lord, have mercy on their souls. Have mercy on your servant Gideon. Grant me victory in your name. Amen."

Silence returned to the mountain air as the trail to Elcurrest came into view. From there, Gideon led the way to the Road to Nowhere.

"Everyone, dismount here and remove your tartans. Now, tie your tartans to your reins. You three men stay here with the horses while I take everyone to safety."

Gideon remained on horseback as he led his warriors into Elcurrest. The orchard had become a dry and desolate place without a gardener's care. The fruit trees had withered and died. Dried leaves and weeds covered the ground. Even in the ruin, Gideon knew where to find the hidden cavern entrance, and he ordered his people to enter. "Everyone, quickly get out of sight. Go into the cave and wait. I will return with our other three brothers. You will be safe inside. We will live to fight another day."

Gideon raced back to the road. "Thank you, men. Now please stand back. Forgive me for what I am about to do." From there the men watched in horror as Gideon stampeded the horses around the Road to Nowhere. Their horror increased when they heard the equestrian screams of terror as each horse came to the end of the road and leaped to its death far below.

The three guards cried out, "Gideon, what have you done?"

"I hope that I just saved our lives. Come, we must hurry. The Romans are not far behind us."

Once they reached the cave entrance, Gideon found a torch and lit it. "We will enter through this narrow passage that leads to the grand chamber of our ancestors. Here, take these torches. I need a volunteer to remain here and guard the entrance."

Gideon led his people single file deep into the earth. "All right, this is home for tonight. Everyone find a place, share your food, get comfortable, and be quiet. We will rest here for tonight."

One soldier spoke out for everyone. "Sir, is it true that you have killed our horses?"

"Yes, it is as true as it was necessary. The Romans will find the carnage and end their pursuit, believing that we all perished together."

"We do not fear the Romans as much as we fear the wrath of the horse goddess Epona for killing her children."

"And again I say to you, there is only one God, and we were made in His image. He alone created the magnificent horse. We have been given dominion over them and all beasts of the field."

"Gideon, we rather stand, fight, and die with honor than to hide in this rabbit hole."

The entrance guard interrupted Gideon's response. "Sir, the Romans have found the orchard."

"Thank, soldier. Go ahead and find a place to rest. Tonight we will climb out of this hole and attack the Romans as Chief Calgacus commanded. It is important for everyone to eat something, remain silent, and rest. Do not worry. This is the safest place on earth."

Earlier, the Romans had reached the Road to Nowhere just as the last Celt disappeared into the underworld. "Column halt!" commanded the senior officer. "You two men ride up ahead and report back to me what you see."

While waiting, some soldiers found the narrow passage into Elcurrest. "Excuse me, sir. Come and see what we have found."

Sometime later, the reconnaissance detail returned with their report. "Sir, they are all dead. All the horses and their riders are dashed on the rocks far below."

The centurion and two others went to the end of the road to see for themselves. The leader was a hardy warrior until viewing the carnage that day.

PART 5—SPREADING THE WORD

"Their stupidity is disappointing. I was looking forward to killing them myself. What a waste of good horseflesh. I have never seen anything like this in all my years of service to Rome. I do not know what to call what has happened here. Is it heroism or cowardliness, sacrifice or insanity?"

"I have seen this before," said the second in command.

"When and where have you known such…such self-destruction?"

"It was at the end of the Jewish War in 73. Decades before the war, King Herod the First built a remarkable hill fortress named Masada. We laid siege against Masada for months. Excitement rose in our camp. Everyone knew that Masada would fall the next day. Our first assault easily breached the walls only to find them defended by the dead. The Jewish Zealot defenders chose suicide over enslavement or death by a Roman sword. They stole our honor with their relentless tenacity and courage until the end."

The centurion gave a halfhearted salute to his fallen enemy and turned to his comrades. "It is late. There is no need to return to base camp tonight. A nearby orchard will make an excellent fortress encampment. Post guards around the perimeter and let the celebration begin. Albeit a hollow one, a victory is a victory. Today we claim a great victory for Caesar. Give extra rations of wine to everyone. Perhaps a little wine will help settle our stomachs over what has happened here."

All was quiet in the cave. Even Gideon was soon asleep, and when he entered dreamland, he found an angel waiting for him.

"The Lord is with you, mighty warrior," the angel said.

"Tell me, sir, if the Lord is with us, why has He allowed these Roman murderers to be victorious?"

"Go in the strength that you have been given, and you will save the children of Albion."

"How can I save the children of Albion? The Curr clan has become the weakest in Albion, and I am the least of my people."

"God has heard your prayer. Tonight, the Lord will be victorious. Every foreigner who has invaded this sacred ground will remain here forever. No enemy will remain alive. After the battle, hide their bodies and all spoils of war deep within this cavern. Then close the cavern and orchard entrances forever. Leave no trace of Rome behind. Their sudden and complete disappearance will send fear throughout the Roman ranks. You and your warriors must then leave this place immediately and follow the setting sun. Do these things for the survival of your clan."

Just outside the cavern, the Roman victory celebration continued long into the night. The wine had finally settled the senior centurion's stomach and numbed his brain. "It has grown late and cold. Have the men bank the fires and sound the call for rest."

Much later, a startled Gideon sat up and relit his torch. "Wake up! Men and women of Albion, it is time to fight. As we enter the orchard, one go right and the next warrior go left. Quietly encircle the orchard. Move to the center once the circle is complete. Take your time. You have all night to kill. Leave no Roman alive. Afterward…"

A frantic warrior burst forward rudely interrupting Gideon. "Master Warrior Gideon— Master Warrior!"

"What is it, soldier?"

"We have overslept. There is daylight at the end of the tunnel!"

"What? Lord, how can this be? You promised a victory that has slipped through my fingers! This is embarrassing, humiliating, and possibly the end of us."

Gideon rushed to the entrance to see the light. He stepped forward and peered cautiously into the Elcurrest graveyard, and then he fell to his knees at the sight of all the destruction. As the angel promised, the Lord had vanquished the enemy in flames while His lambs slept through the night. A sacred wind had swept through the camp and spread the bonfires to dried leaves, weeds, and trees until the ancient volcanic crater became an inferno one last time.

Agricola, the Roman Governor of Caledonia, sent his report to the Senate in Rome. The grow story of vanished legionnaires spread through the ranks until everyone knew that the demons of the Grampian Mountains swallowed an entire company of dragoons. The Romans claimed a great and final victory against the Caledonians, and yet they retreated all the way back to southern Caledonia to hide behind defensive walls until they completely withdrew from Albion by about AD 430.

It took another thousand years for the people of Albion to emulate Rome as a world power. It was then that Sebastian Cabot intruded upon the tranquility of a new land and kidnapped three native people to England in 1497. The

PART 5—SPREADING THE WORD

native tribes and the English clashed for the next three hundred years. That was the beginning of the end for a nation that had lived in peaceably with man and nature for millennia. A plague called civilization and its diseases, greed, war, politics, environmental pollution, and religion brought death to a previously peaceful land.

European civilization expanded the known world with ships, roads, culture, and technology. In doing so, it trampled over every family, tribe, nation, and culture that stood in its path. This imperialistic drive was determined to subjugate the savage heathens of the new land no matter how many innocent people had to be murdered. The Europeans believed that it was their manifest destiny to dominate. These imperialists only desired to see the extraction of great wealth flow across the Atlantic to the capitals of Europe.

The invasions are over, and yet the Word of God continues to be the truth, the way, and the life against these evils of the world. Through it all, the Celts have survived in Scotland, just as the noble Mikmaq tribe has survived in the new Scotland known as Nova Scotia despite the encroachment of civilization.

Gideon Bloodgood is the inspiration of this chapter and friends. He is a mighty warrior that fights for each day of his life. Please join us in praying for this sweet baby boy.

CONCLUSION

Writing this Christian fiction was an enjoyable learning experience. Exploring the root of modern theology was also interesting. However, just as creation is simply trace evidence of the Creator, my religious expressions are simply trace evidence of God's presence in my life. For me, it began in 1959. I was driving through the mountains of West Virginia in a hard rain. Upon entering a curve, I could not help but notice TRY GOD painted on the side of a large boulder. My two companions took the sign as a challenge to God and said, "Yes, go ahead, try, God." A moment later, the 1932 Dodge was sliding on its side until it finally came to a stop at the entrance of a junkyard. From there, my two companions took one road home, and I took another to follow the best advice ever painted on the side of a rock. I decided to take the challenge to try God in my life, and that led to a personal relationship with Jesus the Christ.

Lord, I am thankful for the life that you have given me. I came into this world having no foreknowledge of my life or the ways it would unfold. You have been there along the way in nature, in the eyes of your people, in your Holy Word, and in your Spirit within me. Forgive us as we boast of knowledge, and yet we still see dimly and behave as though there is no God and eternal judgment.

"Jerusalem" is a beautiful song that is dear to the people of England. It tells of how you were seen walking about in the highlands of England. In our lifetime, we can know that your Holy Spirit does walk with many people of Great Britain, and that you, the Creator and Master of the Universe, can walk any time and any place that you wish. Still, there are those who would reduce you to the anthropomorphic limits of human endeavors and say that it was not possible for you to have visited ancient Albion. These same people are willing to accept the historical fact that Gaius Julius Caesar easily traveled to and from Albion twice, and he only thought that he was divine.

Whether you did or did not visit the highlands of England is a moot point when one considers a greater question. Why would you care about something as small and insignificant as man crawling around on a minuscule speck in just one universe of billions? And yet, as I near the end of my life, only you, God, are real to me, and everything else, including the cosmos, is passing away.

PART 5—SPREADING THE WORD

Much of Hannah's story has been inspired by moments in my life. The best moments were spent trusting in you, and the worst moments were spent being self-willed. You were there every moment, even when I chose to turn my back on you. You have always loved me, and if you can love an old insignificant Celt, then boundless is your love and mercy. I will soon join my ancestors, and yet your love for me (and everyone) endures forever. Whatever your reason for loving us, those of us who have sought you have been experiencing the indwelling of your Holy Spirit even before the Pentecost of Mount Sinai over thirty-five hundred years ago. Thank you for the patience you extend to each person so that we may know that your reality is the only reason that we tiny, insignificant humans can have hope, faith, and love. The greatest of these has always been love. For me, a Jew named Jesus personified your love as the propitiation for my sin. It was through the sacrifice of His precious blood on a Roman cross that we can have eternal hope. How blessed we are to still have that same blood flowing thicker than water through the veins of God's Chosen People. How blessed we are to have had the opportunity of life, and to seek you and your will for our lives. The purpose of our lives is to love you with all our strength, our hearts, and our minds. Second to that is your command that we love one another. It is by placing our faith in you that we are saved and not by the works of our hands or by obeying the law. Fortunately, the final judgment of each person is yours alone and not through the theologies of men. Amen.

J. J. McCurry

McCurry: son of God's peace

APPENDIX: GLOSSARY

Aber-, Aberdon, Aberdeen: the mouth of a river

AD (Latin for Anno Domini or "in the year of the Lord.") The Hebrew calendar marks this period as CE (Common Era) and BCE (Before the Common Era).

Alban Eiler: Light of the earth; the vernal equinox of spring. The length of daylight is equal to the length of darkness. It is one of eight time portals where the Druids could easily enter the Otherworld.

Albion (or Alba) is the ancient name of the British Islands. Albion means white (or light) as in the White Cliffs of Dover in England. Most of Gaul later became France.

Albion Arthurian (Light of Arthur) is the winter solstice celebration that marks the beginning of the northern journey of the sun.

Amen: An expression of agreement or concurrence. It is so. So be it.

Andrew Supper: Saint Andrew is the patron saint of Scotland since the sixth century. The Feast of Saint Andrew is held on November 30. It is a day that church members invite non-church guests to the Andrew Supper. Warning: Haggis is traditionally on the menu.

Anthropomorphic: ascribing human form or attributes to a thing or a being that is not human, such as an animal or a deity.

Apennine peninsula: the land mass containing all Italy

Apocrypha: a group of books not found in the Protestant or Jewish Bibles.

Apologetics is the branch of theology concerned with the defense or proof of a religion.

PART 5—SPREADING THE WORD

Appian Way is an ancient Roman road built by Claudius Caecus in 312 BC. It extends 350 miles. The Roman transportation system of road and wheel continued to improve until an entire army could travel from Rome to Gaul in a few weeks by the first century.

Asgard: the dwelling place of the Scandinavian god Odin.

Astrology is the study and the attempt to interpret the influence of the heavenly bodies on human affairs.

Atonement: reparation of a wrong or injury

Aura (or-ah): the Celts called it "fire in the head"—the radiance that emanates from a person with psychic or spiritual powers.

Avon: In this story, it is an imaginary village on the north side of Firth of Forth in Dunfermline, Scotland of today. A village, town, or city by the name of Avon did not exist in England until much later in the Middle Ages. However, Avon being Nova spelled backward was an enjoyable coincidence for the story. Webster's Dictionary shows Avon pronounced as "Ah-vahn" with soft vowels as it is in England. Fifty years ago, in New Jersey, it was always pronounced with a long *a* sound as in the name of the letter *a*. Today, some people in New Jersey have gone to the soft *ah* sound.

Aye: yes (Scottish colloquial expression.)

Bar Mitzvah means *son of the commandment*. Every Jewish boy is automatically Bar-Mitzvah at thirteen years of age. The Bar Mitzvah ceremony did not exist until over thirteen hundred years after the period covered in this book.

Bard: a composer and reciter of ancient Celtic poetry

Barbari: *the others* and the Latin root word for *barbarian*.

APPENDIX: GLOSSARY

Beltane, Bealtaine: May 1 Celtic celebration of May Day. This was still practiced when this author was a child, Maypole and all. The Maypole was a pole decorated with ribbons and flowers that we danced around.

Ben: Gaelic for mountain

Ben Avon is the watershed of the Dee River and Nova's birthplace.

Ben Nevis is the highest point in Scotland at 4,909 feet above sea level and the film location of the opening scene of the 1995 movie *Braveheart*.

Blodeuwedd: owl, Gaelic word meaning *flower face*

Bonnie: pretty (Scottish colloquial expression.)

Bonnie lassie: a beautiful young woman or girl

Brigit (or Brigid) was a powerful Celtic/Druid goddess and later was demoted to Saint Brigit as she remains today in Ireland and Scotland.

Bris or Brit Malah: Hebrew for the covenant of circumcision described in Genesis 17:10. Bris also means birth.

Brose: onions and oats. The blend is stir-fried into the grease that remains after cooking meat. The result is served as a garnish. One in five Scots know the dish. Ancient brose was a type of uncooked Scottish porridge that was mixed into boiling water and allowed to stand before eating.

Cailean (KA len): Gaelic man's name meaning *young warrior*

Cairn (Karen): Scot Gaelic for a mound of stones used to mark a location. Each warrior would place a rock on the pile before battle and remove a rock afterward. The remaining rocks of the dead and wounded formed a war memorial.

PART 5—SPREADING THE WORD

Caledon is a Latin reference to the Celtic Picts of Northern Scotland. Today the Caledonian Canal runs southwest to northeast through Northern Scotland from Fort William to Inverness. The Druids of Caledon practice contemporary Caledonic Druidry to "benefit all life on earth."

Caledonia: Latin for Scotland

Caoimhe (KUY vu): Gaelic woman's name meaning *kindness* or *tenderness*

Capernaum was the hometown of Peter and his brother Andrew, located on the north end of the Sea of Galilee.

Caesarea was named in honor of Caesar Augustus. A Roman regiment posted there consisted of six hundred men with six centurions.

Ceilidh: Scot Gaelic for *a meeting* is the literal meaning, but it is known as a dance.

Celt: a race of Indo-European people who spoke the Gaelic language. To be called a Celt implied that the person was a follower of Druidism. There were at least three types of Celts in Albion at the time of this story: Picts, Scots, and Britons.

Cernunnos or Herne: Celtic god of fertility.

Challah: Jewish bread baked especially for the Sabbath. The *ch* in Challah is pronounced as a hard guttural *h*.

Chanukah (Chanukkah or Hanukkah) is a Hebrew story that tells of the faithfulness of God for His people. The Hanukkah story can be found in the books of the Maccabees and in Jewish and Catholic Bibles. They were a priestly family that ruled Judea in the first and second century BC. Judas Maccabaeus and his brothers defeated the Syrians and rededicated the Temple.

Clan, clann: Gaelic for *children*, and later came to mean *tribe*.

APPENDIX: GLOSSARY

Corneli is a Latin term that refers to the ten thousand slaves emancipated by Cornelius Sulla.

Cornelius Sulla was the Roman dictator that preceded Julius Caesar.

Croft: a small Scottish farm.

Cur: a mean mongrel dog; the Curr Clan said another way is the Clan of the Mongrel Dog.

Decimate: to kill every tenth person.

Diaspora was the scattering of the Jews out of Judea after the Babylonian captivity. Judea was renamed Palestine by the Romans after they destroyed the Temple and caused another diaspora in AD 70. Scots have also suffered diaspora.

Divination is the gift of foretelling the future through prayer, meditation, or dreams. Divination was a way in which the Druids communicated with the other worlds that they believed to exist.

Dolmen: a structure regarded as a tomb, consisting of two or more large, upright stones capped by a horizontal slab of stone.

Doxology: a hymn or statement that gives praise to God.

Drat: a Gaelic expression of frustration voiced by the author's Celtic grandmother Quinn.

Druid: is a priest-like wise man of Druidism; also a belief system.

Druidism, Druidic, Druidry: pertaining to the belief system. Druidism: a pantheistic religion predominantly shared by the ancient Celtic people.

PART 5—SPREADING THE WORD

Dungeon: comes from the Latin word for *keep*. The dungeon was also used as the last stand keep or panic room in the event of a successful siege against a castle.

Dun: Pictish word for *hill*

Ecclesiastes: a book of the Bible containing thoughts about life and its meaning

Eiler Equinox or Alban Eiler: Light of the earth, it is the vernal equinox of spring. The length of daylight is equal to the length of darkness. It is one of eight time portals where the Druids could easily enter the Otherworld.

Epona: a Celtic white mare goddess

Elohim: Gods. Also a name for God meaning the One manifesting as many.

Eloch: God, is the singular form of Elohim: Gods

El Shaddai: the Almighty One (Hebrew)

Faolan (FER gun): Gaelic man's name for *wolf*

Feast of Weeks is also known as Shavuot or Pentecost. (See Genesis 37-41)

Firth: a coastal bay or estuary (Viking origin)

Forecastle: a shelter located in the bow of a vessel, and a castle is located in the stern.

Gaelic: The roots of the Celtic language and their Druid religion are planted in Indo-Europe (the eastern European territories). Both the Latin and Gaelic languages developed in the territories north of the Mediterranean Sea. In Ireland, it is pronounced "Gay-lick." In Scotland, it is pronounced "Gal-ick."

Geasa or Geis: an ancient Druidic curse used to control the people.

APPENDIX: GLOSSARY

Gentile: any person who is not Jewish and is considered by them to be heathen. Mormons believe this as well. The name Gentile is capitalized in this book.

Gilgul (turning in a circle): Hebrew word for reincarnation

Glasgow: Gaelic for *a green hollow*

Glenn: Gaelic for *a secluded narrow valley*

Goblins are demons of any size in human or animal form.

Goy: non-Jewish person with contemptuous attitudes, traits, and customs. Goys are often used by Jews to perform tasks that are considered unclean.

Hades: is the home of the evil spirits of the dead in Greek mythology and the name of the Greek god ruling over the underworld.

Haggadah is the Passover reading that describes the four different types of children within each of us.

Haggis: is the national dish of Scotland. It is made by stuffing a sheep stomach with minced sheep liver, heart, and lungs, blended with herbs and salt.

Hall: Gaelic for salt. Salt was used as currency throughout the known world. The word salary comes from the way the Roman soldiers were paid in salt.

Hallelujah: a Hebrew expression meaning *praise be to God*

Ha-Shem (the Name): is the simplest Hebrew form of referring to God without using His name.

Head hunting is perhaps the strangest if not the most barbaric practice of Druidic Celts. It is part spiritual, part cultural, and totally disgusting. One cannot help but wonder how such a practice came about. Druid head hunting is closely related to reincarnation because of *metempsychosis* where a loose

PART 5—SPREADING THE WORD

eternal being (soul) may enter and take over another living person. In addition to the obvious fear of this happening to a host, it opens the possibility that a victor may not see the approach of a slain reincarnated enemy. Decapitation was the only way to prevent this from happening. A person could not be reincarnated if he was decapitated, thereby sending his soul to the underworld forever. Furthermore, a Celtic warrior gained prestige by the number of heads he accumulated and mounted as household trophies. And the religious carnage did not stop there.

Hebrew: one translation is "the dusty ones." The name was first used to identify "Abram the Hebrew" in Genesis 14:13. Therefore, other definitions such as "to cross" or "Passover" are incorrect because the first Passover took place much later. The Hebrew people are an Eastern Mediterranean ethnic group. From Abram the Hebrew, the Hebrews became a race of people who predominantly followed Judaism. Judaism is the first monotheistic religion based on specific written knowledge of the One True God. Furthermore, it is believed that God gave His written word to His people.

Hill-forts were used by the Celts as defensive positions. The landscape of Great Britain is dotted with the remains of over 1,600 Celtic hill-forts.

Human sacrifice to appease or thank god(s) is a practice found in many religions as it was in Druidism. This comes from the observation and notion that actions and inactions have consequences that result in *eternal reward and punishment.*

Iberian Peninsula: containing Spain and Portugal

Jerusalem: righteousness and peace

Judaism: a monotheistic religion predominantly shared by the Hebrew people.

Judea: the southern region of ancient Palestine

APPENDIX: GLOSSARY

Julian calendar is a twelve-month calendar that was established by Julius Caesar in 46 BC. July is for Julius Caesar, and August is for his adopted son Augustus who was originally named Octavian as in October.

Kiddushim: meaning sanctification, it also is the word for a Jewish wedding ceremony. A marriage between a man and a woman is God's way of perpetuating His creation.

Kinrick: Gaelic for kingdom

Kosher: food prepared under the guidelines of Jewish dietary laws

Laddie: a young lad; a boy

Lass: a girl (Scottish colloquial expression)

Lassie: a girl or young woman (Scottish colloquial expression)

La Tene: a Celtic art form developed around 550 BC in central Europe. One form of La Tene art is known as Celtic Mandala. Mandala art has its roots in Hindu and Buddhist iconography of deity.

Latharn (LA urn): man's name meaning *fox*

Linn is a waterfall or a steep ravine or precipice.

Llyr: Celtic sea god

Loch, lough: a lake or a partly landlocked or protected bay

Lyon, Gaul (France) is pronounced Lee-on, with a slightly guttural *on*. The town of Lyons, Colorado, is pronounced as the plural for lion.

PART 5—SPREADING THE WORD

Maccabees were a priestly family that ruled Judea in the first and second century BC. Judas Maccabaeus and his brothers defeated the Syrians and rededicated the Temple in Jerusalem.

Madadh (MA daugh) is a Gaelic man's name that means *canine* or *dog*.

Maon (Moon) is a Gaelic name that means *hero*.

Manawyddan was the king of the oceans and the son of the Celtic sea god Llyr.

Manna: the food miraculously supplied to the Israelites in the desert. In Exodus 16:15, Moses said to them, "It is the bread the Lord has given you to eat."

Mead is an alcoholic drink made from water and fermented honey. Later, honey was replaced by cane sugar to make rum. Rum is the basic ingredient mixed with water to make grog. Groggy is what one becomes after drinking too much grog.

Metempsychosis is a belief that a loose eternal being (soul) may enter and take over another living person. In addition to the obvious fear of this happening to a host, it opens the possibility that a victor may not see the approach of a slain reincarnated enemy.

Mikvah is a ceremonial building or area for cleansing Jewish women after childbirth, menstruation, or while recovering from certain diseases.

Mishnah is an oral tradition meaning *teachings that are repeated*. It is a resource for Jewish sermons.

Mitzvah: a command relating to the religious and moral conduct of the Jews

Monotheism is the belief in one god.

Mor (More): is a Gaelic woman's name meaning *great*.

APPENDIX: GLOSSARY

Moses: Egyptian word for *drawn from the water*. Sixteen verses in The Christian Bible report that Jesus himself verified the Mosaic authorship of the *Torah*.

Nag: an old or worthless horse, and a person who persists in finding fault.

Nantosuelta, Onuava, or Rosmenta: Celtic goddesses of fertility

Neptune: Roman sea god

Oatcake: an oat biscuit

Odin: principal god of pagan Scandinavia.

Ogham is the Celtic alphabetical script that did not exist before the fifth century AD.

Omen is an event that indicates (portends) that something good or evil is going to happen. Once a blackbird came into the author's childhood home, and it was seen as a portent of death. Of course, death is going to come knocking eventually. The nova in the night sky was seen as an omen of a great future event for the Curr clan, Star, and her twin sister, Nova.

Oral tradition of the Druids did not allow their spiritual beliefs to be written.

Orpha-nus: Latin for *destitute, without parents, bereaved*.

Other worlds were believed to exist in addition to the one that Nova was living in. She was told of places such as the underworld, fairyland, dreamland, and the spiritual world. Closely associated with these other worlds is the eternal being, otherwise known as the soul.

Pantheism is any religion or philosophical doctrine that identifies the divine with the universe. Man and god(s) are all part of that universe or cosmos. In Christianity and Judaism, God is the creator of the universe and therefore He transcends His creation. All creation is seen simply as trace evidence of

PART 5—SPREADING THE WORD

a creator, whereas Druidism followers worship nature, ancestors, and things created by man such as gods and stone idols.

Papyrus paper was (and is) made from the Egyptian aquatic papyrus plant.

Pax Romana: Peace of Rome

Pedyon Haben: the redemption of the son. The father is allowed to redeem his son from the Temple on the child's thirteenth day.

Pentecost: the seventh Sunday after Easter, commemorating the descent of the Holy Spirit rested on the apostles; also known as Whitsunday or Shavuot.

Pharisee: pure or separated

Plaid: is a long rectangular piece of cloth with a pattern of clan colors. It is usually worn across the left shoulder by Scottish Highlanders. A plaid reader could retell a clan's history by reading the combination of woven colors and patterns.

Polytheism is a belief in more than one God as in Druidism. Judaism and Christianity recognize the biblical manifestations in which God revealed Himself to man.

Porridge: a hot breakfast made from milk, butter, oats, sugar, and water.

Poseidon: Greek sea god

Praetorian Guard: the bodyguard of a military commander

Pretani: *the painted people*, was the name the Celtic people called themselves that was first translated into Greek, then to Latin, and finally to English. Pretani became Britannia, the land of the painted people. The Gaelic Pretani was translated to the Greek as Pretannike, to the Latin Pretannia, and finally

APPENDIX: GLOSSARY

to Britannia. Another less likely source for Britannia is the name of the Celtic goddess Brigit (or Brigid).

Promised Land is the land promised by God to Abraham and his descendants. "To your offspring I will give this land" (Genesis 12:7).

Rabbi (teacher): a social and spiritual leader of Judaism

Reincarnation occupied a large part of the Druid faith that did not include a heaven or hell. It was of particular interest to Nova because it promised the chance to be reunited with her mother. A person could return as another life form or in the past, present, or future, because time as we know it was considered to be an illusion. This is an extension of the belief that all the cosmos, including the human soul, is alive and regenerating.

Rosh Hashanah: is the Jewish New Year when it is customary for each believer to reflect over his or her past actions.

Sabbath, also known as Shabbat, takes place at sundown on the sixth day. The Shabbat is welcomed as a loving friend. One day ends and another begins at sundown. Therefore, the end of this scene is the beginning of the seventh day, the Sabbath or Shabbat.

Sadducee: member of an ancient Jewish sect of priests who controlled the Temple. They based their faith on the written *Torah* and its laws.

Samhain (sow-en) is the ancient Celtic name for Halloween.

Samuel: when speaking the name in Hebrew, it sounds like the Hebrew words for *heard by God*.

Sanhedrin: supreme legislative council and ecclesiastical and secular tribunal of the ancient Jews until AD 70.

PART 5—SPREADING THE WORD

Scota: a mythical daughter of an Egyptian pharaoh and the root of the word Scot

Scotland was known to the Romans as Caledonia.

Semaphore mirror or flag signaling over long distances was used by Alexander the Great in 335 BC.

Septuagint: is the oldest Greek version of the Hebrew Scriptures. It is said to have been translated by as many as seventy-two Jewish scholars at the request of Ptolemy II.

Shadchan: a Jewish matchmaker

Shamanism: Celtic Shamanism of today is a sketchy revision of ancient Celtic Druidism.

Shape-shifting from one life form into another life form is an example of Druid magic shared by Native Americans. Their oral tradition often reported a person changing into a deer to escape danger.

Shavuot (Feast of Weeks or Pentecost): encourages the believer to accept the temporal and the eternal as a relationship with the human condition, and to find harmony between the two in one's life. We as the temporal should be at peace with the one eternal God, who without a need of us, chose to share His living Word and His kingdom with us. Shavuot is celebrated on the fiftieth day after the second day of Passover on or about the day of Pentecost. This celebration originated over 3,500 years ago at Mount Sinai.

Shtetl: a village where Jewish people lived separately from the "others"

Sheol: the home of the spirits of the dead in Jewish theology

Shire: a county

APPENDIX: GLOSSARY

Shomer: Jewish funeral memorial service

Sorcha (SOH ruh chuh): Gaelic woman's name meaning *light* or *brightness*

Talmud: means *finishing* or *completing*. It is the written oral *Torah* or *Mishnah* (meaning "teachings that are repeated"). *The Talmud* was put in writing in AD 200.

Tanakh: Jewish Bible. Hebrew scripture uses the first words of a book as the title for that book. For example, the first book of the Christian Bible is Genesis and Bereshith in the *Torah*. Bereshith: In the beginning. The *Torah* is the first five books of the *Tanakh*. The *Tanakh* is the proper name of the complete Jewish Bible. The Protestant Old Testament contains the same thirty-nine books.

Tack: nautical sailing term meaning to sail a course obliquely against the wind

Ta'in (toyn—Gaelic): a cattle raid

Tamay is the Hebrew word for when a person becomes unclean for a physical or perhaps a spiritual reason.

The One: is one of many Jewish ways of referring to God without using His name directly.

Thistle: the national flower of Scotland. This flowering weed was used strategically against invaders.

Torah, also known as the Pentateuch, is the first five books of the Bible.

Trichotomism is the Protestant Christian belief that man consists in body, soul, and spirit.

Triskelion is a symbol consisting of three components such as geometric figures, branches, legs, and arms.

PART 5—SPREADING THE WORD

Torc: A collar-like necklace made from a twisted band of precious metal worn by ancient Celts.

Tu B'Shvat (the 15th day of the Jewish month Shvat): It is their day to honor their relationship with nature.

Vellum writing material (paper) is made from lambskin that is limed instead of tanned. Ward: a Celtic spell that was originally a protective spell placed around someone or something. It is found in words such as reward and steward.

Wean: a child (Scottish colloquial expression)

Wee: small (Scottish colloquial expression)

Ye: you (Scottish)

BIBLIOGRAPHY

BOOKS

Allison, David. *History of Nova Scotia*. Nabu Public Domain Reprint, 1923.

Cahill, Thomas. *How the Irish Saved Civilization, The Untold Story of Ireland's Heroic Role from the Fall of Rome to the Rise of Medieval Europe*. New York: Anchor Books, 1995. (Mr. Cahill presents a plausible answer to how we pulled ourselves out of the Dark Ages and into the Age of Enlightenment. With the fall of the Roman Empire, the vandals destroyed the libraries of Europe except for a remnant of literature that survived in the fringe of remote Ireland.)

Cahill, Thomas. *The Gifts of the Jews (How a Tribe of Desert Nomads Changed the Way Everyone Thinks and Feels)*. New York: Anchor Books, 1999.

Clough, Juliet, Keith Davidson, Sandie Randall, and Alastair Scott. *Eyewitness Travel Scotland*. New York: DK Publishing, 1999.

Cowan, Tom. *Fire in the Head (Shamanism and the Celtic Spirit)*. San Francisco: Harper, 1993.

Davis, Paul K. *100 Decisive Battles from Ancient Times to the Present*. Oxford: Oxford University Press, 1999.

Ellis, Peter Berresford. *The Druids*. Grand Rapids: William B. Eerdmans Publishing Company, 1994.

Erickson, Millard J. *Christian Theology*. 2nd ed. Grand Rapids: Baker Books, 2002.

Falcon, Ted, Rabbi and David Blatner. *Judaism for Dummies*. Indianapolis: Wiley Publishing, 2001. Thank you, Rabbi Falcon, for this great book.

PART 5—SPREADING THE WORD

Graetz, Heinrich, PhD. *History of the Jews*. New York: Wipf and Stock Publisher, 2002.

Gerhard, Herm. *The Celts: The People Who Came Out of the Darkness*. Barnes Noble, 1994.

Goldsworthy, Adrian. *The Complete Roman Army*. London: Thames & Hudson Ltd, 2003.

Green, Jonathan. *Scottish Miscellany*. New York: Skyhouse Publishing, 2010.

Jewish Encyclopedia, Funk & Wagnalls.

Lacey, Robert. *Great Tales from English History*. New York: Back Bay Books, 2007.

Lewis, C. S., *Mere Christianity*. New York: Macmillan Publishing, 1986.

MacLean, Fitzroy. *A Concise History of Scotland*. London: Thames & Hudson Ltd., 2000.

McCurry, J. J. *Khazar University English Language Reading Program*. Baku, Azerbaijan: Khazar University Press, 1996.

McCurry, J. J. Baku, *Azerbaijan Made Easy*. Baku, Azerbaijan, self published, 1995

New International Version Study Bible. Grand Rapids: Zondervan, 2005.

New Revised Standard Version, Catholic Edition of the Bible. New York: Harper Collins, 1999.

Ridpath, Ian. *Stars and Planets*. London: DK Publishing, 1998.

BIBLIOGRAPHY

Spence, Lewis. *The Mysteries if Britain, Secret Rites and Traditions of Ancient Britain*. London: Senate, an imprint of Studio Editions, Ltd, 1994.

Sutton, Maya Magee and Nicholas R. Mann. *Druid Magic: The Practice of Celtic Wisdom*. Woodbury: Llewellyn Publications, 2000.

Michaelson, Jay. *Everything is God: the Radical Path of Nondual Judaism*. Shambhala/Trumpeter, October, 2009.

Sykes, Bryan. *Saxons, Vikings, and Celts*. New York: W.W. Norton & Company, 2006.

Tanakh, The Holy Scriptures, The New JPS Translation According to the Traditional Hebrew Text. Philadelphia, Jerusalem: The Jewish Publication Society, 1985.

The Chicago Manual of Style, 16th Edition, The University of Chicago Press, 2010.

Winchester, Simon. *The Map That Changed the World*. New York: Harper Collins Publishers, 2001.

Winterling, Aloys. *Caligula: A Biography*. Los Angeles: University of California Press, 2011.

Wood, Juliette. *The Celts: Life, Myth, and Art*. New York: Stewart Tabori & Chang, 1998.

INTERNET RESOURCES

Access Genealogy – Micmac Indian Tribe History

Ancient Egypt – Akhenaten, religion, Aten

The Druids of Caledon

Heart of Scotland

    Celtic Mythology and Celtic Religion

    Ancient Scotland – The Picts and Scots

    Celtic Christianity and Spirituality

National Museums Scotland – Pictish Throne

Wikipedia, the free Internet encyclopedia:

    Adminius

    Celtic Trade and Industry

    Cunobeline*

    Hillel the Elder

    History of Aberdon

    History of the Jews in England

    Library of Alexandria

INTERNET RESOURCES

The Druid Network, regular meetings

Weather of Aberdon

Yahoo Answers:

Celtic Trading Ships

*Cunobelinus (one of several spellings for the King of the Britons, father of Adminius).

MAPS were hand drawn by author.

MUSEUM STUDIES
Denver Museum of Science and Nature, Denver Colorado, 7/21/2012.

National Museum of Scotland, Edinburgh, 9/4/2012. EST. 1888

Royal Museum of Scotland, Edinburgh, 9/5/2012. EST. 1997

Both adjoining Edinburgh museums are truly national treasures. The five star Tower Restaurant sits atop the National Museum and with a great view of Edinburgh Castle.

Maritime Museum, Aberdeen Scotland, 9/7/2012.

Saint Mungo's Museum of Religious Life and Art, Glasgow Scotland, 9/14/2012.

Comment: These museums, including Saint Mungo's Museum of Religious Life and Art, did not offer any information about Druidism. There was no obvious mention of the religion that dominated Albion for centuries.

ILLUSTRATIVE OIL PAINTING
Ann Maree Beamen, *The Rabbi*, 2012.

PART 5—SPREADING THE WORD

PHOTOGRAPH CREDITS

Horse owner Vonvalee Adair (Penny) is the photographer of the two pictures of the horse and child in Part 1. The child's name is Sydney Sabins, and the mare really is registered as Goblin.

Rebecca Ewer is the photographer of her crying daughter Sydney Sabins in Part 1.

James and Judith McCurry photographed the pictures not taken by Vonvalee Adair or Rebecca Ewer.

WILDLIFE RESERVE Kincraig Highland Wildlife Park, Scotland, 9/10/2012.

ABOUT THE AUTHOR

The Celt, J. J. McCurry, did his undergraduate work at King's College in Raleigh, North Carolina, and Regis University in Denver, Colorado, and graduate studies at Southwestern Baptist Theological Seminary in Fort Worth, Texas. He has served in the ministry in North Carolina, Colorado, Texas, Ohio, British Columbia, and the Republic of Azerbaijan.

1961-65 USAF—served in Viet Nam and The Republic of the Congo
1965-90 IBM—Engineering
1993-95 Azerbaijan Broadcasting Company—American English Editor
1995-97 Khazar University—American English Professor

Books by James J. McCurry:
- *Hannah*, 2012, copyright number TXu 1-812-448.
- *Khazar University English Language Reading Program*, Khazar University Press, Baku, Azerbaijan, 1996, ISBN 5-7843-0001-6.
- *Azerbaijan Made Easy*, 2nd edition, 1995, Baku Azerbaijan.
- *Azerbaijan Made Easy*, 1994, Baku, Azerbaijan.

THE RABBI
by
Ann Maree Beamen